MAN OF LOXLEY

Man of Loxley

JOHN BRUCE LEONARD

Visit the author's website at JohnBruceLeonard.com to order additional copies.

Man of Loxley

ISBN   978-1-7356691-4-4 (Softcover)
       978-1-7356691-5-1 (Hardcover)

To Jared ~

> *man of Sherwood if ever there were one,*
> *and without whom this Robin Hood*
> *would have sure been lost to the woods.*

Table of Contents

MAN OF LOXLEY

Preamble

I

ark, friends! for I've a tale to tell. 'Tis one you've heard before, I'll warrant, and one you fancy you've known since the beloved days of infancy. And so you will try no doubt to outpace me at every step and anticipate me in every latest word. Yet who am I to wish it otherwise! I say, *that* is the better for the telling: for thus all things under this sun are born anew.

Hail and hearken, then, my deep-eared, clear-eyed friends! I've a tale to tell that is sung and writ for just such as you. We have a legend to yarn, if you be for it. And I say—what is legend? Legend is the iconic renewal of all things, the great re-iconing of this our life: legend is the recreation of the past in the view of the future. We bear through dark time a burning image, not of what we are, but of what we should be, of what we were and so must be, of what we *will* be, with *will* girded round in symbols and seals. And in bearing hence this image, we shatter the image before us, that paltry shadow which is but our own sham present and most meager actuality. Legend is hence resurrection, and resurrection is the balance twixt the weight of time behind us and that ahead. The symbol of legend in absolute is the great flaming bird, child of the sun itself, that consumes its own being unto ashes and from its ashes resprings into being. And that, too, is life, the God-given innermost wellsprings from which we all of us have our birth and being and continuation and consummation. Though legend would seem to be a thing of the past, this is but half its heart: for the dead alone have no legends; and the dead, though well enough endowed of a past, have no mortal morrow. Then we, who look backwards now and grope through the fog of our history to set our hands on some almost palpable thing—we are not looking *backward* at all—

I say, I say again—all things under this sun are born anew. Ho! I have a name for you that you will sure know well: a name, one might say, that stirs a light amidst the ash of all these incinerated centuries: *Robin Hood* is the name that I would sing. A name not so distant as to be unreachable or unseasonable; nor one so near as to be falsifiable or vulnerable to niggling dispute. And we must allow that it is a peculiar delight to see how the historians flock round it in vain, like buzzards about a desert sojourner who will not, but will not die. Not because we would mock at the poor historians, who are an honorable lot in the end and deserve only our tenderest praise; but rather because history is the first science in the old sense that failed to become a science in the new; and thus spirit again reveals itself insusceptible of grosser calculations.

Then hail, I say! What the reader holds in his right competent hands is, first and foremost, *not* a history. What use, after all, should we have of *the* Robin Hood, who lived and breathed and had his name and his trade and his several human, all-too-human failings? If we saw such a man carved out in the flesh, what should we do with him but stand abay, and perchance laugh and shake our marveling heads? "*Ah*," we might say to ourselves then, satisfied in some pauper's curiosity—"so *here* is Robyn Hode, good man that he was—and reeks to boot of being too long in the wilds and clothed too many days in the same unwashed rags. Does his Marian not take womanly care of him at all? Ill-shaved he is, and coarser of his speech than we had right to expect, and considerable shorter, and somewhat stouter. Ho, *that* is the laugh of Robyn Hode? Say, was that sign of mirth, or a donkey's braying? By troth, seemed more a drunken hiccough than either! For I swear it, he drinks his share of ale, does good Robyn Hode, and goes his way merry *indeed*, and hacking and stinking to the skies. Goodness, and how he fumbles with his bow! And what an unbecoming smile he wears as he does it, the slickard, as though he knew all eyes were on him, and he the bawler and backtown charlatan of all regards! See how 'truth is more interesting than fiction,' for it turns out our Robyn Hode here is naught but a naughty gambler and cheater of the state, who, in flight of debts and attempt to win him liberty of his own license, became an outlaw, and was crafted *Hobbehod* by the people and derided for it, and now is this silly saucy swain who gets himself into brawls a-many, losing them to a one—"

So here's the truth, then—we might confide to ourselves in all impertinence, shaking our heads again, after we have scraped away the crust of time, and scratched out the lines delineating this "historical figure" from his "historical context"—*here's the truth: that Robin Hood was a man as any other!* And so we modern men, who—let us confess it!—are in truth petty souls enough, cutting no prettier a figure in the world, might sleep soundly for knowing that nothing special did wear this name.

But I say, friends, all that is but tar and feather on the truth. Friends—is it not so? We, who do not build this work of envy, nor worse yet of the desire to bear all facts to their last and final grave; we, who ply neither the factitious nor the fictitious; we, who are no paladins of a shallow transparency, but who war nonetheless against the shades—we have us, say I, finer quarry to poach.

II

Well, here then is stuff enough to commence: the name, the time, the place—these simplest dramatic elements that have confounded our right honorable historians time and again, and which yet form the very framing and substance of our work—its palpating skin and its beating heart, as it were; the shell and meat of the seed. And so, to well begin, *Robin Hood*: where and when was the man that bore such a name, and what *was* the name he bore, or that bore him?

Let us train our minds a little. What is *Robin*, if it is not diminutive for *Robert?* Then let us seek us a Robert—a Robert Hood. Indeed, some have even declared, with that back-and-forth logic of legends which is the only proper way to reason about human things as such, that the very "Robin" we have taken as the diminutive name of this man, is quite superfluous, insofar as one can rest quite content with "Rob." For then we have us "Rob-in-hood," which surely devolved to Robin Hood by dint of use. And so far so well. But this leads us to the next natural question. What means *Hood?* Is that a sur-name—as was common in those days, for example, amongst the makers of hoods, who, as was common to common folk, called themselves by their proper trade? Then perhaps our Robert Hood was a tradesman after all, the crafter of useful headgear. Or perhaps he was descended of such. Or perhaps he really was only Rob-in-Hood—that is, one chap named Rob, who made a habit of the cowled habit, so that, contrary our Robin Hood with his feath-ered cap and his sunny disposition, we must picture us instead a lurking sulky fellow who in eternal shade goes about his grim work...

Or perchance we abandon these notions altogether, as being unpalatable and unoriginal, and note well the fact that this *Hood* might in dialect of the day have been simply *Wood*—so that we treat here of a man of the wilderness, a woodsman or one who lived in the forest. But that does not get us very far, if we would be historical, for where in our registers may we seek out a *Robert,* who dwelt worlds away from those places our registers are meant to register? Perhaps then we delve deeper still, and find us in this *Wood* a profounder sense. Perchance this Robert Wood was a bosky sprite, a spirit dweller of the greens, the very personification of spring itself—for who ever heard of Robin Hood's winters!—a figuration and anthropomorphism of natural, wild forces and powers that lead us back to the very roots of the upper countries, the old style of our pallid, hale, Northern ways—

Ho! That is heady stuff—liqueur for our intellectual man. We would but right the draught of it. Let us be neither shallow nor deep. For to stop up the undercurrents and crack the fundament-meanings of any legend, is akin to declaring that the world on which we ramble be but shell. Yet, contrariwise, to insist *too much* upon these profound, elusive matters, is to strip the skin off the world, and seek to bed hot on the core of things. And we are neither superficial nor salamander enough for either of these routes, being but human beings, and so find ourselves in a pretty tangle!

Thus I fear that Robin Hood evades us yet. For was he not *even so* a man in flesh and blood, and did he not truly find himself in the Sheriff's ledgers for voiding the Bishop's purse, and did he not once knock good John Little a good bump upon his crown, and split an arrow in twain by the true flight of his dart? And if he did not do all this, and it is but allegory, or worse yet, mere vulgar sounding, then where is the substance of it such as we might sink our teeth into, and how account for this man's continued presence among us mere centuries anon? And if he *did* do all of this, then what good does it do us, to dream that he was in fact a touchless sprite or boneless "symbol"?—And if he was the one, was he not the other?—And if he could have been *both*, then—

Well! We are in a merry muddle indeed! Nor will it do us any good to dodge the issue modernwise, by supposing that we are not dealing with a name at all, but merely an epithet, since, as is well known, *Robehod* and *Rabunhod* and the like were but monikers lent to criminals, so that "Robin Hood" was but an ennobling title of a bad profession, and our man a thief. What! Robin Hood! A thief! And this is news? Such workaday logic must be marvelous indeed, if it permits us to discover what any schoolchild knows! And still another objection presents itself here: these historicizing etymologies upset the order of things, mistaking effect for cause. For Robehod, or Robehood, or what you like, far from being origin of the name of our man, is surely derived from the same: Robin Hood is no ennobling of Robehod, but Robehod rather the *corruption* of Robin Hood. And this title "Robehod," which was in liberal use already by the opening of the fourteenth century, is therefore the only really valid clue we have found thus far: for it intimates at least this much, that the original name *Robin Hood* was invested in the popular imagination already by the turning of the year of our Lord 1300, so that our hero did far antedate that annum. But—what in heaven's name was he, then, that lived before the year 1300, and was called Robin Hood, and got up to such mischief as has been passed down by tongues and quills abundant, to find himself still alive in this very late day, and evidently as hale and healthy as ever, and standing grinning moreover before our very eyes?

Then back, back, and back still a ways the more—back to the root. Our records are threadbare. Let us doubt them. Let us doubt even our logic, tempered and conditioned as it has been by *science* and *history*; aye, let us doubt our rationality itself, in the name of a higher reason. Let us employ an other, the very logic mentioned above, the logic of life itself. In God's name, my friends, let us lend a bit of wonder to the name that so makes us wander! There is need here of a little dexterity—is there not? A little dancing round or *straight through* such an historic briar patch?

Now, it is largely taken for granted that the name we ascribe to our hero was his given name—that Robin Hood was some Robin, Robyn, Rob or Robert. For we reckon that *we* should call a man as he was named. But we do not adequately consider the state of things in, say, 1200 *Anno Domini*. Names were not in 1200 what they are today—nay, nor the world and its courses what they seem to us. Names then were not some static repository of our audible "identity," selected by our parents more or less arbitrarily and generally left unmolested by kith and kin. We do not consider that much better than half the population of the commoners bore in those days one of a meager handful of names; that to shout "John!" in the street might cause the turning of a full fifth of its beards.

So a man christened "John" would never be called such simply, but perhaps, for instance, *John Lackaland*, or *John Twain*; for he has no right homeland, has our John, but is a rover and a vagrant, and speaks with a forked tongue, and seems often to balance more than a single meaning upon it. And from *John Twain*, hence to *Twain* alone. Thus Robin Hood, we submit by way of probable hypothesis, was born no Robin at all. Nay: nor Robyn, Rob, Robert nor any other name robbed from the census books. His name was given to him, and given, in the way of all true names, by way of some intuition into the nature of the man, his situation, his right activity and habits, his destiny. And if this fresh hypothesis be valid, the which is suggested already by the fair imbroglio into which our histories get themselves while searching out an "historical" and "factual" Robin Hood, then already *by the name itself* we are deceived—as is indeed only fitting if one considers the protean wile of the character in question! Indeed, let us assert here the full rights of our newfound *logic of life*, and assert them readily: this modern mess of ours is the very *proof* that Robin Hood was *not* Robin Hood, that his being called such throughout the centuries, has resulted in just such a jest as should have tickled him and made him sneeze with laughter!

III

After such reflections, the faint of heart among us might be fain, not so much to cut to the chase, as to cut the chase *off* entirely. Why trouble ourselves at all—they might fairly inquire—with this hunt for the "historical Robin Hood"? Even supposing the man existed, he lies too far swaddled in the tenebrous past for us to ever discover him. If we cannot pursue us a Robin Hood who was born to that name and who responded to it from his toddling up, so that we may trace out his figure from the records of the day, then already the way to *history* is closed. And we are even tempted to wonder: could it ever be otherwise? Is this not always the way of such inquiries, such artistic excavations into the past? What would it even mean for the records to be clear? Would such lucid documentation not at best form a paper-thin skin stretched clumsily and arbitrarily over the face we seek? What *could* it tell us, that *we* would want to know...?

So we stumble all inadvertent upon a truth which should serve us in any human investigation: at any point in the recorded past, be it near or far, *history is but a skin worn by prehistory: any visible moment in the past is underlain by a bedrock of prehistory,* and the life of the moment is to be found *only in that prehistory*—and furthermore, we cannot get to that prehistory, by means of history alone...

Well! That is a fine turn of events! In this case, Robin Hood may as well not have existed at all, for all the good it would do us! Why not then presume he was but a figment of the popular imagination? Why not simply paint Robin Hood as we please, without bothering over models, precedents and origins? If non-fiction cannot oblige—why, then, let us satisfy ourselves with fiction, pure and unabashed, and have done with it!

Ah! but what, friends, is fiction? What is invention, if not a subtler kind of discovery? And where is the line between the one thing and the other, that we may neatly decide on which side of it to stand? And how if there is *no* line whatsoever? For let us be clear: even if we take headlong innovation as our standard, we are yet hunting *something*, some *one*; we have indeed put a pretty price upon his head, and do pursue him with all the zeal of the legendary Sheriff of Nottingham himself. We shall not leave this outlaw in peace, but shall hound him to the end, until we are satisfied that we have prisoned Robin Hood, and Robin Hood alone of all men, and the true Robin Hood to boot, whoever and whatever he might prove to be. Aye, we shall chase this singular ghost of Robin Hood through dell and dale, bramble and briar, and cleave to him in his bosky hideouts, whether they be historical or fantastical or the both together, and we shall haunt his heels though he is swift and sure and evasive as a shadow. Even were we the most consummate of artists, still we must go to him where he is to be found, for it is unlikely enough he will come to us. And so, friends, we find ourselves already—lost to wildernesses, lost in Sherwood...

And speak of! There is another tidy riddle, against which many heads have beaten in vain! Everyone knows that Robin Hood had his way of Sherwood Forest, and menaced the roads that passed therethrough. And this Sherwood is just north of Nottinghamshire, where had his post the aforementioned and most notorious nemesis of Robin Hood, namely, the Sheriff of Nottinghamshire, whose jurisdiction fell as well over the wood at that town's borders. There are problems rife that issue from this simple enunciation of the "facts." Here, for instance, is a spiny one indeed: the earliest tales of our Robin Hood have him living in Barnsdale, some fifty miles north of Nottinghamshire, in Yorkshire, country that had its own and diverse sheriff. But it is an unlikely tale that a single outlaw, even one so bold and versatile as Robin Hood, menaced a road two days travel distant from his home, only so as to goad the sheriff of a county different to his own! Then to further complicate everything, there is *Loxley*—is there not? That *Loxley* which later was said to be the home and birthplace of the true Robin Hood, though Loxley is neither York nor Nottingham, to say nothing at all of Barnsdale or Sherwood...

Then there be the lesser inconsistencies, which are easily dismissed as so many accretions of too many writers and raconteurs—for example, the simple fact that Robin Hood was originally figured in garb of red, but has come down to us in our day donning his greencloth. Or confusion about the true King of the day, be he a Richard or an Edward or a John. Or the absence of Maid Marian in those early tales, who figures so centrally in the later, and the presence instead of another maid, let us say even, the *prototypical* maid, of a name not much diverse. And was our Robin a cheerful ne'er-do-well, a jack of the greenwood, as spry as he was lackadaisical? Or was he a dark and gloomy dreamer intent on venging his father's wrongful murder? Or was he violent and proud and overweening, and got he into his outlawship *by* murder? Or was a silly and ludicrous sort, who was always at the butt of other men's jests and staves? Or was he pious to the point of recklessness, philanthropist to the poor and a good and charitable Christian, forced into his hood by the distortion of the times...?

Ho! A nice and Gordian knot we have tied for ourselves, or been tied up in. And it will take some finesse finer than that of an Alexander to cut us loose again. For here is the secret we have reserved till now, which makes matters so much richer and more complex and so much the more ticklish, that they shall have *us* sneezing ere we are done: all that has been said about Robin Hood with voice clarion and and in spirit true, *has been the very truth itself...*

That is a riddle. That is *the* riddle, if you will, of legend. And we are riddle riders, and riddle righters, and writers too of riddles—and lo, dear reader, have patience and heed me! For it needs a book now, to speak the truth that has just been uttered.

There is a tree down Sherwood way—or was, ere it fell before the huntsman's axe, to be burned of an evening flame to warm this man and his family, or parceled to lumber for their furnishings—a tree that once rose towering and proud in a place but few men knew and fewer still frequented. And this tree was scarred in a special way by skyfall, and long bore in its flesh a certain arrow, for it was fated from among all its million brethren to be host and witness to certain calamities of heaven and earth. Beneath its boughs it shaded many a needful soul from sun and rain, and covered the tracks of animals and wayfarers, and did attest to oaths and duels, bonds and deaths, and attended one day a contest of blades between two men, and one of these was slain, and his blood soaked the earth and fed its roots. They had come to settle an antient dispute, which revolved around the violence of the one and the reticence of the other; for the first had o'erstepped the right bounds that the second had lain. And they stood before one another like faces reflected, and the one drew steel and the other answered. And that tree drank up the blood of the fallen, and grew taller and stronger for it, and all that happened in the shade of that tree after or before this event was marked by it in some special way, until the tree itself was razed and its roots rotted off, and nothing left there but a shade and memory.

Merry Men

John Little

as five years and thirty-one days since I set out to seek me a man my better. The length and breadth of England had I tread, to find me one who could vanquish me by might or wite. I knew by my troth that such a man there was, for God hath made men equal in their immortal soul, but diverse in their traits and features, such that one must be best over all. And I knew that I could not be that best, for though mighty of body I am weak in the head. I had decided me to follow that man as God had ordained first among men. For a man should follow what's best in this life, or he be not a man at all.

I have lost count of all them as I defeated with my trusty stave, but they were legion, and some of them I allow were solid men. Now a stave is the only honest weapon, and that to be sure. For though a man should ken the use of sword and dagger, knife and bow, if he cannot face ye square up with a measure of solid wood in his hand, and knock ye flat with it, or permit himself to be knocked flat in turn, why, he is no man at all, or no decent one, by my troth. Do not trust these sword players that are so many these days. They wield a creature they have not builded, and it is deadly, not for their own strength, but for its edge, granted it and honed by an art foreign to theirs. And these bowman also, as ply by treachery, and kill a man at a dozen paces—pah! But a stave, now, is only as good as the man as holds it, for it is but a length of wood, and if ye with a stave in your fingers get at a barehanded man of true caliber, he might knock your rod out of your hands and take it for his own, and leave you a bump on your skull with your very weapon to know him by. And ye can kill a man with a stave, but only as your own strength and craft permits it, but not for some merit in the weapon independent of you. That is why I carried with me my trusty oaken stave far and wide across the face of our England, and used it and it alone to mark out the caliber of my contestants, whether it was weakness or clout to hold them, and would face no man with steel nor bow, save in spirit of sportsmanship and to keep my hand practiced in the way of all art of war. For I say to you, boy, that this world beneath God's peaceful Heaven is war against Satan and his minions, and only an honest man can prevail with it.

Now today there is many a man that struts about with sword trussed at hip. 'Twas not always so, but when I met Robin Hood there was much respect yet for the stave, for the times dark as they were were better than these now. That is progress for you, and mark it; we were better off when we were worse off. Pah, all is gone to the devil, boy, and pansies and milksops are at the helm of things. That is the way of the world, that it falls ever the lower if we do not hold firm and strive mightily to raise it. For there is something in the heart of this world, boy, like to a rot, and it does gradually gnaw at everything. That's the Fall I warrant, and the Sin it brought into this world. By my troth, boy, a man must be of strong wood.

Now I say, five years and thirty-one days I had been a-seeking, and I the man to count them, for I was hungering ever to find one my better. I had passed lately through Nottinghamshire, and had had good hopes there, for rumor had it that men were lusty in that place and goodly of sinew. Pah, there was not much show for it. I recall one man at a fair there, a queer monkeyish sort with but a single eye. He was not a limp hand with the stave, and had the better of me in the contest of the bow. Yet I think him probably a sly and sneaky sort, and do not hold much hope that he was a man of honest mettle. Yet I never did run 'cross him again to learn the matter straight, nor knew aught of what became of him.

Now I was passing on from Nottingham, for I had found none there as I

might name my better, and had ventured into Sherwood, from which I had
been much forewarned, for they said that a nasty band of thieves lived there
and would rob any passerthrough of his possessions. I told them that I feared
nor thief nor murtherer, for I had but little on me that one might rob by
treachery, and if a man should set designs on my life, I would know the reason
for it. I will tell you, boy, a secret of this world, that if you rove with your purse
heavy with gold, then your fear will grow heavier for the weight of your bag;
but if only a single coin is bouncing in your pocket sufficient to pay your next
meal, then you go as light as a sparrow in the field, though ye be as heavy a
wight as I.

’Twas a footpath not far from the main road, and I was passing there to
make the shorter way to Barnsdale, where it was said there were many a
scrappy swain. Now on this trail there was a footbridge, boy, and it over a nice
little stream, a rivulet if you will, which might have been deep as a man and
wide thrice his length. And as I was coming upon this bridge, I saw before me
some movement in the brambles—for it was uncommon thick at that place,
was the wood. I did not tarry, but bethought me some animal was out there
jostling in the bush. Yet as I approached mesaw ’twas no beast at all, but a man,
and that a man of decent height and slim build, all dressed in forest green, and
with a cloak upon his back, the which’s hood was down. He was a bearded
sort with a reddish chestnut beard, pointed of its tip and its mustaches, and he
had about him no mean face, but seemed comely and descended of the better
sorts. And I saw he was making for the same footbridge, and was like to arrive
there just ere I had passed. Yet he had seen me, I wager, for he hastened his step,
in such a way that we did meet at the dead center of the bridge.

Well, I stopped up and put my stave before me and my hands on it, for I
was in the mood for a clash. He asked me passage in decent terms, but there
was aught in his voice that did not like me, for it seemed by my troth he was
laughing at me in some secret way. And I saw that his eyes were strange, for
they were not like mine eyes, nor yours, boy, which hold each the same color
and are in accord the one with the other and as it were in harmony, but rather
the right one was blue and the left one was green. And I tell you boy, this did
not please, but riled me, to think that the nature of this fellow should be at

odds with itself. So fast I stood, and said to him, "I be John Little, and for all I am concerned this is my footbridge and mine alone for the whole duration of my passage 'cross it. Lo, I am seeking out a man as can best me in single combat by might or by wite, and if ye be not he, then name the man ye know of such a caliber, and if ye do not know him, then step ye down and find ye some other way, or swim the crossing, for all that I care of it!"

How he smiled! and said to me, "Truly, I doubt your words from the outset, for I should call you rather Little John, in appraisement of the heft and girth of ye. I am the man called Robin Hood, and respect to you, Master Large, but all within the forest's edge belongs by rights to me, this footbridge well included. So I fear I am duty bound to hold my place, and must ask ye what single combat ye prefer."

"I will fight with nothing other this stave, choose ye the weapon ye will," said I, and glanced contemptuous on his bow and his dagger

"I have no stave," said he, "but only bow and blade."

"Pah," spat I. But that fellow turned back off the bridge, and for a moment I was set as to follow him, to give the coward a whelp on his noggin in any case just to recall me to him by; but then I saw he was out to get him a proper arm, and I held up and honorably abided.

Now he went to the edge of the wood, to where a gnarled oaken sapling had been felled by coarse weather, and he pulled a hefty dagger and lopped that sapling of all its deadening branches; and then stood with it and by my troth pulled it straight clear of the ground, though it had been a tree the size better than of a man, and must have had roots well sunk. Yet he pulled it out, and down half of it stripped it of its bark, and cut the crown from it so that it had no weak and wafty upper part, and came to me with it. And I saw as he came that it was not right, this length, but was all gnarled and crooked and looked its part like an unstrung and ruined bow. "Master Hood," I said to him, "how do ye intend to fight with that, which is no stave at all, but an overgrown corkscrew, and cannot be balanced in straight combat? What is your meaning?"

"To use as I find," said he, "as do I ever in life." And by my troth, he was grinning, so that for a moment I even took him for a madcap lost in these woods, who had conceived himself Robin Hood and now went awandering by that false name to get himself into high trouble thereby. And I even thought to stand down, for fear of hurting a fool of God; but saw as he was ready to fight me, so I resolved to disarm him and lay him flat without much harm, and then to go on my way in peace.

Came at him then with my stave and all it was worth, and, by my troth, he and his mongrelly weapon met me at every blow. And it was even hard to match him, for that damned bent wood did not follow the straight coarse that a right quarterstaff would follow, but seemed to dodge and duck in very the air as it flew, so that on several points, I was even in danger of receiving a clap from it. Yet I kept to, and resolved to break that piece of wood in half, so much had I conceived a loathing for its twisted nature. And I set aside my wonder at the skill of this man—for listen well, boy, and know that wonder is the enemy of manly equilibrium—and flew hard at that fellow, and beat him back a few steps. Aye, and with a skillful turn I smacked him hard on the crown, and felled him, flat on his back, though his hands would not leave his ridiculous implement. So I came to stand over him, and said to him, "Was well fought, Master Hood, but I am proved your better."

Now here lithe as a deer he jumped up on his feet, grinning once more, though I saw he was bleeding from the wound I had planted straight on his scalp, and he seemed inclined again to battle!

"Man," protested I, "I have felled you fair and square."

"What felled?" said he. "Or do I not stand before you yet?"

"But a moment past and you were felled," protested I, "and flat on your back. And look there, you've blood on your brow to prove it."

"Let bygones be bygones," said he with a shrug, "for truly the past is hard of deciphering." And came at me again, so that I was obliged to defend myself. And we were at the fight once more. And I confess he seemed faster and surer this time, and that damned stave of his was flying at every odd angle, so that it was all I could do to keep time with it. I marked my will once more, and re-solved to cudgel that fellow back into his senses, and give him a walloping that might leave him with a broken bone or at least a bold bruise in memory of me. I was resolved to hold back no longer. Now I knocked him off his guard in a movement that is special to me, and that leaves your foe but no time to respond, and was coming round fast with the gracing strike, when of a sudden and I cannot say how he had taken the force I gave him, spun clear round and swung back at me out of the blue, striking me fast and remarkable hard on the shoulder, so that I lost my footing altogether and let fly my stave which by God's grace landed there balanced on the footbridge. I was none so lucky but did go tumbling down and sank full in that river, depth of which I fathomed at once was greater even than my height.

Now boy, I am an uplander, and lived always where the water was scarce e'en to whet a man's own thirst, and have never learned me to swim. And I would have drowned me there in that tub had Robin Hood not fished me out and borne me blubbering back to shore, where I lay on the bank regaining my breath and thoroughly beaten. And when I had my air again, I stood, and went looking for my stave; but he laughing presented it to me at once, and seemed present to the fight again. "Nay, good sir," said I to he, "but you have conquered me. Never has this back touched earth but as I lay down of my own full will to rest under God's golden sky. Five years and this the thirty-third day of that fifth, have I been looking for one my better, and by my troth, I have at last found he. Friend, are you truly the man they call Robin Hood?"

"True as named," quoth he.

"And do you truly live here in this wood, and rob of the men as go along the road through it?"

"That I do! Yet not all such, Master John, but I do select those as are elect to the robbing."

"And would you have robbed me then, Robin Hood?" I asked of him.

"You, friend!" he laughed. "Nay, not on my life. For I did know that you were a brave man and a Christian, and I do not make habit of robbing from my brethren. Nay, I was this day about a stroll, for I am fain to wander, when I came upon yon footbridge. Master John, you swing a mighty stave, and have a heart to match its oak: and I wonder if you would not be pleased to join me and my merry men?"

"Friend, you are proved my better, and I shall do as you bid willingly and with gratitude," said I, and I offered Robin Hood my hand, the which he took in firm and manly grip, and smiled at me. But a doubt o'ercame me, and I said,

"But I say that I join Robin Hood for Robin Hood, and not for his men; for I am inferior of no man alive, save that which stands before me."

"Then Master Little John," said he, "—such I christen you true, for all's in a name—ye shall be henceforth, and for as long as you stand unfelled by any hand but mine, my first and last man."

And since that day to this have I been Little John, foremost among the Green Folk of Sherwood and of all men everywhere, with only Robin Hood as my better.

Sheriff Robert de Vieuxpont

ill, will, will. Will, will, red as a pimpernel. Say, now what *will* be? But a knave and a trespasser, a shady sort with no antecedents and a vulgar cropping tongue. A thing sprung up like a weed, and cut down as readily by the hand that wields the keener sickle. The leader of a motley of tramps in the bramble. A coward and a villain, and a two-bit liar to boot. Tell me, *will* I have the better of him, and do as the King hath appointed? Will, will—I say, *will!* Tell me, oh say, *will* I put this dog down? But will I, oh will I! For I have got me a name.

Now, good *Robin Hood*, fair fiend, they say ye are a sprite of the forest, a dark woodland thing that is rose up from the moss therein to trouble the right folk of England and dispossess them of their coin purses. The peasantry speak of *justice*, the curs, as if that were a word signifying anything at all, beyond a shadowy dream in the heart of the oppressed. I say, men are born to their station; it shall suffice to us, earthy folk in our earthly home, to note that some man is born of a queen, and another of a slut; or to perceive that, while Sir Thomas has him breaches of silk and a lacework tunic, Master Toad fetches his back in rags and malprised stretches of leather. *That*, Sir Hood, is the fact, all your thousand arrows notwithstanding. It is useless to beat one's face against a fact; and so one must invent a woodland spirit in which to lay one's very hope, thus overturning what most palpably *is*, for some callow and fleshless and impossible *should be*. Oh, but here's the hook: for I know that Robin Hood is *not* a demon of the bosky deeps, nay nor an angel, nor an *ignis fatuus* of some lowly heart's slavering after comeuppance. Nay, for such creatures as *that*, exuding from the fumes of swamps and fens, have no names but those we wilfully set on them. They are not creatures of reason, and cannot be reasoned *with* nor *about*; and that is why they are without right appellation—and thus shan't exist. For we name them by their essences, and not, as is common and fitting, by arbitrary sounds meant merely to differentiate *Samuel* from *Hesper*, and render them unique to ear, while in no way touching on the root of the matter, which is best left 'neath heath and heather, mold and mildew. And by this same iron-clad logic, which I defy any to defy, so I know, Robin Hood, that ye are no will-o-the-wisp, nay, but another and more solider *will* altogether—for I have got me a name.

A name, a name, tacked down in register and scrawled in most terrene ink on a most mundane page, to show me that this *Robin Hood* got himself dirtied as we all did in the slough and slick of parturition. A name, a name, to lay absurd rumor to rest, and refresh men to their abandoned senses. Aye, a name to expunge this absurd "Robin Hood" from the memory and the ledger alike, and to supplant it with a *fact*, proved by our very sciences and by all that's known solidly of the world. *Robin Hood*, I slay ye with a word—and that word is, *Will*.

One William de Loxley have I here: a recreant youth, though for the better part of his greener days quiet in his disquiet. He got up to small mischief as a small man, and yet nothing that we shall consider exceeding ordinary bounds or worthy of our high note. His father, one Gilbert, a fletcher; his mother, a woman of wide-touted beauty named Avice, who died rose-young and at the pitch of her loveliness, that his father turned a sot and a self-pitying wreck of a fool, and let his work fall into desuetude. Young William the single product of their coupling; no siblings does he have—or none legitimate, for it would seem that our good Gilbert had himself at least one other natural son, though it be devilish tricky to capture me facts about *him*. It would seem Will learned his father's art, if we are to judge of the use he makes of its product; but he was never a working man, proving too slothful for gainful activity, or to find his right slot in our nation's great economy. Will Scarlett, they called him, for his habit of dressing dandy-like in brilliant red, a feather standing straight out of his cap. Must have been a womanizer, this Will; oh, a regular popinjay and good-for-nothing he must have been. He took up the lute, it would seem, and got him a reputation with it. He passed his youth a loafer, at intermittent blows no doubt with my colleagues in Loxley, and slipped away at last to go a-wandering, from which *Lehrjahr* in vagrancy I wish he'd ne'er returned. But alas, he did, persistent as a flea.

At the borders of that self-same and loathsome stretch of wilderness which he calls his present home—that woody ill-bred acre, which by rights must one day be laid low under the mortar of men and mitered to an earthly order—our callow William de Loxley happened upon two members of our very lawkeeps, who were holding guard there under the orders of my predecessor, Lord Bardulf. It would seem that this sprightly Loxley adroitly convinced those guardsmen, who most surely were bored in their watch, to try him for a game of hazard. Two of them sat down to the dice, then—one of our guardsman, and this Red Will—and played a series of rounds; the which, our guardsman tells us, this Loxley won in kegs. But now, our guardsmen, and woe for them, dreamed a simple calculation: two armed men of th'order, against a single strutting coxcomb with a turn of luck to his favor: and *why* should the stronger pay out to the weaker? So they refused him what by a gambler's honor they seemed to owe. But even so they must have miscalculated, for Loxley insisted on having what he had by merest chance won, and when he was not paid, took the wages out of the loser's flesh. He drew his sword, slew his competitor, disarmed that man's companion with unusual skill, and struck it for the woods, where he has been in hiding in abject shame almost ever since.

Almost! Almost!—And not forever?—Nay, alas! not forever. Imagine the cocksure creature strutting about in the light of day after proving himself an assassin! Yet so he did; and could afford it, because he had poltroon-like been hooding himself under foreign names. He had told my guardsman his name was Alan-a-Dale, and for a time indeed we may track him under that moniker; for it seems he wore it during his stint of vagabonding. And in consequence he was well protected, the liar, under false appellation. Thus he could come straight out of that forest as William once more, and without fear of reprisals; the which he did, when circumstances were sufficiently rancid to lure him to their scent.

For though he was some year's time in Sherwood, and, by what rumor has reached me, caused much exasperation to my predecessor, and in the end e'en poisoned him to his demise, yet shortly after the untimely death of Lord Bardulf, our man of Loxley vanished altogether from Sherwood, and quiet came back once again. So much so that I, taking up the Lord Bardulf's fallen mantel, believed and hoped this business had found an end by some mysterious but inevitable means, and thought myself free of battling this absurd cockamamie disrupter of rule and right. But not so—for he was up to mischief on grander scale, and was bound by his bad star to return to th'war with me.

Alan, Robin, Will—this multinomered falsifier—had caught wind of rebellion such as his pathetic person could never dare to accomplish alone; and so ran to the scent as a dog will get to a rotten fish. For these were the days that Fulk FitzWarin was coming up hard against the King, and seeking to win the lands of which he had been dispossessed. He had already been to field with Hubert de Burgh, who fought him in the name of the King. Loxley joined FitzWarin, it would seem, under yet another false name—Reynold Greenleaf he called himself—and made war on his part against the King, and so filthied his false name with true treason; but then with FitzWarin and his companions, was pardoned by the King, to the end of one great rebellion, and the seeding of another pitiful and small. For with this pardon, Loxley was given leave to serve under me; and I, ignorant as I was of his antecedents in my own domain, did take him on, and planted that weed square in mine own garden, nay, beneath my very nose. He must have ingratiated himself well with FitzWarin, for I was begged to treat him kindly. I had no truck with this Greenleaf and do not believe I ever spoke to him, but I saw him once or twice—strange fellow, tallish and not poorly made, handsome enough, all told. Sour apples will wear bright skin. Gave him easy time of it, as well, for his work was light and he could keep his stomach as full as he pleased of my larder. He could have loafed his life away, the loller, had he not something twisted in his soul that troubled him out of all consequence. They say he grew bored with the quiet life, and yearned again for adventure. Tripe, say I; it was trouble for which he was yearning. I think him sick of heart. All I know in fact and form is this: that he up and disappeared one day from my premises, and with him the silver of my kitchen, and my best cook to boot.

I knew not at the time what my oversight had cost me, more than silverware and plates and the skill to garnish 'em. Nay, nor did I comprehend at first the subtile connection between various events. Here, one loafer vanishes; there, one outlaw springs up. Here, one varlet disappears; there, one villain arises. Here, a little disorder in my house; there a large disorder in my wood. Ah, but there is not much related in these facts to tie them the one to the other, and the thread that does connect them is thin as hair to this human eye. I might have wagered that the man known to me as Greenleaf had lived up to his name and had gone to live like a brute in the bramble; but I should have as easily wagered that he would be as irksome to the forest thugs as he was to me, and perhaps laze about all day and refuse to thieve as he must, or perchance rob the robbers before all was done. Instead, nay, *that* man, that loafer and gourmand, and the one as cowls himself on the Great Highway—those two men are one and the same!

I learned it from a fellow of the thieves, an ugly wretch that I should have liked to hang, if he had not slipped away from me. 'Tis no wonder they say that Robin Hood is a ghost, so light does he move—pah! But devil take your ghost. For I have got me a name.

I say, this boy of theirs calls himself Simon. I do not know if it be his given name or not. I had not the time to straitly investigate the matter, and frankly care not a whit; for men of his class may as well not have names at all. This Simon was caught bandying words with a strumpet, and baring his criminal heart to her in return for the bosom she had bared to him. He must have been drunk, for he was yollering like a hound, loud enough for the whole whorish district to catch ear, and one of my guardsman on watch was lucked enough to o'erlisten. I shan't ask what *he* was doing in those parts at a time of the day when he should have been on duty. A good turn of the hand deserves a good turn of the eye. And this guardsman took Simon on a hunch, or perhaps mere on the chance that this fellow was not simply boasting vainglorious for the whiskey he had in his paunch or the itch he had a sight lower, but was spinning tales from true yarn. A useful man, that guardsman. I fancy I shall have him promoted.

That is how Simon fell to my care. I let him sober up, for if any truth is to be had in drink, 'tis locked in folly embrace with sham. And then I set on him. I swear, he was hard as rocks. I had not expected it from one of so tender a face, yet I could not pry a word out of him that he did not willingly yield. So I set about doing what the miner will do with a rock as has gold in its core; I cracked the fellow open. It took but a little branding. Well, now, that was something. At the touch of physical suffering he opened his petals like a flower, and would not close 'em again, so that I then needed not graze a hair of his head to get what I craved from him.

What is your master's name? asked I him.

Robin Hood, quoth he, but in no jesting vein.

I mean his right name, boy—that with which he was born, and not this ludicrous nickname you forest folk have put on him.

I know not, replied he.

Give me not such slyness, or sure ye shall suffer for it, vowed I.

We call him Loxley, said he, after a pause.

Loxley! say I, much surprised, and ticking away already in my head. And why Loxley?

I cannot be sure, but methinks 'twas his birthtown.

Now, now, that *is* of interest, say I. And his given name?

That I do not know and have never known, says he. Robin Hood has never spoke it to us, and none of us has ever asked him. He is Loxley to us, or more and more is Robin Hood.

So says my prisoner—and I believe him. But I pursue: And tell me, what does this master of yours seem? Say, what mark does he have? Is he abnormal tall, this Loxley, or uncommon pale of hair, or the contrary? Is he fat about the midriff or about the temples? Has he some malformation, or what? Say—how does a man that does not know him, distinguish this Loxley out from other men?

His scar, said Simon after a stretch, a scar he wears upon his brow.

Hah! I could have kissed that scoundrel, would the stink of him not have clung to my lips for days against all saffron and clove. So old *Robin Hood*, that weary, deceitful title, comes crumpling off this forest larcenist like so much motley, and now the canaille need no longer lie when they bark of a woodland scamp. Will, Will! I shall cry that name to the heavens, till I've got a Scarlett Will under my will, and with whip or knife or executioner's ax can dress him up crimson as I please.

All the more so for this business about Simon. I left that whelp locked in Nottingham's deep to season there like cheese, and meant to go back another day to bleed some more out of him. For I was much enthusiastic by my discoveries, and had direct work to be about. Only that the day after, and Simon was gone, and no one can tell me how; and that is a stain on this entire affair to rile me almost to forgetting what I have gained, that a prisoner should vanish from out my stronghold like a puff of wind. I suspect foulplay in mine own men, and must be vigilant about cleansing my house. For I am in need of strong obedient arms now to do much building, and there is an entire flea-bit forest in want of structure. And it is particular shame, for I had other questions I would have put to that wretch.

At least this much I got out of him. For pursuing the point with him, before his evasion, I asked him, Man, where does this Loxley hide?

In no one sort of place, he told me, but he moves his camp often, and will surely have done so by now, realizing that I am gone; so do not hope me to lead you to him.

And how many men does this Loxley command? I asked.

Short of a score and a half, with the numbers e'er i' the wax.

And where does he find so many ruffians to tally to his numbers?

They find him, said he.

What, like dogs will find a bitch in heat? Say—what draws 'em to him? Is it the smell of gold?

Gold! spat Simon, as though he could not hold the word in his mouth without suffering some urge of vomiting. Not a man among us cares a whit for gold, he said.

No doubt! exclaimed I, much sarcastic and not a little peeved. And what then moves your master?

Justice, says he, in all seriousness and without so much as cracking a smile. Robin Hood would bring down the high and mighty, and raise up the low and downtrodden, as Jesus did.

And a blasphemer to boot! said I; and I admit I laughed much at this admission, and cheerily dreamt to myself a fanatic dressed in green cowl and wielding a holy bow to the righteous death of his dev'lish enemies. Some Jesus, I said to Simon and not without a sneer, as robs and murders, against all telltale law and right course!

He robs them as has been robbed, replieth he, but never murdered a man.

Whatever ye might think of his deeds in Sherwood, I know of a fact, told him I, that his hand has blood on't.

He's come down on *you* with hard enow a hand, said Simon; and so I much came down on *him* with a hard hand, and let him feel the welt of it.

That was that.

But oh, matters do not end here, with one criminal vanished and another yet on the sly! Nay, but upon my sword they shall not end here. I have had Simon, and I shall have Will, and Simon again to boot, and all the numerous tribe of those filthy ragtag skulkers. By dawn one month from to-day, I do solemnly swear it before the might of the Crown, I shall see the true name of Robin Hood on the eyes and on the lips of all the folk of Nottinghamshire, and the echo of it shall summon William de Loxley to me. And within a semester of that date, I shall have the neck of the same Will in a noose before those same crowds, that they might learn the matter of this mortal flesh they have made such stuff of, and he *will* sway until the light goes out o' him.

Hawise

peak not to me of that man! If *man* he can be called. For I have heard many a *real* man as beat the stuffing out from him, out there in the greenwood, and bested him in wit, brawn, stamina and every other manly quality you could name. Believe me it, and my father to justify me, for as Lord of Nottingham he knows this hamlet in and out, as no other soul does or could do, and can tell you tales many. Why, I could heap on you names on names of those who had *flayed* Robin Hood, if ever I wanted to, but I see no need to prove what every other stable-boy knows. Or do you dare doubt your Hawise?

You silly lad. I see you are in love with an outlaw and a villain. No, no, don't deny it! Hawise can see right to your heart. Why, you've fallen for him, haven't you? Perchance you'd rather be with *him* now, than with your own Hawise, and wed *him*, and live with *him* forever in his dank forest grotto? Hah, look how the boy blushes! Poor fool, you know not what Robin Hood is, else you would not lionize him so. Do not attempt to defend him: it is useless trying to convince *me* of what I know to be false. I call him not Robin, but Poppinjay, name more fit to his character. Yes, of course I've seen old Poppin, with my very own eyes! Why, was I not there when he lost the archery contest like a bumbler, straight outmatched by no fewer than four of the Sheriff's archers, and was uncovered because his beard fell off when he was trying to beg me for a kiss, and was beaten by the Sheriff's men and taken straight to jail? And *should* have rotted there, had some sneak not sneaked him out of there. Why, he is not even comely, but has the pinched face of a starving fox, which he tries ever to cover with his famous hood and his beard, and that is why he goes round like that, to cover up his ugliness, but in vain. Why, I should not wonder if he had become an outlaw from the first so as to escape the hisses and jeering of the mob.

How dare you challenge Hawise! Very well, serf, I will tell you how Robin came to Sherwood, for I have heard it from my father. He murdered my father's steward in cold blood over a matter of a small wager, and fled like a coward into the wood. That is how he became an outlaw. How does that like you? What? Of course you have never heard this story; 'tis secret, for my father, noble man that he is, is ashamed of the business, and wants to bring Poppinjay to justice to make him even. But *I* do not mind if it is bruited about, for I would have Poppin denounced for the criminal he is, not held up like some kind of popular hero.—No, he did not fight with the steward, you dunce! He stabbed him in the back like a proper coward!

You are ever one to talk! You have heard too many fables from common mouths, that like to make up stories because they are born hopeless. Then I will tell you another story I heard from my father, who heard it from the Sheriff of Nottingham himself. There was a tanner who went into Sherwood, and Poppinjay stopped to try to filch his gold, though the tanner was a poor man and had almost nothing on him. (Aye, that's how your Poppin works! Some *hero*!) Anyways, the tanner was stopped in the road, and Poppin demanded him to give over his purse, but this tanner, unlike Poppin, was at least a man, and said that if Poppin wanted his purse he could sure come and seize it. Poppin turned as red as a turnip at this and practically fumed over, and said he would have the purse one way or another, and came at the tanner with a knife, but the tanner just tripped him flat onto his face and went on his way whistling. That's how little he thought of him! Then up popped Poppin and came at him again, but the tanner tripped him a second time. Then, when he came the third, the tanner decided he had had enough, and gave Poppin such a beating as he had not seen in all his days, and even broke one of his arms, and tanned his hide as if it were one of his pelts, and sent him racing away like a cottontail into the forest. *That's* your Poppinjay for you.

Noble! You dare call him *noble*! He has not a drop of nobleman's blood in him, or my name is not Hawise! He is commoner through and through, a yeoman and naught better, with a yeoman's airs and a yeoman's arts and a yeoman's farts. It is no wonder you would think so highly of him, being what you are. Perhaps you dream he will come and snatch Hawise's purse and give it over to you, and that with her own gold you can finally *wed* her, and that's what all your murmuring is about? Hah! Now just listen to this silly boy! *Happy* to be poor? Why, no man could ever be happy to be poor, idiot, just as no man could ever be happy to be common. Blood does not lie, and that is why villeins are villains. As for you, I need not even see the color of your veins to know what you are about. Your hope is always in Hawise, for you understand nothing of the world.

No, no, lay not your commoner's fingers on me! Hawise won't be pawed by a penniless infant infatuated with a scallawag. Go find yourself a tavern wench, boy, for after today you'll have nothing more from *me*.

Guy of Gisborne

On this day 27 June of the year of our Lord 1207, I, Sir Guy of Gisborne, Knight of the Crown of England, do write and record, for purposes both legal and personal, my encounter with the villain William de Loxley, commonly known as Robin Hood, which meeting was the matter of this very afternoon, and came to no good ending, but left me much vexed of mind and much wroth of spirit.

I proceeded to Sherwood to find him, having been hired by High Sheriff Robert de Vieuxpont to pursue him and bind him to justice, for William de Loxley has years now been a living menace to the good peace of Nottinghamshire, and has in particular measure terrorized the road through the wood in that area called the Leen Valley, where he has purloined from passersby of substance, and got his living of the coin of other men like a bandit boor. I took him for a rapscallion and a sly fellow and divined that there were no other way of having him out than seeking the viper in his nest. For had I awaited his return to Nottingham, then I should have loitered time unforeseeable, and much would depend on chance, that I were in the right place at the right time, or had spies well posted, or set a bait sufficient to lure him, all the which subterfuges I abhor. If however I advanced in active search of him in Sherwood, or garnered me a contingent of men to scour the wood, then likewise he and his men should sure conceal themselves, and, being more capable woodman than me or mine own soldiers, should as sure evade us or lay for us in ambuscade. All the which determined me on a single course of rational action, by which I might discharge my duties to Sheriff de Vieuxpont and defend my good name: the which being, that I would personally go straight to Sherwood with some few of my most trusted men, and present myself there to the mercy of Robin Hood, in hope that he in the spirit of agonism or derring-do might be persuaded to meet me in private combat, from which engagement I was sure to emerge victorious, by dint of my honor and my virtuosity with the blade.

Trusting then to valor and boldness, set I out with four riders, armed all of us with sword alone, for I knew the shrewdness of those woodland bandits, and would not tempt a battle ere honest steel could be drawn. I am one moreover that does abhor the use of bow as a species of pusillanimous chicanery, the which has been assumed by the lower classes to shield them against their own recreancy and inborn weakness of arm and fiber. We instead were stewarded by our bravery and our willingness to face dire peril and death if need be, and went as it were into the den of the jackal with iron ready to our hands.

We had not far penetrated into the wood, nor had long passed the monastery there at the edge of the Vale of Leen, when Loxley and his men descended on us, as though they were fruit plummeting from the very trees in durance of a windstorm. They must have been in twenty to our five, and yet I wager that ours would have been the prospect and ours the day, had those poltroons but laid down their wood and set to with man's steel. Yet well I knew the vanity of this hope, for the character that invests a man informs each and every of his actions, and if he be himself of poor or friable mettle then nothing he can do will show aught of solidity or firmness.

So they circumscribed us, and I awaited that Loxley would step forth, once more without setting my face to hope, for I wagered that he, being brigand through and through, might not so much as risk to show face. Yet in this calculus I did dismind that Loxley was also head of brigands, and so constrained to act his leaderly part to set them to their place and to hold him to his own; and if he had sent another to do his work, particularly in circumstances that put him in no way in personal danger, then 'twould not need long before some brazen underling determined to supplant him. So it was indeed Loxley that stood forth from that motley crowd, and approached me and my men, cowled and sneak-like. I knew him by his own admission.

"Say, good fellow, but where will you be passing?" he demanded of me.

"By this road, man, seeking me one who goes by the name of Robin Hood," responded I.

"Then my Lord has found him, for here stands one robed verily in hood."

"And might I perceive the one as I address, or needs must he secret his countenance from my sight?" So I challenged him, peeved by this hood and the clandestine shadows it cast upon his face. And truly, I suspected him of defiance, that he would not lower his cowl, but remain so occultly arrayed. Yet to my surprise, he drew down the hood at once, and I found myself looking into an agreeably arranged but impishly expressioned visage, which might have been beautiful were it not marred by an ugly grin. For I find it to be a deep flaw to masculine beauty when a man express mirth in the face of life, and a sign of lightness of character and wont of noble sobriety. In a woman 'tis more becoming, for these are frivolous and lightsome creatures to start, the more congenial as they are winsome. But in a man excess of warm humor is defect that can never be remedied, and prohibits such a one from looking straight on the truth of things and the character of the world, and sure corrupts all manly activity in him. There was indeed another detriment to that countenance, and this one of a physical and not spiritual origin: for his eyes were not twin to each other, but bore two distinct stamps, and whilst one was green the other was azure. This I found most disagreeable, and attributed it as well to manifestation of that man's deeper temperament, or his deceptive and scurvy soul.

Forthwith I announced my reason for coming. "William de Loxley, I am Sir Guy of Gisborne, come to you this day as you see me, to challenge you to personal combat with me, you and I alone and without the intercession of our men, the which battle must decide the matter of your errancy; for if you are found victorious, then sure you shall continue your life of vicious outlawry, until such a day as you meet inevitable and infamous end by dint of the King's justice; but if I am victorious, than you shall give word to your men that they are to disband, returning hence to a life of peace, finding their right place beneath the King's reins, and your blood here upon this forest floor as bond to that pledge."

"Sir Guy does put the matter succinct," said he. "And pray, what weapons shall be the pen and the ink of our contract?"

"But those befitting a man," said I. "We shall draw steel together, and by the honorable blade of sword shall sort this thing out."

"And where the arena of our testing, Sir Guy?" asked he, and I responded, "Why, here, on this very road."

But he contested the matter, saying, "Nay, but I know some more fitting locale within yon forest's bower—a glade that has been trampled down in a bowl of trees, all girded round with wildflowers and the song of bird and the strumming of the cricket on his little lute. If I should die, no better place than that could I find to call my end."

"Ye skirt cowardice to dream so immediately of demise," exclaimed I. "I say the contest shall be here."

But he returned me this word, nor spoke poorly, saying, "'Tis not cowardice, Sir Guy, but art, that should with care and deliberation arrange the commencements and the endings of life, in stern obedience to first and last things. Hear you then my proposition, and see if it is to your liking. Not one contest but two shall Sherwood see this day; the first, to determine the where of the second. In this first, we shall draw arrows together, striking toward a mark of my Lord's choosing, and the winner shall have his choice of place. If Sir Guy should defeat me, then verily I shall meet him here in personal combat, upon this very footpath and gash of civilization. If instead I should take the day, then we shall repair to my forest home, and there Sir Guy shall sit with us and sup and be our good guest; after the which, I shall draw steel with Sir Guy of Gisborne within the glade, and this I swear to him upon the righteous and Christian name of King John."

"Yet I carry no bow with me," pursued I, in truth of my honorable nudity in this respect.

"Then, Sir Guy, you shall borrow mine, a truer piece of oak than any that can be found in all of England, and so we shall walk upon an even field."

"I find this agreeable," acquiesced I, persuaded both by his eloquence and by his reasoning and by his unexpected show of good breeding, and I dismounted. Now I am a fair sight with a bow and arrow, for I have passed me time practicing at it for th'hunt. I do fancy myself the equal or the better of most men of my rank. But I say, the bow is a weapon at which one marks one's merit by not excelling immodestly; for only men of low station have the time or the need to master it. And truly, I was much outsighted by this Loxley. I chose me as our target a crotchet in a tree, some thirty feet hence; and though I did strike the tree and near to the target, Loxley centered the goal to perfection, and was an honor to his rank. I conceded to him his victory, and did submit to follow him through wood, to that place he called his home.

We struck for the forest, and I was much surprised that these dwellers of the wood did not bind us or shut our eyes, but invited us freely and with open vision to follow them. And yet I saw at once the motive for this seeming liberty: that this forest was a labyrinth, and it should need a woodsman half wild to retrace the path we followed. For we spiraled much and switched back at turns, and took needless round-abouts through gullies and hollows to reach our destination, which was deep in this wilderness. But by and by did we come to it, a kind of extended shanty town there within the wood. And I could see it was a city builded to be dismantled and transposed. I could not get me right count of the numbers that this Loxley boasted; but somewhere 'twixt fifty and sixty sure there were, which was a greater host than I had before credited to him. And to my wonder men and children I saw there forsooth, for this was no gruff encampment of warbound warriors, but instead a kind of false shire.

We sat us down near to one of these tents, where a fire had been kindled, and food was called for. And there we dined, though I refused the venison, knowing it to be cut of the King's deer, and not wishing moreover to break bread with the rabble that Loxley had at his beck. In the meantime, William de Loxley and I had us discourse.

"What thinks Sir Guy of my moveable city?" asked he.

"Methinks 'tis wanting in refinements," said I, for I was in no mood to be civil to these beasts.

"Troth, troth," said he, "though we do what we may." And at once he snapped his fingers and was brought a lute of some quality, which he set minstrel-like to playing, and sang to its accompaniment. Verily, he played a clean board, and his music and his voice were fine, so that I was strangely calmed in my soul, and might have feared me bewitchment, but for my great contempt of this riffraff folk. Then he had done, and the instrument was withdrawn, and he turned to me, saying, "I have it on my faith that a man will carry his refinements with him wheresoever he may stray."

"And yet there are embellishments of life that cannot be introduced into savagery," countered I.

"My Lord speaks true," he allowed, ever with that irksome smile, "but hardly do we of the forest engross savagery. Methinks that liberty is an embellishment of such worth, as pays for many a lesser."

"And is this liberty," challenged I, "to be penned in a forest hole, and denied all passage to and from the thoroughfares of men? Is it liberty to be refused commerce and right intercourse with the subjects of the Crown? Is it liberty to bear a price and a law upon one's head, that others seek ever to extricate? Or prithee, is it liberty, each double fortnight, to be obliged to tear one's own very home up from the ground upon which it stands, to displace it some number of miles, in quest ever of that sanctuary one has forfeit?"

He conceded me the point, saying, "Truly has my Sir Guy proffered description of social or political liberty, by which my little band stands condemned. And true it is that my example is flung in the face of society, and should wreak there havoc general."

"Then you admit that if all men were to follow you, it should mean the wreck of the world!"

"I do," replied he, all tranquility

"And stand you not then condemned?"

He smiled a curious smile then with that unpleasant turn of his lips that I had afore noted, and quoth he, "Were all men butchers, or fletchers, or else warriors like my honorable Sir Guy—why, indeed, if all men were prophets or priests or kings—then in any one of these cases particular, it should mean the wreck of the world. The absurdity of a uniform and hypothetical humanity is no just response to the vital fact of its diversity. 'Tis said, is it not, that the house of God hath many mansions?"

But I waved off these sophisms. "You do not meet the point, Loxley, though ye seem to," said I. "For the principle is this: if all men were to contemn the law and abridge it, were all men to transgress upon the very borders of social order, then all things should come to an end, and societies be rubbled."

"And were *all* men, my good Sir Guy, to follow unjust laws as sheep and kine, life itself should be stripped of your very social order, and a gray and tedious world it should be that's left behind, full up of tyrants, victims, and abuse."

"Tedium is no evil, but a petty irritant that a just man will neglect e'en to notice."

"Your just man, Sir Guy," said he, speaking sudden in a way that riled me, "is hardly even alive, so strictured is he! Why, he seems to me a kind of turtle, dragging about the burthen of his duty on his back, slow moving and careful not to trample upon the grass. Yet tell me—does the lawgiver slave himself to his own unrighteous law?"

But I interrupted him, saying, "Enough of this hash of words." And I rose then, for the heat was on me, and I would have this matter out in a more decisive manner. "I would extract what was promised me, William de Loxley. Let us to the duel."

And Robin Hood rose as well, with something on this face that pleased me none. I felt a tug of my belt and struck about, but it was late, for before me was a smirking peasant, decked in green, who grasped in his hand my very sword, the which he had darstardly robbed of me. "What means this!" I cried. "What is this mischief?"

"I beg honest pardon of my Sir Guy," said Loxley, "but it should be pity to stain so lovely a blade, or so fine a day, with bloodfall. Let us lay aside our strife for some other moment more opportune. There are, I wager, chances enow in this world to kill one another! I say, my Sir Guy and his men need not trouble themselves over the fare that has been brought them, and e'en the Forest Tax this day is waived. That I do consider the just price of our hospitality."

"Loxley," seethed I, for I was grown wroth indeed, "I had you on your oath!"

"I swear I swore on nothing solid," bantered he, his brow rising, and he smiling that wretched mocking smile once more.

"I had taken you for a man of honor," said I, "and find I am much deluded."

"It is sure a question how a man ought measure his honor," laughed he, which riled me the more.

"Or what are ye, Robin of Loxley, but a yeoman and a knave?"

"I, Sir Guy? Why, I am the lord of all of Sherwood; and that methinks makes the extent of my rule something well in excess of the piddling fiefs and demesnes that my Sir Guy might claim as his own in Gisbourne town."

"I have seen ye this day a coward," I said to him, and arrant was my scorn. But he only grinned most abusively, and began to arrange his men to guide us away. And mine own men were tempted, I know, to draw steel and die in glory, but I held them off, saying, "Sheathe your swords away for this day. We did not set out to hunt dogs. We shall find Loxley in another, and have his blood by combat manly."

By and by they put us on our horses and aimed us toward the forest road. And as we were going, I saw that Loxley was set to stay behind, I said to him, "My sword, man, I would have my sword!"

"Does my Sir Guy value it so greatly?" he asked, gesturing to the villain that bore my sword yet in his fist; the which brought it to Loxley and handed it to him. He took it in his fist and tried its balance, and though he rightly praised the blade mine eye did detect he was not sure of himself in its play.

I spake again. "It is the blade of my forefathers, Loxley, an heirloom of many generations before mine own, and I would have it."

"Then my Sir Guy *shall* have it," said he with a nod, "for I would ne'er offend a guest. Yet not this moment, for I fear that the blood that is hot on my Sir Guy should lead him to principled recklessness this day. So heed me. Soon when my Sir Guy and his men have been led to the Great Road, let them set out for Nottingham; and when they have come to the edge of the Leen Vale, they shall find there a monastery, set in the thicket to their right, nestled within a dale. Thereabouts the road curves widely, running almost half a circle round in the course of e'en a mile, and in the cove of that arc, deep and hidden in the closure of the trees, there is an oak tree of more years than Sir Guy's ancestral blade. It is a mighty bark, and spreads its canopy wide o'er the wood surrounding, and is in all things a marvel and a spectacle to witness. I have gone there atimes to meditate on matters of near concern to me. Now, this oak tree was stricken once time past by a bolt of thunder, and was sundered behind its mighty bole, so that in its regrowth a sappy crag has opened in its hoary woodflesh. I say, Sir Guy, and I make this promise on my very life, that you, passing round that tree as I have instructed, shall already find your blade secreted within that nook."

"Ye are a liar, Loxley, as has already been seen. If it is to be your men that lead me out, how can it be your men that precede me to this tree? Nay. Loxley, I shall not make me twice a fool this day."

"Look to the tree, Sir Guy. This day I rob no man."

"Then what, oh man of Loxley, is your desire, this day or any other?"

"That Lady Luck should reign again," said he, and spake no more, but smiled his horrid smile.

He gestured to his men, saying, "Bear yon pollard back to his horn," and with these infamous words, they gathered our horses by the reins and led them forth. And as we went I perceived the sword of my sires glittering in his fingers.

We were left where we had been found on the road, and I, in much fury and righteous dudgeon, disposed my men to ride hard for Nottingham, for I wished to precede Loxley's man to their destination, and to apprehend him, in the off chance that Loxley were not a rank liar. Elsewise, I had determined that, if I should not reclaim my father's sword, I would lay siege to the very forest and burn it down ere I find me Loxley. We came to the point he had indicated, and left our steeds upon the curve of the road, with a single guard, the rest of us to hack it through the underbrush. So we proceeded until by strait luck we spied the oak tree, of description such as Loxley had given. I wheeled to its far side—and lo, there was indeed a gap, black and pitchy, even as Loxley had promised, and sheathed within it, in a sheathe even of some craft and quality, was the blade of my sires; the which I took and tried and even struck light against the same oak tree, fearing unreasonably witchcraft or deceit. But it was doubtless my blade and none other, and no sign of the man that had bought it hence. In my anger I left me my own gash in that tree as even the lightning had done.

And yet my great wroth was not by this assuaged, but even now waxes in my heart the keener, for I have been mocked and sullied by this woodland fiend. And I repeat now the great oath I took beneath that oak as our druid forefathers were once wont to do, that I shall haunt this man's steps wheresoever he should go, until such a day as I might extract from him the battle he has promised me, and take his life forfeit to it.

The Saracen

will tell you why the Lord Robert has it out for him. I will tell you sure. It wasn't just one event, neither. 'Twas the Saracen as done the worst of it, but that come later. 'Twas all before your time, for you had not yet arrived to Nottingham at that time. These events is common knowledge here, you can ask anyone. But I'll tell you the story most cannot of that first day, for I myself saw it, while most did not. Why, of course I was there—the very day it happened! I was e'en with the Sheriff when the news come in. And so naturally I was one of the men sent out to catch him. Had it not been for Father Steven I think we might have. But he got away, and put Lord Robert to shame, that he did, more than just once even on that day, and I'll tell you just how.

It was the last day of May, on the feast in honor of the visitation of the Virgin Mary to the mother of St. John the Baptist—the day, you might say, when Jesus meets John. And Robin had come in to communion. Yes sir, communion! I knowed it not at the time, of course—no one knowed it, apart, I reckon, from Father Steven—but we all knowed it afterward, for it was at the doors of the very church we almost catched him. Aye, at the doors of the very church! Can you credit it? I have heard rumor he will not miss a mass to Mary. Well, this time, he almost hanged for it.

So the lad as brung us the news gone first to Lord Robert, and Lord Robert dragged the boy to the Sheriff, where I happened to be, as I was bein' hounded on some business concernin' tax collection. The Sheriff was a stickler on his taxes, he was. No, no, not the present Sheriff, but Sheriff Bardulf, who died before your time. A hard man was Bardulf. So the Lord Robert arrives with this lad, and this lad tells what he knows, that Robin is afoot, and the Sheriff says, "You're sure of it?" And the lad just nods stupidly, mouth agape, like a imbecile. So the Sheriff asks, "And how do you know this man?"

And do you know what the lad says? He says, "I do not, sir." So the Sheriff asks 'im where he saw Robin prior, and he says, "I have not, sir." The Sheriff asks 'im how he recognized Robin of the Hood, then, and the lad says, "I did not, sir."

Now, that Sheriff was a patient man—in that, at least, nor a spot nor a speckle in common with the current one!—and he says, "On what grounds precisely, lad, do you make your claim?"

The lad just nods and says, "He seemed a hunchback, sir, but I spied beneath the shadows of his hood, and 'twas no hunch! But rather the curve of a bow his cloak so rides upon. And I ask myself, sir: now why would a man bear arms into the holy church? And why be he dressed as a beggar so? And I says to myself, sir, I says, *there* is a outlaw, if ever I seen one; and what outlaw is famed for the bow, and what would be so daring, if not Robin of the Hood? And is there not a fine prize upon Robin's head? And am I not a boy in need of gold? Well, then, sir—that was my reasoning."

And the Sheriff sayed to Lord Robert that the lad was not so stupid as he seemed. And he sayed that time had finally come to go out and catch 'im once and for all. And I warrant he would have, had not Lord Robert craved all the glory. For he interfered, he did, and sayed that he would be the one to take Robin Hood. The Sheriff had no choice but to let 'im to it. And a right good thing for Robin Hood!

So out the Lord Robert ordered us, and out we went, to the church, where the faithful was just departin' mass. And there he was, sure as day, a hunchback with his hood up, limpin' from the church. But guards had already been put on either side of the doors—that was the Sheriff you see, so sensible a notion would never have crossed Robert's head! And Robert wasted no time but he called out, "You, Robin of the Hood! Drop your hood and drop weapons, for you are catched at last."

Well, Robin looks around him, and sees he's surrounded, and he starts to take off his cloak. I was sure it was over, I was, and that we had 'im. "Well, well," says I to myself, "ol' Lord Robert's got 'im at last." That's what I sayed! Little did I know! I think every one of us thought the same, and that was prolly how he could pull his next trick.

See, one of our fellows walked up to 'im to seize his weapons. Well, what happened next happened so fast *I* could barely make it out! All of a sudden, Robin's cloak was right over my comrade's head, and he had his bow in hand, and he was loosin' arrows among us like a devil, he was. He must have felled ten of us right there! And then he taked off like a hare right through the middle of us. I never seen a man run like Robin run. And every man of us was in such a state of shock we just let 'im race right by, off into the square.

Now the Lord Robert, he was just standin' there, stunned as a goat! It was the Sheriff as woke us all up, roarin' like a beast, and we come to and took off after him. Well, he couldn't get out the far side of the square, because here again the Sheriff had thinked ahead and had posted archers. But there was a gallows there set up in the center of the square, for a man was to be hanged next day, and Robin runs right up to it and mounts it at a leap, standin' there right next to the noose like it was meant for him. Lord Robert catched up at this point flappin' about like a goose. And he cawed out, "Fool, do you not see you're surrounded? Give it up, now, or I will order you killed!" And might have sayed more, but that the cap he wore speeded off of his head like a bird, pinned on the point of a arrow, and he fell flat on his face holdin' his scalp.

And Robin, bold as you please, called out, "It wasn't skill as missed your skull, Robert, but mercy! So watch your next words." Well, I for one seen how he shooted that day, and I've heard the stories, and for my part I wager he was tellin' the truth. He could have shot Robert through the eye if he'd so desired! Though as to why he didn't kill him then and there, your guess is as good as mine. Well, Lord Robert was bleedin' from the head, and he yammered at his men to get Robin, and they swamped in like a pack of wolves, and Robin disappears under them. But then—swear on my soul!—I see 'im climbin' up on top of them all, pullin' himself up the rope of the noose, and he walks over their very heads like they was steppin' stones, and jumps down on the far side and starts racin' across the square again, now goin' the other way! And none of my fellows seen 'im go, for they was under him, but for I and a few others who was farther back. *We* seen, alright, and we start after him. He runs to a buildin' on the corner of a road, shootin' men down as he goes, and vanishes around the corner. One of my comrades comes up to that corner, and slows down, no doubt because he figured that Robin Hood might be waitin' in ambush there. Well, he comes up to the point where he's just about to peak 'round, and suddenly I hear a arrow come loose, and it comes whistlin' 'round the corner. What do you mean, what do I mean? I mean it come *'round* the corner! Swear it on me mother's gravestone, bless her soul! It curved in the very air, and struck my comrade straight through the heart! No, not *right* around the corner, but easy like, curvin' just enough to hit its target. Never have I seen such sorcery as that, but that's how it happened, or my name isn't Ralph! You don't believe me? Why, the fellow that was shot—John Pretlove's his name—you can ask him yourself how it happened, for he survived it! Right, I said he was shot through the heart, but that was a figure of speech, friend. He took it in the arm, if you please, but he ne'er so much as seen the fellow as loosed the arrow, and that's the truth. He told me his shadow had fallen before him and alerted old Robin that he was comin', so maybe his shadow got a glimpse of how Robin done it. Go on and ask him, he'll tell you...

Well, we was all wary about comin' up on that corner now, let me tell you! And when we did, what did we find, but that Robin of the Hood was long gone. We followed the trail of his blood—for he had a good cut of the sword in the fray—right to the doors of the church. And Robert wanted the Sheriff to storm right in there and take him, but the Sheriff naysayed him. Sayed that he would not trespass the boundaries of Church property. Well, the Lord Robert was wroth over this, and almost gone in himself, but the Sheriff pointed out to 'im that the Pope was a worse enemy to have than a dozen Robins, and told the man to step down, which he done—first sensible thing he done all morning! And the Sheriff sayed he himself would talk to the priest and demand the criminal be handed over.

And he done as he sayed he would—waited there all mornin' until Father Steven come out, then given 'im a bit of his mind. But Father Steven refused to hand Robin over. Wouldn't even allow he was hidin' in there at all! Oh, he talked around it somethin' wonderful. The Sheriff sayed a villain was in there, and Father Steven asked 'im if the Sheriff didn't know the church was a hospital for souls, and every day full up of villains. The Sheriff sayed that by harborin' a criminal Father Steven was breakin' the law, and Father Steven sayed he must obey the law of God first and foremost, and only then the law of man. The Sheriff sayed this was wickedness as would stain the church, and Father Steven replied that the church could not be stained by acts of charity. Aye, acts of charity! Well, the Sheriff was right sore at that, but could see there was nothin' more to say to so stubborn a man, so he stationed men secretly about the church (I was one of 'em, which is the way I knowed it) and gone back to wait the thief out. And we waited, and waited, and waited.

Well, me and another of my fellows was there—Peter Pinchpenny, who's long since dead now—to watch the south side, where there was a small door of exit, and we taken turns watchin' and sleeping, and never once seen a man exit it, neither day nor night, if not Father Steven and the Deacon. Five days and five nights we waited there, and then we was called down by the Sheriff hisself. He came round to ask us if we done our duty those days, and we told 'im by God we had, and he told us we were no longer needed there, but that we were to organize a posse and comb the town for the criminal. Well, I myself was weared out, and I asked him, I says, "My Lord Sheriff, what is this? Has Robin of the Hood got out?" And the Sheriff only glares at me and goes on his way.

Well, in days to come, I heard what happened, I did—or as much of it as any man knowed then or knows now. Which is to say, that the priest gone to the Sheriff and telled 'im that the thief was flat out of it. How Robin done it, the priest either himself did not know, or else would not say. I do know it riled the Sheriff considerably, for I later seen 'im starin' at that church like it was a riddle and he the man to figure it out. He passed all that afternoon walkin' around it, just lookin' at it!

As for Lord Robert, he did not show his face for a week, on account of the bandages he had to wear for that arrow, and when he was seen again, he was scowling, ever scowling. Not that he was ever just bright as sunshine to begin with, but this done 'im over, and no question. I seen how it riled him, I did, for I went to the Sheriff that evenin' to tell him that Robin was nowheres to be found, and the two of them was together in the Lord Robert's rooms overlookin' the square. The Sheriff was standin' there at the window and had his great big back to us, and ne'er once turned as I gived the news. But he heard me out, and still without turnin', he says to Robert, he says, "'Tis sayed there is a mighty Wheel that turns us all upon its back, men and kingdoms entire — now risin' us up to glory and fortune, now throwin' us down to wrack and ruin." Well, Robert didn't get the gist of this, and asked the Sheriff what the devil it was about, and he jus' points out over the square at nothin' at all, and says, "I reckon that man there learned to ride it," meaning Robin of the Hood, of course. Them words stuck with me, they did!

Well, I have never seen anyone so angry as Robert was at that moment, and I taked my leave fast, I'll tell you, for fear I might see a chair fly at me head as the bearer of bad news. And ever since then he's had it out for Robin of the Hood. He even set a trap for 'im of a archery contest, thinkin' the fellow would just saunter in and try the contest for a gold arrow. And God's boots if he didn't! Have you heard that one? The time Robin dressed as a old man and come in and winned the prize by splittin' three arrows in twain? No, no, it was three, not one! Three, one af'er another, it was. I was there, I seen 'em, every one! Three in a row. And then he took that gold arrow in hand, and gived a great blow of his horn, and the whole town was full of 'em, Robin's own men, and they killed some thirty of Robert's best men before all was sayed and done, and losed not one of their own, and fleed the town, gold arrow and all!

What's he like? What, you mean what does he look like? Oh, he's a fine-lookin' man, he is. Dark of hair and dark of eye, bearded, cleanly lookin', though they say he lives like a boar in Sherwood. Aye, a fine-lookin' man he is! An' he knows how to talk, he does. Has the *gift*. Why, I heard 'im talk to the Sheriff as he took the gold arrow, and what words he sayed! Oh, I can't recall what they was. *I* haven't the gift! Though I *do* talk a lot, hah! *He* plays on words as he played on his bow that day. I *do* remember this, that he went straight up to Maid Marion and kissed her, the bold dog! What, you don't know of Maid Marion? God's boots, man, I allow you're new hereabouts, but have you truly heard nothin'? The Maid Marion was the Lord Robert's charge, till Robin up and robbed her from 'im! Aye, come in and took her away, just as easy as you please, and she never heard from again! Loveliest lass in the whole of this shire, I reckon. Who can say what fate she met out there in the greenwood... *Tha's* no place for womanfolk, I'll tell you that.

What? Of course he's still out there. And may God preserve him! That's right, I do say it—and proud! If you want *my* view of Robert and Robin, one alongside the other, I'll tell you this: Roin may well be a fox, but that Robert is a weasel. And if Robin's a fox as robs only golden eggs, Robert's a weasel that robs from the coop for the joy of robbin'. They be two different kinds of Robs, they be. Those were better days. Sheriff Bardulf was hard about taxes, but he ne'er stole a parcel of land from a poor soul. I need not tell you whether his successors was so honest, and you'll have heard what role His High and Mighty Lordship has in all that.

Alright. I'll show you what kind of man he is. I'll show you what kind of man the both of 'em is. You know, don't you, that one of Robin's band is a Saracen? That's right, a Saracen, swarthy as a dyer! I'll tell you how it all come about. It all started with King Richard, bless his soul, who on his Crusade once captured ten thousand Muslims at a blow. Well, the cowardly Moslim King Sladden, cursèd be his name, ordered his army sneak up on a thousand of King Richard's men in the night and slitted their throats while they slept, so King Richard in his anger gone to these ten-thousand prisoners and told them they could convert or they could die. And when they chosen death to a man, death is what they had. But one of them Saracens had a little boy with him, and King Richard could not bring hisself to kill it. That is the kind of man he is! He was for leavin' it behind, though it would like as not have died there anyway, but one of his knights stepped up and sayed he hisself would take it on, and make of it a servant boy, and bring it back to England with him. And this is what happened.

But when he come back to England he found here a foe fiercer and fouler than the fiercest and foulest of the Saracens, waitin' for 'im in his very house:

his own wife! Why, she seen that Saracen boy and ordered her husband at once to release it. She sayed she would not abide a mere boy doin' the work of men, Saracen or no, not in *her* household; and when her husband replied it was a Moslim child, and a slave, and he could do with it as he pleased, she told 'im it wasn't like to become Christian if it was made to live a slave to Christians. And so this fellow, who had slayed hundreds of Saracens on the Crusade in Acre, found hisself conquered by a shrew in Ol' England, for there is nothin' in this world so formidable as a huswife. So let that be a warnin' to you about marriage, my young friend!

Defeated he was, but not ready to give in all the way. No, sir. He wasn't about to free this child—no, not he. Why, he'd hauled that boy all the way back from Acre! Was he to let his troubles to go for nothin'? So he up and selled it on the sly, and sold it moreover to a certain lord some leagues from his own town, so that his wife would ne'er get wind of it. And I believe you can just guess the name of the lord as buyed it. Aye, 'tis so, the very same! All this was before your time, too, which is why you ne'er heard nor grunt nor mutter of it. Boy's name was Nadir. Still is, I reckon. Must'a been better'n ten years of age when he come here to Nottingham, and this was already better'n half a decade past, so you can reckon his age now!

You can also guess how he was treated by our ven'rable Lord Robert. He lived in constant terror of that man, he did, and I don't blame him. I reckon he had scars on his back to show for his lordship's hospitality. Why, if he decided at last to break for the hills, that was only because he, though a Saracen, ain't a fool. Only, he chosen the wrong moment to do it.

See, the Lord Robert's wife one fine mornin' found that her prized necklace was gone. Rubies, diamonds, em'rals and sapphires on a chain of purest gold, gone. So she sets up the ol' hue and cry, and what a voice she had for it! Like a chicken at roost. Soon the whole of the town's out and about and lookin' for the thief.

Well, our young Nadir, hearin' this righteous hubbub, decides it's do or die. He sneaks off while everyone's out lookin' for the thief, not bethinkin' himself just how that would seem! Too bad for 'im, but they sees 'im runnin' down the road and into the forest, and they think they've spied the thief. He's a fast boy, and he gets a ways in—lucky lad, as you soon shall see!—but he ain't fast enough, and they catch him, and haul 'im back in, and accuse 'im of stealin' the jewels.

Poor Nadir protests his innocence. Says he never lain eyes on this necklace, and doesn't know what he'd do with it even if he had it. Says he was just tryin' to get away from ugly ol' Robbey, and that's that. They search him, they do, but of course find no necklace, for *he* wasn't the one as had taken it, as you shall see. But do you think that satisfies the mob? No, sir, it does not—nor does it satisfy good Lord Robert, I might add! For he has it out for this boy. He is certain, certain to his very bones, that this boy took the necklace and throwed it into the briars as he run through the wood. Search parties is set out left and right to find it, but they come back empty-handed. Well, Robert is still not ready to give it up, so what does he do? Why, he does the charitable thing: trial by ordeal, then and there, right outside the town! The boy will prove his innocence by holdin' a hot rod of iron, and then they'll see jus' how quick it'll heal; and if it festers, and he be proved guilty, Robert says he will cut it off, and take a eye besides, to teach that lad ne'er to set nor his remainin' hand nor his remainin' eye on a lady's jewels again. That's what he says!

So they get up a fire, and put a iron to it, and when it is red hot Robert himself takes it up in a pair of tongs, and orders that boy to hold out his hand. By God the lad done it, or I ain't a Christian! I ne'er seen such stalwartness in e'en a Christian man, not to speak of a Saracen mite. He holds his hand out and looks Robert square in the eye, he does, and not even a shudder from him! Why, I'd be proud to be his father. And Robert is just lowerin' that red rod to the child's skin, and it's comin' down and comin' down, and it's *just* about to touch—when he gets his second scar from Robin of the Hood. For Robin had no doubt been there in the wood, and seen the boy tryin' to escape, and was sure not goin' to let any pambly-nambly nobleman lay hand on a child. That arrow comes whistlin' down the way, right out from between the trees, and flies straight into Lord Robert's pretty little hand, and he drops that iron rod like he hisself was holdin' it, and goes off wailin' away clutchin' his feathered fingers, fearin', I do not doubt, for his very skin! Well, I tell you, there was chaos at that moment, and the whole lot of 'em in a uproar and men throwin' 'emselves this way and that and flat down on the ground—*anything* to get out of the way of them arrows, let me tell you!—and the boy takes to runnin' again, straight for the wood—bright boy, I say!—and disappears into it, and is ne'er heard from again. Not, that is, till rumors started comin' in about a Saracen in Robin's gang. Then it was clear as day what had come of little Nadir. He growed up a woodman, he did, and one of the most dangerous of the lot!

And do you want to know the best of it? The best of it is this: the very evening after these events, the very same, the Lady Robert is diggin' about in her dressin' room, when what does she happen across? Can you guess it? That's right: her own necklace, right where she left it! She'd been hollerin' for the thief all afternoon, only to find that the thief was what she sees in the mirror e'ery blessèd mornin'!

So that, my friend, is a short history of why the Lord Robert so actively loathes Robin of the Hood. You might say he hates 'im from his own head to his own hand, you might. Oh, they've all been tryin' to catch 'im for years now, old Robert first and foremost, but I reckon they never will. Nah... Robin and his gang'll keep a step ahead of 'em, for Robin of Sherwood is cleverer than any man of Robert's or the Sheriff's, or my name ain't Ralph! You can count on it: he'll keep a step ahead of, 'em, alright till the day he dies. A step ahead of 'em—or a step right *over* 'em! Hah!

David of Doncaster

swear it by my honor, the fool had letters patent from the Sheriff himself, justifying the hunt! He was right proud of them. Puffed up as a peacock he was, and out he went with them stuffed into his pockets, and that was all the excuse he needed! Well, it happened that he first thought to patronize a certain celebrated tavern there (so as not to forge into the woods dry) and got himself a mug of the first-rate ale that this tavern could offer, and boasted a while with the locals about his intentions. And then he asked the most excellent and notable *Proprietor* of that most honorable and well-famed *Establishment* if the man knew aught of Robin Hood.

"Who don't?" says the Proprietor, lapidary as is his wont.

"But have ye e'er *seen* him?" pursues old David.

"Seems I have, once or twice, mayhaps. A man never can be sure," says the Proprietor, with smart prudency.

"But could ye *recognize* him if ye saw him again?" presses David.

"That's for God to tell," equivocates the Proprietor.

Well, that fool just says to the Proprietor, he says, "We shall know, and soon enough. For look here: I'll be back this very day with Robin Hood in company." This very day! And he really believed it, the poor deluded twit!

Well, the Proprietor just scratches his beard and nods steadily, and away our boaster sallies, as sure of himself as Old Scratch.

Into Sherwood with him then, and down the long gauntlet, and he just marching on as if sooner or later he'll walk right up to Robin and strap a rope about his neck and march him right back away again to the Sheriff's gaol to be tagged, caged, inspected, itemized, pulled apart, and gallowed! Hah! Well, so he walks and walks, does poor David, and no sign of any soul taller than a squirrel for many a mile; but he is undismayed, is good David, and walks some more, looking straight ahead as if there were no left and no right. When suddenly, up ahead, what should he spy, but a fellow garbed all in red! And he, brave David, strides up to this crimson stranger, and announces himself, the amazing fool, declaring, "Well met, Wayfare! I for my part am David of Doncaster, and I am looking me out for Robin Hood, for I have a layman's warrant on his head, signed by the Sheriff of Nottingham himself, and intend his arrest! See here, where 'tis all writ out: 'The Bearer of this Letter is hereby granted and authorized express Permission and Encouragement by the Shrievalty of Nottingham to perform all deeds necessary and requisite to the Apprehension of one Robin of the Hood, dead or alive, as the said Bearer shall see fit, by the Will and Acumen of this same Bearer, in return for which lawful Service he shall receive that Amount of gold Coins currently set upon the Capture of the said Robin of the Hood by the Law of Nottingham.' So see, I shall find this man and take him back to the Sheriff's gaol and earn me the reward posted upon his head. Say, Master Wayfare, have you seen him, that I might apprehend him?"

And the other just smiles as wide as you please and lays a hand on David's broad shoulder and says to him, "My good man, you are in special luck this day—for it happens I am just come from Robin's encampment!"

And good David does not bat an eye, nor ask himself a single wondering question! For no doubt he imagined the whole affair to unfold in just such a manner, for the greater good of Nottingham and David Doncasters everywhere; and he says, "Excellent good! Then you can lead me off to him at once, and we shall show him these letters patent in the hand of the Sheriff and bring him back with us, and by my word I shall give you a quota of the reward on Robin's head. What say you to a tithe of the total, as finder's fee?"

"Fie, say I!" cried the other, as if in dismay, "that is a sight too generous of you, Master Vigilante, for so little work as shall be required! But hear me this, that I will lead you before Robin Hood, and you will take the whole prize for it, but I in return will have all that's in your bag there."

"In my bag?" cries David.

"In your bag, cully," says master Scarlett.

"But my bag is full up of naught but various of my personal effects!" protests he. "To wit: ten silver coins; one small knife; one spool of woolen twine—"

"Then these are the effects that shall be mine own," says the other.

And David, looking for the first time as though he verges on surprise, says, "If you would take them over a quota of the profit, then so be it! There is naught in it I cannot easily purchase or find again with so much money." And on this they shook. Then David says, "Lead on then to Robin's encampment!" but the other puts up a hand as though to halt him, and replies, "Look here, friend, I have other notion. For Robin's encampment is full of Robin's men, and we just two. 'Twere better to set a vigilant trap, think ye not?"

"On my honor, I abhor deceit!" says David, but the other says, "Deceit 'tis not, Master Vigilante, but straightness, for a man as lives by deceit is honestly ensnared by the same." And David, who is no philosopher, ponders on this a moment, scratching his poor pate, and finally agrees that it has its share of sense. So Master Scarlett says, "Hear me, then. My mouth's dry as tinder and my legs weary from long walking. Let us get us to the nearest tavern and weigh our strategy over a flagon or two of cool ale."

"This notion likes me well!" cries David of Doncaster, who never in all his days let a drop of ale slip by him.

"Good! Know ye an establishment suitable to these purposes?" queries Scarlett, and David, reflecting on it, says aye, he does! For he has just come from such a one. "Then forth!" says his new colleague, and off David goes, and Scarlett behind him, to the selfsame tavern he had only just quit!

Now, the most excellent and notable *Proprietor* of this most honorable *Establishment*, observing the return of that man he had only an hour past bid adieu, and finding him moreover in certain company, looks them both over long and hard; but as any proprietor of any tavern, he is much inured to wonders and knows to mind his own business, and so when a table is requested, he but shrugs and sees to it. Ale is brought, and ale drunk, as poor David keeps trying to lay out a plan for the capture of Robin, involving snares and falling cages and pitfalls and ambushes. But Master Scarlett only draws him in circles, saying ever, "No need of such machinations, Master Vigilante, for sure we will bag him well." And the other: "How bag? Will we not need such and such a treesnare—"

"No need, no need, Master Vigilante! For bag him will."

Now, David knew the art of drinking, but never once learned the art of ceasing, and by and by he was so deep in his mugs that he forgot the art of staying awake, but fell into a long and snoreful slumber. By and by he comes to, all at a start, to find the Proprietor frowning over him. Well he groans and tries to rise but only falls over, and rolls about a moment on the floor, catching his bearings, when suddenly by a mighty exertion of will he realizes that both his new red friend and his precious bag are nowhere to be seen! Well, you can be sure that this epiphany awakens him at a blow, and he manages e'en to gain his feet, and grabs the Proprietor by both arms, screaming, "Where has he got to, that crimson scoundrel? The one I came with?"

"What, mean you Robin Hood?" responds the Proprietor, incredulous.

"Zounds!" cries poor David, and lets his hands fall, that he might better scratch his poor pate. "*That* was Robin Hood?"

"What did you take him for?" asks the Proprietor, brushing his shoulders discreetly.

"But why did you not *tell* me it was Robin Hood, man?"

"And did you not say to me yourself that you would return this very day with Robin Hood in your company?"

David ponders this a moment, and grows distinctly red about the brow. "Why," says he, "then I shall now go forth and find him and flay him alive, by my troth, and tie him up in these very letters patent—bah, but what! For they are gone!" And 'tis true! For though poor David gropes diligently about his person, it is all in vain: the letters patent have gone the way of man and bag. He turns despairing to the Proprietor, and cries, "He stole even the warrant on his own head! Why, I will find him and make him swallow it…" And boldly sets to depart the tavern and enter again Sherwood, does our dogged David, but alack!

for the *Proprietor* blocks his way, saying, "You may go wherever you durst and do whatever you please to whomever you fancy, but first there is the bill to pay!"

Now, David stands astounded for the first time in all his many years, and stares at the proprietor with blank eyes. "Bill?" echoes he wanly.

"Aye, the tab! For as Robin was leaving, he promised you would make good on your common bill."

At which, David sets to such a mass of cursing that I am not sure I have ever heard so thick and wide a river of imprecations in all my days (with my ears, mind you, that have received veritable marvels), and I do not doubt but he would have dismantled the very furniture of that tavern in a rage, had he not been foggily aware that it would have only accrued to the debt he owed. But by and by, regaining mastery over himself, he cries, in a moment of divine inspiration, "Good Master Tavernkeep! I cannot pay you e'en a cent of what is owed, for all my moneys have been seized with my bag by that thief, liar, caitiff, scamp, deceiver, rascal, blackguard, perjurer, malinger, misleader, defrauder, mischiefmaker, and—shrimp—Robin of the Hood, including my own bag, in which were contained various of my personal effects, to wit: ten silver coins; one small knife; one spool of woolen twine; fourteen buttons of size miscellaneous; four fragments of pottery; six marbles; one lock; one piece of bread, wrapped in one piece of gray homespun; one dead beetle—"

But the proprietor interrupts him here, saying, "Your misfortune afflicts me most gravely, Master David of Doncaster, as does the loss of your possibles, but I fear that despite it, the bill stands as before."

Now David lets out at this a great wallop that echoes through the entire fine establishment, rattling the windows and startling the guests, and cries, "Hear me, and have my word on it! I will within this very day find Robin Hood and return here in his company, and he himself, the vagabond, shall pay you full what is owed. My word, Master Tavernkeep!"

"And if you find him not?" inquires this most excellent Proprietor, who is, if nothing else, then certainly a shrewd businessman.

"Then I shall hence to my home and gather there the moneys owed and make right this bill, until I can find Robin Hood and extract from his hide the debt he owes me!"

Well, the Proprietor made this calculation, that while the claim seemed wild, so too it had done the first time, when good David had carried it ne'theless; and who could guess the future but God? And this besides: that a penniless David standing before him was about as useful to him as a bump on a log, while a propertied David returned might bring him some modest gains. And finally this: that though he could of course set even this poor David to menial tasks about the tavern in defrayed payment of expenses owed, it seemed on the whole more amusing to let the rascal go and see what wasps he might stir up, though it mean the loss of the debt. For to the tavernkeep, my friends, stories, too, are a kind of currency.

So away he forges, brave David, once again into the forest! And strides along that road with his fists balled and his arms a-swinging, and he the very picture of determination, looking neither left nor right but only straight ahead. And he must have made good time, for soon enough, what does he spy ahead, but the outline of a figure that seems known to him, sauntering nonchalant down the road and whistling even? And though this man wore green where the prior had worn red, our David is no longer to be fooled by appearances. He picks up his pace and strides right up to that man and taps him rough on the shoulder, and when Robin turns—for Robin it is—cries into his astonished face, "What is the meaning of this!"

"Prithee, of what, cully?" says the other, all amazed.

"Of this dastardly joke you have had on me!" says he.

"Alack, no joke have I had on any man this day," replies the other, in an air of wondering sadness.

"You are a liar!"

"By my faith, I have been all honesty with you!"

"And I, filled with ale, and left to sleep?"

"Tut tut, Master Vigilante: was it my hand that filled your belly with this ale, or laid your head upon the table as on a pillow, to betray your own vigil?"

"And you, who never told me you were the Robin I sought?"

"And you, who never asked it!"

"And you, who robbed my rucksack with all its contents, including various of my personal effects, to wit: ten silver coins; one small knife, one—"

"Owed to me by our very agreement here on this road, upon which I had your hand, and you had mine."

"But for this exchange you had promised me the price on Robin's head!"

"So I did, good man! And as promised, so delivered; for duly and truly I did give you full the price on Robin's head in yonder tavern, and I right hope you paid it, for the excellent and notable *Proprietor* of that most honorable *Establishment* is an upright man and earns his wages fairly by a steady hand and a polite tongue, and the superior quality of his beer."

"I shall have your skin for these abuses!"

"Whoa, Master Vigilante! For this skin is most wed to these sinews. Say, Master Vigilante, by what right?"

"Why—by that written in the Sheriff's own hand on those very writs of warrant that you have also stolen from me!"

"What now, these writs here?" asks he, and plucks them from his pocket and waves them before the irate David.

"The very same!" cries that poor David, nigh carried away by his ire.

"But my good man!" exclaims Robin, shaking his head, "This will not do! These writs are not writ out to any David of Doncaster, but only to their own Bearer, the which at present am I; and they do grant to said Bearer the right to apprehend Robin Hood, dead or alive. Well, my good man, I declare and solemnly avow that I have done as they bid, and to the letter, for I have appre-hended Robin a life entire, and do fully apprehend him now! As for the rest, I would have him living and not dead, as is left to my arbitrium, and I am will-ing to waive the prize as we have formerly agreed upon, all the moreso now that I have gotten me divers treasures in this fine rucksack. So withal I believe we can call this writ satisfied."

"You caitiff! *I* will have you dead, and not living!" roared David, and set upon Robin in a flash. Down onto the dust they went, and David set upon bending Robin into a form much unlike that which God had given him, and Robin fighting for his very life. Now, David was a mighty sort, powerful in thew and of formidable physicality; but Robin held his own with a strength I do not believe David was expecting, and they rolled about in the road a good long while, wrastling like bears, and David yelling from time to time, "Kill ye!"

as though it were a wanted formality of their contest. Until at last, after long and mighty struggle, David had the better of poor Robin, and pinned him face down in the dirt. He grasped then the warrant, and held it triumphant in his fist, and said, "Who now is the bearer of this writ? You by the law it represents are to come with me, and I shall drag you before the Sheriff himself, if need be, and he shall have your neck, and I, my prize! And if you will not come living, then you shall come dead!"

"Then let it be living," laughed Robin into the dust, and David rose him up to his feet, smiling triumphant. But Robin, rising, said, "But hear me a moment, Master Vigilante, before you would drag me to yon Sheriff. For as you have a note from the Sheriff, so I have a note all my own, in my bag here, which I believe is pertinent to our case." And David looked at him in sudden perplexity, his brow knit, and, scratching his head, said, "What note is that?" And Robin said, "None but this!" and drawing his horn out from David's own bag did blow a powerful wind in it, and the ringing of it filled the greenwood, at which David cried, "Rascal, fibber, bandit, trickster, fraud, deluder, and— oyster! For this I shall take only your hide to the Sheriff, lifeless as a wineskin!" And flew at him again.

Down they went a-wrastling, and Robin holding his own once more, but barely. Who knows how it might have come out, had not the men of the greenwood come upon them, summoned by Robin's trumpet, and separated them, and Little John himself held David back, he being the only among them of main strength to do so alone. Will Stutely came up then and said, "What is this man, Robin, who has assailed you?"

And Robin, laughing, "A vigilante who has come to claim the price on my head!"

"What! An enemy! And how shall we deal with him, then?"

"How indeed? He has earned the price he seeks, that much is certain, for he has legal writs in his hand that justify him to them. It needed only my apprehension, and he has certainly seen to that. But I say, he has yet to decide whether he would have me living or dead. Now let him go a moment, Little John!" And Little John did so, and David stood before them wide of eye and scratching his head. And Robin said to him, "Good David of Doncaster, you have only to choose my fate and withal your own, as it is written. And before you make your selection, hear me an offer. For I say, I have never been wrastled so well, nor met such determination in a man, mounting recklessness on courage. You are welcome to bear me off to the Sheriff, for verily I have been defeated this day, and by my troth not a man of mine shall harass you if you elect to walk away with me in chains—though your bag, and all its contents, by our prior agreement, shall remain with my band. But on the other count, if you would grant me liberty, then you are most welcome to join our merry clan and partake in liberty of all good things here in this our kingdom of Sherwood, and lend your brawn and you wilfulness to our many endeavors. In return of which, I gladly give you back your bag and all your various effects in sign of the respect I bear you, with but one alteration: that I shall retain your ten silver coins and your single lock, the first to pay our common dues with the Tavernkeep, the second as fit gage of your loyalty. In their place, I shall set the full number of coins presently riding on my head in Nottingham, that the contract you hold in your fist might be duly fulfilled." For indeed it was the case that in this whole last bout of wrastling, David had not once retracted the warrant from his hand nor dropped it to the earth, but had held stupidly firm to it, holding Robin at bay even thus encumbered.

Well, David looked at the papers crunched in his fingers, and he looked at Robin, and he looked at the men about him, and, eyes narrowing, said, "And this another trick?"

But Robin cried, "Why, has there been e'en one yet this day? But test my veracity, David of Doncaster, by any means you can conceive, and I swear you shall find me an honest man!"

David scratched his poor pate a moment, and then, by God, if the widest smile he ever wore did not spread across his great bearded face. And thrusting forth a hirsute hand, he declared, "Verily, Robin of the Hood, I came out this day to find me a criminal, and found me a friend instead. For God help me, and I cannot e'en say why, but I ne'er liked a stranger as well as I like you. I take your offer with your hand, and glad is me heart for 'em both!"

Then Robin took his hand and the band struck up in jubilations, and they determined to feast and sup of ale in honor of their new companion. But as they were about to depart, Will Stutely said, "But what shall we call him? For David is a workaday name and not fit for a man of Sherwood."

"Let us say he is Smith," said one, "for certainly he has the brawn for it!"

"Nay," cried another, "but the Tanner! For surely he has tanned Robin's hide this day…"

But David drew up with a great frown and said, "I was christened David and David shall I die, and no man set a name on me that is not my own!"

And so the others fell mum. But Robin rose smiling, and said, "Then good friend David, David we shall christen you a second time! Now take your rucksack, and we shall away to the greenwood, where I shall pay you what is owed you by law and fair treatment."

David took up his bag, and thrust into it the warrant, and took from it ten silver coins and the little lock, and presented these to Robin, who held them up in his hand, turning amidst his men.

"To the Merry Band of Sherwood!" he cried, and their cheers rang out in every corner of the forest. And such was meet; for they were filled with joy at the power of their leader, to transform even his enemies into his friends, were only they right of their heart.

₩ill Stout

hey was the saltiest landlubbers these eyes had e'er clapped upon. I knowed 'em for what they was on'y subseq'ent, *that* goes 'thout sayin', by mouth of a certain sailor; they was to me and our men just a pair o' red devils on the deck, and like to each other as these two feet. 'Twas them as ru'ned it for us, for the rest was merchants, and 'twould have been easy pickin's but for the two of 'em that a'most lone-handed kept us at bay. Pass the rum, now.

The sailor b'y hisself, he that told me all, well, he's now one of our own men, and a decent 'un at that. I've seen worse by a long sight, and no mistakin'. Minds me of meself at his age. Aye, we get on like a pair o' old dogs. He holds his post down and don't flinch afore a man's fight, 'spite his age, and I reckon he speaks true 'nough. Well, his is a story all its own, and I tells on'y one tale at a time for each tongue I bear 'twixt me teeth. I tell ye on'y this much, that this b'y—name's Gamain, 'tis—come to us to stand with real men and no longer with those pambly dandies as ride with the merchants. Merchants! Pah! Blind me for a rat, but turn him any way I might, I cannot get me hands 'round a merchant. Do these merchants not crave gold like the next man? Then why in the blazes do they not take it for their own? Why trade for half when ye can grip whole with yer hotblooded hands? 'Tis like a man as cuts a lamb in twain to eat a chop of mutton for supper, and lets the rest to rot, when he could be feastin' the whole mo'th long. Foo's, say I, the lot of 'em, and devil bring 'em down in deep for stupidity, and fill their daft lungs with the brine! Now, rum, says I... Fill 'er deep!

Well, we knowed at once 'tweren't no merchants as was defendin' that ship, that much I can tell ye plain and easy, with three of us down fast with wood stuck in 'em, and we not even halfway near enough to lay a plank over! Made ol' Cap'ain Stringfast hold up, I can 'sure you of it! Made *me* hold up, too, and no doubt. I had me head down un'er a barrel there just as fast as ye please, and like as not would'a stayed there, right next to a red corpse with a dart in its neck, if the first mate hadn't planted a right hard kick straight on me rump. 'Tis all that got me movin', and I'm not shamed t'admit it! 'Tis one thing slashin' it out man to man, riskin' skin and bone for a pretty prize and stakin' one's life to't; 'tis another to stand about like a dummy waitin' to be pricked through by some whistlin' barb! I'm not one for vainglory, no friend, I'm not one for that. But better to die by a dart, than have that pig of a first mate on your hide. The on'y good as come of it all, I swear by the Kraken, is that that pig was skewered through, and as good as roasted in the battle as followed. Rum, man, rum!

Well, the captain regained hisself and ordered speed on us; then two more of us was down, Morris me bosom mate o'er the edge of the ship and food for the sharks, and I never to clap eyes on his face again. I can tell you that followin' that I was red as a devil meself, and couldn't see me very hands for the rage. The darts like as not picked up then, and by the Kraken, if there's only two men behind 'em all, they was as good as ten! We came in astern, and by the time the first plank was laid o'er, must have been twelve of us down on the deck, wounded or killed, and the blood sloshin' 'bout our feet like seafroth. Well, those damned merchants had heartened thanks to these twin devils, and was rarin' to go by the time as steel touched steel. I was the first 'cross for good ol' Morris, and blast me for a gull, if those two didn't have sticks in their hands in place o' sabers! They was wheelin' 'em round like a pair o' little booms and sendin' our men flyin' port and starboard, and it was just *crack, crack, crack!* Wood on steel, wood on bone, man. Had I heard their intentions aforehand,

I swear I wouldn't'a given 'em a fig in odds, not I, but by the blazes with these sticks they had anon secured the two planks and dead set 'gainst us, and there wasn't a thing for't but retreat. The bigger'n was beatin' down men afore me very eyes. The cap'ain saw it, he did, and called us back.

Well, I can't rightly say if there's e'en a merchant in the fight, part from our b'y Gamain. Mayhaps those two alone droved us back. By the blazes! if we had a pair like that on board, you can be 'sured we'd be kings by month end! No merchantmen, those, and ye can set your mark to't. I reckon they're out in the wood, as 'tis said, and do e'en as we pirates do, but for the land side. I know not what profit's in it thereabouts, but I reckon those two are fat as cows if they rob half as well as they fight. Aye, I reckon they've got a pretty penny stored up by now, a real man's hoard. I've had half a notion to seek 'em out meself and hire 'em on for the crew. On'y they'd have to learn the sea, the shoredogs. Say, where're ye hidin' that rum, ye no good...

'Twas on'y as I come back on deck that I see the cap'ain hisself had took a barb in his thigh, and it was a close cut of it, I tell ye, for he a'most bled out there, and ne'er have I saw a man more pallid than he as he come out through the worst of it. The whole adventure set us back some month or two, I can tell'ee, 'twixt curin' our men and gainin' a new crew for all the hands we'd gave over to the fishes. Some few wished to leave for the bitter morale of it, so at Cap'ain's word we slit an' sunk 'em, and some three or four was ca'tured by the merchants durin' that there dog fight, and well as not strung up for't on the mainland. That's the life of a pirate, by the blazes, and ye can reckon it in brass or gold, as ye please. But I swear I'd rather hang a buccaneer'n die in silk sheets a fat merchant pig, and by the Kraken ye can reckon *that* in brass or gold. A rich man as must obey the magistrates and the prelates is no better'n a dog by me reckonin'. Now a man as can sack town or seize wench, board ship or disboard as he please by his own sover'n lights with not a "by yer leave," say as he will to any man and ne'er bite his tongue or hide his thought, spit in the face o' whom he will and slit the neck of any as murmur—thar's a man, matey, thar's a man, and free. I don't set no store by dogs, not me—not e'en those with leashes o' purest gold.

Aye, we fled for't, and wouldn't ha' got far, neither, was we not in a smarter ship than 'at merchant squaltrap, and had us a certain advantage in Gamain. See, we din't leave empty-handed, no, not we, but took the b'y with us as a hostage like; and if he took to piracy thar'af'er, that's for he's a smart b'y. 'Minds me of meself, he does, at his age. Why, I's not a day ol'er when I run off and set by on a whalin' ship, where I learned the ropes meself. 'Twas a man on board that ship by the name o' Murchadh, an' me an' Murchadh was real bosom mates. 'Twas he as brought me to piracy, for he cleared out the whaler when we landed, and the two of us cut an' run, an' later wound up aboard the *Saltbane* together, as he knowed a fellow there. We lost 'im in a dogfight off the coast o' Spain, and I myself skinned the dog as killed 'im. I been a buccaneer since Murchadh brought me on, and not a wink have I turned back in regret. Killed me first man not a year af'er I come on, and by the blazes, 'twas like fire in the veins. Yo ho, like this rum, this rum here! See how it burns ye, see how it fills ye? That's what death is like, me matey, an' killin'. Feed me beaker, man, and be fast about it...

Well, I on'y learned later how it had all fell out, and that them two thar, they was landlubbers born and raised. Learned it from the b'y Gamain, I did, and that's a fact, for he tells it straight, does Gamain, and a fine b'y he is, a fine b'y. As fine a b'y as ever was. Why, a finer b'y, I ne'er...! Well, he to'd me they was shoremen they was. (Rum, by the Kraken! Can't ye see I'm dry again, ye lubbard?) Why, one wasn't e'en a member o' the crew. The one as was, now, why... What's it they called 'im... Will, Will Stout! That's it, that's it, or me name's not Tenney. Right name for'm, for he was a stout fellow indeed. The b'y Gamain says he come aboard a month prior for reasons as wasn't none too clear. I smell trouble on't, by the blazes. A man at odds with house and home, I reckon. A pirate can smell *that* a league distant. But he... As for he... That'n... Well... Argh! blast me for a dog, but I can't recall what in the blazes I's gettin' at... Why, get your hands off me rum, ye scurvey...! Ah, you was to fill 'er... fine then, fill 'er to brim, and that's a good fellow. Now, as I was sayin'... What was it I's sayin'...? Aye, those two scalawags... Why, I'd find 'em and commission 'em, I would, if Cap'ain Stringfast'd give me leave, I would. Aye, ye said it, 'twas that thar Will Stout as come on board first, and he knowin' straight naught o' the sea, but they took 'im no'theless, the merchant dolts, the lousy grubbers, for they was short on hands and worried o'er pirates. Har!

Th'other? What other? There's on'y one merchant ship, no "th'other"...
What're ye on about, ye damned...? Ah, th'other *land* devil! Aye, aye. As for
'*im*... Well, he wasn't nothin' but a stow'ay, he was, snuck aboard to get at that
Will. Rob they called 'im. Rob... Hod, I think 'twas. Funny name, that'n.
Stow'ay! Why, a man stows on board *our* ship, ye can bet yer gold tooth he'd
be slave or sharkbait by mornin'! But the b'y Gamain says that Rob could talk
his way off the gallows. One eye, but two tongues. Bah, where's me damned
cup got to, now... Ho! Thar she blows. Aye, the gallows... What's I sayin'...
Gallows... 'Bout our b'ys, as got caught up and took to hang on the main'and,
'sthat it... Swingin', swingin', to the lights go out. Aye, life of a bucc'neer. First
the free salty wind, then ye hang... Gold an' silver, an' then... What's that?
Rob? Rob what, now? What are ye on about, Rob... Oh, aye, Rob *Hod*! Well,
those merchants are weak-bellied, you can be 'sured of't. That Rob just pops
up one day, says Gamain, he does... an' they don't do nothin', not they... an'
he... well, he, uh... Argh, blast it. Devil take it, but I'm boiled! Aye, aye, that's
it. Ye said it, ye did. He come on board just like that, and got to arg'in' with
that other fellow—what'd I say his name was? Aye, Stout! Will Stout. That's
it. And they two, Rob an' Will, arg'in' like a pair o' dogs, and all those dolt
merchants just standin' there and oglin'. But just then the call come down:
they spotted our own ship on th'horizon, so the arg'ment was stymied, and
not e'en the b'y Gamain knows what end it made.

Argh... By the Kraken... Me head's a-splittin'... More rum, that's the
medicine... Anyways. Those devils... Why, I've thought it o'er a hun'ed times.
I go an' find 'em, ye see. If on'y the Cap'ain'd leave me go. I'd go, but he'd slit
me throat, he would, like ol' Sander and Cane. Th'Cap'ain's a devil, he is. Elsewise I'd go, and you can put your tooth 'gainst that. Not that I like... Well, I've
no love for the land, me... but... Right, that's it! You said it, me worthy. Just a
fortnight! Why, you can be 'sured of't, har har! Men t'our board. *Real* men, no
dogs. That cyclops Rob... and ol' Stout... Too many dogs at sea, e'en in our
crew. Jus' 'twixt us'n two, you un'erstand. I wouldn't want the Cap'ain to...
Why, if he heard me now, he'd... Aye, i's jus' as the lad Gamain said! Lovely b'y,
the lad Gamain, me fav'rite b'y. I love 'im like a son, I do. I ne'er had a son, not
I—leastwise not as I e'er seen. I won'er where he's got to, that b'y. Should fin'

'im... Say, why don't we go off an'... What's 'at, now? Them two *what*? Two devils? Are ye havin' me on, ye scurvey seadog? What's this balderdash 'bout devils? Why, ye listen for a moment, ye rotten... Ah, *them* two! Well why di'n't ye say so! What are ye talkin'—devils this and devils that! 'Tis no won'er a man gets right mixed up, talkin' to *you*, what with all yer blabb'rin'... Devils, pah. Well, as for 'em landblub... blandlub... fellers there... I can't rightly say. Ne'er heard 'nother breath off 'em, not I. Right as not they're back 'broad. Fire eaters as them, and they on a merchant ship! Pah! I'd have 'em both on *our* old ship, I would. Mateys like good ol' Morris. If on'y the Cap'ain... An' right good they'd do for's... Imagine it, me matey... What a force, we would, what a force to reckon with... Imagine all that gold... Bah, but they're out there on land, sure's daylight. I tell ye, though... tell ye... What's it I wannad... Ah, well. Sure'y don' wanna go up 'gainst 'em two in a dogfight 'gain, no, no, no! Not I. Agh, poor, poor Morris! Down under, with the sharks... But on land, on land, aye, that's where they be, and me gold tooth on it... Out there with the gallows. Why, give the king's men hell and raise a right ruckus, and then swing for't. Tha's a life, me matey, a seadog life. Ver'table land pirates, they be. Tha's a way. First blow, then swing. Set fire everythin'! Burn it all! Fire, me matey, fire! That's the devil's own orders, by the blazes! *They're* the men for't. Ye can reck'n that'n gold or brass, ye can. Brass or gold.

Maid Marion

ould that you had seen it, Avice!

I suppose I should have liked to, my Lady.

He came, in very midst of his enemies, in such a guise, despite all warning! Fearless, Avice, that is what I call him. I have never seen nor heard the like of it, save in the old tales. He is no man of this time, that is certain, but of every time—a man for all ages.

Calm, my Lady! But is it sure they have not caught him?

Nay, Avice, rest certain of it. I have seen the dour countenance of a certain lord of our mutual acquaintance, who I know should have bartered his honorable name just to see my Robin strung upon a noose. Imagine his wrath now, after what he has witnessed! He is a jealous man, and has even doubted the intentions of the King with me.

Well, my Lady *is* a beauty, and no doubt...

Is that just grounds for jealousy, Avice? Is there some necessary ligature 'twixt a lovely face and a false heart? Or is it that my sex in itself is frail of its intent, and must be inherently mistrusted? Yet I defy any to prove that the heart of woman lacks the constancy of man's! Bring against me Helen, but I say, count every Penelope that remained in faithful stead of her warrior, and we shall see which side numbers more. Bring against me Clytemnestra, and I shall answer you with her own sea-bound daughter. Bring Electra, and I shall answer Antigone; Delilah, Deborah; Medea, Lucretia; Xanthippe, Hypatia. Set before me the entire hordes of the Bacchae, and I will match them with the Vestals and the serried ranks of our own Christian Sisters and virgin martyrs, who outnumber them a thousand to one. Or name me, as you will surely do, Eve! Yet then I will reply with the Second Eve, our common Mother, the Virgin of purest heart and unshakeable faith who stood in the shadow of the Cross itself. Nay, our womanly hearts must be stronger than those of men, as our fists are weaker. Then what equation can stand between beauty and disloyalty? Beauty attracts, no doubt; but she as wears it perchance has in her the reason and sense ever to repulse the repulsive.

Well, *I* sure wouldn't know much of any of that. But, if my Lady doesn't mind my saying so, she does not *much* repulse Master Robin! I can rightly understand my Lord's scruples.

You fall on the wrong side of this matter, Avice. Robin is the sun to me. Fie, what times! Had I been born a little more at my liberty, and were not heiress to all these strictures of birth and blood, t'were Robin I had married!

Have a care, now, my Lady, even to grant utterance such wishes! *He* does not live in such a palace as this. My Lady has some pretty dreams in her head, but she doesn't know a pin's tip of the world down below, and I'll beg her pardon for saying so. But I *do*. I know all there is to know of it, if my Lady will permit me, and I say—'tis best Robin Hood keeps himself to Sherwood, and my Lady to Nottingham.

I would forfeit palace and riches and all for him. I would go and dwell with him in the forest, and be his huswife there, and tidy his hut, were it even a shanty with a dirt floor to it and drafty daubed walls, or a damp grotto in the face of a hill. I would go to him!

Aye, and no question my Lady *would* do such a thing, if anyone were mad enough to let her! I don't mean to doubt the truth of my Lady's words—only their sense.

What folly is there in adoring what is good and high and noble, and not mere show of such? Or living to the crux of life, and not amongst all this peacock display, that, were it unplumed of its finery, should show forth so many chickens and barnyard fowl? Why, my very guardian is a knight of the crown, has battled in foreign wars, has seen aught of the Orient and has traced this world to its extremity, and yet he carries on his shoulders the most frivolous head I ever despised. What good is it to live in a palace if a man's spirit squats ever in a stye?

Easy, easy, my Lady! I had no wish to rile. I was only stating fact. And fact *is*, peacocks or no, there is much comfort in this house, and that is not to be taken for granted. My Lady's lived in silk all her life, and would not easy come to homespun.

I should lay the very hairshirt upon my skin, if my soul were drawn in better cloth for it! But Avice, you did not see him this day, or you would understand! How he stood out there, before the eyes of all those who would have him dead, and yet his hand untrembling, for his aim's as true as any that's ever been known... And you shrug, Avice!

I can't see the point of it, my Lady, and I've no fret in saying so. So he came here out of the woods—to what, spit in Sheriff's eye? A fine deed, that! And d'you know what they're saying in the servants' quarters? Why, they're saying that the Sheriff planned it all in advance, that he *wanted* Loxley to come—

Oh, for shame, Avice, don't call him that!

—that he *wanted* him to come, my Lady, and set up this entire contest just to draw him out. Now just what manner of fool does that make your Robin, praytell? And I don't mind telling my Lady, that *I* think these rumors probably not altogether hacklebrained. Say, what'd call out a boaster, better than a chance to boast?

Narrow minds will interpret great events narrowly. To me he demonstrated far more noble motives. Nay, but Avice, you cannot know what it was! For you did not see him. Neither during it, nor before.

Nay, I didn't see him, my Lady. And I reckon I didn't miss much, other than a swaggering fit of cockiness. These men, they're always the same! They want to be *first, first, first*, and you never *can* tell the why of it, or what it might gain 'em. First over all! As if the angels in God's blue heaven cared a whit what man could shoot his arrow best. I'll tell my Lady what: not the finest archer in all of England could shoot into heaven's lowest window with his best shaft.

And I don't set much more store by my Lord Robert, begging all forgiveness, for I think he wants Robin's head for the same reasons, at the end of the day. Why, beggin' my Lady's pardon, 'tis all silliness, stuff and nonsense!

Ah, Avice, you have ever been much confounded by the physical aspect of things.

I don't know much of that, my Lady, but I am sure not too trusting of one as goes about in a mask, beggaring people of their gold and pilfering coin-purses.

He is the least avaricious man I have ever known.

Begging pardon, my Lady, but *that*, I might well doubt.

Look, Avice—look what he gave me!

But what—is that the golden arrow?

The selfsame, Avice. He gifted it to me after the contest, saying he would yield it to the fairest creature there. When he had called victory his own, he stepped before my tent, where I was seated with our Lordship and that intolerable girl, and he bowed before me, and handed it to me, and kissed my hand as I took it, saying, "My Lady, if my aim was true this day, 'twas by the gravity of such beauty as I now dare to look in the face." All in the tent with me were much riled, of course, and I believe Lord Robert suspected everything already, for he rose in his seat. Robin backed away, but his false beard did catch on my fingers and chuck loose, which is how they knew him. Then the tent fell upon our heads somehow; there was sudden confusion, and when I came out of it, he was gone. I still cannot say how 'twas he escaped! They so many, and the guards summoned to boot! But I am certain there were others of his men, there in the crowd, though I cannot be sure, for then everything became mad and the people burst into a sort of frenzy... There was even fighting, by my faith. I mocked that I had lost the arrow in the chaos pursuant, for I knew elsewise the Lord Robert would have it, but truly I pinned it up in my skirts.

And no doubt. It's a pretty trinket, that I'll say for it...

And worth a prettier penny, or would you not say?

I would, my Lady.

Well? Shall that, then, mark greed on this man? Why, I have seen him hand a purse full of gold coins to a mendicant, an old toothless woman dwelling in a lean-to. I heard it directly from a traveler down the road of Sherwood, a butcher and seller of meats, that Robin Hood stopped him in the Leen Valley, and drew out a little chest of gold, much in advance of the worth of the butcher's worldly possessions, and gave this to him in return but for his meats, his cart, his horse. I have heard from men who would know that when he was but an orphaned lad he gave his last coin to the the church coffers, and almost starved for it, saying that God minds the sparrow. Now—would you say that these are the signals of a ripe cupidity? Don't hesitate so, Avice, speak! Are these the signs of greed?

They are but stories, the most of them.

Stories! And if he came all this way this day to lay his hands upon this golden arrow, then how do I hold it now in my hands?

Well, this is not his reputation among *my* people, at any rate. And who can say what he weened he was bartering for! Methinks my Lady is most childish generous.

I, generous, Avice? Nay, but say it is Robin Hood who is generous, and so to a fault! And courageous, and courteous, and valiant. You have made little of his deed this day, as if it were mere blustering and vain display. I tell you, nothing shows out a man's character as danger, nor reveals what caliber he be at the heart of him. For in fire of hazard and the pressure of the crowd all foppery and pretense and play-acting do burn away, and all that is or can be left is the raw truth of the man himself, undisguised and unabated. They say that war is the test of men, and I do believe 'tis so, Avice; for when a man goes into battle, and all he has ever claimed of himself can no longer protect him, and even his cold reason is enflamed with fear or the burning desire for glory—in *that instant*, if he is not at core a fine man then he shall perish or flee. And it is much harder for women, for they do not have this proof by fire, in which they might demonstrate their quality; nay, but we must show it in constancy and continuance at every hour of every day in the most plodding and wretched circumstances, revealing ours to be a fire not brief and hot and red, but long and white, and this is why fidelity and constancy is prized so acutely in our sex. Now hear me, for today Robin Hood stood before a crowd of eyes, full half of which should have had him hung on the spot, had they known what he was, and yet he came before them unabashed and without the merest tremble of his fingers. He was dressed as a mocking old man, and I swear even I would not have known him, had I not seen him before in such raiment, and had I not perceived his eyes. He stood out there, I say, before all of us, in the very crucible, and yet outshot a dozen expert men, until he remained alone beside the finest archer of the county, and maybe of all of England, who had been, I do not doubt, hand-picked to contest with him. Two shots each they were granted, at a target which stood fifty yards hence. The other archer, known to all as Gilbert of the White Hand, and the Sheriff's favorite, was given first shot, and struck true to the target, a little short of center. Robin discharged another, which hit a touch farther, off-center on the other side, favoring Gilbert i'the match. Then Gilbert flew a better arrow, which drove home to the precise heart of his goal, at such a perfect center that it was proclaimed outright he had won, for naught could Robin do to regain him. Yet Robin, against all proclamations, and in absolute despite of what everyone there believed, suddenly drew up his bow, and without even seeming to take aim let fly. And that arrow that had been at the center of the butt, that arrow of his competitor, why, 'twas twinned!

How's that, my Lady? He struck the center as well?

Not only, Avice, not only! But with a single deft stroke he did sheer Gilbert's arrow in twain, and pierced, not only center, but the very shaft that had pierced the center!

God's angels...

Aye, Avice. I say—a man as can do such a thing as that, in such a moment—he is no ordinary man! Or a man who, in such guise and such stead, could come before all his fiercest enemies afterward, and look them in the eye one by one and accept his reward from their very hands without for a moment shaking or doubting; who could stand before *me* at such a moment and speak to me in honeyed words and perfect dignity, and not a single one lose to stuttering or confusion. That is no ordinary man!

Perhaps, perhaps not. Yet he is ever a man.

What mean you with that, Avice?

Why, my Lady, I mean only that Master Robin Hood, for all his fine shooting and dashing looks, is still as much flesh and blood as me, my brother, or any fishmonger, and wants the same piggish things that all men want, and when it comes time, the Lord God will judge his soul just as any other—aye, right aside Gilbert Whitefoot, Tom Baker and the King of England.

Have you not heard me, Avice? I tell you—*this very day* he was judged!

Of his case I know not a whit, and reckon it's none of my business. But I'll say this: *my Lady* sure has been judged. Has been judged the silliest and sweetest bird in any of the golden mews of Nottingham. Nay, nay—I've heard quite enough tales of Master Robin in the Hood this day, my Lady Marion. Spare your sweet breath, there will sure be more to tell of him in another moment, for I am sadly certain that I shall have my ears filled up with his antics until the day the Lord bears my soul home. In all this bland chattering, I shall try to spare me some space in my poor old head, to store away all the nonsense about him that my Lady believes with such dear faith.

You judge us wrongly, Avice—both him and me.

Time will tell, my Lady, time will tell.

Yes, time will tell. For his is a name that cannot die, and when the monikers of all the scamps, ruffians, miscreants, and perfumed noble nitwits of our entire age have burned back to ashes, he shall still be remembered, and shall find his fit place among those whose recollections have been armored by virtue and hallowed by worthy recollection. And if I do not merit a place there beside him, in fact if not in memory, then by our Lord and Savior Jesus I do not know what this life is for!

Easy now, girl! *Avice's* name will sure be forgot e'en tomorrow, but I'll tell you this: 'tis a better thing to see the solid truth about this world, and to live in avoidance of constant disappointment, than to fall for all this fine display of virtue and glory and be taken in by it to a broken heart. You will know all of this when you are older and wiser and have seen the ways of men, not at the beginning, but at the end. 'Tis not the courtship, my lady, that measures a man, but the marriage; and there was not yet one of them that proved himself anything more than an "ordinary man" in that. This I know by experience, not supposition and pleasant dreams, and I am here to remind you of it to spare you the pain of learning it before the time comes. Nay—let's leave be.

No doubt my Lady is right in all, and I am but a poor pea-brained crone with too many years to my name, grown gray and bitter with my own disappointments and my coming eldering. My head aches for it, and all I know to a surety is that I have been trusted by better heads than my own to look after a certain Maid Marion, with all her mad fancies and her wild flights of girlish whimsy, and to keep her from getting into greater trouble than can be got back out of. That is work enough for poor Avice, and you can swear by it. Leave the matter there, my Lady, and I shall do as much meself. Now let us see to your corset.

Clorinda

ut it in, my lass, put it in! Haste now! Aye, and the seeds of the columbine, and dove's blood, immixed with blackberry and elderberry. Dust of foxglove and the three prime petals of three blooms of lobelia. A cup of water of the first rain in April muddied in silt, bone of swine, dried leaves of anemone, and a wilted yellow lily... And the hair, the girl's hair, else it shall all be powerless, and all our work in vain! Enough, enough! Aye, now stir, my lass, stir! And so we shall wait, and let it brew, ere the incantations—for time is needed with all things, and all things come to power only in time...

Agh. Get me a chair, girl, and gather me a shawl, for I am cold and grown weary of the damp with these years. There is a chill on. Another year may be much for me. Nay, nay—don't ye naysay, girl, 'tis much of a truth. I have naught to lament, save as what's fit to lament. For aye, so 'tis, that I have lived in this abandonment since your birth, my girl. I know, I know—'tis harder for you than 'tis for me, unnat'ral old crone that I am become. You would see something beyond this crag—and see it you shall. By the powers! You shall be fifteen ere another moon has passed, and a beauty worthy of each of those years. You see that my spells have not been unvirtued? You see that old Sagen has not been idle, and has learned her arts well? No, no, not unvirtued. I have

waned as ye have waxed. That is how I willed it, and that is how it's been. Time
for time, my lass, ye cannot cheat time! They that live to unnat'ral old age, 'tis
from the blood of babes they do so. But I have turned the law upon its end. I
have bartered for ye and bartered well, and your time is almost on us. Then
listen here, girl, one of these days when it comes upon you, you must up and
leave me. Aye, aye, no naysaying now! Hear me how I would have it: I would
wake one day and find ye gone. I would wake and find ye gone, I say! Hear me,
girl, and do as I say: catch yourself a rich young fool, not so far up the ladder
as to make for a chasm 'twixt him and you, nor so low as to make a burden on
your shoulders, and do as I have taught you, and teach your sons the same. For
I have bartered, not only for you, but for them, and as I have bartered, so they
shall gain. That is how I would have it.

...Ah, thank ye for this seat. That is better, and now that I am sitting my
sluggish blood might catch me up. What's that, now? Why... for shame! What
questions do ye ask me, girl...!

Nay, nay—but a moment, my lass, do not blush so... You are right to want
to know it, after all... I can only imagine the nonsense they've filled your head
with, those nasty village children... That your mother is a siren, a slavern... 'Tis
bad enough I know the art of turning root and bloom and blood to secret
powers. Men are envious of the powers, remember that always, girl. The world
is to the strong ones. They would know what we know, and do as we do, but
they are unwilling to pay the price for it. They call me liar, forked of tongue,
but that is only because I know how to turn my voice to my benefit and bend
ears to my will. Yet I have never once lied for hypocrisy's sake, coward-like—
not before nor since the day they cursed me and drove me out of their city, and
you remember it, girl. *They* lie from fear, that is the difference between us.
They are weaklings and unsteady, and in need of a faith to pull 'em up. We are
strong, my daughter, and you will be stronger still than your mother, for the
virtue I have put in it. We are of the weaker sex outwardly, but the stronger
inward, and these men shall bend to us as straw for the powers. You just remember what I have taught you, and see how they shall bend.

So heed not their rumors. Now, you will know the truth of it. Yes, the time
is come. Listen well, Isabel, and I shall teach you certain things that you are old

enough to know. And by the powers, whether you are old enough or are not ready matters little, for I have nigh spent all I have of life and must tell you all I am able ere I o'erstep the threshold.

You know your father's name already, girl. You have heard it spoke by the village children, of that I've no doubt, and perchance by others as well. He is called Robin Hood, though that is not his right name, but a moniker gave him by chance. It does not matter what he was called before, girl, for to you and to me and to all the world abroad, now and fore'er more, he shall be Robin Hood. He branded himself with that name, and so 'tis his right name.

How did I meet him? Why, girl, *he* met *me*. I was a shepherdess in those days, damned by my folk to live in the country with the sheep, for I was a beautiful and wild colleen—I know, 'tis hard to figure now. Time has made me ugly. Time is cruel to man's will. Aye, my girl, I was much like you, though not so fair, for none had aided me with the powers. My father and my brothers were jealous of me, they were, and would not have any of the young boys clap e'en eye on me, not to speak of hand or wedding bond! When I was old enough to fret over they sent me to the sheep, thinking it the only way to secure my innocence. And perhaps I would have been saved there indeed, had I not been found by Robin Hood. But find me he did, my lass, and fell in love with me for the charms that were in me e'en then; and do not listen to the slander which would have you believe he ever loved another! Blast and barmy, and a pox upon 'em all! Nay, *I* was his one and true, *I* was, and I would have married him, had they not killed him. Aye, and my brothers and my father could rot, for all that I might have cared! I would have run away with him, and he with me. But that was not to be, and I was left instead abandoned and with squirrel. When my father and my brothers found out, they gave me a fine beating, and tried to bind me to a local burly. But I say, girl, I would have nothing of any man but Robin Hood, and I refused. They would have forced me to it, but I fled, girl, to the wilderness, where I had learned well enough to do for myself, and built here this cabin—aye, girl, e'en while I was large with you, built it with my own hands, and lost blood and earned callus for it—and birthed you myself in it and tended to all by my own hand, alone and abandoned and forgotten by the world! Oh, I fancy they all knew where I had got to; but I was no longer of any interest to anyone. My family rejected us and has since pretended that I died out here in the wilderness, and you with me. What friends we have we owe to the potions and the tinctures I have learned to concoct. An old goat woman of the hills taught me the powers, an old crone. A sight to see she was! with wispy beard and huge eyes and long ears. She found me not long after you were born, and died not many years after, and she taught me the powers—arts loathed by the many because the many fear what they do not know, the timid fools, and are blinded by the rancid smoke of their faith. Such is our state. (Say, girl, stir the pot as I speak, or its virtues shall not stick; the fellow as asked it is sick with love, and I've promised him a potent elixir.) As I was saying... What was it... Ah, yes! Robin Hood *would* have come, had only he been able to...!

Oh, what was he like? God's bodkins, girl! He was the most handsomest man I had ever known. He had him red hair, and eyes green as a clean pool of water. As for his person—well, you know what he is, d'ye not? He that makes sport of the fat prelates and all these church puppets, and lives at his liberty in the wild woods, free to his will and his want, a king unto himself, who could kill or drink or rut as he wishes. Oh, he had a time of it with those nasty rich sorts and brought all their high airs down low. He went about robbing from fat men to feed hungry ones, and made sport of the King's law against poaching, to show the folly in holding fast a forest of venison, when folk were starving in the towns. Ye have heard the stories, have ye not? Well, *that* is what kind of man he is.

What's that? Violent! Blast and barmy. They call him violent, and a thief, and a coward, and many other things, the insufferable idiots. What do they know of anything! If he is violent, it was because he is strong, and if he is swift to anger, it is because they madden him recklessly. The world is to the strong ones. My girl, heed not their evasions. 'Tis envy that wags men's tongues. But... here, my lass... *I* will tell you a story, that maybe ye have *not* heard (for few enough know it), that has everything in it of Robin Hood. And you can meditate on this tale when they slander him; for in this tale lies the truth.

When he was a young man he lived in town—aye, girl, up in Barnedale, like my own family. His father was a tanner, methinks, or perhaps a fletcher, and he and his brothers took up their father's work and so upheld the family. I cannot remember now what he told me of his sire; 'twas little enough. Methinks the man died early, and perhaps the mother, too. He had himself a brother, as well, and a sister, who was known by all to be the most fairest maid of the town, and whose beauty made itself a fine reputation indeed. She was much courted, and yet she clung to her modesty, the little fool, and would hear nothing of proposals of marriage.

Now this girl, whose name was Agnes, was a happy lass, but when still very young met a local rake names Lew. And Lew was a quick young man. He wasted not a minute in convincing her of love undying between 'em. He rambled on in poesy to her, and made great speeches of devotion. He would carry on before her for hours, at times, and came chanting beneath her window, risking his limb—for her brothers would have taken him apart if they'd caught him. He would sing there in the dusk, and she would lie awake in bed and listen to him, the fox, and his sly words would fill her ears like a spell, until her head had spun around so far she couldn't think straight. She was a romantic sort, as is the way of young and foolish girls, and she fell into his snare, the old spider. What was to be done? She so young, innocent of the ways of foul pigs like him, and full up of fool fancies. Blast and barmy! Fact of it was, my girl, that one thing gave over to another, and by and by she found herself with squirrel, and the man that so filled her of a sudden could not be made to recall so much as her name. Nay, but like a spineless skulker he vanished those several needful weeks, gone to all the world, hiding like a wretch, and may a pox and vex be upon him until the very last breath he breathes for it...!

Yes, I'm fine, my dear. Not to worry, 'twas a fit of ague, is all. I'm my own again. Back to the tale...

Agnes went to her elder brother, Will, in tears, and begged him to go and set this Lew straight. For the gallant young scoundrel had forgotten his great love for her, and she, the poor wight, thought he could be convinced to remember it. Such was the gullibility of that wretched girl! Ah, but she learned, she did. She grew up right fast, and learned the ways of the world, and the hearts of pigs, and how to avenge herself—

But that is neither here nor there. Her brother, Will, was an irascible sort.

Had him a mean streak, and that is no doubt. Speak of violence! He confronted this Lew down the road a ways, and the lad's responses I warrant did not satisfy; for Will drew a dagger and slew him.

You can imagine it! A pretty plight that family found itself in. Both parents dead, Agnes neither nubile nor wed, and the elder brother, the only of 'em as had any gainful employment, fallen awry of the law, and like to be punished. And it would have gone badly with them indeed, had it not been for Robin Hood.

Now it was a peculiar fact of them, Robin Hood and his brother, that they looked greatly alike—I say, could atimes be taken for twins. It is true that the elder brother was somewhat slighter and of character utterly diverse. The younger had another certain peculiarity. But those who did not know them well might have taken them for one and the same man.

When the Sheriff's posse came to take the brother and throw him into gaol, well, he stood forth stoic and dark, ready to accept his fate. That was how Will was, my dear. A real man. But just as they were about to carry him off, that Robin Hood jumped forth, and proclaimed himself the murderer, and demanded they take him instead! And his brother tried to object, but Robin Hood was the faster tongue—oh, my girl, he knew how to talk, that one did!—and at last they took the younger in the place of the older.

I do not know how he escaped from them. It was methinks along the road to the keep. He was wily and quick, and much stronger than one would have thought to look at him. At any rate, he broke free of his bonds and his captors, and fled into our own Sherwood. And that was the how and the why he became an outlaw, my girl, who otherwise would have made himself I dare not imagine what, back in the days that I knew him.

Now, Isabel, when they speak evil of your father, you recall this story, which is the only one that need concern you, and remember whose blood you have in your veins. Heed not them as say that your mother was fooled by fast words, for they are liars and pigs, but remember always this. And listen neither to those wretches who slander Robin Hood for any of his acts. For in whatever came later he had his hand forced; but in this he acted on his own liberty, and as a free man.

Sir Richard at the Lea

eloved of my soul, the tidings that you have forwarded me cast a pall of shame upon our land, and I pray to learn soon that the news be proved mistaken or impish rumor. For if it stands as you say, 'tis a lawful man fallen into hands of criminals then, and alas, all is head under heels in this our England.

Of the man himself, you have asked me of him and done well. Much falsity is spoke of him, more than of any other wag or wain a man could name, for that is in his nature and in the nature of our times. I pray you, Beloved, do not idly ape what you have got from ignorant souls, and remember ever that it is the bent of the low to slander the high, as they shall do viciously and until the end of times. Did the mob not crucify our Lord? Then imagine what they might do to a mere man of noble mettle! And as for you, keep well out of these invidious disputes, Beloved, though you shall know the truth of them, for men have been killed over what this man is said to have done or not done, and disputatious tongues are oft leashed to violent fingers. Do not seek to stall a dog fight when you have but your hand to put in it. Rather pray to God ceaselessly for peace within and without, and pray as well for him who has been taken, but do not fear for him, for he is bound to outlive us all. A hundred years hence, and all men shall be speaking of his gests as though they had been carried yesterday, taking the pith and truth of these events from the paps of mother time herself.

What I will tell you is God's own truth, which I can vouch for by these eyes that saw and this memory that recorded, and may God return to me and without fail the whole of all I lived through that I might transmit it to you, for by my troth, I have spoken nothing of it since twenty years. I am not fain to speak on these events, for as I have said these are evil times, when truth is held in contempt and even its mouthing can prove even a hazard to a man. These are not the first such times in the history of our race and until the Antichrist reveals his face to men they shall not be the last, but they are our times, by God, and we must live accordingly in them. By troth, I would be reticent even in better times, for I am an old man and have no patience for disputations or idlers, still less for historians and scholars and all those dust mites that fossick about in the past like rats in the ossuary.

About this man I will tell you my business with him, how came myself to know him, and how we saved each other, first he me, and then myself him; for so it was, that he left me with a debt I did repay, and would willingly repay again a second time in this very moment if the possibility were mine. But first I must withdraw a step, for you can understand nothing of these doings if you do not first know the scandal that was on me.

You will recall my father, though a good man at heart, was hard on his bottles and on his pockets, and it fell out that when he was dead and in the ground, his debts were disinterred and came to life, and these landed at once upon my head as the eldest male of our woe-begotten clan. I saw to them as I could, but there is a limit to all things in this world save sorrow and the grace of God, and it was His will that I should suffer the first before being delivered by the second. For in tying the most pressing of my father's loose ends, I found myself tangled in them, a poor man dwelling in a nobleman's castle, and not but ten shillings left for all my title. And as misery pursues misery, my own son, the light of my eyes and the pride and joy of my manhood, in joust with a knight of the Crown, inadvertently slew this same, and was imprisoned by the late Sheriff of Nottingham, where he was sentenced to pay the same penalty that he had unwittingly wreaked on his peer. For this Sheriff held a cursed grudge against my father on account of an ancient dispute between them of which I have been able to divine little or nothing, and now, being a malicious and insatiable man, wished to revenge himself on the dead by means of the living. And he set upon the release of my son from his bondage a bail of four hundred pounds, at default of which he would surely hang my child at the gallows pole.

So gross and disproportionate a condition he had set on purpose, for he knew it lay so far beyond my means that it would send me to desperation if not to ruin, and such it was. Wide I wandered in those days in search of a creditor who would succor my need, but my father, alas, had burned a wide trail indeed, winning our name ubiquitous reputation for frivolity in debts, and the very men from whom I was forced to seek solace were the same I had but lately repaid, for which they were reticent to throw themselves into the very ditch from which they had lately scrambled. The name of the father clings to the son, Beloved, for good or more often for bad, and it shall always be so.

Unbeknownst to me, the Sheriff in his bad ambition had designs less on my son than on my entire line, and was conspiring with a certain Abbot of our mutual acquaintance to use our great misfortune to build one greater. Or so he reckoned things in his material fashion, though I am in dispute with his conclusions, for it were better to be a serf side by side with my living son, than to stand a rich man upon his grave. Already I knew this Abbot, a man as fine as can be found anywhere from him to himself, and I was well aware that he was a lender of infamy, one who always used to be taking wicked advantage of every wretched soul who asked him for moneys and who used never to turn a generous hand when a heavy would do. I avoided his unscrupulous name as long as I was able, but when I had exhausted every other possibility, in my desperation I set myself before him and heard his terms, that he would pay the bail of my son, and I to set on that the gage of my lands themselves, and to repay the debt I had earned, in a period which was schemed to conduce surely to my downfall. These terms he did impose, aiming at my utter dispossession, and at his—and, as I was later to learn, also the Sheriff's—own fat enfranchisement, knowing that my great need would conquer my native prudency, and that I would cast myself full into his power thereby. And so it was, for I accepted his conditions, and took his money to his occult confederate the Sheriff in order to free my son. I swear, Beloved, that though the sadness of our near ruin did weigh heavy upon our hearts, that night my family rejoiced and celebrated the return of our boy with a joy that not even penury could have disrooted from us.

As I did not misdoubt, the day of reckoning came fast upon me, and me unable in the meanwhile to raise a shilling more than I had erstwhile possessed. I told my wife to ready herself for our shame, and with darkened heart I set off down the Sherwood way.

I was walking and ever walking, as one progressing to his own execution, for truly, this was the way with me. For on the morrow I would stand before the Abbot, and have subtracted from me my means and my sustenance, my good name, my inheritance and all that had ever nourished me in this world, and would be turned out a pauper with my wife and my family. So I was going and ever going, until at a wide turning on that awful endless road I was set upon by a band, as I perceived them, of miscreants, the which hotly desired, I would have sworn, my final misfortune and wrack. But from so low a point as that to which I had declined, little more could they have filched from me than my own and very breath, and almost would have done me a favor thereby. I say almost, for dearly did I loathe to abandon my family to inherit the shame that had rightly been my heirloom, facing its worst consequences without me. And for this alone I was not so cavalier in my dealing with these hooligans as otherwise I might have been, but met them still with sangfroid and a manly demeanor and demanded to know of them what it was they willed.

They responded that they would take me to a feast ordered by their lord and leader, and not to delay but come at once with them. I asked them who there leader might be, and they responded that he was none other than King Greenleaf, sovereign of the wood. I smelled mockery in this, though the nature of it I could not fathom, for, as I was sorely outnumbered, any kind of planned ambush would have been redundant in the extreme, unless they wished to play me as the cat will play the mouse. They must in any case have noted the skeptic eye with which I regarded this entire affair, for they swore by their souls that their intentions were pure and asked me again most cordially to join them, in such terms that I might have even mistaken them for the ill-garbed heralds of some noble household, as fallen on disaster as my own. They inquired even if I had a hunger on me, and I avowed I did; for I had been eating slender in those weeks for want of means, preferring to feed my family rather than my belly, and had been fasting hardly in prayer for some several days, and they told me again in lively and jovial tones to come. I would know if I must, and they said no, they would not constrain me, but I was to join them of my own will and volition. At which assurance I said I would go with them, and welcome.

Still I believed that they intended sport of me, and supposed that they would not have let me go even had I sought the liberty they declared they willed me. Yet as an honest man I will treat each and every man, according to his word, until his deeds give me reason patent to do otherwise. Nonetheless, as we were going, I was ever trying to devise a route of escape, should such prove necessary, that I could return in peace upon my mirthless errand, but I knew it would not be easy, for ten men were walking with me there and they were going on their way always laughing and making merry. They were a motley lot, old and young, mismatched and vested in fashions divers, and some with glibs upon their brow and some with long hair and some with short, and seemed nothing unified them if not their will to bring myself where we were going.

By and by they led me through a wind of forest paths and to a gully and a glade, and there in the callow a great bonfire, and the sweet sound of lute, and the smell of a savory feast, and some four score men and women busy at all manner of work and play. And some were setting a great long table hewn as I perceived of the trunks of felled trees, and others were keeping the fire, and others were roasting by it, and some were sitting and chatting in the green. For a moment, Beloved, I did fancy I had been abducted by the little folk them-selves and was to lose my soul in some fey realm for the sins I bore upon me and those that tarnished my name; but this illusion thanks to God was quick dispelled, for I was brought before the lutist, a most handsome sort with a sly and vulpine face to him. But though I was presented there before him, he did conclude his music, which was very fair, before rising to greet me, and as I watched him and his cunning features I did believe a scoundrel was in it. With fair manners he introduced himself with the name that is upon him still and which stood in high infamy in those days as in our own, and informed me he had sent his men out to find one with whom they might break bread that evening, for the day had been unusual prosperous, and it was good to share good fortune, luck being but another name given to the visible gifts of the invisible Lord of hosts – gifts which He apportions to us, not as we would have them, but as He perceives we need them.

I was taken much aback at these fair words from the mouth of an uncouth sleeveen, and my host laughed at my amazement and asked me my name, the which I gave him, for never has a forked tongue lain between my cheeks. He invited me then to his board, where myself was seated as guest of honor, and given all the choicest foods, which were abundant and of comely aspect. Still I did fear trickery of that band, though they seemed a jolly and peaceable lot there in that glade, and I admit I even at first suspected me some poisoning; yet he himself, seeing my reticence, partook first of all I was to eat and prove me its goodliness, though it was rather his own he was ever more revealing.

Now we ate long and well of fine foods that were all out of joint with the modesty of that manner of life, and such was the merriment at that table that even my heavy heart was aught lifted and my weary spirits somewhat refreshed. At the end he rose, as though to lift his glass, and did indeed, and drank a toast of it to me, and asked if I would be willing to offer a gift of some moneys to his band in support of their good works. At which I fell dark again, for I saw as methought it the signs again of the miscreancy I had first feared I glimpsed. I told him I could not do as he requested, nor even with myself willing, for twenty shillings were all my riches in all the world, and these the single flimsy barrier staked between me and disaster, and I kept this poor treasure such as it was in the trunk that weighed so regrettably light upon my horse's flanks. And I told him that he could have even these twenty if he would spare my life and my mount for the sake of my wife and my children, who were already fallen into domestic disaster, and would have need of my strong arm and a good beast in the hard times to come. And he looked of a moment grave, and told me that he would ask nothing of me at all, neither gold nor life, if I would not give it, but that he prized honesty above all things, and would know if I were dissembling, for while the meal was free there was a tax in Sherwood upon the lie, and so bid me measure my words before I set them again across the length of my tongue. But I emboldened by the truth in it repeated my assessment of my holdings, detailed even unto the objects I bore on my person, and he commanded his men to check me against my word, and they did, and found me an honest man.

At which he sat in his seat in amazement perceptible, and asked me how ever it came to pass that a man of my birth and rank should be traveling so unburthened. Had I found in him but the disillusioned highwayman I should never have responded, but for the sincerity in his eyes I began truly to believe there was a man in it I had not in the least understood, and some angel prodded me then to speak openly before him and his men, Beloved, and to tell them frankly the whole of my miserable plight. It was long telling, for there was much to unwind to them that yourself have already seen rounded on the spool, and by the time I had finished it was far into the night and the bonfire had burned low, for not a man had tended it in the meanwhile, so intent were they all on learning the outcomes of my tale. So I came then to that very night, and how I was walking that road to bear my paltry gains before the Abbot, and how I would not flee this duty, but had bound myself to it by word and troth, and would carry it through, by God, or I were no Christian.

I told him further I would gladly have paid him and his jolly men ten times what I had in my possession, if only such riches were mine, for I had been well treated indeed by them, and, what is worth more than gold, had for a while found my spirits raised and my megrims assuaged; and I told him moreover that he was welcome to what little I had, for little could it succor me, who was about to lose everything; and in truth, I would rather he, who was rumored to be kindly to the poor, take and use this small sum of money, than that it should fall into the Abbot's greedy and self-serving hands.

And when they had listened full of it, suddenly he leapt to his feet, and exclaimed that they alone had much to fear of the wilderness who who were possessed by their possessions or disordered in their souls by bondage to vice; for that which such men craved should remain in the wilds to taunt and debase them. But, he declaimed, he himself ne'er stole a cent from a man as had none to give, nor from any as could not spare it. And suddenly he ordered his men to bear before us a certain trunk, the which was clearly known to them all. As I look back on these events, I do not know what amazes me the most still now, Beloved, whether the command or the alacrity of the men at carrying it out, for surely there can be found in this world some few such as he, who value money to its right place and do not set gold before things of greater worth; but a community of men so constituted I had never seen in all my days and do not think to see ever again in this present world, if not in this or that religious order set apart by God for purposes divine. But here it were no religious vows that abetted such attitude, but rather only his singular will, and I think there can never be another like him.

This chest they did bear before me, and laid it at my feet, and he, pointing to it, said that it contained all that I should need to satisfy the Abbot, and more besides, and that he would yield it to me then and there as one honest man to another, that I should be preserved from the talons of cruelty or the roasting spit of my enemies. I avow I was bewildered, and knew not how to respond to this gesture, which seemed at first to me some new trick, but for the avidity I then saw in him to do right before man and God. I told him I could not accept such a wealth from strangers, and he said that we were not strangers, for no servant of Christ is stranger to another, but that we were in troth brothers and must act to one another as brothers would act. And I was moved deeply by his words, Beloved of my heart, and to this day as I remember them am put deep in that mood again, and deep in me the spirit is stirring. So I said to him that as he had proclaimed, so it would be, but that I could accept no such gratis largesse even from a brother, but must, one year and a day from that very moment, return to the Sherwood way, and stand upon the piece of road where I had been intercepted, and gladly repay my debt to him and to his band of men, and my word as my slauntiagh, and he accept this offer or else rescind his own. He smiled then widely, a smile I am not soon to forget, and we shook our hands upon it in bond. I passed the remnant of the night with them and was yet awake from this vigil and off ere dawn, a wagon drawn behind my horse now that they had given me, and I on the wagon, and behind the wagon the chest, and in the chest my salvation.

I was going then fresh as though I had slept all the night, and I in constant prayer and thanksgiving, for God through his servants had recovered me beyond any hope I had ever possessed of salvation, and showed His puissance ever and ever again. I took those pounds before the Abbot, and a great bemusement was on him at seeing them, and I could see he was trying ever find the answer to the riddle of where I had got so much money, and still to get out of it and find some way to stablish again my ruin. But failing this he stood mum as an omadhaun and boggled at me. There was nothing for it but to accept my gold, such as was due him, and it please him, and me to go home with the considerable amount that remained of it, to use it toward gaining the amount I would need to repay my new and, this time, most welcome creditor.

Beloved, I shall not belabor the point, but I did indeed amass the quantity required in the arc of that year, and even advanced a shade beyond, and on a year and a day from that night did stand in the Sherwood way, now with my eldest son, and was as before met by the merry men of Sherwood, and brought again to the face of their captain with all that I owed him to the cent and more besides, and I brought what is more food and spirits and good ale in aim of celebration. And we passed that day in feast and merriment, and the telling of stories long into the night, and by the time myself and my boy left, and returned to our castle at the Lea, I would count that man a bosom friend. Yet I never believed my debt repaid, for it is one thing to give a man the material he has lent you, and it is another to match him his spiritual boons.

Yet I strongly fancied that I would never see him again, for occasions I had to pass his way were few, and reasons for him to pass mine fewer still, he hidden for countless sound reasons, and not the wandering sort, and so I believed that I must trust to prayer to do what these human hands could not, and to bring him some semblance of a grace as that he had bestowed on me. Yet fate was to disprove me in this, Beloved, for it came out that one final time we would stand in each other's company.

The circumstances were peculiar in the highest, and to this day I am sure I know not enough of them to recount them clearly. I will detail all that I know.

There is a certain fortress in Sherwood that the Sheriff was building in those days to siege the forest, thinking in this way to force to heel the brigandry he perceived there and to establish himself a presence where he had none. I think it stands now as a symbol of the vanity of our human projects. When this fortress was nigh on completion, and only a fortnight before it was to be manned and armed, it seems that my friend and his men snuck upon it and dispossessed the builders of their work, hostaging them in the inner gaols and riding a makeshift banner over the fort as though it was their very own, and my friend the rightful prince of that castle. What intentions they had of it I cannot say, for surely they did not hope to hold it long against the King's very armies, and I suspect they were making their usual sport of the high fancies of high men, to remind the Sheriff that a lone fortress cannot long tame the wildness. It is likely, Beloved, that they wished only to stay there a night or so, and to enjoy themselves liberally upon the stores of that place, and perhaps to get up to like mischief ere they depart the fortress, having left thereupon the indelible traces of their stay and their mastery of that entire region. But very nearly they paid full for the misfortune of their risk, for unbeknownst to them one of the builders had escaped, and like an exile raced back to Nottingham to inform the Sheriff what had transpired.

There was a flurry of action in town, and all the men the Sheriff could seize were brought against the intrusion, and hounds to boot, and I do believe the Sheriff was set to lay siege to that fortress and raze it to the ground if necessary, so as to bring its momentary indweller to bar by dint of arms. As well he might have, Beloved, if word had not been carried first to the forest men of what was afoot, in advance of the arrival of the Sheriff and his ranks. The messenger was not far afore the Sheriff's militia, and the men disbanded from that fortress with danger hard at their heels. Indeed, by the time the last of them had quit its premises, the Sheriff was already upon the outer walls and had divined their flight. He wasted no time, for he has a cool head, but rounded the fortress at once and found my friend and several of his close associates issuing thence, they being the last to leave that place, as is befitting to commanders. The rest had slipped into the woods, but these were forced back into the walls, which were neatly surrounded, and three men inside to bear the coming wrath.

Night was near fallen by then, and the Sheriff determined to set upon the stone lodgings in the dark, counting on the full force of his numbers to bear any pursuant casualties. Some hours they waited before setting to action, and then laid ladders to the sides and climbed over. They spread out over the fortress premises, seeking the three castaways, but to their surprise, and the fierce displeasure of the Sheriff, came up empty-handed. Meeting his men at the center of the fortress, the Sheriff was nigh upon madness, when the bay of dogs beyond the wall awoke him to what had transpired: their quarry, anticipating just such an assault, had hidden themselves in the very battlements under blankets like so much masonry and materiel, and awaited the passage of the men, perchance even being tread upon there, before employing their selfsame ladders to escape. But the hounds were on them now, and the ring of their yalping could be heard through the wood. The Sheriff regrouped at once and spurred his men to follow. They found their dogs slain already by arrows, and it is a wonder, Beloved, that these men were of such a mark that they could seek out a beast in the nightclad wood by the mere sound of its throat. But so it was. Yet the Sheriff was not to be dissuaded, and pressed on with a large contingent of men dead set upon the hunt. And those three, alas, had not gained such a distance that they could safely hide nor silently flee, but went loud enough through the wood to mark their passage, and the Sheriff was determined on their capture.

The flight that followed must have lasted some several hours in length, with men chasing men through the greenwood. It was nearing dawn that the three fugitives broke the bounds of the forest, with the Sheriff's lot hot behind them, and I do not doubt but an end would have been made of it there in the open field, had it not been by God's will and guidance my own castle grounds they had stumbled into. I was out at that early hour as is my wont in every season, for I am enamored of the sun's first rays. You may imagine my utter astonishment when I perceived my own friend, the man who had saved me from mere ruin, racing at the utmost brink of exhaustion across the lawn, and arrows falling about him as he came. I wasted no time, but took him and his two companions in by the gate and had it raised at once. I came then to the ramparts above, and saw the Sheriff irate below me, shouting his complaints in no uncertain terms and demanding the consignment of these men, whom he called already his prisoners; but though my friend had begged me not to set myself between him and the wrath of the Crown, I will betray no kith nor kin,

Beloved, nor any man who has opened his palm to me in generosity and brotherhood. I told the Sheriff he would have no prisoner that day, but that the men I was even then protecting were my own guests, whose safety I would vouchsafe save as I cut the honor from my brow. This sent him into a wrath, and he menaced me every way he could dream, in the name of the King or of the sword he carried at his thigh, but I was not to be moved, and he, swearing vainly, demanded of me several mounts for him and his nearest advisors, to get them hence to Nottingham. And these I did furnish, for honor bade me meet him by his rank. They rode thence for Nottingham and for my doom, leaving the remainder of their footsoldiers at the castle's gate to make certain we would not try to escape. To these men I had provender borne. I should have done better still for them but that I feared treachery if I allowed them to breech my walls. And with that, we awaited the judgement from on high.

I knew, Beloved, that the Sheriff would take his lamentations before the Lord of Nottingham, but that this Lord could as my peer do nothing. So word would be then brought to the King of my infidelity, and the King himself or, more like, one of his legates, would come to me to wreak upon me the price of my tenacity. I steeled myself against these ends, though my friend urged me to lay him to justice and to shield myself from the penalties that would accrue upon his head; but of this I would hear nothing, and told him as much, for as he had saved my life, so my life was gage to his, and I would not repay him that brought me freedom and life with imprisonment and death. And I in turn entreated him to fly, but he would not, saying that even as I had staked myself upon his cause, so he would do on mine. I swear but not a child born of the womb of my own mother could be so brother to me as this man, and I gave oath that day that his fate was bond to me, but I find that now this bond is broken by a strength greater than my own; for if things stand as you have said, I can do nothing in succor of my brother. Yet I will to the King and plead his cause with the every art I have of persuasion and diplomacy, vain though it be, and seek to win this man his freedom, though it should mean my own downfall. This I swear by the same oath I took that day, for a man such as he must not perish in such case, like a lowbred criminal.

We were together five days before we were saved by as unlikely a turn of events as any I might have dreamed. And it is strange to say but we were in high spirits as we awaited our doom by the King, and did not at all pass our time like criminals on the vigil of their punishment, but more like old friends in intimate visitation, whose hours are numbered merely by the time apportioned to their meeting. And I learned much about him that I will not commit to word here or anywhere else, but will take with me to my grave, for these are not secrets that are mine to reveal, and I have it on his word he has told them to no other man than me. I found his company stimulating to the last, for he was endlessly fascinating in his speeches, and could discourse on whatever subject was broached, and we were of a common vein in all things and spoke like the brothers we had become. It is likely we both would have ended that season together in a final disaster, had not, against all foretellings, the banner of the lions approached the gate.

I was told of its coming and could scarce believe the news nor even my own eyes as I raced upon the ramparts and saw it blooming in an eastern wind. But so it was: three lions passant-guardant, a blazon of or on gules. King Richard had returned to England and regained his throne not two weeks since, and the news first reached me in the person of His Majesty himself.

My very household was in uproar, and I determined at once upon a course of action. I demanded of my friend that he conceal himself with his companions, and though he was loth to part with me I impressed upon him the essence of matters, and he agreed to do as myself had bid, saying only that if gall should tincture the honey of this news, and I be arrested by the King's men, he would out his hiding and join me in my infamy. What could I do but agree to this, the time being too narrow, and he as hard-headed a man as has ever been born, and all things coming to a point at such a pace? These three then were secreted away, and I made ready to meet my long-awaited and yet so altogether unexpected sovereign.

I tell you, Beloved, that my obeisances to the King were as sincere as any man's, for to this King the wolves of the forest themselves would bow. He came in that mercy and philanthropy which was his hallmark, and, before justly reprimanding me for behavior against the law of the land, was asking why I had acted as I had, and what I had saved in an outlaw, and what sort of man was in it. And I recounted to him all that had transpired from the passing of my father on, through to the events of a week prior, and how I was bound to the fate of this outlaw, and would rise or fall by him. And the King weighed these words, and said he must take rede with himself, but that in the meantime myself should prepare a meal, for whatever decision he came to, he would first break bread with me, as a man who knew how to defend his own honor, and to honor friendship. What was undecided, he told me, was how to weigh honor and friendship against the iron law of the land, that could not be traduced save at the expense of the general order. But he would break bread with me, even were I a technical criminal, and I in all due humility thanked him and commended myself to his mercy and wisdom. Never once did he ask me the whereabouts of my friend, and never once did I proffer a word on it, nor made myself a perjurer.

We dined that eve at my board, and over the fine wine that I brought my liege and my king, he stood and declared that he would bring no action of law against me, but that I was from then on to closely follow his every command and never bewray the just and pious word of the King for any reason on earth, and I to swear an oath by it, so help me God. This oath I gladly swore, and this oath I have since most gladly obeyed, and though we passed an eve in merriment, and he asked me keenly of news of my friend's doings in those parts in recent times, and I recounted to him the full of it that I knew, yet not a word again was spoken of the presence of the outlaw in my house. His Majesty departed the day following, and it is a blight on our land that he has since perished, for a king like that rises once in a century, and that when a kingdom is lucky. As for my friend and my brother, he tarried on but little longer, saying that he must get him back to his own realm, where his own companions and fellows would be wondering at his fate.

So he went, and so he has gone, and I never gripped his hand in mine since, though my thoughts and my prayers have turned upon him daily, and, by his word, his on me, for we are brothers in Christ, and our bond pertains thus to a heavenly realm and a divine kingdom far beyond the terrene shores of this our England. Methinks that though there was a time of peace beneath King Richard, it afterwards degenerated again to disorder, and in this disorder my brother was returned to his prior dubious place and his erstwhile work. I do not incriminate him for it as others do, though it is a tight line he walks. It is taught by our faith, Beloved, that we must obey the law and bend our knee to authority save as it would press us to ungodliness, and I have followed these precepts all my days save in this single transgression I have just recalled. As for him, to this extent, little could it be said that my brother in his way of life has more closely followed the strictures of God. Yet I say that while the Way is straight and narrow, there are perchance as many individual ways as there are men that God has crafted of clay, each of them in strict accord with a single law but each marked out by myriad idiosyncrasies its own owing to chance and to individual character, and each man of us must return to God upon his own path like so many rays of light returning to the sun. Each epoch of men has its character and its just reply in fairness and honor. When times are good, good men withdraw to deserts and wild places, and when times are bad, they appear to shine the brighter for the contrast. What does our Christian history teach us, if not that it is sometimes incumbent on men to make themselves outlaws, that they might rightly honor the law? What counts, Beloved, is whether our spirit is God's or our own, and whether we seek our own transient glory, or His eternal. It is for God to judge my brother's soul and what was right and what was wrong in his actions, but for my part, I say this, against all those who have called him miscreant and faithless: my friend and brother made no rebellion but his own, and never once incited mobs nor overthrew townships nor ambited for rank and the honors of the kingdoms of men nor craved their corruptible riches, and all he did he did for those who suffered and were lost and wandering, as even I was that day in his wood so many years ago when he by these very acts that I have here recorded succored me. To mine eyes, he lived as true a Christian as any man I have known, right to his blood up to this very moment, and has paid for his honesty and his constancy in infamy, confinement, and chains. If he dies in it, it will be truth he dies in, and God save his soul.

Wolf's Head

I

he Right Honorable High Sheriff of Nottinghamshire, Derbyshire, and the Royal Forests sat before his ample desk, and contemplated the tablets on which the late collections of the King's
taxes were scribed. Feeble flame of a guttering candle was the aid
to his figuring; for though it was bright day beyond the walls of his office, yet
there were no windows furnished in that place, but he sat and worked in dark
inscrutable security in the heart of Nottingham Castle, in chambers of stone
that were fortress-like, and protected by the arm of state itself.

"Fie!" sighed he after a time of these calculations, rubbing his stubbled
gray head, and speaking to his lone self, and gazing upon his lone companion
in that room—a jawless skull that was set upon the corner of his desk in eternal *memento mori*, and which gazed at him now from its hollow desperate eye
sockets beneath its everfurrowed brow. "What times these be..."

Now it happened at that very moment that his deputy was upon the door,
which, though it had been closed, was a drafty old affair of dry-rot wood; and
so his deputy received this comment as though it had been spoken into his
very ear. At once this deputy was put into fouler spirits even than before; for

the ill-temper of his master, which seemed to him always superfluous and un-accountable, was ever a rowel to his own. Thus wrothful did he knock; and wrothful enter, when at a moment he was summoned.

Thomas de York—such was this deputy's given name—shuffled his way into the room with the disagreeable crab-like way of moving he had, and, stooped and gray and frail-seeming as he was, though still a young man, came up before the Sheriff's bureau, and hovered there in glum silence with his head bowed and hands folded before him, as though it had been the Sheriff to summon him, and not he to request audience. And the elderly Sheriff, by now entering his eightieth year of life, muttered something under his breath and leaned forward and drew a cankered hand over his bearded white face. As he saw that the other still refused to speak, "'Sblood, man, what have you come for?" he demanded at last, with a rolling baritone that betrayed none of the weight of those decades.

"To report an altercation, my lord, with a man of the town, on the matter of taxes," came the dry response, in an edgy voice.

And, at the Sheriff's prodding, duly he did report it.

They had come across the fellow in his home in the lower acre of Notting-hamshire, and at first had thought him drunk, so belligerent was he—a most sturdy man, said Thomas, and not at all stingy with his fists, as several of the Sheriff's men could unhappily attest. They had proclaimed themselves come in the name of the law, and had been greeted on this appellation with knavish words prickling to their sanctioned honor. They had demanded forfeiture of taxes owed, citing the rule of the King; but he said he would pay no taxes to the King but those he could afford, and with this he offered them coin inferior to that demanded of the ledgers, inviting the King himself to come and claim the remainder if it so vitally interested him. When the guards began to seek out the balance of his debt in his hut, he came at them with a club of wood he fished from beside his fireplace; and thereupon he had to be subdued forcibly, with such vigor of reply that he lost his consciousness in the encounter. They had taken him into custody and ported him to the dungeon; and now Thomas de York had come to inquire what the Sheriff made of it, and what the consequences would be.

The Sheriff duly pondered these reports, 'til at last, reckoning the balance, he pronounced. "He's in the right with our reason, but in the wrong with our law. And so he's in the wrong with our reason as well, and must pay the usual fine, which is much in advance of those same taxes he withheld. 'Tis a shame, for it well might break him; but if a man lives in the city he must abide the city's rule, be that rule cut to his pockets or not."

"He said it lacked in *justice*, my Lord," said Thomas de York, with a sneer.

"Fie!" grunted the Sheriff again, and gazed about a moment as though seeking something. "The day that men propose to live by *justice* and not by *law*, we shall be in a sorry way indeed. Then you will see, master Thomas, just how various and absurd are the notions of men, and how ill-suited they be to informing principled action."

"There is always the Church to compensate," offered Thomas scornfully.

"And always will be—if the Church be believed. But the Church's justice is not the justice of man, who is unfit to live even by his own humbler law. Let the Bishop see to the Church, Thomas de York, and let neither Bishop nor his Church fret over affairs of state. This I will affirm, most solemnly (and may God forgive me if forgiveness it doth require): man's man, and if the Church were to determine the worldly law for man without the intervention of the state's cold calculations and colder steel, all her flock should stray into lawlessness in the arc of no more'n a generation."

"Then perhaps we want a good king," ventured Thomas de York with a sly glance, for he knew his master's mind in such matters, and did not worry to step falsely with a phrase so weighted with untoward implications. He liked atimes to stew his master to treasonous speech, simply for the sport of it.

But the High Sheriff merely chuckled a dry chuckle and shook his hoary head. "No, Thomas de York. What we want is a good *man*. How then could we pretend to constitute a good *king*?" And rose he painfully from his arm chair.

But even on that moment, as he stretched his long rheumatic limbs and, wincing, drew him up, the High Sheriff was confronted with another intruder on his beloved solitude, and one moreover that did not rest on ceremony at the door ajar as Thomas had done, but rather with all habitual authority, burst in through directly.

This newcomer was a fat man, and of no great height—particularly compared with that long sallow Thomas, or the heighty mass of the Sheriff himself, who even in his old age still wore the impressive figure he seemed to have come into this world with. A heavy man indeed this newcomer, weighty to suit his office, and decked out in the purple of the Church. He was huffing in great indignancy, and a ruddiness seemed to flush and glow from his round cheeks that bespoke too rich a diet in too poor a constitution; and he stood before them almost in defiance, as two retainers scrambled in behind him, evidently only now catching up with his evident rush to arrive. He fixed his bewildered eyes first on Thomas and then on the Sheriff, before he began in a rush of words, carried on by a thin womanish breathless voice past trembling spittle-dampened lips.

"Lord Sheriff, pray do forgive our arrival thus; we saw the door agape, and permitted ourselves to enter. But upon our vows, Lord Sheriff, there is substance in our haste, and the Lord Sheriff is certain to pardon when he learns the motive for our great urgency."

"Your urgency is all apparent, Your Grace," replied the Sheriff mildly, who had already regained himself. His surprise was ever a short-lived beast, and had already expired. He gestured with brusque elegance. "Prithee, Your Grace—do catch breath, and let the matter be told, all with calm."

"My breath is caught already, Lord Sheriff, has been caught now some hour's time of travel—and thankfully so, that I still have my breath to catch it!" babbled the Bishop of Hereford, in heat and animation, his fattish limbs flailing about with much the same urgency that his arrival had indicated, and his eyes two perfect circles of outraged wonderment in his face. "Disgrace!" he wailed. "Far we travelled the road 'twixt York and Nottingham, Lord Sheriff (which, if I am not mistaken, does fall beneath my Lord's jurisdiction), that parcel of road which runs through Sherwood forest—may that wood burn to the ground and be built up into goodly cities, let God hear me!—and seeking for speed, for that is a foul and demon-kept wilderness, full up of blackguards and worse still. We kept to our cab with the blinds drawn—for we do not like the way the shadows have the best of the sun in that place, and our imagination conjures horrid visions for us in those dark crannies—when of a sudden we felt the horses halt and heard our guard call out before us, and—oh!”

Luck had it that Thomas de York, though in general a lackluster sort, had his wits about him that day, for had he not swung a chair round at once to minister to the Bishop’s failing girth, then that mass might have dumped to the cobble-stone floor, and who knows what damage caused itself, or the Sheriff’s appurtenances. But the sturdy seat materialized to catch the Bishop as he collapsed, and the Bishop sank into it with grace to belie his weight, nonchalant at the fortune that upheld him, and brought a fluttering hand to his sodden brow.

“Saxons! Highwaymen! *Treachery!*” he cried out shrilly in final and fatal explanation; and the white-flecked brow of the Sheriff did rise thereupon.

It had happened, as the Bishop proceeded to tell (albeit in a somewhat more wandering and inconclusive manner than the following presentation might suggest) that midway through the forest, their defile had been brought up short by a tree fallen crossways upon the road. The avant guards of the Bishop had dismounted to remove this impediment, whereupon they were laid upon by bandits—a group of ten filthy ruffians or so who were led by a lightly bearded fellow in a cowled robe of forest green. (At this description, a glance passed between the Sheriff and his Deputy; but the Bishop was too absorbed in his late misadventures to note it.) This thief and his henchmen had surrounded them and promised that many more of their sort lurked ready in the leafy shade. “And what cause had we to doubt them!” cried the poor distraught Bishop, to whom evidently the thought had only now occurred that he might have taken the bandits’ word with a deal less alacrity. This hooded bearded criminal himself had irreverently drawn aside the curtains of the Bishop’s cab with the nock of his bow, and mockingly demanded to know in precise enumeration the treasures that the Bishop held in his train.

“And prithee, did Your Grace tell him?” queried the Sheriff coolly, with a glance out of shrewd gray eyes.

The fat man drew up in renewed indignation. “Lord Sheriff!” sputtered he, “we are honest, sworn to truth in all and for all! But,” added he suddenly with a slightening of his pique, which showed a kind of unctuous cunning unbecoming to a man so nobly arrayed, "God and the Church have imbued our noble office with the weapons and defenses necessary to protect it from criminals and iniquities and the various agents of Satan; and foremost amongst these, the right to white deceptions in the face of black snares, toward the wardship of the Church's holdings, against her enemies."

"Of a course, Your Grace," nodded the High Sheriff with a certain weary indulgence. "Your Grace did not furnish him with the knowledge he had requested."

"Nay!" frowned the fat man, drawing his head down into his abundant chin and chuckling at the Sheriff softly as though at one who would appreciate such a ruse. "But rather some figure short of the true," he admitted with an generous wave of his flabby arm. Suddenly a sly smile crept onto a single corner of that sensual mouth, which had but moments before worn so tempestuous a frown. "For see you, Lord Sheriff," he said, glancing about him and almost snickering as he spoke in a voice low and confidential, "we have made abundant provision for just such an affliction. We carry a meager chest of gold in a wagon behind us, a box that rattles with a sorry pair of gold coins, to give idea to these scoundrels that our full wealth lies there; when in fact we have located a richer and more excellently endowed chest, below the seat of our very cab, and our own holy person. For it is a brigand's work, no doubt, to lever into wooden crates; but only a devil's own child could dare to lay unholy hands on the consecrated cloth of a Bishop of the Church!"

Yet this brigand had done just such a thing. Informed no doubt by some hellish imp of these hidden riches, he had sniffed out that second chest of gold with beastly nostrils and had known precisely where to fossick for it. And he had ordered the Bishop with rough and vulgar terms to issue from his cab. When this had been refused with righteous umbrage, this bearded man had laughed a horrid laugh and had snapped his fingers, summoning two of his toughies, who had come in and pried the Bishop bodily from his house, bruising his legs and his arms in the process and leaving the marks of their impertinent fingers on his skin.

"And so these wretches stole all from Your Grace?" demanded Thomas de York, shaking his scowling head, in every outward sign of sincere umbrage.

But here a curious doubt stole over the Bishop. No, he admitted. No—not all. That is, in despite of God and law, these murderous robbers *had* filched the gold beneath the Bishop's own person, all of it to a penny.

Then—not all? ventured poor Thomas, somewhat baffled by accounts.

Nay! affirmed the Bishop. For they left the *other* chest, the almost empty one—surely in plain mockery of those from whom they stole. *If* they had not merely forgotten it there, fools that they were!

The Sheriff nodded, drew a hand to his chin, which was rough with some days lack of shaving. "What was his aspect more precisely, this hooded man?" he inquired at last.

"A Saxon, through and through," said the Bishop with scorn. "Tallish and lank, as is their tendency. Bearded of face, wretched to look on—oh most wretched!"

"A name, Your Grace? Did you procure the name of this fellow—their leader, I mean, the one who came to you in guise of a cowl?"

A name! No... Why, certainly not! What did the Sheriff crede? Or did he expect there had been moment for introductions and pleasant exchange of acquaintances? Nor had the Bishop thought to ask, given his plight, what was the given appellation of the man who was derobing him. Nor even had he heard the man referred to by any title at all. No—no names had been sung. "But by God and by his Majesty the King, my Lord Sheriff," concluded the Bishop in a new outlet of rage, "pray do find this brigand and reduce him to the full might of the penalty!"

And the Sheriff sighed. "I am the King's man," affirmed he, and guaranteed the Bishop of Heretoford that in the name of the law he should do all within his might, and with such dispatch as he could afford, to gain back the gold of the cloth. At which his gray eyes wandered haltingly about the room, as of late they had begun to do, as though he suddenly were no longer reviewing his immediate surroundings; wandered, until they tarried tired at last on the tablets before him, and their arcane tallies, and the skull.

II

e need not relate the much that was contained in that glance between Sheriff and Deputy, nor how it announced in a moment what the good reader has already inferred: namely, that the existence of an outlaw responding to the Bishop's description was no novelty to them, that they had already known trouble with this selfsame cloaked figure, who had indeed been making a nuisance of himself in acts of petty theft along the selfsame Sherwood road. His victims were ever men of a certain rank, but never before had a mark of the Bishop's stature been heeled; and, as the going interpretation had it, the Church, the Crown, nay, all of Norman rule was challenged by this misdeed, and it was soon strongly suggested to the Sheriff from the hierarchy above him that a deal more will and moxie might be required to set things back to their prior order.

He began to ply the usual routes. Bounty signs were duly hung in public squares and thoroughfares, images of the criminal himself sketched thereupon as though in effigy. It was an old strategem that worked on certain levels of psychology. On the first and crudest level, it was a simple ward against further incursions of lawlessness upon the town. For say that John-a-Leech from the far westlands has been pilfering under the name of Charles de Norfolk: what is to stop this good John, unknown as he is in these parts, from parading down the streets in full public view, hiding behind his true name of John, and with a grin on his face to boot? Nothing at all, if he fears no recognition. Hence these portraits, drawn up in poor hand and crude likeness, and posted in places where the many would see. The Sheriff did not hope *much* that they should directly aid in the capture of our clever John; for what stranger, happening upon so equivocal a sketch of a human person, might be both able and willing to direct the law to the very hiding place of the same? But John-a-Leech might hesitate before too boldly showing himself in a town that warned its citizens against his likeness in every major point of passage.

Beneath this likeness there would be the writ, itself still less effective than the sketch. For in these days of high illiteracy such announcements were mute, and needed fleshy voice if they were to speak sensibly to the better part of ears. Enter then the voice of the written word: enter the town crier.

"*Oyez, oyez!*" went this one a-crying, for instance, ringing a brass bell and pointing emphatically to the portraits as he went; and the people about him paused their business and interrupted their conversations and plucked a hand up to their ear, that each and every juicy word might find its right place and not go sliding into obscurity. "*Oyez! The Thieves of Sherwood at their wicked work again! Stole thirty coin of minted gold from His Grace Bishop of Hereford! Wanted most in particular: leader of these Thieves, bearded sort in the prime of his youth, robs in a hood...*"

And so this voice, and others like it, did transfer, from one ear to another, the message of the Sheriff and his law. And what had begun as a double phrase of thrice partition, rose to become a hydra of rumor thirtyfold, and went its way monstrous and strange to the seed that had planted it.

Now there was in those days an alehouse in the town of Nottingham, a common place of gathering for the commoner, where plenty of ale was drunk admixed with rowdy speeches, and plenty of speeches were spiced with ale; one of those forcing beds for bavardage that spring up by necessity wherever human communities are founded. This particular tavern was a broad old wooden structure that might have been conceived a barn for how wide it was within; and full as it could be with wooden tables worn smooth and oily in the use alone and splintry benches and stools for the sitting, that the proprietors might never run short of patrons, and have always spot to set any newcomer as should come craving a beaker. A good thing too that ceiling hung no lower, for with the merriment that was usual there, and the occasional enraged brawls that could spring out at a single wry word, greater space yet was wanted to house all the noise and cries and blows that therein intermingled, and it was a wonder that this structure never burst for the verve it contained, or split its very timbers.

The evening in question was no more pacific than any surrounding; was perhaps a touch the more riotous than usual, on account of factors beyond the scope of our tale, having to do with variations on the small routines of common folk. The talk had been much and diverse, and we enter into it on a point of high gossip.

A certain fellow known as Tom Dandy for his fine way of dressing and speaking was standing amidst the tables (as was his way) and had called for attention from that assembly, which attention he was beginning to elicit, both by the nature of his speech, and by the fact that he was well known to all as one who would divulge matters of interest. For he was a ferret of novelties, was Tom Dandy, and (by what channels none ever divined) had his knowledge in advance even of swift-footed rumor. Yet, as was also the norm, his speaking did not go uninterrupted, but was punctuated throughout with intercalaries and interjections on the part of his lively audience, who after all felt themselves as entitled to the public ear as was good Tom, though most of them could not command it with such aplomb as he.

"Have ye heard the latest of our King?" shouted he, already jolly; and already was held up, as another voice called out, "Now *what* king would that be, Tom Dandy? And mind yer tongue! For 'tis sure ye would not dare to speak of our new and present and most honorable King John!"

"*I*, Aldous Felter? Why, never would I dare it!" replied Tom Dandy with an expression of wounded innocence, his eyes twinkling merrily. "I am of course speaking of our present and most pious and reverent *King Edward the Confessor*, whom I do rightly call Edward, for he is most prosperous indeed!" he added, playing on the etymology of that name; and much merriment rose up at this.

"And just what has King *Ed* got up to?" laughed Aldous, cleaving to the game without missing a beat.

"I say, he would marry an Isabel!" cried Tom, casting his arms out and making his eyes clownish wide.

"An Isabel, ye say?" wheezed an old fellow from beside him, a bitter old man who was not much disposed to merriment. "Pah! Fine news that is! Why, you dolt! He *has* married Isabel, long time ago now! She is the very Queen!"

"Nay, old friend," corrected Tom, with an admonishing wave of his finger, "you are right without being i'th'right. For Edward has married *one* Isabel, but now would marry *another*!"

"What? How's that, Tom Dandy? Are you having us up?"

"On my honor," said Tom Dandy, and drew his brows up, one hand lifted solemnly roofward and the other elegantly pressed against his heart to protest his honesty and good faith. "For as we know, our good King Edward hath married Isabel Countess of Gloucester—or is it not so? And she had been a fair and faithful Isabel, though only half a one, inasmuch as our pious King could not lay his royal hand upon her, she being his first cousin. Aye, she was, I say, a right good Isabel, until the King knew Isabella of *Angouleme*, who, being tart of her years and beautiful to boot, and not so much as even third cousin to Edward, and on top of all engaged to another, was the very most ideal Isabel that an Edward like our King could ever hope for. And now ye see, the first Isabel no longer *pleaseth* our good King Edward, but he would ravish himself the second. For, being *such* an Edward, the man *is* rather short on Isabels, this I think we must allow His poor Majesty!" And nodded in mock solicitation at the crowd, which by now was full in his possession.

"Now that *is* some news, Tom Dandy!" acknowledged a younger fellow, an ingenuous surprised sort, who took all things as they came and never quite got his hands all the way round any of them. "And say—will they let Jah—that is to say, *Edward*, I mean," said he, interrupting himself and blushing and gazing 'round as if he had committed some unpardonable *faux pas*, "I say, will they let *Edward* get away with it?"

Tom Dandy shrugged a loose and whimsical shrug. "Who could say, my game young rooster? But then, why *not?* He *is* the King, is he not? And the King, 'tis rumored, can do whatever the devil whispers into his ear. Why, he's free as free, is the King, and if he would throw off one Isabel to take on another, or choose to marry 'em both like a great good Edward indeed—why, them's his affairs, my lovelies, and may he sire a dozen Edabels from each. Or at least, God be pleased, from she as is *not* his cousin!"

Laughter general arose at this, and much chatter, as about the room this news whirled rampant and began to assume its many eddies, and some would speak of John in it, and others of Edward, and a few confound it all and tangle themselves in this web like flies.

"That's a fine story, Tom Dandy!" rose a sudden voice from somewhere amidst the mass; and emerging from that drab fray there debouched a balding and himself none-so-slim fellow of perhaps forty-five years of age, who was grinning a toothless grin and glaring round him with remarkably round eyes. "A fine story, and no doubt. Yet I say, it does not touch us as near as this one. Did ye hear the latest, Tom, about a certain fat Bishop and his mislaid hun'ed-pence?"

"That I did not, Spander!" replied Tom Dandy easily, drawing back and looking at the coming of Spander with canny eyes. "Unless it be that this Bishop had hisself a hun'ed pence, and with 'em bought hisself a gigantic roasting pork, and roasted hisself alongside it, believing all the while he could swallow down even his own tremendous person, and so more than double his formidable stature..." A roar of laughter; but Sander drew on ineluctable.

"Nay, nay, but a true tale, and one pleasing to weary ears; for a Bishop is better roasted *inward* than *outward*. And nothing roasts a man of the cloth more fiercely than misplacing his coin purse—"

"Tha' minds me!" called another voice—a wiry fellow who leered round from ale-spent eyes and spoke from a toothless mouth. "D'you hear 'bout the Thieves o' Sherwood—tha' fellow, wha's his name... the hooded fellow?"

The chump and balding Spander spun his great nose round and glared irately at the drunkard who had let loose this cry. "That's what I was just *saying*, you hedge-born drate-poke!" he cried.

"Ah, take it to your grave, Spander, you're always tryin' to be one ahead of the crowd!" laughed Tom. "Le' someone else give the news for a change."

"What then, you'd hear it from this tankard here?" demanded a much irritated Spander, evidently wounded in his vanity and drawing back and looking about him, his eyes eloquent with their hurt.

"And why not?" parried Tom. "Good ale never harmed a good tale, as me grandsire would say!"

"Right!" cried Sander, folding fat arms over his chest and looking defiantly about him. "Then as ye please! See what good ye can pry out of *yonder alekeg*!"

And glum and petulant slumped deep onto a bench to scowl about him.

"Le's hear it, then, Tim Tenpint!" cried voices all round. "And best make it a fine tale!" shrieked a tart there who lounged, half undressed, in the burly arms of a great drowsing fellow. "Show ol' Spander here how it's done!" So the drunkard rose wobbling to his feet, a skeletal manic-looking fellow of some age twixt two- and three-score, and grinned stupidly around him in a kind of mindless ecstasy, his beaker shaking precariously in his scrawny fingers. "*Hear, hear!*" they began to chant when he would not speak, lifting their mugs to one another and laughing and drinking, and when their cries had died down to an expectant murmur, all eyes a hundred turned to watch him.

And he, chuckling and hiccoughing, rose to his stooped height, and grinned about him, and, even giggling somehow, with an expression both uneasy and affectionate on his rubicund and shining face, chirped out, "Hiya! Tha's right, now. But say—hear just *wha'*, now?"

A roar rose up, laughter and cackling and cries of indignation. Spander leapt up to his abandoned post triumphant and drew a stiffened finger into the air. "What did I say!" he called out uselessly in the din, shaking his finger and twisting about, seeking a sympathetic face. "What did I say! What d'ye expect from a tongue soaked in brandy!" A beefy hand flew out of the crowd to clap him on the back and he stumbled forth. "Whoa!" he cried, and clipped around to find the hand that had so struck him; but it had retreated back to its rightful owner amongst a dozen men, and all were laughing uproariously in his face. "Who was it...!" he began, raising his fists to show his readiness to defend his wounded honor. "Who...!"

No response had he but jeering, and it drew up harder still as two men mimicked fisticuffs, and pranced about each other in circles like crickets before collapsing in hilarity in each other's arms.

But then a lanky old man that some had been eyeing the evening long, for he was not known to those parts, and sat silent among them—a limber old fellow, with a belly-long gray beard that was as thick as horsetail, a face clear of wrinkles and sparkling eyes to belie his years, and an old rank straw hat smeared it would seem in mud or manure—why, this old man began to call out to the fray; and when the fray would not mind his feeble voice, to the wonder of all he leapt off his seat and onto a table, tipping over tankards and mugs and bumping into men and using their shoulders as his ladder rungs to their groaning complaint as he danced up over them all with weird crooked spryness. And standing there arms splayed, did shout over all, in a curious placeless accent, "Ho there, friends! But tell me, I say, tell me, if you would—for I'd know it fast: what *has* this Robin-a-hood been at?"

"Robin-a-Hood!" echoed Tom. "Tha's a nice 'un! I like that! But what's it worth to you, old man?"

"Call me a collector and mime of the tales of knavery," called he, grinning about him through his beard; and it was to be seen that he had a spent tooth at the front of his mouth, so that he almost whistled through it as he spoke.

"And then what'd ye do with your collection of tales, old man?" called out a smooth tenor, a sneer in its voice. "Tell 'em in the square?"

"I'll sell 'em back to *you* for better'n I paid, my gabbing friend!" riposted the old man, grinning down on all their heads. "Or keep 'em rattlin' about in me poor pocket for posterity, to feed some morrow to me many grandchillun alongside their daily bread. Or better yet—I'd act 'em out and live 'em over and over, and see how they might be improved upon in the play. Ho! Heavens me! Is a man not permitted his wonder, for reasons private to him?"

"This fellow wants to tell worn tales in the square..." repeated the smooth voice, still sneering.

"Man, I am not deaf!" roared the old codger suddenly, with a voice surprisingly vigorous against his evident years. "Heard ye the first time, and care as little now as then! Now, someone say at once and without any further preliminaries: what *has* this Robin-a-Hood been at?"

"I'll tell you what, *I'll* tell you, boys!" yollered Spander over all other voices, waving for silence; and by and by, against all probability, this silence did come to him, and eyes turned beerily his way. "Our Robin-a-Hood has been at nothing less than *high robbery* and the *shaming* of proud heads! Why, on the very road beyond these alehouse doors, 'twixt here and Barnsdale, in the deep dark of Sherwood, he cut down *five* of the Bishop's guards—"

But once again to his great vexation he was silenced, as "Pah! Cut down, rot!" barrelled out over the heads of all, in a baritone to make everyone start and turn. It was a tall burly sort as had interrupted him, a man who did not stand up from his table, despite the forcefulness of his outburst, but only shook his greasy head coolly, as though in general displeasure at the ubiquity of human folly.

"Rot?" repeated poor bewildered Spander, interrupted now a second time on his way to a telling tale; and glared wide-eyed at the man who had so challenged. "Now tell me just who ye be, and how ye might come to know—"

"Name's Holt Gilpenny," cut in the other brusquely, "and me and Jack Mouse here, we're of the guard of the Bishop." The burly fellow made this affirmation dryly, nodding his unshaven chin decisively, and indicating a mum fleshy monster sitting wordlessly beside him. And in wake of this revelation, the attention of the hall fell to him by magnetism unanimous, and Spander once the more was left bewildered and deprived beyond its circuit.

"Then *tell* us, *tell* us, my good man!" cried the old fellow on the table, as he achingly descended from his perch, evidently much tried by rheumatism and the joint complaints of the elderly. He kneed and knocked and laid his hand on the heads and shoulders of several complaining fellows as he came, but paid them no heed, using them as so many aids to his descent, and staring all the while fixedly at Gilpenny. "*Tell* us what you saw in Sherwood, and just what Robin-a-Hood got up to there!"

"First things first!" called out Holt Gilpenny. "No blood was ever spent this day in Sherwood Forest. Let that be known—nor thief nor guard this day has shed a drop! Even so there *could be* no fighting properly speaking with that lot, for they came at us with bow and arrow a-pointed at our hearts."

"Bows!" exclaimed someone, much surprised.

"Aye!" affirmed Holt darkly. "English longbows, by the looks of 'em. That's how it started, by my troth! This arrow comes a-whistling out of the brush, and drives in right through the carriage wall, in which was riding His Grace the Bishop. I say, a force was in it, gentlemen. It did pierce that wood, which I know to be hardwood three fingers thick, and came splintering almost out the other side, the point of it staring the good Bishop right in the face. So we stop up, and out they come. Come out like cowards a-hiding behind their barbs, and surround us just so. Tell us to lay down our weapons, the which we do, and they gather up our swords, which they carry off, never to be seen again. So, having disarmed us like dogs, they unhook their arrows and circle round us."

"They did not e'en draw a sword?"

Holt shook his greasy head. "Not an inch of steel did these marauders show," said he, "save as hung at the end of their shafts."

"And then? And then?"

He shrugged. "Then that *one* stepped forth—that *Robin* as you call him, old man—a tall slight fellow by the looks of him, and all wrapped up in green and a-cowled like some manner of monk, so that you couldn't get a clean look of his face. Stepped right up to the carriage of His Grace the Bishop, and drew aside the curtain just as calm as you please, and all politeness asked the Bishop to tally him out a running list of all the treasure we had with us. The which our Bishop did."

"What? Jus' up and told him? And he the Bishop and all?"

"Nay, me lads," smiled Holt glumly, staring before him and indicating the air, as though he were reliving the very scene once more before his eyes. "Nay, but tried to pull a quick one on our Robin here. Told him, to be sure, how much gold he bore in a chest we was towin' in plain sight behind his carriage, the which we all of us knew more or less; but unbeknownst to any of us, and still less (I'd have wagered) to these thieves, there was another box of gold he carried beneath his own seat."

"The clever old codger!" cried a voice.

"Aye, sly old fox! But not so sly as this Robin. For Robin looked about him, left and right, and smiled, and peaked under the carriage, and said, still all smiles, 'Grace Bishop, your carriage is riding unusual heavy upon its larboard!' To which His Grace replied none pleased that he himself was no waif for his poor horses to pull. 'Nay,' said this Robin, 'but methinks 'tis not the weight of holiness that so trains upon it,' and said something about his Grace being too spiritual to set upon the balance, and asked His Grace to step forthwith out from the carriage. The which the Bishop did without murmur and fast as a squirrel, and so two of these thieves went in and come out with a lockbox not the size of that little ale keg yonder, but they was a-huffin' and a-strainin' something powerful to bear it, and you could just smell that it was full up of metal. Now the Bishop was sore at this, and protested hotly, but the thief said he was doing the work of the Church, filling the dearth of poor bellies with the wealth of rich ones. Then this Robin thanked His Grace—that's right, thanked him, just as gracious as you please, in all the tones of a regular lord!—and vanished into the wood with *our* weapons, and *his* lock box. Aye, silver and gold they trucked behind them, boys, or my name ain't Holt Gilpenny, and we standing there, poor and armless as wenches. But I'll be burned in hellfire if they didn't leave that other chest..."

"What's that? The one o'the carriage? Just left that gold to the Bishop?"

"Aye!" affirmed Holt, but shook his head in perplexity. "Took the better part of what there was to take, mind you, for His Grace had trusted more weight to his hidden chest than to the other. But—they still left a pretty penny behind them in that other chest. I can assure it, for I saw inside that box, as the thieves took to counting."

"Could be they forgot about it?" suggested someone.

Holt chuckled grimly. "Man," said he, "no thief I ever saw was foolish enough to forget his booty behind him. This Robin least of all."

"Now *there's* a tale!" cried the old geezer of before, rising up unsteadily once more, so that it was feared he might launch back onto his table, or even come clambering down off his equilibrium, landing hard upon one of them. But instead, with his strange crooked sprightliness, he simply made his way toward Holt, cheeks rosy and eyes a-twinkle, and peering into that fellow's face, affirmed with much animation, "Now that's a tale, by gum! A robbing robber too much a damn fool to rob all that glitters! That'll earn me a pretty penny for a laugh at large, I could swear by it!"

But Holt guffawed and shook his head. "Old man, this Robin might be whatever you please him to be: but *fool* he is not. I knew him for what he was the moment I saw him."

"Ah! Robin Hood no fool, no fool!" cried the old man, peering still with such queer intensity into Holt's face. Then, "Ah hah hah *hah*!" he cried, and began to laugh openly, dancing weirdly about the floor, nimble as a kitten, his arms akimbo and his head down.

III

ow these tales, even as they were letting fly in the tavern, sought themselves other routes into the ears and hearts of the people; and some still more direct even than this. As for instance in a small household of the outskirts of the city, a humble hut twixt Nottingham and the dark forest beyond, wherein dwelt a likewise humble family—one peasant, a tender of another man's pork, together with his homely wife, their three daughters and one son. And the imbalance of this family's gender had been a great cross on their shoulders. For these were folk that counted on the brawn of their progeny, and these were times when boys were greeted as blessings from God, for the simple reason that boys could bear the greater brunt of the family's ceaseless and needful labor. But alas, of this poor pious couple had come but a single son (discounting another, which had died an infant), and he a miscreant sort, who, though strong enough, did not care to fill his father's turnshoes. And as soon as he could call himself a man, though the down was but shading on his upper lip, and his voice still shrilled and cracked, he set off to find himself a more prosperous destiny than that promised by a plowshare and pigs. Long was he gone at first, and no word came back to his parents of his end, till the day he showed upon their threshold bearing them some little money, and then was gone once more.

But thereafter he would now and again come back, and bring with him gold, source of which his father suspected too well. And he, greeting his boy with words both glad and bitter, would object to the coin he brought, but take it nonetheless; for the ligatures of necessity proved more binding than the strictures of pride.

The hut they called their home was a two-roomed structure, with pigsties in one wing and human abode in the other. In this latter, the furnishings on the hard clean earthen floor were crude and simple—whatever might serve most cheaply and durably. No chairs were there about a large ancient table, but benches of rough-hewn wood; and upon it bowls carved likewise from logs. Silverware there was none, for these folk ate with their hands, and cut with the same crude knives they brought to their work in the fields. Wattle and daub founded on stone were the stuff of the walls, and the beds of the daughters were of straw, and curved-out logs to serve as pillows. Upon the walls hung curing pork and a few coneys that their father had snared in the fields that very day. Several chests were there, in which the family's few poor valuables were stowed. In one of the corners stood a small loom where the mother would work, and a board game of ninepenny marl for the girls. A fire was carved in the middle of that room, and no chimney to bear its smoke hence; but the thatch roof was high, and there was a hole at its center, that the fumes of the flame might gather upward and seek out the heavens, sooner than sink to a reeking vapor to clog these human lungs.

This eve had gathered about the fire the three daughters. The father had but late returned, on the very cusp of dark, from his duties in the field, and stood with his arms extended over his head, hanging the rabbits. In the great hanging cauldron over the fire a stew was cooking of potatoes and cabbage and boiled root, a watery affair that might sate need better than hunger. No lamb nor pig nor beef nor bison to be found in that mix, for in general meat was what a soul might sell, and not what it might afford itself to consume; but there would be a bit of the rabbit that the mother was in that moment skinning and preparing to cut it into pieces and cast it in. A dog whimpered at the feet of the table and poked his nose about prematurely for the offal it knew was coming its way.

Such the humility in which this family dwelt. Yet penury often makes merriness an unexpected company, and there was no melancholy or despair to be found within these simple walls, but the girls laughed and jested, and the parents exchanged pleasantries as they went about their work, and all was warm and cozy.

Oh, materialism! Oh lust for gold! Defend yourself from this charge: that there is no natural proportion between the tinkling of money in one's pocket and the tinkling of mirth in one's breast; that as easily as one man may smile in his rags, so may another scowl in his robes! Yet such is the misdirection of our human appetites, that a man nonetheless will glue his eye to wealth, and aim his entire life's bark toward that miser's polestar, as though it alone and by alchemy mysterious should improve his lot, when in truth for a dour man a full purse is heavier than an empty one. And herein the one misery attached truly to poverty: not want itself, but rather the vain wanting after want's elimination.

Of this latter spirit had been the son of this family, who had grown to his youthhead a somber and acid swain, his family's indigence riding heavy on him. And only of late had he become lighter in spirit, now that he had been abroad and in the company of certain foresters—for nothing graces the natural verve of young men, so much as a bit of adventure.

He came to the door of his old home that very evening, and heard from within the delight of his sisters; and smiled himself for the joy he found already, and for the joy he was about to bring. And paused there on the door though his heart was beating, in warm expectation of his welcome. He was a handsomish sort, though callow yet, and with wideset blue eyes that were someway dreamy, and a receding lower lip that lent something winsome to his visage. His nose however was a peasant's nose, trait that had come of his pigkeep forebears as though in recollection of the very beasts they kept; and so it shamed him. Large and crooked, it hung over his mouth and loomed between his eyes, to mar an otherwise fine masculinity. His brown hair was loose and longish, and his limbs were limber, and he was (by the standards of a pigkeep) clean and fresh. He drew his cloak about him, and, smiling cockishly, burst in through the door without so much as a knock.

Well was he prepared (but not well enough) for the gleeful shrieking of his younger sisters, the cries of pleasure from his eldest sister and his mother, the cloud about his father's eye. A flock of girlish affection accosted him at once, and he was a moment disentangling himself from all their many kisses and plump embracing limbs. Laughing, he urged them down; then greeted them then one by one, kissing their glowing faces. He suppressed the will to reveal his gift at once; but from some mixture of sanguine solicitude together with an actor's instinct for more dramatic staging, inquired first after the news of his family.

And news there was indeed! For fair Emma, their eldest girl, now entering into her fourteenth year of life, had been engaged to the butcher's son. She blushed deep while her mother, clutching her hands at her bosom and bending her face red with maternal pride upon her daughter, declared the fact. And it was in this way that Simon—for such was this lad's name—find fit moment for his own announcement.

It came in the form of a leather satchel, which he pulled from out of his cloak with a flourish somewhat attenuated by his awareness of the eyes on him, and laid it on the table, with such a clanking and clinking that no one could doubt its contents. "See here, Sister!" quoth he. "*My* contributing to your dowry." And flushed with pride, and stood a little taller in that little room, thus nearer the acrid cloud that was yet striving vainly to escape.

Gasps abounding, and all eyes were turned on that sack and its invisible, but yet so very intuited, interior. His mother held her hands trembling at her lips, and her eyes were welling up with tears; and it seemed as if Sarah might faint. But the first voice to speak was not that of girl nor lass nor lady. Simon's father, Thomas, asked in a hard voice, "Boy, where did ye come upon this coin?"

"By my work, Father," said Simon, with the phrase he had picked out for response to this query—for he had long anticipated this encounter. Only his voice trembled as he spoke, for he was still a young man who dwelt in the shadow of the paternity that had engendered him.

"By which ye mean ye've pilfered it," stated the elder man firmly.

"Husband Thomas!" cried the mother; but husband Thomas did not so much as glance at her.

"A man as robs from a man as robs, was never a thief, Father," replied Simon in his pride, poorly echoing words he had heard once, not from the man whom he merely feared, but from that whom he loved as well. But he felt these words flat in his own mouth which had been so rich in that other's, and the blood rushed to his cheeks.

"Nay? Pray tell then, boy, what is it ye'd prefer to call him?"

"A justice—" stumbled poor Simon, whose fantasy had been insufficient to predict the conversation so far as this late point. "That is, I mean to say, is one as *looks for* for justice—"

"Justice!" laughed Thomas. "Boy, I will tell you where your justice will find you, one of these days: with your head in a Norman satchel and your neck in a Norman loop."

"That is *not* the punishment for theft," exclaimed Simon, hot now and growing fiercer of his temperament for this obstruction to the gratitude and praise he had so craved. But this heat and this ferocity were inward working, for his father was yet terrible to his eye.

"Nay, 'tis not!" allowed Thomas. "But for poaching the King's deer, 'tis." And he lifted his finger to point past the door, to the dark forest that even from their hut could be made out in its superior part against the pale hue of late evening, and to the dumb mute beasts that rustled there through the brush. And Simon scowled and bit his tongue unto its bleeding.

"My boy is no poacher!" objected his mother in horror.

"No?" sneered Thomas. "D'you not see him, he that loiters out in the woods with those thieves of Sherwood? Look to his dress, woman! Look to the pelt he wears, and that handsome dagger at his hip in its sheath of deer-leather! And what do you suppose they feed on there in the wood—pine cones and acorns? Or locusts and honey mayhaps?"

Simon rose then, and announced with wavering voice, "I leave this bag here, on this table, Father; and if you see this coin is bad-earned, then you may take it back to whomever claims it."

"Who's 'at?" escaped from one of his sisters, the youngest, a wide-eyed round little creature whose curiosity would not be contained.

"The Bishop of Hereford, girl. Now mind your tongue," growled Thomas, who was kindly toward his youngest girl despite himself.

"Why, the *Bishop*!" cried his mother once more, and turned her horrified eyes to her son. "Simon, tell me this is not so! You would never rob of a holy man!"

"How would he not!" laughed the father once more with his embittered laugh. "D'you think the thieves of Sherwood stand on ceremony? Why, the news is high and wide, what these bandits have got up to. The law is out for them—all of them—and when it has them, I warrant they'll *wish* they were a-hanged."

"Husband Thomas!" pleaded the poor old woman, covering her affrighted eyes as though there were some ghastly presence in that room which she could not bear to glance upon.

"Ah!" sighed the father then with a wave of general frustration, and rose. "I will go to my pigs," announced he, and made for the door.

"Father!" cried Simon despite himself, and his father paused and set a hand upon the lintel of the door.

Then he turned to face his son. "I am a trouble to my women and a hindrance to my son, for my women prefer wild fantasies to the fact of things, and my son prefers madness to sense. Then I will go to my pigs, for they are more reasonable than the one and more sensible than the other." And with this, opened the door and stepped out into the night.

They were some time soothing their sobbing mother, but at length they did manage it, so that her tears stemmed and even her heaving and worrying bosom began to swell the less visibly. Then all at once as if by an act of grace she regained her wits to her, and ordered her daughters to see to the sack of gold, to hide it in a place that she named, in a pocket in the floor beneath the chest; for if she knew her husband (as indeed she did) then he would say no more of that gold once it was past his sight, but would let it pass. Later, when he was at his duties in the field, they might count it with care and split it nicely into thrice partition, and dole it out in secret to the daughters of the family for their various marriages, prospective or hypothetic as these might be: one third for the marriage even then imminent; two thirds apart and stowed away for happy days to come.

"But what shall father say when we draw it out!" cried Emma.

"*You* mind the gold, and *I* shall mind your father," quoth she, with a curt nod. And only after she had so secured the safety of this their common treasure did she turn back to her boy, to whisper unto him, "Now say, Simon, to your mother, who knows better, that it is not so, and that you did not insult the Bishop so, nor take his coin!"

Simon rose, surer now that his masculinity was undisputed in that room, and spoke, saying, "But be sure of it, Mother, I and my band—or rather say, Loxley's band, for Loxley is our leader and soul—stole it right out from under the Bishop's own nose. And had there been a hundred Bishops, and Cardinals too, and the Pope himself, that passed that way, if only they were as much pigs as this Bishop, then we should have robbed all of them, to a man!"

"Oh!" cried the mother, "Speak not such blasphemous speeches!"

"Blasphemous? Mother, this Bishop has got rich off money that other men have made him—my father, and yours. You think he is a man of Christ? Why—then—so am I! He is a fat man—you should see him—a gross man, real swine, who needs an entire carriage and four horses just to haul him about from one village to the next! What man of Christ is that? Where do you suppose he got the coin for so fat a life, Mother, if not from simple Saxon folk like us? And would we simply sit quiet and work our hands to the bone in the field as our fathers do to pay for his fat belly? Nay, but I say—we must stand against this injustice!"

And though his mother recoiled from it, her daughters would know the tale; and Simon told it to them, as the girls looked on in adoring wonder at their brother and provider, and his mother listened through the fingers she pretended to keep pressed up to her ears.

"It was Loxley that knew he would pass," said he, posing full the game young rooster, though he had been atrembling that very forenoon as the Bishop's retinue drew nigh. "It was Loxley that knew just where to lay the log, and how to arrange our men. He has seen war, you know, has Loxley, real battle where men fought and died, and so these are as hobbies to him. And it was Loxley which waited there beside the road, not ten paces from that bait, and let fly the arrow that stuck right into that carriage—Loxley never misses—and stopped them peacocks up short! Why, and so they did, looking around like dimwits. And then ten of our men came out—not me, for I was back in the brush, and holding up my arrow in case there should be battle, and ready at any moment to let fly against any resister. And ten of our men, I say, with Loxley at their head (he alone with his bow and his arrow drawn), and he called out to the Bishop's men to throw down their weapons. Only not just like that—but you must hear him speak, Loxley, to know how it is! He has a way with words that is a match even for the most schooled sorts, and a voice he has, does Loxley—aye, he sings, even, and plays the lute! And any-

haps, they all threw down their swords, the cowards, as they saw us gather round their retinue...

"Then Loxley, he plucks off his arrow and sheaths it, and walks round the whole line of men, and looks them up and down, smiling all the while, like some general just inspecting the regiments. And then he tells the guards to gather together some distance away from the carriage, some twenty feet, and strides right up to the carriage of the Bishop himself, and draws aside the curtain. And you should have seen His Holiness' fat face pale at the sight of the King of the Thieves of Sherwood!"

Here the image of the distraught prelate appeared before poor Simon with such vivid absurdity that the lad, overcome, burst into an attack of restless giggling that had him crying by the end; for in his divers challenge to authority, his person was exhausted to its roots. All those tensions that had so whelmed him for such length of time needs must be spent out one way or another. So he laughed. And as he cackled, his sisters and his mother listened on, and giggled nervously with him, though to them that amusement was not so near nor so evident.

By and by he remastered himself, though the tears of hilarity were fresh on his now ruddy face, and continued, stuttering at first and breathless, in a high voice, "Ah! Pale as pig lard, I tell you! And Loxley said to him, 'Your Holiness, I would know how much gold you have with you here' (only much better than that, for Loxley has a talk to him, as I said)... And the Bishop muttered out some reply, for he was all in a tumult, and pointed to the cart behind his carriage, where there was a chest in plain sight. Our men went and counted out the gold of it, and it was as the Bishop had said. But Loxley knew better—I'll be blasted if I know how, but he knew better! Why, he squatted down and looked under that carriage and said that it was a heavy carriage indeed, and at that the Bishop owned himself to be a fat man, but Loxley said, 'Nay, this is not the weight of Your Holiness,' he said, and said also, 'If you would kindly step down.' You have never seen a priest or a bishop or even a hare of the field move so swift as did this fat man, but he at once leapt up, so that it seemed the carriage was tipped over, and got quit of it. And Loxley himself stepped in and knocked about, and found him a chest of gold hidden beneath the Bishop's own seat, and brought it out, though it was very heavy—for you would marvel at how strong a man he is! And he handed it to our men, and said, 'Your Holiness, we who are poor wretches and in a state of dire need thank you for your generosity,' and bowed low to him; but the Bishop was hornet mad and said we were defiling the Church, at which Robin says, 'Your Eminence, with this act I do Christian good to clergy and laity alike, for I give to *them* the means to eat, and take from *you* the means to sin,' and prodded him right in his piggish paunch! And then we took our gold and went on. And here is the marvel, that he bid us leave behind that other chest of gold...!"

"What? Why's that?" cried out Emma, her plain green eyes wide.

"Why, one of us asked him that very thing, later, and I overheard the talk of them. And he turned to this man, smiling—for he is always smiling—and he said to him, 'We *must* pay our taxes!' And later I heard him say to another one who asked something of the kind, 'It was a fair gest.' And I heard our men grumbling over it, that it deprives us of gold. But I think it splendid, that he will repay honesty and punish the lie..."

Some time the longer they spoke on the events of that day in Sherwood; and spoke of other things as well, pertinent to the family more than to our tale. And by and by Simon's father returned to them, cooler now of head; and though he glanced at the table, at the space that satchel had occupied, it was as his mother had predicted: for he said not a single word to mark its vanishing, but joined them in silence punctuated with grunts. And by and by did join too with their conversations, until such moment as Simon, recalling to himself the danger into which he might be placing his family, took his leave of them, and, with many farewells from the womanfolk and but a nod from his sire, retired once more to Sherwood, and to his wayward comrades there.

IV

he Right Honorable High Sheriff of Nottinghamshire was by name Hugh Bardulf, born on a date unbeknownst to him around the year 1120, son of landed gentry in Suffolk. Had lived a youth of no particular record, entering the court of the King in various rolls of high submission only in his sixtieth year; and by way of these roles, was noted for his astute mind and his thoroughgoing knowledge of jurisprudence. From this had proceeded to him an annual judgeship, and he had been charged with dispensation of the law of the crown. Though a man already of years drawing on, he commenced with Richard on the glorious Crusade, attending him as far as Messina; and dwelt there a time in that bewitched land and spent long hours gazing across the sun-speckled sea and meditating on the world and on the life he had lived, which, it seemed to him, was fading already to a dream, and would not be much longer in its tarrying. As far as Messina had he come; no farther than that, but from there, against the pressing surge of the Crusaders, he set back for good England. For he had learned in that long voyage that the great hardiness of youth had fled him, and he was indeed become an aging man. His heart kept a rhythm that his body could no longer match. And so he made formal request, and with the blessings of the King returned to country, and never laid eyes on Cyprus and the Dominions of Saladin, nor Acre nor Jerusalem, nor knew aught of the spice-laden lands that lie beyond the cast of Europe's eye, past the gleaming waves of the Mediterranean. And bitterly did he regret this; but nigh on seventy years already he did call his own, or they called him theirs, and he would strain his heart defunct did he try to force it to the crossing.

He brought back with him letters patent in the hand of the King's chancellor to recommend him a post under Hugh de Puiset. The King had heard his request and had nodded in silence a moment ere speaking, as was his wont. "Though I regret the loss to our expedition, my Lord Bardulf, yet I rest content with the knowledge that I am sending back what is required most in England: a *mind* fit for a *heart*," quipped the King, playing on that given name shared in common twixt Bardulf and de Puiset. And so Hugh Bardulf hewed back by stately roads and measured paces, back to the soil of his birth.

By special request of the King he was made justice once again; and in particular justice of the eyre, at a time when the law was crumbling about the question of secession and thence succession 'twixt Richard and John. "I can abide your reticence at voyaging to the very edges of our world, Sir Hugh," had said the King, "for that is much to ask of any man, even one i'the prime of his years. But I pray you will at least venture the length of our own small land in honor of your loyalty to the name of your King?" Even Bardulf in his aging felt better than equal to this lesser task, and agreed with much alacrity to become one of these itinerant justices of England, who travel with the law riding upon their shoulders.

Those were complicated days for a man who held before him the rule and order of state as his canon of experience and his lodestone of guidance. He was such as would never but never desecrate a cause by attending to the wrong aim; was one of those who believed any battle to be a right one, that had as its sun and moon the law. He might even have nodded when Machiavelli centuries on would coolly declaim his *dove non è iudizio da reclamare, si guarda al fine*; supposing only he had seen in that *fine* the head of the perpendicular hierarchy of human affairs. Never has a man been so dedicated to jurisprudence as our good Hugh Bardulf, and never so tried in such a stance by the adversity of the times. He sided with John when Bishop of Ely William Longchamp besieged the Castle of Lincoln, and so was excommunicated by that same Bishop in reprisal—matter which did not seem to sit too ill with him. He sided with Richard against John by defending Doncaster, when this same John tried to overthrow his rightful King, and so indisposed himself to the contender for the crown. But being also a sworn vassal to John, he would not besiege John's Tickhill whilst defending Richard's Doncaster; and so he was at the same time denounced as a traitor to the crown. And it is a marvel that a man who had made himself simultaneously repugnant to Church, to Crown, and to Pretender to the Crown could pass through this thrice partitioned fire unscathed.

Yet the good Justice did so by means unknown, or perhaps through intercession of the King himself, who must upon his return order the kingdom his absence had condemned to chaos. And this left its mark on Hugh Bardulf; for he who had drawn about him the cloak of the law felt himself immune to the lesser buffets of this mundane anarchy, and found once more within the constitution of the state, matter sufficient to elevate and armor the corrupt and vulnerable flesh of all-too-mortal man.

With the underwhelming return of Richard in 1194 there was indeed much to set aright. The alarums of war had dimmed to a reckless clatter in a distant land; but there was much racket yet in Richard's very house as he set foot once more upon English shores. The kingdom had been lost to something like civil war for nigh on a decade, and loyalties, indeed the very sense of loyalty itself, had been at countless points unhinged, and at many more rusted and made ready to burst. But return the King did, and imposition with him of the rule to which blood had once and always entitled him. He had been too long away from his own marl, and was come now to till the field. He needed him strong and capable men to go forth and sow the silver thread of law once more into the unraveling fabric of England; and he laid this charge, among others, upon Hugh Bardulf, calling him justice of eyre once more, and setting him out to county, town, and shire, with the mandate to clean that country to a line.

Before Bardulf became the Sheriff of Nottinghamshire, he had served in a dozen other shrievalties, and knew the lay of the land and the law that governed it better than perhaps any other man alive. He was given the postment of Sheriff of Nottinghamshire, upon the death of Richard, by none other than John himself, who had once used Nottingham Castle as a pivot in his campaign to seize the crown. It must be that John recalled to himself the ills done against him by Bardulf during the warful years preceding; yet he would also have recalled that Bardulf had become traitor to Richard, so as not to besiege his liege lord. And John would have bethought himself, that a man so strictly loyal to the law was a rarity indeed, and the sort of human being that could be easily cast into any pose, like the molten bronze that be poured into whatever mold the lawgiver should choose. Besides which, Hugh Bardulf was a respected man in those days, having been one of the arms to restore order. Then let him lend his glowing respectability as well to the aura of the new King. And so Hugh Bardulf was granted anew the title of Sheriff, and relegated to the Castle of Nottingham, where need there was indeed for a strong and lawful arm, and such qualities as the right honorable justice above all other men could claim.

For in those days had been trouble twixt Nottingham and York, on that road which cusped the wildness once known as Shire Wood. Bandits had dwelt those woods as long as society had been, or the difference between citizen and outlaw. A century before Hugh Bardulf took his post as High Sheriff of Nottinghamshire, a law had come down from the conquering Norman king of England, William of Normandy, whose lust for venery was keen. It was the design of this Forest Law that the flora and fauna of the King's wood be protected from any harm but that brought by the King and his men, on pain of capital penalty. Thus did the woodlands become places sanctified against the encroachment of society, palisaded against settlers, bolstered against the plow and steeled against fire or the ax, and mailed against all arrows, spears, bolts of crossbow and stones of sling. Yet this became, against its aims, a reciprocal action; for inasmuch as the wood was rendered safe from civilization, so the uncivilized were made safe within the wood. And thieves and criminals and men craved by the law, and the hermetic and anchorite as well, and also the unclean and the scoundrelly, found refuge there, and mainly built themselves a sort of society past society (for no human animal, save, as the Philosopher allowed, beast or god, may live without the ordered company of other men). And these refugees fleeing from their variety of catastrophes, lived in liberty or squalor or dignified retreat, as their various cases may have it.

Yet well had the King laid down the bounds of those forest places; for they had become a manner of border within his Kingdom, to the exclusion of the same. The people that populated them became as foreigners, and built themselves a sort of city in contest with the cities of the Crown; and as foreign nations are wont to bicker upon their confines, so too these forest-dwellers tormented the purlieus and the abbeys that had intruded into their wilderness. The monks in particular had voice to spend on the wrongs that were done them; and as they were part and parcel of a larger spiritual order, these voices beat against high-placed ears, and were heard. And when King Richard returned and set his iron hoops of order once more upon the land, many hoped he would extend them also to those dark sun-slashed wildernesses; and some began to weave plans for the banishment of the devilry that dwelt between the walls of Nottingham and York.

Yet one knows the way of these things; one knows of that constant backlogging of human desires, and how intentions are laid as layers of earth on on the next, until by the pressure of gravity alone some are smothered and others forgot. Never very far did these designs on Sherwood proceed, on account of the endless more pressing disorder of the nation as a whole. And as it would be useless for a man to sweep his basement, when he find his living room clogged with dust and riddled with cobweb, so did King Richard see fit to lay his priorities elsewhere than on the wild margins of England, when those places so-named civil were yet disrupted and unhashed. Perhaps in his kingly wisdom, even had that center held strong, he might have disdained to bind the wild extremeties.

But while Richard spent his final years in refreshment of his throne, John was come into a throne already stablished. And he found glory for the taking, in taking up unpressing but popular tasks that Richard had never begun. He turned his eye greedy upon Sherwood, and in sound instinct, sent forth a capable man to deal with the miscreants there.

Sherwood—that weird wood, with its hoary old trees raising their twisted arms toward the sky, and seeming to become monstrous lurking things when the common fog sank down over them and draped them in its gauze. Sherwood—with its endless corridors of ivy and bay and oak that hid the woodland denizens from all civilized eye. Sherwood—that labyrinth of countless ways that led ever to the same enigmatic and ubiquitous heart. It was a curious thing, that rotting mass of life and death that stood eternally savage over the last rubbled wall that any Roman had ever raised. And it was a strange thought indeed that in those untamed places men dwelt, men cut off some way from the links of the city—aye, lived and had their livings, and somehow persisted in vague reflection of the manners of society. The new Sheriff of Nottingham turned his own falcon's eye coldly upon those dark places and the dark men who lived therein, and set his hand to work.

And by his labors, by the right provision of patrol house and waystation, and the judicious distribution of watchman and sword, he brought many a break-neck and villain to the hand of justice—hand which was as firm, by his watch, as any gauntleted knuckle. He himself rode the patrols, by day and by night, and seemed a thing indefatigable despite the encroaching gripe of time, or the growth of the ashes that consume this flesh. It seemed that the value in his outings was more in the way of a scarecrow that keeps the pests at bay, for never saw he a bandit save once. It was as if they divined his coming by some hidden sense of hazard; but that single time there came a band of them upon the Sheriff and his men, and steel was drawn and several men of them slain. And though the Sheriff did took neither life nor blood that day, nonetheless he was there in the fray of it, and would not have backed from the peril had death itself advanced on him in all its terror, grimacing at him with its sword naked and its teeth bared. For though it is true that these muscles shall flimsy, and, at the last arc and wane of our years, shall be but strings on sticks where once ligaments ran true to bone, yet nonetheless this heart, surest muscle of any, shall in a noble breast hold out till it burst. The heart is an organ wrought to a line: or it be right in its main, or it be wrong; and nothing lies between, save the mystery of the contrast.

He was but a year into his office before the effects of his work began to be felt. Travelers began to ride the Sherwood way with countenance less grim, eyes less alert. The settlers on the border of the wood, folk whose sires or grandsires had built huts and habitations before the Forest Law had been, felt themselves better secured against the gloom of the wilds. Those dejected in society; those who had rejected the law, or been rejected by it; those whose sense of life was not qualified by a feeling of ethics; those, in short, who were susceptible to criminal acts for the great myriad of factors that might birth or condition the same, no longer viewed Sherwood as their refuge and haven, nor fled there straight when the law was at their heels. Nay, but farther north did these rogues venture on the lam, into the truer wilderness there, for they sensed that the foundations of society itself had been laid down into the rich mulch of Sherwood's soil, and must clog its woody efflorescence with solider stands of soldier and lawman. And by and by, what breath had been expended in the commons, in jest or warning of Sherwood, was now transferred subtly but most perceptibly to grudging respect for the Sheriff, instead.

And I say grudging respect, for there remained a bitter edge to it. The High Sheriff of Nottinghamshire had this toll to pay to public opinion: that he was come into his new office at the exchange of the throne from one king to another, and one who was of a very different tenor and conviction to his predecessor. And this new King John laid into his people with novel taxes for a novel crown—nothing, to be sure, compared to what was yet to come, but an irritant nonetheless on the already burdened populace. And it was the duty of the Right Sheriff Bardulf to hound these taxes to a penny, to ascertain their amounts and to secure their income. Work which he did, as ever, to the precise letter of the law, and severely, in despite of all lament, complaint, or rebellion.

Thus he cut himself an infamous figure of two faces. Even as the money his fingers squeezed from the King's subjects jangled harshly in their memories, yet the sound was someway sweetened by the fist he brought harder yet against the enemies of order. But even these his merits were set upon a hard tense balance: for while the Sheriff was content enough to give the forest to the forest and the city to the city, leaving each to its own domains and seeing to it merely that the overlap between these two concentric spheres should be as narrow as possible, yet King Lack-a-Land was not so tolerant. The King would have the forest made city, and cleared of every man who would train a dart upon the King's deer or who would live without due obeisances to the Crown. He dreamed of ownership therein, propriety of the wildlands themselves, a control as absolute over the wooded glades of Sherwood as he could boast of in his very hall. And he pressed the Sheriff the harder, the more it seemed his deputy was succeeding. The Sheriff was thus obliged to press in turn, though he was painfully aware that in pushing so firm against the line of orderly peace, he might bring it one day to snap.

"We have done it, My Lord—have cleaned this forest out," exclaimed to him one bright day, in excess of triumphant pride, the young man he had taken on for his servant and pupil; a smart blonde fellow of not two and twenty years.

"Nay," informed his apprentice the Sheriff, indicating a black mar in the blue sky, "but have attained a victory as small and fleeting as yon crow's flight."

"My Lord is dire where there is cause to rejoice!" exclaimed this fellow, whose name was Robert. "For where are gone the outlaws of the wood who once troubled our domains and robbed from innocent men and abused our womenfolk and estates?"

"They are a-hiding in the shadows, my lad, ghost-like may be and without substance, to take on form and flesh the very moment we lax our hold. It is but a sliver's edge between complacency and ignominy in this world."

"But have we not instated order?" cried the poor boy, in an outburst that was such as to make the Sheriff laugh, as much a laugh as ever he emitted: a dry and mirthless chuckle.

"Ho, lad!" he exclaimed. "The law is not something to instate *merely*, that we may found it once and leave it stand there like a statue, forgetting the madness beyond its purview. This is a holy battle, boy, endless against disarray, and we must be constant and vigilant always, to be even one instant victorious. For as our order grows the mightier—and mark it well, young Robert—so does chaos grow strong in the shadow cast thereby. By our victory itself our enemy is strengthened, and it is but a moment that we grow flaccid and it outpace us and gain us better. Heed me in this, if you would learn nothing else from me in all our days together: we are as the string, and it the shaft, of the bow. And as we pull taut so we tense the yew, and must hold against the very tension we breed, lest the line snap in our hands, and bloody violence be born."

"But then, My Lord," exclaimed Robert, his eyes grown somber, "we have *not* won? And never *will*? What then are we about, if we can ne'er one day rest content with what we have done, or spend our elder years in peaceful repose, blessed by the tranquility we have afforded to our children and our grandchildren? What is this work, then? I say, what are we about?"

And the man before him—already by now standing well within confine of those elder years of which the ingenuous lad spoke with all the facility of young men—smiled a wry smile, and commented only, "My son, a man must be warrior."

V

hat had been the way of things; and the Sheriff's words might have seemed prophetic to poor young Robert not six months on, when trouble sprang once more from the dark and moldering soil of the wood.

It began with mere skirmishes, a spate of highway robberies—a matter most common in those days, and, being most common, nigh invisible in its stranger aspects. But the Sheriff had eyes for such matters, for his vision was the last vestige of his once invincible health. Or perchance it was his nose that smelled the way. Yet be it for the one faculty or the other, he sensed already from the first that something differed in these crimes, that there was an element here that had before been lacking—an intelligence, as it were, or the sign of such, that made these events conspicuous. Or perchance there was something in them of charm, the impish charm of common legend, that could summon the senses and inspire the mind—

Charm! There was a word to pin to so gross a fact as robbery! And where did our Right Sheriff come cross that word, that notion? And how did he let this notion, indeed, *charm* him, as he sat blank hours at his desk, his hands balled as if in mute prayer beneath his chin, his eyes gazing deep into the candle's endlessness, or the empty eyeless sockets of his eternal companion there? How did our Sheriff fall into the trap of such fantasies, that were so foreign to his staid and stolid nature?

It began in one of the earliest accounts of these thieves and their work. Four men, known to the Sheriff by repute and ill fame, had entered into the forest—local confidence men and bilkers who had been in and out of trouble with the law for months. Into the forest they went, armed well and carrying some small bit of gold—and out of the forest they came, much the same but for certain alterations that had soured their countenances. For where they had borne swords and daggers of steel, they wore now arms of wood, that had been carved by the forest thieves and afforded in place of those stolen; and their purses were clunking almost inaudibly with coin of perfectly disk-shaped stones that had been fished from some woodland stream. And had presented themselves to the law so accoutered to lament their misuse; word of which lamentation had finished in the very ears of the Sheriff, who found himself hard upon a smile.

Aye, even this mistreatment of the Bishop of Hereford—oh, to be sure, it riled the Sheriff deeply, to behold such contempt of order, and in the very borders of his jurisdiction! But then again, the Sheriff's exquisite reckoning had perceived something just in it, as well—something even to touch the frosty visage of the Sheriff with a slight loosening of the tissues and a certain fussing of idle muscles, that in another man might have qualified for signs of humor. But in the breast of the Right Sheriff of Nottinghamshire, there was somberness aplenty, that any tick against it would be beaten back with a blow. Whimsy gave way to indignancy, and the strong will to cut the legs out from under such untoward acts as these.

He employed his usual methods for expunging the ills of the forest: increased the garrison of the road; brought harder penalty, and harder still, to bear on whomever was found in despite of forest law; sent men to test the edges of that wood and to fish out ill-doers from the periphery; and spread word among those whose purse could bear the weight of it, to arm them well with private guard, must they pass alone the Sherwood way. But these new thieves were canny, and had buried themselves deeply in the very tissue of the forest, as though when they entered it they vanished like spry woodland creatures, or sprites or fayries. Were invisible until they chose to appear; and did appear only so long as they chose. Then the road would be once more clear and the forest a great echoing mass of feral things that responded to no voice with voice, but seemed inhuman and untouched and pristine of all mortal machinations. Every step it seemed these bandits anticipated the Sheriff; did seem indeed that they had scried his very thought, and knew whence his next word would issue and what intentions it would carry. It was eldritch in its way, for the Sheriff was a lawman who had long accustomed himself to attributing stupidity and lawlessness to the same genera of human qualities, and had long believed that folly and disorder were kith and kin.

It was one such jest that riled this Sheriff at last to act: a jest, humorless this one to his eyes, which transgressed far the bounds of proper decorum, and called too much into question the order of the Crown—which, it was supposed, should provide for the safe passage of voyagers along its thoroughfares, and particularly those voyagers whose station in life might have justified them to suppose themselves immune to mishandling.

Of such post had been Alfred Clarke, one of the under-deputies to the Sheriff, charged in particular with the unpopular office of gathering unpaid taxes. Save that this was a man to whom such work was in its way agreeable, for he was viperous and saturnine, and delighted in needling poor. And he would come to the door of this or that establishment or home, and demand of the indwellers their taxes in arrears—with such regularity of presentation and of speech, that he became known himself as "Sir Arrears," for that phrase with which he greeted an opening door: "Master So-and-So, I come in the name of the Sheriff of Nottinghamshire, who does urgently require payment of all taxes in arrears, which amount to the sum total of such and such a sum." The Sheriff knew all this, and despised Alfred Clarke; but knew him as one who would do his duty impeccably and would draw the law to an unambiguous line.

Now Sir Arrears was, like many men of his ilk, a frightey and nervous sort who went his way under fear of harm, and would not step beyond the shadow of his own roof without the protection of his closest-trusted guards. 'Twould not even do to say that Sir Arrears recognized the public detestation of him, and therefore sought to armor himself against its cruder displays; but rather that he was in himself a paranoid side-glancing sort, who felt himself threatened by every breeze-blown bush. And it happened that Sir Arrears proceeded on horseback once down Sherwood way with five well-armed men, along that Great North Road, and passed through Leen Valley, where the late highway robberies had been blistering out. He went thence by the order of the Sheriff himself, who had tasked him with a bout of surveillance, a kind of marching guard to alert the bandits of the wood that order was now to bear upon it. And poor Sir Arrears, who was a lion at his taxes, proved a lamb at this new task, and did now fret on his horse as he went, a scare-crow like figure with overhanging brow and gaunt cheeks, and dark black-cropped eyes that fussed to and fro and scanned that dense woodland for merest sign of menace. Had told his men to be at the alert, had Sir Arrears; but he had also selected men hardened to peril, and so men who were not of the sort to mind it.

Had they been sharper, would they have noted the lurkers in the dappled deep? Or were those thieves there too limber and foxy, mimicking the very brush and the wind that soughed in the oaken boughs? Idle questions. Fact remains that at the blink of an eye these passers-by found themselves surrounded, and a hooded man stood smiling by Sir Arrear's own harness. And though the town mercenaries did seek to do what they had been commissioned to do, they were quick disarmed, and one of them fell upon his back to the ground in a tussle, and would have been slain there by one of the woodsman, a long fellow with a white glove, but that their hooded leader pulled the fellow back at the last instant and saved the life of the fallen man, with a few sharp words.

Thus it happened that, sometime nearing darkfall, six horses came a-straying leisurely into Nottingham, and on their backs rode six men, nigh bereft of belongings and weapons alike. And these men were not mounted as men are wont to mount; nay, but had had their hands tied in their laps, and their mouths stuffed with leathern satchels full of the only coins they had retained. Their legs were fastened under their horses' bellies, and they were sitting backward, and facing mutely and powerlessly the rear of their going.

Alfred Clarke, as he described the ambush to the Sheriff, had about him the look of a man startled by some most rude awakening, to the hazard of the world and the precariousness of life. He shook as he told the tale, like some poor leaf last clinging to an autumn-blown tree; and the Sheriff listened with silent patience as this bewildered fellow rattled his way through account of the misery that had befallen him.

"Did you recognize any man of them, Sir Alfred?" queried the Sheriff.

"Nay, not a one, my Lord Sheriff, not a one!" Then, bethinking himself a moment and scratching his pointed chin, "Or at least, I could not be sure. These commoners, you know, all look alike, and alack, I see so very many of them in my work..."

The Sheriff nodded drily, then wondered at the satchels of coin that had filled the mouths of the unfortunate band, and asked what the leader of that band had said about these. "He said, my Lord Sheriff," replied Sir Arrears, blushing deep—whether out of embarrassment or anger it could not be rightly told—"that he was sending his taxes in arrears."

"A queer thing," muttered the Sheriff, massaging his temple with a great hand.

"The words of a madman, My Lord Sheriff."

"I shall tell you, Sir Alfred," said the Sheriff, letting his hand fall and turning frankly to his interlocutor, "much as seems sensible in this world is dead dearth of sense, and much seeming nonsense have I heard, was but seeming on seeming, and had 'neath its clownish mask a face of somber verity."

But alas, dear Sir Arrears was not of a grade to mount the steps of this steep logic; and he let the matter nest on those heights whereupon it had soared.

VI

ow it happened that these events led to a curious unbalancing of reputations, and a readjusting of the scales of human perception. It somehow seemed that the acts of Robin Hood, fame of which spread with lightning's alacrity to all the hovels of the county, incited the common imagination and unleashed therein that resentment which had been festering silently 'neath the weight of taxes and the harshness with which they were requisitioned. The Sheriff had hitherto enjoyed a dual fame—the darker half of which was formed up by his pinioning of his populace through excises, as though they were fowl for the pantry; but the brighter half had ever been his ability to render them safe and to stamp out the stubborn sparks of plunder and rape that threatened their towns and the land surrounding. Now a curious alteration could be perceived: for the threat of those outer lands had returned, but would not vex men of little means. Indeed, for all that the Thieves of Sherwood grew in celebrity month and month, yet

never were they known to steal a stray farthing from any of the common folk, nor defraud any whose purse was slim. It seemed they had care only for the fatter prey that hobbled down the Great North Road, opened their ears at the jingle of horses and the creaking of wagon and the rumble of carriage, and turned a blind eye whenever it was a cart and donkey that made its humble way down that thoroughfare. Subtle seemed the distinction, but the people felt it. They sensed in this Robin Hood a champion; though the interpretations they put on his championing were various indeed, and in many a case, contradictory amongst themselves. Here was one who challenged the pride of wealth; who countered the high-handedness of the noble with a fine legerdemain; who opposed justice to law; who strove to reconquer the forest for the common man; who stood against the arrogant Norman for the downtrodden Saxon; who gospelwise impoverished the rich to enrich the poor.

Be his motives what they may, Robin Hood became to them the *good thief*, a man who made no menace to them, but at the same time spat full in the face of authority in a way which was most gratifying to the oppressed and downtrodden. And so it happened that the very forces that the Sheriff had pleased his constituents by smothering out, suddenly transformed into as many folk heroes before his wondering gaze. Whatever had counted to the Sheriff's favor in his battle against lawlessness, became a second and even stronger mark against him; and his reputation declined precipitously for it, till he, that tireless battler of villains, at length found himself playing the villain.

Where did the sign of it show? Only in the murmurings of the people; those whispers they reserved for walled chambers wherefrom no sound could creep. Or in secret glances, cast between the eyes of commoners, when the Sheriff or his men ventured within sight. Or in that slight hesitation, that moment's snag of suspicion, when the townspeople confronted the forces of order. Or in a thousand other subtle signs, which could not be read by men of grosser perception, but which the Sheriff with his subtlety did note, or at the least surmise.

Had that been all! But the favor and indeed the whole valuations of a people show prominently in their games and their festivals. And when those puppet-players with their vivacious dolls got into the town squares, and the folk gathered round them to gaze on laughing at the ludicrous spectacles, well now, what did the Sheriff perceive, but a cowled figure dressed in green that made mockery of those who would oppose him? And had this not been clear enough, the hero carried bow against men of sword, and like a pert and turfy rascal threatened a man at ten paces with a dart that flew with deadly speed. Oh, there was no question—*that* was Robin Hood, that green puppet; and his enemies there that were brought low with a puppet's ease were none but the men or patrons of the Sheriff; and as the people adored the one, so they ridiculed and scorned the others.

Or note how the children in the street had begun to play, decking themselves in rags that much liked to cloaks; or see how they no longer beat on each other with sticks, but now made play bows of wood and twine, and each strove with his tiny peers, straining at targets distant. Note whom they called their foes in these games, that had but months ago been forest bandits; for now the children themselves who strove with each other to enjoy the honor of playing the thieves. Change was afoot, to be sure; and the Sheriff stood in the swallowed underbelly of the crashing wave.

And came these changes, as was only fortuitous, at a point of great turning on a scale much larger than the small happenings of Nottingham or the shires about it. The behemoth of warfare itself was transforming—that terrible beast with its steel-bladed claws and its blooded maw. Had been not two hundred years ago that a man's honor was wed fast to the sinews of his arm, and the natural and breakless continuation thereof, his sword. And still so it was amongst the nobles, whose great and just pride lay in the skill they could oppose in melee combat. Archery was a talent they might cultivate for the joust of it, to show in contest of friendly rivalries, and far from the red ferocity of battle; or for the hunt in bosk and greensward, and the seeking out of mastery over stealthy beast. But to bear a bow against a living man was beneath their high condescension, and to hold an arrow pressed against the space twixt flesh and flesh, was to them the business of lower souls, cowards and triflers and classless folk.

Nor did they altogether err. For a yeoman or a fellow of the commons, who was no waif nor peon, yet less still a Duke or Count—such a one, if he had a sword, would have no metal in it such as could compete against the fine steel of the aristocracy, but only a scrap of iron that dulled on the blow and crafted against tempered blades. And as for armor, he should be counted fortunate if he could strap to his chest brigandines of piecemeal leather, or bear in front of him a buckler wrought of the discarded lid of some old keg. Against a knight with his noble breastplates or his chain-mail, shining like scales on the back of some glistening drake of war, what was a commoner to do? And this to say nothing of the absence in education—the lack of training, the lack of means and the lack of funds. The sword was high work indeed, an expensive and complicated instrument of combat that one must learn to play as the lute itself, and which would sing only for studied hands.

But the bow! Why, a sapling uprooted and a length of leathern twine could suffice to contrive from the very wilderness a weapon of defense and death. Arrows could be wrought from the green wood, at no cost but the time it took to cut, slim, and dry them to a length. And while gold was lacking to the commoner, time was abundant. As for the point, sufficed it to sharpen the shaft and burn it to a hardened charcoal tip; or to strap on a nib of stone or chipped agate. Even iron points were not so very spare to come by, when compared with the lengthen cost of a dagger or the worked matter of a spearhead. And this economic convenience melded fortuitously with a growing interest in bowplay on the part of military tacticians.

Late wars had seen conquests by virtue of archery; had brought to the field, nor only the plated warrior, but also hordes of yeoman bowfolk. And by and by it was seen fit, by that same aristocracy, itself so contemptuous of archery, to equip the lower orders with the very weapons it disdained. Bow fashioning was encouraged, and new orders of labor emerged, dedicated to the cutting and casting of wood for war. And even as the blade grew a symbol for the upper classes, so did the yew become for the lower. And arose then custom to sport this skill in practice and in competitions, and to show one's craft and measure it against others, and to pride oneself, were one yeoman, on one's marksmanship. Years were fast approaching when the law of the land would embrace this development and encourage it to a fault; but these were the heady days underpinning that later legislation, which could only come when the sprout of law was ready to shoot out from the soil of prior consuetude.

Then this thief, this Robin-a-Hood, this scoffer at those upper orders, came out his umbraged green with his arc and thistle in hand, and a deadly mastery of the both: and that was a hero in the making for the people, who were but lately finding their way to such arts. He was one of their own, welt in his hands the sign and symbol of this kinship. He was one to hold a threat over the heads of those who were more and more the oppressors of the common folk, or a front for the same. He was anonymous and faceless; one could apply to him the name and countenance one's imagination best pleased, shroud that figment in cloak, and stick a bow and arrow in his hand, and—lo! He was true a doppelganger, this Robin Hood, a myriad-visaged phantasm to the public consciousness, and a universal incubus to that of the powerful.

And now money was pinned on the head of one who went by the name of Robin Hood, and a weighty purse hung round his neck; and suffice it for the lawman with the lawman's patience to await the weak point in this long, very long train—if it would be the treachery of one near to him (for who could count long on the honor of thieves?) or some misstep of the man himself (for what thief does not sooner or later trip on his vainglory?); if it would be knowledge come by on the part of a townsman who had his memory jogged by the summoning ring of coin, to say where Robin Hood had come from and where he might be presently found, or perchance some member of his family to at last turn against the black sheep nurtured at its hearth, to reclaim its good name by betraying a robber and outlaw, even one reared of the milk of its own bosom.

Sheriff of Nottingham Bardulf did not let the matter lie so facile as that, however, but pressed his work at every point he might. And he knew that intelligence regarding Robin Hood was to be had more than anywhere in a single place: amongst the band of men that the knave had already gathered round him. Word was given out on all sides that gold was to be had, not only for the apprehension of Robin Hood, but also for any of his cronies. And he spoke with especial emphasis on this point to his deputy, and ordered him to put any suspect to extraordinary inspections. "For the law gives to us," as he put the matter drily to Thomas de York, "range sufficient of means, I do believe, to extract the knowledge we seek..."

VII

he events here recounted occurred on the threshold of a great and public fair that was held in Nottingham, and the town was soon bannered and ribboned in gay festoons and rich bright colors, and a new aspect came to the houses and hovels of the shires and villages. The open lands about the town were filled to the brimming with tents, and by and by that space had been refashioned and rendered unrecognizable to quotidian eyes. Oh, this stretch of bare dust beneath our very feet: what was it worth to anyone ere today? And this bald spot of earth, which before had been but a harbor and congregation for dust mites and fleas and the occasional crossing of swift-bound hound or stalking cat or racing child—why, look now at the shape that has sprung up from it, in form not dissimilar to some curious fungus of wildly foreign lands: a cloth or canvas shack as big as the house of a dwarf or fayrie, and no mush in this room at all, but men or women at the peddling of things outlandish—spices exotic, perfumes bearing scent of nations obscure and distant to knowledge, stones of every hue and quality clefted from the black bosom of the earth, cloth of every weft and weave and dignity, goods crafted by dark hands in parts far beyond the ken of these pale northerners or their pale northern sun. What weirdness has here been born! Just look: I knew this plot of ground; once I saw Kevin Smith eat an apple here as he was disclaiming after his way on the doings of Miller Tom, and here he dropped that apple's carcass straight down and let it lie. Why, is this the tree that has sprung thence? Is this the germ that apple's pit carried? Then what marvels yet remain in this world!

Within these tents congregated a crowd of the ne'er-arrived, a host of the ranging and the sojourning, a moveable city of rootless folk, come and gone within the arc of the month. Singers there were, and men in motley who strode round on pegs and jested at themselves and at the dwarves they had made of normal men. And folk who swallowed the very flame, or fed upon live scorpions borne hence from strange lands; and midgets and giants and boneless men who twisted their unnatural limbs to impossible angles; and women who had hair upon their faces, and men who were lacking in limbs or bestowed with claws in the place of hands, and children mottled of skin as though they had been reared of speckled cows. One they called the Goblin had strange growths about his skin and bones, and seemed to have a face that was halfway melting. Jugglers and tossers, and men who strode confident across single ropes and even would cartwheel and caper thereupon without breaking pace or falling to disaster. And old women of the wood who with occult cards, or gazing into palms or lining out the wrinkles of faces, would scry the fate of the folk before them and declaim the doom of their very patrons. A fair fest it was indeed, and a sight to behold; and crowds came aplenty to divert themselves for a transformed day, and forget their daily woes.

Now it happened that the Sheriff was tasked with seeing to order in these maddening revelries; for the franchise of this fair had been allotted by the hand of the King himself. And the Sheriff and his men strode slow down the dust-capped roads and vigiled over the unfolding of events, and kept all things under eye, that they should not have to force them under hand. Several times the Sheriff tasked his men to put an end to some scuffle or to decide fair outcome of some dispute; and the Sheriff in all cases was arbiter and final judge.

He was dressed ceremonially the day, and the silk and satin was strange upon his skin. Yet one item in particular was lacking from this outfit, and it was Thomas de York to notice, and to comment.

"Lord Sheriff!" murmured he then, distraught. "Your sword!"

But the Sheriff only grunted and nodded, and replied curtly, "'Tis grown heavy on me, Sir Thomas. Leave steel to the arms of younger men."

"At least a dagger, My Lord, would be becoming—"

"Becoming, bosh!" the Sheriff shouted him off in impatience and irritation; for he was out of sorts that day, and feeling the years upon him. "I am for order, man, not seeming." So it was that he went about unarmed the day, though his men about him were girded and ready even for violence, should it come to that. But never it did. For the people were full of mirth and high spirits the day, and such trouble as began was of so effervescent a nature as to swiftly bubble off and vanish to the sun like the froth of good beer.

Now in this fair were many events and sportsman's contests, of every sort—races, and tests of strength, and contests of wrestling, and tugs-of-war, and battlement of stave, and matches of archery. And the Sheriff, much for purposes his own, and little for his disport, saw fit to watch several of these contests that day; and so was witness to a most unexpected and spectacular spectacle indeed.

It began with a show of muscle—men who must lift a series of ten stones above their heads, each larger than the last; and he as carried the greater stone would be the winner of the day. Many a burly sort presented themselves to put their musculature to the test, and to demonstrate their superiority over all lesser men. Fat men with tough muscles hid beneath their layers of flubbery bulk; stocky farmland men of solid tawny brawn; working men of capacious torso and powerful arm. Yet one among them stood out for various reasons, he being, first of all, nothing to compare to the great bulk of his antagonists, but rather in the contrast almost even a scrawny fellow; for though his shoulders yea were wide, and his hands had some evident power to them, and his waist was neat and trim, and he not at all a short fellow—yet what could he hope from that nice girth, to match against these behemoths and ogres that accompanied him to the stone's queue? Yet came he smiling with them, in much misplaced confidence.

That was not the only thing go draw attention to him. For he was also arrayed in odd gear, and seemed almost like some man of the sea, or corsair even; dark garb and a tight skull-cap that covered his hair to the temples and the nape of his neck, and a great long beard that seemed almost cut from the tail of a horse, so coarse and gross and thick-growing was it. And most startlingly of all, an eye-piece, a patch of black fabric that covered his left eye, tied about his skull cap by a length of dark twine. Came he then, this corsair, and smiled strangely brilliant teeth through his pitchy beard; and gazed about him with a striking blue eye; and so of course was noted and wondered at, so that many laughed and made skeptic comments at his sanity and his fitness for this contest.

Began then the work of it. A butcher stepped forth and beat his chest and grinned wide-mouthed about him and crazy-eyed. The first stones he carried, all the way up to the fifth, a monstrous piece of the earth he must take in both his arms and stress to lift. The sixth defeated him, and he let it thud back down to the ground with a grunt of displeasure; yet he glared at the next man in line with a haughty glance, as though daring any to gain even the rock that he himself had wielded.

Next a blacksmith and worker of iron, whose body was thick from the weight of his labors and tense from the constant glowing heat of it. His piggish eyes looked upon the stones as upon challengers. The sixth he brought above his brow with great trembling and a low moan, and let crash before him with a yell, the veins standing out upon his neck and in his eyes. But the seventh was beyond his strength.

Came next the corsair, who strode to the stones with a long light step, grinning about him as he came, and reviewing the boulders it seemed from every side, amidst the cries of encouragement and derision that met him. "Get to, half-blind!" cried one voice. "Why, if only you had muscles to match your beard, we'd be in for a show!" added another. "Lift that fourth stone, friend, and I'll call myself a one-eyed Jack, and wild!" cried a third; and laughter general. But the fellow was unfazed. He grinned about him as though these jeers were intended for some other man altogether and he himself would second them, and began his lift.

First, second, third, fourth stone, swift as could be, floated up over his head, and plummeted back down with an easy mastery that made the crowd hush. And after the fourth, he looked about him, grinning his flash of pearly teeth, and called, "By my faith, where's gone our cyclops Jack?" And he lifted a hand over his brow, and peered into the crowd from his singular eye. But Jack would not reply, and the pirate laughed a brilliant laugh and shook his head.

"Five's the trick!" called the butcher then, who had been glowering since the blacksmith had felled his record.

But five, though a strain to be sure, came as well. Thew had been a-hiding no man could guess where in this seeming scrawny fellow; aye, stuck out plainly now, muscles stark and moulded well with veins, bulging incredibly; and his neck of a sudden wide, and his face a vivid red. Stone five he carried over his shoulders, over his head, and then let fall, clapping the dust from his hands as he did and smiling wide; and now the crowd was his.

"Ho, but the smith!" someone called out. "The smith has had number six!"

"True!" he replied, "The smith has right forged us a path." And so he passed to number six, stepping round it and eying it from each and every angle; then, with a great heaving, lifted it, too, above him. The blacksmith, his bear's face reddening now for another reason than his recent strain, put a fist before his frowning mouth and shook his head.

"Seven, now, good sir—take the seventh, and I shall swear you are not as you seem!" came a woman's voice from the crowd, a bold lass who watched him with fiery eyes. And the corsair stepped to number seven, boulder as it was, and looked at her as had spoken, and said, "M'lady, for thy fairness alone shall I hew this stone!" And put his hands below it, and, with a great cry of the force of it, heaved that rocky ball to his chest, and his chin, and—'twas done! For there he stood, that queer fellow with his liar's form, his muscles trucked to a fantastical strength, and a rock above him such as would sure crush and kill him, did his strength fail him now—

The crowd cried out and applauded and was generally much amazed, and the girl in whose honor the thing had been done blushed as she was not wont to do and brought a flighty hand to her lips. And from the stands to the side of it, the Sheriff watched on in sudden attention.

The eighth stone, however, had its way of the good corsair, and though he tried it with all he had of his strength, he could not rise it above his knee caps, but it remained with its perverse recalcitrance, tending toward the dark center of the earth. He let it fall and clapped the dust from his hands and laughed, speaking to the stone thus: "I shall not trouble you more, O stone, nor try your will, which is proved more granite than mine own. I leave you as a grave stone indeed."

Several other men followed to try their power against weight, but not one of them passed the fifth; until a great giant of a man, known universally for his daftness of head and his proportionate puissance of form, and one moreover who had the record in this contest, heaved those stones over his head one for another, until he had come to nine; and it, too, he hefted up. Stone Ten had never been lifted by mortal man, save, legend had it, by King Arthur alone;

indeed, this entire contest was arranged around Stone Ten each new year, for Stone Ten was almost become a monument in the otherwise empty field, and men said of it that it had fallen from the sky and contained a principle which imbued it with unnatural weight; and this day, too, Ten held its stubborn place against all flesh, though the giant crouched above it and screwed his id-iot's mouth into incredible contortions, as if he hoped to frighten the lump of rock to flight.

Several more pursued, though by now the crowd was diminishing. Truth be told, one of the last managed eight. Yet that dumb enormity of a man had still won the prize—and the corsair, the crowd.

VIII

magine then, the furor, when he showed his face again at the tourney of staves! And once again the crowd entertained itself in judging the outcome of events before they had moment to pass—arguing whether the corsair should be a miser at this con-test, or a hand, or merely mediocre. And as every human being is in his desire a prophet, so every head of the public opined as to how this matter would out in the end.

Now fighting by quarterstaff in those days was a common art, for simple question of economy. If the sword was a rare measure of costly steel that could not be easily fit in the commoner's purse, the quarterstaff was a weapon as common as the trees of the wood. A length of straight ash, a cut of upright oak, and one held an arm that could in many cases overcome even the blade; for a sword was a heavy blundering thing, and clumsy in untrained hands, and slow to its cut, and not near so long as a stave. Then it was well to the com-moner's merit that he learned to wield a weapon that could be to him shield or spine, as the case might want. Thus the origin of such contest as this.

'Twas organized thus: that in a large arena carpeted in white dust, men were paired to battle, some sixteen pairs to the start of it. And a turn would carry until each of these pairs had settled account. Victory was won simple, thus: that the man who fell first, his hands, his butt, or his back touching the earth, was loser. At the end of each turn, ranks were checked, the losers of the bout set aside, and the winners paired amongst themselves, and so forth, until at last a final pair remain, and of that pair, a final victor.

Thirty-two men then stood forth at the call to count, and in long line faced the crowd, as though they had been gladiators at salute of their emperor. No emperor was there, nor king; but the right Sheriff of Nottinghamshire was, for it was his business to be, and his eye was keen upon the corsair.

A motley bunch they were, of all shape and size, and even of age; for among them was a tough old man of better than seventy year, and also a boy, but a sapling himself, whose face had not even the first down of its maturity. But two of these stood out most particularly: the corsair, for the rumors flying about him, who contemplated the crowd in fine repose with his hands behind his back and a curious grin upon his obscured face; and another, a giant of a man, who stood a head taller than the tallest of the others, and something yet more than that beside the corsair. And as they were so assessed by the crowd, the corsair leaned in to the giant—for that man was stood beside him—and said, peering up at him, "Good master giant, I should have seen you at the stone contest some hours ago. Methinks you would have shamed even him that shamed the rest of us."

"I need no show of force but that my stave can grant, I warrant," scoffed the other. And then suddenly stood out before the line of men, as though he would present himself. He who was calling out the rules fell uncertainly silent, and all eyes turned to the great man, who looked about him for a moment haughtily before beginning.

He was, as stated, an uncommonly tall and also powerfully built man, with shaggy hair that verged hard on red, and a long feral beard; and his eyes were a timid kind of green, though the look they held was rather one of challenge than of timidity. Out he stood, and out he bellowed with a great booming baritone:

"I am called John Little. Five years now I have wandered the breadth and the length of this our England, in search of a man my better, or such a one who can, by might or wite, defeat me in hand-to-hand blows. I have yet to find this man, though five years and sixteen days have I sought him. If he be here amongst these today, let him now lay me low!"

And evidently content with his pronouncement, he stepped back into line, and folded his mighty arms before him. The corsair eyed him merrily, evidently well amused by the scene; and the voice uncertainly resumed its call of the rules. Then the men were handed their weapons and ordered about the field in pairs, to square off amongst them. The corsair found before him a mouse of a man, who held a stave that must have been thrice his length; and the giant before him a hopping intent fellow who was all nose and mustache and will to win. And, at the fall of a red flag, and the cry of "Begin!" these rounded each other, and so the other combatants; and before long was heard the hollow drum of stave beating on stave, and the grunt and sharpened "Hie!" of men as they sought to strike each other to pain and defeat.

Had passed not so much as a minute before the fellow with his nose and mustache was sneezing on his back, as the dust rose up and embroiled itself in his upper-lip whiskers beneath an astonished pair of nostrils. The mouse lasted a time the longer, as the corsair seemed catlike to play with him. But at length, he, too, fell.

And while this was a-going, the crowd had its sportsman's way, and called out support of this fellow or jeer of that, encouraging Tim the Winder and praying aloud that Sam Steward should fall face first into the dirt and be pleased to never rise again. It was clear as matters proceeded who was the wiser in this business, and who but a tyro; and it appeared swift to the public eye that four or five good souls on that pale and cloud-swept stage were superior to the others. Among these, the giant and the corsair.

Several phases and these thirty-two men spinning their greatened toothpicks and spiraling about one another like dancers had been reduced to four; two pairs now dueling it out to determine who should be in it for the championship. And in one of the pairs, the giant and a spidery figure with great long arms; and in the other, the corsair and a nondescript fellow who was, despite his not seeming much, a solid hand with the stave. And so these two pairs rounded each other, like twin clocks set to roll counter each the other there upon the salty floor.

Now the spidery fellow had long wide blows that had knocked the better part of his competitors off guard by reason of the impossible length of his reach, those tentacle-like members he called arms that flew every which way and knew to find a man with their stave nigh eight feet away. But now this squid-like man was paired with a man as tall as he, if not as gangly, and one who moreover was better versed in the art of this thing; and of a sudden all his advantage was annihilated, and the sparsity of his technique showed forth stark. By and by the inevitable blow was dealt him, and he fell backward, his arms spiraling like twin flags of a windmill, his unnatural large mouth opened wide in the shock of it; and came crashing down, a great serpenty creature fallen in the dust.

The nondescript fellow proved the longer. He, for all his lack of trait, had compensated well with his knowledge of this business; and if the corsair kept on his feet, it was thanks to his own skill and that alone. They wound about each other long before the corsair, almost at a stroke of luck, managed to plant his enemy's stave hard on the ground, and with a second blow that seized advantage at once of this fortune, drove its keeper down after it.

And now the giant and the corsair were twinned for this final duel, and the crowd, which could never recall a tournament so engaging as this, were heightened to the peak of all tension to see how this thing would resolve. Some for the corsair, and some for the giant; and the odd fellow here or there who, from sheer cantankerousness or from the will to stand apart with unique opinion, was for neither, or both together, or would be for whomever should win. "The fight is to the best," quipped one such fellow sententiously, with that smile peculiar to those who pride themselves on their superior notions. "Then who'd be fool enough to cheer anyone but he that'll win?"

But even these wiseacres were hushed when the dance began; and even the skeptics had hidden somewhere away in their hearts a vested interest in outcomes. For it is in the nature of all human beings to choose out, be it even on basis of perversion or bias rank, the better over the lesser, and to prefer the one to the other—aye, even in matters of no import; even in the trashy day-to-day tumble of affairs. And so 'tis seen again, that this human spirit is innately discriminatory, and—thank God!—shall always be; lest the heights should be but a relative point in space, and Satan alone be tongued.

Now when the call rang out, John Little came at the corsair with everything he had, and was a veritable flurry of devilish wood. And it was a marvel to see how the corsair mirrored these blows and withstood; yet he did, and seemed only slightly troubled for it. John Little, seeing that his adversary was none of the flimsy grain that had preceded him, redoubled his wild attack; and yet once more was repulsed by a series of meet replies. 'Twas a series of clacking clicks almost too fast for the eye to measure; and yet these two men at least gauged well enough the pace of it.

By and by it happened—and no spectator, nor even the most expert, could say when—that the defense was spun about, and the corsair began to gain on the giant. Came at him with a marvelous dexterity, and a fluid race of strike and counter that threatened to put that great man down. Seemed he even had the better of the situation, the better of John Little himself, and would spurn and rankle him until the end. And a strange expression began then to grow on the face of the great man, a kind of mute wonder at the force of the fellow before him—a startlement, nay, a bewilderment, that he should be at the reverse end of the weapon which he had always been the king of. He looked on the corsair with bemusement, nigh goggled, as he raced to match the blows he was sent. And—lo! Could that glimmer be omen? Is that a drop of sweat upon the brow of John Little, who has proclaimed himself the first of men? And does it portend—?

But no: John Little would not be brought down this day—not by some pirate in a black shag of a beard; not by some cycloptic fellow blind from his left eye. Nay, but John Little rose up then, flaring with his pride, and caught a right swing with a hard upper thrust, and drove his stave down and around in a sweeping arc to exploit the instant he had gained; and it was only by the flight of the corsair and his swift sure instinct that that man saved himself a sundered skull. For as he fell back away from the onslaught he recovered and raised his staff with incredible velocity, and so intercepted the blow, sufficiently to save his head; even as the crown to adorn it was lost. For with this blow that fell upon him like the paw of a bear, he came crashing down upon his side, his legs up, and his eyepatch flapping—which he was quick to rearrange.

Above him then the laughing giant, John Little, who himself offered his adversary a hand to help him stand. "Good fellow," bellowed the great man like a bull, and chuckling while he shouted, "I do confess, I have never seen so near defeat as today. My compliments to ye, and those sure. Ye are as fine a stavesman as ever I have gone against, I'll ready admit it. I offer you my hand in congratulations and camaraderie."

And the corsair, wonder to see, was laughing as well, as he took the proffered hand and dexterously regained his feet. "Mayhaps, but I warrant ne'er so fine as John Little! For a better dance than that you offered me, I do not believe has ere been seen in this our England." And the two gazed on each other gamely, and were well pleased with each other, so that even a fondness might have grown there had it but been given the time. "But say, friend!" exclaimed the corsair, his eye suddenly narrowing in merry speculation. "Is this cudgel your sole art? I mean to say—master John Little, do you perchance shoot bow as well?"

"Do I!" huffed John Little. "Why, if I did not pride myself so on my quarterstaff, I should fain call myself an archer."

"Excellent! Then you will partake of that contest, too, and give me the chance of making an equality between us?"

But John Little's eyes grew fierce once more, as he grunted up and lifted his chin, and avowed firmly, "No bow shall sing prettier this day than John Little's—nay, not even yours, my fine fellow!"

"Then it shall be will's pleasure to bow twice before John," replied the corsair, coy as a rook; and smiled most toothily as he himself turned to present the crowd its champion.

IX

The archery contest was high work indeed, archery being an art, as before noted, much in fashion in those days, and of clear and obvious utility to men of low station. And as the eyes of authority had just begun to look favorably on fine preparation in bow and arrow, means were found in advance of the other tournaments to render this one particularly attractive.

The largest space of the fair had been set aside for this competition, and fully forty men were set to participate, in an arena decked round with bright banners and flags. Butts of hemp filled with sand had been hung at a distance of two rods from a long black line of soot, a pitchy gash along the earth to indicate that limit beyond which the archers must not pass. The contestants should be set to groups of five, for reason of the arrows that were provisioned by those as had arranged this event; for though the contestants of the event should furnish their own bows, which were to them as trusty dogs or as appendices of their very body that had grown old with them and worn to the shape of their hands and the strength of their sinews, the arrows were to be an element equal to all. These shafts were drawn and checked for uniformity, and had about them only a single differentiating characteristic, this being the color of the fletching. The pinions of geese had been stained in five tones, and a number of bandanas of similar hue had been prepared, to tie each flown barb to its originator; blue, red, green, black, and white. Then each contestant in each group was assigned his own color. In the first round, both John Little and the corsair drew arrows of green; for they were of two different groups. And a man of the contest came round to indicate to them all the mark they were to strike, and seemed to hover in particular earnest before the corsair, who laughed. "Hey-ho, man," cried he, "what's this solicitude, now? I am not blind!"

Then they stood forth, and took their ready aim; and at the call of a bugle they let their arrows fly, a curious whistling flock that drove hasty out like so many long birds and bit into the sand-filled butt. Then the act was doubled, and each let loose a second arrow. At which a judge passed each of these and called out the color that had on the balance struck truest. In the groups of John Little and the corsair alike, green had the day.

These eight contestants were then drawn to two groups of four, and the colors once more were allotted. The bags were moved back then to four rods. And again, the archers stood and readied their arrows; and again let fly at the call. And again, and to the final round, with but two men still standing—'twas the corsair and John Little, and the crowd was wild with delight.

As the targets were moved back to fully eight rods distant, the rules were changed for this last round, and were announced thus: that first one of them and then the other should shoot, and then the same a second time, and the verdict be determined thus. Straws were drawn to win the first flight, and John Little came out with the longer. But suddenly the corsair popped up beside him, the shorter straw pert in his fingers, and held it up as though for inspection. "I say, my fine friend," quoth he, "that the man that's won the stave round deserves the privileged spot here; for let us not leave to luck what can be assigned to justice." But John Little, though clearly pleased by this gesture and the words that accompanied it, would not have the favor of it, but waved it off and urged the other on to shoot.

The colors of the precedent match were allowed for this, as well; and thus it came about that the corsair wore his arrows milk white, John Little, blood red. They stood beside each other a second time that day, and though each man eyed the single butt that had been made their joint target, neither forgot the man next to him. A boy had gone to dislodge the arrows of the prior match, and as he did so, John Little seemed to gaze arrows of fire into that target of sand and jute.

But the corsair was loose and easy, and gazed up at John Little, smiling his curious smile. "Will scarlet win out, think ye?" he asked, peering at the giant with his glittering eye; and seemed somehow to wink. John Little said nothing, but notched his arrow and lifted his bow, until the call had him send off.

It was a fine shot, and not a doubt. The arrow had flown true, and driven its head deep into the central circle of the butt; and its path was followed sure by much cheering from the crowd at so skillful a strike. John Little smiled, and beamed at the crowd, and bowed to his rival, who smiled as well, and bowed the lower in return.

Then the corsair, who let fly an equally true shaft; and when the judge came by to assess the mark, he called out that the two men were matched. So came Little John's second shot.

He stood a long while, gazing at the target, holding his bow elevated but loose, and then drew, and stood several seconds like that. Not a sound in the crowd, not a breath cast to air; then he let fly, and the bolt was true, for it struck near the center, and the crowd began a maddened din in its excitement.

In the midst of which the giant turned to his competitor, saying, "Truer than that there cannot be, friend. Call this contest mine, as well."

"Yet I swear red will have the mark," replied the corsair with a broad smile. Then he rose up swift and sudden and lifted his arrow, which none had seen him even pluck, to his chin, with a consummate ease; and turned smoothly toward his target, and let fly: all of this in so swift a motion that a man blinking might have risked losing the half of it. Yet notwithstanding this speed of act, which seemed to preclude all deliberation and all right aiming of vision or dart, the arrow flew true, and outpaced even poor John's, but sunk dead center of the butt, and half the shaft vanished from sight. So quick had it happened that the crowd did not even know for a moment to cheer; but gaped instead, and ogled the target that now inexplicably had twin bars of wood protruding from it, and tried to give account to itself as to where that fourth bolt had leapt out from.

The judge was called forth at once; and raced indeed to the learn what had befallen. It was adjudicated in an instant, for the outcome was clarion: the shaft that bore white had flown more truly, and had struck with greater force; and this not to speak of the cavalier means of its release, which displayed indeed an unlike mastery of the bow. Nothing could be said in further favor of John Little's last arrow, though it had been flown with great adroitness, and would have been the death of its target, were such a living body of flesh and blood. Nay, though that was a true shot, the corsair's was truer.

And John Little rose up wide-eyed beside his rival, and exclaimed, "Now *that*, master bowman, was as fine a shot as I e'en have ever seen! Though I have proved myself this day your better at the stave, I must and manly concede, my bowmanship beside your own cannot contend. Compliments—nay, but true compliments! Master bowman, I would know the name of the man that beat me at this contest, for none has ever done so before!"

The corsair smiled and cocked his head and seemed to sway, and said, lively as a monkey, "My name, Master John, is long since forgot, and best so. Call me Locken de Ribbon, sir, and that will be that, for some backward sorts have been known to call me by such a moniker, and there is nothing about it that does displease."

"Locken de Ribbon," frowned John Little, stroking his great beard. "A curious name, that."

"A hash of a name, Master John, a hash of a name no doubt!" conceded the corsair, shaking his head as though in good-humored regret.

And so saying, he turned and bowed once more to the mob, that beast of a thousand heads that had lost all of them at this display of virtuosity.

Before the corsair went to collect his prize from the mayor of the town at his gaudy booth, John Little stopped him, and said to him, "Now Master Locken, I shall say to you what I have said to rare a man: and that is this, that I do hope one day to vie with you again."

"And right good of you to say it!" grinned the corsair, and proffered his hand, which was warmly taken in the giant's great mitt. "I second this hope most warmly, and do suppose even—if I may be permitted a glint of prophecy—that today is not the last day John and Locken shall cross their paths."

The corsair was then duly summoned before Nottingham's own Lord, Robert of Doncaster, who had sat in state in his gaudy box and watched the contests with discerning air and bored eyes. His Norman nose, which seemed to span a mighty distance between eyes and mustaches, defiantly faced the corsair as he strode before the box, peering up at Robert with an almost impertinent twinkle in his eye. "Good archer," quoth the nobleman, "you have shown fine display this day, and have won the prize. I congratulate you. May I know your name?"

"Will Gamewell, m'Lord, and let no man mistake it."

"Well, Will Gamwell," began Robert, stuttering a moment over so many like sounds, and proceeding only with some difficulty, "and…just where did you learn to fire with such a handy hand?" A slight perception of red could be discerned in his cheek, and the corsair's jovial smile was only somewhat obscured by his great beard.

Yet he made no sign of his mirth in speech, saying only, "I am afraid I am in no position rightly to recall, m'Lord. As to the the fire to which my Lord alludes, a man might say it came to me on a breeze midst trees."

Robert of Doncaster appeared to weigh these words, and whether or not they indicated some oddity of mind in the man before him. "I see," he allowed at last. "And what is your work, good man—your station in the town of your origin?"

"God save me from such devilish torments!" exclaimed the corsair. "Nay, but I am a man for the country, and please it my Lord. May I remain so until my days have trickled out."

"What is it, then? Woodsman? Shepherd?"

"Aye, m'Lord. Woodman to be true, and king yet of unruly flocks."

"Well, this day you have earned you a pretty prize, my good man, which shall certainly fetch a pretty price in market, to aid you in your pasture."

And with a gesture indicated to his retaining man to extend the trinket, a silver medallion bearing the profile of King John. The corsair took it in hand and held it glimmering in the air before his single eye. Then, perceiving it well, he said, "I am surely most gratified by this trinket, my Lord, and will indeed sell it for the prettiest price a man could dream. I intend e'en to barter it forthwith, and not to idle about as some men do upon their treasures, as if they could carry 'em straight into the afterworld. Nay, but I would exchange the head of a king for a kiss from the loveliest lady here present—if only my Lord will allow it, and *she* grant my humble self so great a favor."

A single of Robert's eyebrows raised slightly, and he said, "A most chivalrous offer, master William, worthy of a man of greater rank than your own. No doubt your request shall meet with just dessert. I pray you proceed." And with an elegant gesture of acquiescence, he inclined his face to the seat near beside him, whereupon his own daughter was perched, plain and fattish for all her finery. She for her part seemed wholly ready to accept both the offer and the price that was put upon it, and was practically wriggling in her throne, the poor plump dear, her reddish cheek outstretched in anticipation. But the corsair cried, "I thank you, my Lord!" and spun him about suddenly to a lesser wing of the same noble box, wherein a young lady was seated in a recession as it were and beneath a canopy of shadow. To the astonishment of the Lord and the indignation of his daughter, the corsair strode dauntless to this corner and, setting his left hand upon his chest near the neck, bowed deeply, and straightened, and smiled, and with his right held out the medallion, shimmering in the light. The figure before him stirred, and lifted her face to him, where the sun caught dark strident eyes, lips of carmine and formed like the very bow the man had late wielded, strands of gold about her brow, and a chin to brook no challenges. It was a visage of rare comeliness, and it regarded the man with a certain coolness and remove. "My Lady," proclaimed the corsair, evidently none put off by the seeming haughtiness of the girl before him, and gazing throughout the entirety of his speech boldly into her eyes, "though I may seem half blind to men who are fully so, my efforts at this contest have proved that I am in troth keener of sight than most; and by this gift of clairvoyance which God alone has bestowed on me, I swear, here and before all the world, that there be no fairer lady in this entire arena as she who sits now before me, nor—and this I will wager against any challenger—dwells there such in all of the countryside surrounding it, from Nottingham to the King's own castle, and beyond the very strait of England. And if some benighted fool should dare dispute my solemn declaration, I swear I will with a single true arrow shoot a flying falcon out of God's great sky to demonstrate my right in't."

Murmurs of approval from the crowd surrounding accompanied these words, ere the corsair continued. "Fair Lady," he said, "our Lord Robert has granted me kind permission to request a kiss in exchange for this coin, but though I am not one to quail before hazard, I grow faint before my own prior audacity. I would therefore beg of you no kiss at all, unworthy of such tremendous grace as I plainly be, but rather two simple boons only: first, that you do me the homage of preserving this trifle in some back drawer of yours until death should find you, though it be a faded relic amidst brighter treasures, that I might boast from this day to my own demise, that an item upon which I have set my hand dwells in some dusty corner of that same house which shelters such beauty; and second that you grant me the honor of your name."

A moment of silence, and all the crowd seemed to hold its breath. Then: "My name, good archer, is Marion," said she in a voice as silvern as the medallion that hung before her in the sunlit day, "and I gratefully accept your gift. Yet the modesty that accompanies it I must disavow, for I find it unbecoming on a man who has elsewise evinced such skill and bravery."

And leaning forth, she took hold of the medallion in a gracile hand and met his lips with a fleet brush of her own all in a single movement, before with-drawing once more into the shadows and her aloof silence there.

"You have had your will most pertly here, master archer," interjected suddenly Robert of Doncaster with a sharp reproving glance toward Marion that the girl seemed either to ignore or disdain; and though the corsair stood for a moment en-raptured at the unexpected bounty he had received, and obviously did not wish to tear his gaze away from the lady who had granted it, yet perceiving something dark on Robert's tone, he bowed again before the damsel and forced himself back to the man, saying, "Nay, my Lord, but at most have been robbed in it, insofar as this will is entirely the Lady Marion's. But in fairness, the act was neither mine nor hers, but your very own, my Lord; for you must allow it was done on your al-lowance, and while the lady Marion is only to be praised for generosity in the face of a poor archer's poverty, as for mine own defense, by my troth I requested much in deficit of what was my right. For I am a poor merchant indeed, and ought to stick to archery."

"It seems your shortcomings in bartering have not worked much to your detriment," noted the nobleman drily.

"Truly is it said that God's eye is on the sparrow."

"I say once more, you are most pert!"

"My Lord is wroth! I should be sorrowed for it. But I fear I must confess I am not: for after the blessing just now afforded me, none can cast dun on so bright a day."

"Nervy man! I give you leave to leave at once."

"Leave I shall, my Lord: leave my silver medallion in golden hands, my poor wit to dream upon rich memory, and my unruly heart to remain with the mis-tress who will fore'er chasten it. Adieu!" And with that, he bowed again to Maid Marion, turned his back upon the frowning nobleman and his huffing daugh-ter, and made way out, followed by all the eyes in that place and by a delighted whispering of the crowd which only deepened the wrath rising in the noble-man's cheeks. And accompanying him as he went were sure the sweetened eyes of the Maid Marion, who regarded the vanishing figure in quite another mood than her warden's.

Now it happened some ways on, as the corsair proceeded, dreaming hard upon these most recent events, that he passed near by the Sheriff of Nottingham, who had been present as well the competition of bows, ever in his capacity as the center of the law in that region.

"Compliments on today's show of prowess, Master Archer," called the Sheriff with a bow of his head, as he spied the corsair. And that man arrested his long stride, and turned to the Sheriff with much attention and even solicitous curiosity.

"But fair antics, these!" replied he, shrugging as he approached. "'Twas nothing, my Lord, but as I owe to luck."

"To luck?" guffawed the Sheriff, shaking his head. "Nay, not even the very luckiest man could prove himself by such demonstrations—in three contests, nonetheless. There was rather skill in't, I will wager, and more than is common."

"By certain fashionable reasonings, all's luck in the world, My Lord, when one traces the arc of time's arrow back or forth to long enough a throw. Why, the world itself—'tis lucky there one at all, crede you not? And so must be luck as birthed the world. Or what, do I err? One might say I have e'en blasphemed. Yet I am certain I speak altogether by a logic too common to our day, which my Lord might readily admit."

"I should know nothing of such matters," said the Sheriff with a frown. "'Tis a species of idle talk, meseems. Or philosophasting perchance. But listen here, set aside that, I have solid business to propose. I before you am the Sheriff of Nottinghamshire. I find myself in want of men. Skill such as yours would fetch a high premium with me. Would you join my ranks for a going rate, and work in service of the law?"

The corsair smiled illegible, and replied, "My Lord Sheriff is well met indeed. I am nicely acquainted with all his fair work, and how he has purged the forest of sneaks, and such not."

"Then you will join me?"

"Nay, I am afeared I *will* rebut this most generous offer," said the corsair, with a bow.

"How now? And why?" demanded the Sheriff, vexed, after a moment's waiting, when it became clear that this refusal would have no sequel.

"My Lord Sheriff shall understand," the man shrugged, opening his arms and his hands wide before him in gesture of surrendering some finer point, "I was made by God a free man in rag of poverty, and do intend to go to my grave in that same divinely simple attire."

"Man, would you not be free as agent of the law? Or what is freedom?"

"Why, 'tis the fall of lightning, that need not ask the sun permit to shine—but which shines as the sun when it shines well!" averred he, all enigmatic, and blinked—or winked, for 'twas impossible to say which of the acts he was about, or if with him the two gestures had somehow melded to one.

And the Sheriff might have replied, save that at that moment cried a voice somewhere not far in the fair, that caught the breeze and carried to their converse. "By my mark," it cried, "that fellow with the eyepatch, why, he plied that bow as well as Robin Hood hisself, at moments!"; which announcement carried strong over the three assembled men, to an almost imperceptible jolt on the part of the Sheriff.

"Ah, Robin-a-Hood!" exclaimed the corsair, his eye widening. "Marry, I know one as goes by that name!"

"Do ye indeed, Master Archer?" perked up the Sheriff at once, and glanced with awoken curiosity at the fellow before him. Then, turning, he set to rummaging in one of his bags, and pulled therefrom a certain parchment he carried ever upon his person, as though in memento or talisman, which he now unrolled before the surprised eye before him. Upon this parchment was the image of a bearded and cowled man—the best depiction that had yet been wrought, and meant, no doubt, in close imitation of Robin Hood, though it was characterized more by a general masculine anonymity than anything approximating meaningful characterization. The face so portrayed was rugged and strong-chinned and bore an expression of cunning and willfulness. "Is this the man?" queried the Sheriff, not concealing a certain urgency.

The fellow before him inspected the portrait closely with glittering eye, seeming somehow pleased with it, before at last replying, "To be sure, he is coarser. But no man could mistake it!"

Thomas de York rose up now as well, though not without that attitude of skeptic jeering that he carried ever with him. "What, now, a friend of Robin

Hood? My stars! Truly, this is a lucky day indeed, for you will be able to tell us at once: who *is* Robin Hood?"

"A man," replied the corsair, turning to him, peering and grinning.

"God's bodkins, what would you have him be, a goblin?" uttered the Sheriff, scowling. "Even the grass knows as much. What man is he?"

"Why, 'tis the man you should be seeking most fairly!" parried the grinning fellow.

"Don't dare frolic with me," scowled the Sheriff. "If you know who he is, then speak out, and if not, then watch your tongue, man, for I do not lightly tolerate light minds."

And the corsair shook his head, all good cheer. "Knew him once, My Lord Sheriff! On the very road to Nottingham. Why, I had long commerce with him there, for he is a game sort, and wont to chatter, though in truth he tends well to his own affairs. He has indeed a fluent fair tongue, and much wit and much silliness slide eel-like from it by turns."

"You yourself possess that gab, methinks," muttered Thomas de York, riled yet at being earlier ill-used.

"'Tis better to possess and to use, than dispossess and abuse, as the Master Deputy might well attest," quoth he, with a nod toward Thomas, who was at a moment's loss to comprehend the meaning of this come back. Yet before he could understand, the corsair had continued on already, saying, "Yet to possess the gift as *Robin Hood*...? Well, I fathom not the weight and measure of such things, and shall leave it to the custom's house and its comptroller to determine. But I will say this," continued he, lifting a finger to his thick-whiskered chin in air thoughtful. "We were not out of harmony, I and this Robin Hood—oh, begging your Lord Sheriff's pardon! Of course I come down on the side of the fair—come down hard, you might say, and 'tis well known by all my friends, colleagues, acquaintances, peers and superiors, that in any conflict 'tween one fellow and another, I am sure to give my hand to him's as truest."

"That says little while wanting to say much," commented the Sheriff, and lifted a pressing finger to his temple, which had in all this show of folly begun to throb.

"Does it! Does it, now!" cried the corsair, in a moment's expression like to being appalled, that was yet belied by a tugging at his lips beneath his sable mustaches. "Well, had hoped the adverse!" he added with a light shrug. "But we must content ourselves with what comes out of us, must we not? There is a straight tack 'twixt the word and the soul—now is there not? And if we doubt the one, then surely we doubt the other, and if we doubt the other, why—"

"Enough of this glibness, man. I've not the time to bandy words. Have you aught concrete and substantial to say of Robin Hood? Said ye before, ye knew what man he was. Is there meat in that claim, or is it but the fat?"

"My Lord the Sheriff should not so negligently disregard the lardy parts!" reposted the corsair in jolly air, and leaned in with even offensive confidentiality, raising a didactic finger before him. "They are often the best and most succulent bits of the morsel, even if from one side the least nutritioning. Yet there is nutriment as well in enjoyment, men say, and the meat is often too lean to sate—but my Lord the Sheriff grows rightly weary with my rambling, and I fear my state if I try not a solider word. Well then, I will say what I know of this Robin Hood, though I can but faintly hope that it will better satisfy than my own game rovings. Robin Hood, Robin Hood. Was born in a glade in the hills, abandoned there straight by man and woman, kept by God alone and raised to manhood by a dove and a serpent, and fed on the milk of boars. A sapling bough in the wind taught him the use of bow, and a robber jay to sing. The lute he learned from the cricket, the bee and the nightingale at turns. His trade he took from the rook. His right name, if I do not me err, is Well-Helmed Lock; but my memory for such things is pitiful scandalous, and 'tis likely I have somewhat strayed in some smallest way. Or I should not put much a bet—"

"Enough of this playmaster," said the Sheriff in gruff disdain. "I've business of more matter to attend to than this brazen espousing of nonsense." And rode on at once, scowling and scorning the bearded cycloptic man, who bowed behind him grinning and slipped away into the crowd. Thomas de York followed his going with a glance of disgust.

'Twas some time on, that the Right Sheriff of Nottingham, grown all pensive for few long minutes, and sitting by the tables, his finger rubbing hard at his temple, jerked toward Thomas de York, and said to him, his voice affretted,

"Nay, but I want that jester again, that gamesman. Methinks there was something behind him."

Thomas de York paused, considering. "What jester would that be, Lord Sheriff?"

"Why, the fool with the skull cap and the eyepiece, Thomas! Be wakeful a moment and rouse yourself!" exclaimed the Sheriff in great vexation. "Go and find him out for me, or a pox upon you both!"

And Thomas de York did as he was bid. But that corsair, the favored champion of the day's fair and the talk of the entire run of tents, had most mysteriously evaporated, and nor man nor woman nor child could, or would, attest to his passage, nor whither had he gone.

X

It was on the day direct following that the Lord Robert of Doncaster himself presented himself before the Sheriff in the latter's bleak study, and sat down unceremoniously before him, a nervous hand at his lips, and he gazing at the Sheriff as though he was awaiting something from that man. Until at length the Sheriff was forced to inquire, "My Lord Robert, to what do I owe this unforetold honor?"

Lord Robert put a hand upon his head as though to assuage an ache there, and said, "My Lord Sheriff, there was a man at the fair yesterday, the winner of the contest of bows—a mongrel of a fellow with only a single eye, and dressed like a villain."

"Yes, I knew him," replied the Sheriff. "What of it?"

"Rumor is making its rounds: they say he is none other than the criminal known as Robin Hood."

The Sheriff nodded. "It has been averred by witnesses that Robin Hood has both his eyes, and a fair beard on his chin. The winner of the archery contest fails this description."

"An easy costume!" cried the nobleman, evidently much incensed still by the man that had snubbed his daughter. "A matter of apparel, and nothing more! Are we to be taken in at appearances?"

"My meaning is quite another, my Lord," said the Sheriff with a self-mastered calm. "The charge is threadbare to our law, and thus is not made to suit us. First, there is naught to prove the common identity of these men. Second, the one-eyed man of yesterday broke no rule of which I am aware for which he might be independently disciplined. Finally, even if he had so done, he is presently irretrievable, and doubtless shall remain so. His presumed equality with this Robin Hood is at best a matter of baseless speculation, and can have no solid bearing on any point in the latter's case."

"But my Lord—the impudence of it!"

"Robin Hood has not hitherto been renowned for timid propriety," observed the Sheriff with a wry frown. "My Lord Robert, I assure you I am doing all in my power to apprehend this man and to bring him to the bar of justice. Yesterday's events are hard of reading, and can change nothing of method or outcome within this investigation. I beg my Lord to let lie, and to leave me to my work."

"He made certain play of me and my daughter," blurted suddenly the nobleman with force, his face strained remarkably, like an animal's. "He dared bestow compliments and favors on my ward, Marion, in evident contempt of my own offspring, the scoundrel! And did so before an entire mob of onlookers!"

The Sheriff observed the man a moment. "That is surely unfortunate, my Lord," he began, "but alas, there is no crime in—"

"My Lord Sheriff has perhaps failed to understand," interjected the nobleman, rising upward in parallel to the length of his great nose and peering out over it with unnaturally widened eyes. He perched his hands upon the Sheriff's desk, and in that attitude stared down like some manner of tremendous owl. "I and my family have been humiliated publicly by this upstart, and I would have it out of his flesh. Do you hear me, my Lord Sheriff? Out of his flesh! When he is taken into custody—as you should pray he soon will be—I would see these outrages met with their just desserts!"

"I am for justice," stated the Sheriff evenly, neither rising in his place nor averting his gaze from his visitor's.

"As am I," replied the nobleman between clenched teeth.

"Robin Hood will be punished full for each and every wrong he has perpetrated against our laws, to an item."

"The punishment had better be full indeed," quoth the other, and without another word turned from the Sheriff's presence and strode out the door, not bothering even to close it behind him.

XI

Here was rumor: that Robin Hood had the strength of ten men, the eye of a falcon, the ear of a hare. That he could disappear as even the woodmouse, and was as flight as a swallow through the glade. That he had spies in every acre of the wood, men of such habit and feral quality that not even a hound could tease them out. That he feared no man, dreaded nothing, and was of perfect confidence to the world. That he had the forked tongue of a warlock and played a tune upon his lute sufficient to bewitch the right senses of men. That he welt a magic bow which never failed its mark. That he was as good a Christian as ever walked the Path. That he was no man at all, but some fey force of the wood—

So they said! And yet, the Sheriff, at least on this last point, knew better. Perfect immortality this Robin Hood had not; he was a man as any other. Aught of blood ran through his veins; aught of the scent of death he had about him, as any human animal. Aye, the Sheriff knew this well. For the Sheriff had secured to his custody a man of Robin Hood's ragtag clan—one of the Thieves of Sherwood, to be short with it. Had secured this man to his custody, and had made full use of the privileged vantage he thereby had won himself. Aye, he exploited his prerogatives to the full, did this Sheriff of Nottinghamshire, for he had a sense of time's wane, and would have this Robin Hood behind bars ere his own flame were snuffed.

Now, the boy in question was one Ralf de Nottingham, a seventeen-year-old lad who had shown some spunk indeed when they brought him in, but decidedly less after the had had done with him. For long he would not speak;

but when at last they had cracked his hardened shell it was as a cascade of water from past the icy dam. Alas, but much of what he said could not be put to good use. For example, when he pressed about the precise location of the thieves, the Sheriff was to learn that they were as vagabonds in the wood, and would not long stay in any single place, but as often as once a month uprooted stake and shifted tent, thus securing themselves a certain secrecy that accorded well with their illicit trades. And thus, in such a case as this, when one of their own had been brought to the hand of the law, they could easily melt once more into the moss and bark of the bosk, and so premise themselves safety. Or also this: that amongst themselves they used names not their own; so that Ralf de Nottingham, for example, had been called Chattel, as a pun on his unwillingness to speak and his evident indifference to personal possessions; and often enough, they did not even know each the others' proper names. For Robin Hood loved to name, it became evident, and put some special significance on the way a thing were called.

But information more utile than this had come to the Sheriff of Nottingham as well, of the character of the man against whom he struggled, and his habits and ways, and much else besides. And it gave the Sheriff much to ruminate on for long nights; for his sleep as of late had been troubled and threadbare, as though he would milk his dwindling hours for every drop that might be squeezed of them.

This Sheriff sought to turn what he had garnered to his benefit, but it did not seem much to avail in the practice; as though this were truly some wood devil against whom he was struggling, ethereal as the fog on the town or the mist on the hills. It seemed he was playing a game against a charmed hand, and every move he made was countered with greater skill and seeming foreknowledge of all cards at play. And indeed, not even a single more of Robin Hood's men made such a blunder as Ralf de Nottingham had made; and so it was that poor Ralf kept quite lonely in his prison chamber, nor was granted company from among his group of ne'er-do-wells.

This signifying solitude rankled the Right Sheriff much, that he should be confronting failure in his profession at so late an hour as this, when indeed he ought to have been in perfect maturity and mastery of his work. For though he was by now an old man, his head was right on his shoulders, and his mind as clear as ever or anon it had been. Nay, for certain things, it seemed he had become clairvoyant with his advancing years, and it was whispered about that he had sources of knowledge that no man knew the well of. 'Twas so much bosh, the mutterings of common folk who could never trace the finer threads of logic. His secret fount was but his ratiocination, a nigh centennial experience of the twists of the criminal mentality and a mind that was keen yet as a well-honed knife. But alas! for this intuition of his remained mute as ice when it came to Robin Hood, and it was as if some smothering wall were builded about the affairs of that man, so that no reason nor perpendicular rationale could climb over it break through it.

It was wondrous to think how this troubled the Sheriff, how it irked him and dug at him like a spine in his thumb driving straight to some minor but agonizing nerve. Never before had his cool equanimity been perturbed by trouble or crime or this or that malfeasance. He had sailed through his life on levelest keel, and even in moments of great outward crisis and the unbalancing of state and society had not betrayed aught of inward agitation. But now, for the shadowy figure of a woodland runagate, the poor Sheriff was tormented anigh, to the loss of sleep, repose, and all serenity.

Now it was a day of particular such vexation for him that he determined to act at last, be it only in the most precursory way, in a sort of personal reconnaissance of no mean hazard but tantamount possible gain. For he had received word that the Thieves of Sherwood and their leader Robin Hood had seized a justice of the peace and had stripped him down to his stockings ere they had sated their greed. To be sure, the justice in question wore a corrupted and long-befouled robe; but that was hardly for a forest hoodlum to adjudge. This act was dire indeed; dire enough that word had come from King John himself, urging the Sheriff to resolve the matter with purpose and promptitude, for the longevity of two crowns—that of England, and that of the Sheriff himself. And Sheriff Bardulf sat before this missive, which bore on it the royal seal, and reflected on his late reunion with Lord Robert of Doncaster, and more particularly on this man's various connections with persons of higher rank; and lost in these contemplations, much disturbed of mind and soul, he rubbed his temple hard, and glared away into space.

When of a sudden he started up, as though come upon by an epiphany, and rang for his majordomo, who was tasked with the getting of Thomas de York. This last came in shortly, though still tarrying a period too long for the suddenly impetuous Sheriff. Yet appear he did, still righting his leathern jerkin, and stood lean and hungry-looking before the desk of his employer, his hands folded nervously before him. "Thomas," said the Sheriff, "I have been deep in this trouble in Sherwood, for it has much distressed me and has occupied my mind to distraction. Our strategies are threadbare. They needs must be rewoven, since to date they have failed to serenely clothe us. Before aught, I must know the man we are against, his temper and his cast; and since we are evidently lackluster in bringing him to us, this alone remains to us—that we must go to him."

And thereupon revealed his plan to the widening eyes of his deputy.

Thomas was indeed nonplussed by the scheme his master presented him, for he thought it jeopardy in the extreme, and likely as endangering to the life and limb of the Sheriff as to his own (and perchance by this calculus still more precious) person. And he intimated as much, though the terms he used wore the due garb of civility and respect.

Nonetheless, at their merest utterance, the Sheriff grew wroth, and towered up over poor Thomas de York as some fortress giant to rage down at him. "By the blood of God, Thomas of Pork, if you are too much a coward to see to this affair then perchance ye should seek other employment than that of deputy to a Sheriff of the law! I say, man, that there is no risk here that is not a hundred times countersigned by what might be gained. If ye worry for me, then desist at once in it, for I am a wretched old dodderer and stand to lose no more than a few sorry lame years and another hundredfold wrinkle and sore to body and mind. While if it is for your own skin you fret, then by the Crown, I say—get ye behind me, coward, and find ye another métier! For I shan't abide beside me nor now nor anon any craven fellow shivering in his trousers!"

And what could the poor deputy sheriff do upon so hot a rebuke, but ready the Sheriff's horses, accouterments, and men?

The day was strange beauteous, though that was a beauty that had never much penetrated the Sheriff's generally stolid gaze. Today the sunlight streaming down through the sparkling verdancy above cast upon him with a kind of malignancy. He felt a swooning of his head for the heat of it, but kept himself upright against it, and would not fail. But he glared out from his window at the light that ached him so, precisely for the pain it inculcated in his brain; and by the edge of that pain kept himself alert.

'Twas not long he had so to machinate. For even as he had dreamt it, at a certain crossing of the wood, a point where the road was narrowed between two flanking walls of thicket, suddenly a dozen men or so sprang out of the undergrowth, as though they had been until then a portion of the brush there, and rounded in catlike silence about the carriage, which at once halted, the horses drawing up nervously and snorting in the air, thrusting their heads about like great crows. And to the side of the carriage there came a light-stepping and tallish man, who drew off his hood at once as he stepped up to the portal from out of which the Sheriff was peering. He was a handsome man, lightly bearded with hair of a reddish hue, and though the slant of noon light cast hard shadows against his eyes, so that one could not well note their color, there was something of intelligence sparkling there, and aught of sprite good humor as well. And he, placing a hand clothed in a closefit hide glove impertinently on the sill of the carriage door's window, said in an easy and smooth voice, "I beg pardon for this interruption of my honorable Lord's passage, but I am one charged with the care of this road, and needs must I know who goes 'pon it, whither they tend and what their business is, lest I treason my charge and fail this most imperious duty that has been laid 'pon me by greater power than mine own."

"This will be Master Robin in the Hood, as I presume?" queried the Sheriff mildly, setting his heavy arm upon the free part of the window ledge and leaning unafraid toward his momentary captor; and Robin Hood laughed aloud a mirthful laugh that sounded of crystal, and countered, "Ho! So I am, if chance has not changed my moniker. And so, my men, let us welcome to our humble wood the honorable High Sheriff of Nottinghamshire."

Up plucked the Sheriff's bushy eyebrow, and he leaned forward to peer out more closely at this Robin Hood. "D'you know me then, Master Robin?"

"Why, my Lord Sheriff, a public figure of such celebrity! Each and sundry should know my Lord's face."

"And yet 'tis not so," observed the Sheriff.

Robin Hood shrugged jauntily, saying, "Mayhaps for those as have one eye forever closed. Or do I ere, my Lord Sheriff? Yet in one thing, at least, I am well certain, as 'tis the very stuff and substance of our present encounter. Good Lord Sheriff, know you there is a tax upon this road, established and esteemed by the people of Sherwood for their mutual betterment, the upkeep of the highway, and the general good of the common weal. It is a tax that depends on the weight of my Lord Sheriff's carriage, and is determined fair and square on such a basis, depending as it does to a just accounting of the whole. Might we inquire, then, as to the full value of My Lord Sheriff's procession, and how much coin and stuff of gold or jewel or other good, minted or un-minted, there is to be found in't?"

At which, with sangfroid entire, the Sheriff did relate to an item the possessions of his carriage and impedimenta, as well as that of the men that followed in attendance. Robin heard this list out with some patience and steadiness of interest, his head cocked slightly to the side, and when it had concluded, snapped his fingers and called out neatly, "Pick-a-nick and Tarryho!"

Thus evidently he summoned two men to their work; for a few of his forest worthies stood forth at once at this, and with neat integrity combed that company with a care that was almost exaggerated, attending the list that the Sheriff's tongue had proffered them. And during all this process, the Sheriff, and Robin Hood, and all the men on either side of this quiescent dispute, remained in utter silence; only Robin Hood whistling quite like a bird, and seeming lost to his fancies, and the Sheriff watching him as though he were a viper rather than a vireo.

When the two inventory-takers had consummated their inventory and returned to their captain, Robin Hood stood before them, smiling easy, and queried, "So, my men, what have you found? Did our Sheriff tally the truth?"

"The truth, Master Robin—and not a cent in excess or dearth!" cried Pick-a-nick, with something of amazement. "Why, there's not a rubbed farthing more than the man declared."

Robin's brow did rise, though there was perhaps less of surprise in that expression than the gesture itself might have suggested. "My merry men, heed me well! It would seem against all reckoning that an honest man has been posted to the shrievalty. Tell me, my fine friends, do you not think we should pay this honest man's way ourselves, and let him out our borders scot-free? Say—shall there be no incentives in this world for a frank word?"

"Nay!" came an echo of voices in the wood. Others joined it, and one fellow, a bold dark sort, bearing a white glove, stepped forward, and declared, "Say, Master Robin—here is opportunity indeed! Should we not take this Sheriff's very hide, while we have it in our grasp, and pin it up as a trophy on some tree? It would make a fine bark, I say, paler than poplar and rougher than pine!" Several wags snickered at the jest, and the guard of the Sheriff shuffled and turned nervous; but the Sheriff's keen eyes did not waver from Robin's face, and Robin himself but chuckled and rose a steady hand. The dark fellow's arms fell to his side as he seemed to read his master's intent. "Robin, it were shame to let this fellow go..."

"Then we must not shame ourselves over shame, at least," smiled Robin, "for a Christian man of any station and any circumstance is welcome to me as my own brother." And, turning back to the Sheriff, "My Lord Sheriff, I give you leave of free passage in this wood whensoever you would take it, supposing only you come as you have today, with your sword wed faithfully to your scabbard. We leave you go, my good man, and call ourselves the richer this day for having spoken to that rarest of all beasts in the King's England: an honest man."

The Sheriff but nodded, evincing no surprise, and leaned out his carriage to say, with some emphasis, "Master Robin, I thank you for your generosity of spirit and your fair dealing. But prithee—may I ask the honest name of the man who so fairly treats his victim?"

"You see?" cried a voice from the dusk. "Here is how the lawman repays a good turn!"

"Nay, but you misjoin the mark," returned Robin slowly, not taking his eyes from off the Sheriff's face. "We have before us, methinks, not just a candid man, but a witty one beside—a man, I warrant, who knew how to play this game ere we e'en set the trick. Did you hear, my men? He tallied us like he tallies his taxes, and came boldly out to our Sherwood way, certain of his safety! I might even wager something the more—he came this way fishing for *us* this day, did our brave Sheriff. And caught us to boot, skillful as he is! Ah, but marvel to the heavens, that a man of Lack-a-Land's should be no'theless a man! Nay, nay—but Sheriff Bardulf, you are forthwith twice-blessed now to my heart, and not only will I spare you your way unharmed, but I myself will attend to your safe passage, and guarantee it by my blood."

"I thank you for this unsought beneficence," said the Sheriff, grown however impatient. "Yet I must ask again your name, man; for it is uncivil that I should speak to one who knows my style and surname, when I am not equipped to reply in kind, save with this abhorrent nickname they put upon you." And as the the Sheriff insisted this once more, he peered in all intensity at Robin Hood.

But Robin Hood smiled and cocked his head. "My name *is* Robin, my Lord Sheriff, or Robin-a-hood, if you will have the full of it; a robber and hoodlum as any that was so accused. My surname is bird's call, if your tongue be lithe enough to mock it, or the whistling of the wind in these hollows. As for that name which came to me upon my birth, given from my mother's sweet tongue and my father's dear lineage, certified unto me upon my baptism and remained common to me until facts of my history set on it the seal of silence—I fear that *that* name, my good Sheriff, has long fallen into desuetude, and is fading fast from the ledgers of men. Do not trouble yourself with't. Robin will do duty as well if not better."

"A man's name is not so easy forgot," remarked the Sheriff, persistent, "and is not such a secret as any may long keep. If its wearer will not speak, then certes it shall do so in his place, will or nil!"

"Indeed, Sheriff!" declared Robin, laughing. "And we are no gods, after all. A man's name does stick like a varnish. 'Tis trouble in a sound. It has been heard by all my men, for instance, that My Lord Sheriff is called Wolf's Bane, on account of his good Saxon surname."

"And it is known by all mine, that you, Robin Hood, are called Wolf's Head, on account of your occupation."

"I say!" laughed Robin again. "I should rather merit such ekename for my very ownmost deeds, than have it imposed on me by slander. But have it as My Lord will. Our names so presented have said the much that need be said, have they not? My Lord the bane to bite me; I the wild whelp to fly him. And there is time yet to see if I be fleet-footed enough to evade the destiny My Lord has crafted upon my future!"

"Not so much time, Master Robin, as all that," countered the Sheriff, and was intent and much severe. "For I am counting my hours. Mark it! You will wonder to hear it, but I, almost despite myself, think you a goodly sort, misguided to acts of violent seizure by a feeling of illegitimate resentment against power, or some like figment. Methinks had I my way I would fain leave you to your forest to do as you please, Robin-a-Hood. But I am the King's man, and you have forfeited the right to be called such by your standing contempt of the King's law. This forest is his; the meat you heap upon your plates is his; this earth beneath your feet, this timber, these stones by which you build and bind your caravansary, all his. To say nothing of the gold with which you plump your purses."

"And the flesh to clothe my bones, and the air I breathe to my lungs, I wager!" mocked Robin. "Forget neither the water we sup from the stream. Forsooth, even the light by which we guide ourselves on our forest ways can hardly be our own! You call mine resentment; but I swear, not a grudge bear I against the King, nor any man living or departed. Resentment is what the bull must feel beneath his yoke, Lord Sheriff; we who have unyoked our necks, what resentments may we carry against man, high or low? Sure the King is a right good cockerel, and I'd be pleased to drink a tankard of the royal ale with him. Besides which, he makes for fine sport to my part, for it is by the King's crooked law that so many puffed up roosters come a-striding down my road, ripe for the plucking. Nay, I protest: the King is a fine dandy and a decent friend of mine. Little enough be he a monarch as a Christian subject could hope, as for instance good King Richard once was—but what concern is that to the free birds of Sherwood? It is said, truly, that the sparrows of the field must not fret. But though I am right fond of John, he is better set where he keeps his throne, and I where I keep mine. Call it a difference in philosophy. Or perhaps only in understanding: for heed well, Lord Sheriff, you who are

the *King's man.* Are we not then all *of the King*, are we not all *his* right property, with which he might dispose as he please? I say, are you your own man in
the end, or but a bit of flesh pinched off from the kinghead, that he might
work on you as on his own body?"

But the Sheriff was grown impatient by now, for he had become irate as an
old man, and easily peeved. It was much he had not accosted Robin Hood in
mid speech. He meanwhile reddened, however, and when this last question
was posed, pointed a swollen and bent finger down the road, back toward
York, saying as he did, "Hear me this, or certify yourself a fool, Robin in the
Hood. The man who lives in that town yonder may well be but part and parcel
of the state; but for that price he need not live in the wild, to be harassed and
hounded by the first who would do him ill. For his status as citizen, he is also
held under protection of the state's mighty arm, and should any seek to wrong
him, as for example some band of paltry thieves who ramble in rags i'the greenwood, then the state shall see to it that those wrongdoers are punished, and
the basic peace preserved. Yet if instead he choose to live here, in this wilderness and away from the sword of the guard—if he should choose, I say, that
state of war which is the state of things bereft of human law—then nothing
may protect him—"

"— but his own arm, what fortune succor him, and the good will of the
living God and His Son, Savior of all our sorry hides, King's men or no!" cried
Robin Hood. "Aye, Lord Sheriff, 'tis true and rightly spoken, and *almost*, I say,
do these matters stand as my Lord Sheriff has avowed. Say what, then: keep
you your state and guard, your balance and your law, and be you blessed with
'em. I for my part will see to mine."

The Sheriff nodded curtly, control regained him, but a look of wry displeasure wrinkling yet his thin white lips. "Know then, Robin-a-hood, that I
reckon it my duty to hunt you even as you hunt the stag of the King. All in my
power to hound you down, man."

"And all in mine to flee My Lord's flea-bit hounds, High Sheriff, and live
by mine own ken, as God provides, and before all men as mine own master in
these glades!"

"You think yourself a man at his liberty, Robin-a-hood?"

"I do claim the liberty of so thinking."

"There is no liberty if not under the law."

"No?" cried Robin, and seemed delighted. "Yet methinks you do not err, good Sheriff. Only that your word tolerates interpretation. For who shall be lawgiver?"

"You hint at anarchy!" spat the Sheriff in disgust.

"Tut tut," replied Robin Hood, shaking his head and wagging a finger before him. "I never did. My Lord Sheriff has plucked the string of his definitions from a winnowed tapestry. I say *free*, and he echoes *anarchy*! Anarchy is that mood which comes on the envious, when he learns to his dismay that he is not master of his house. What use have I for anarchy? I am the liberalest man in England—though 'tis true, the King almost touches me on this score."

"You dare claim parity with the King?"

"God forbid it!" cried Robin. "My reason should abhor such misuse of the truth. For by my troth, I am his superior by a *hair*. He lives walled in a castle and fettered in his gold and entrained in his beloved satin and silk, and must pass his days in slavish attendance to his ten-thousand subjects, and bend his thought constant on the ways and means of his fat kingdom, glutting himself ever on the land that he lacks. Whereas mine own kingdom, as you see," he concluded, gesturing gracefully to the forest thick about them, "is lean and canny by its own head and takes well enough care of itself, leaving me to a leisure and a liberty our poor King can only dream."

"Methinks you are a braggart, Robin-a-hood, and it is a depressing fact," said the Sheriff with voice grown hoarse, "for I see you might have been a man of some quality, had your upbringing or your education not so spoilt you. Yet I believe despite that you do not know the danger you tempt, nor the pitfall that stands gaping on each side of you. Hear this well, Robin-a-hood, and beware that my word is my troth; I am as the law embodied, yet ever still I am the law, which you perhaps know how to play as a strummer his harp. But by the law, Robin, know this: my days are run thin to ruin. He who follows me shall be no kith of mine, and there is much that I would not do for lawfulness and decency, that such a one will not shrink from but e'en will quick embrace. For he will not love the law, but gold."

"Then he shall be almost as welcome as my present Lord Sheriff!" announced Robin Hood with a laugh of delight. "The present Sheriff, for the weight of his mind; and this future one, for the weight of his purse. Now on with My Lord the Sheriff, for afternoon is drawing nigh to dusk, and I have it on my promise that he and his retinue shall pass this way unhampered. Knows my Lord Sheriff: Sherwood is no safe place when the veils of night are drawn. Word has it there e'en be bandits as haunt this wood." And with this he winked at the Sheriff and chuckled through his white teeth.

At this, rage was born anew in the Sheriff's heart. "I say to you, scoffer, you shall die by the King's blade!" And when this met with no response but a suave smile, "Loxley!" cried he, in utter wroth, "Ye shall die by the King's own sword!"

So he roared from out his carriage, borne away by that strange emotion, which not even he could name the nature of. 'Twas some reaction merged deep in in his soul at the pleasant insolent insouciance of this outlaw and common thief. And as that carriage had begun to move, upon Robin's light slapping of the flanks of the horses that pulled it, that cry was the last word to fall in this conversation, save the mirthy response of the king of Sherwood ringing through the green weald, in a voice that seemed nothing flummoxed at this secret name called so openly by the mouth of the law. But he rose upon his bow, and brought a hand to his mouth, that the arrow of his voice might fly the truer; and so called out, laughter in his voice—"Tallyho, my fine Sheriff! He that has died by the sword, has sure lived by it!"

And the Sheriff's barge tumbled wide down that corridor of trees, as the laughter of Robin Hood's men vanished to the foliage behind him.

XII

he Sheriff that eve was much distraught and bemused, though he sought with all his power to master his wits, and to this end did sit in stern meditation behind his desk. His faculties tarried on unwonted ends, his mind was set like a dog on its tether to roam

about the same fixed point. He felt light of head and impassioned, and feared a weird fever was cast on him. The skull seemed to leer at him. He set him to scribe some correspondences that were long since due—for he had lately been uncommonly dilatory in his writing—but found his mind in a state of great agitation unto confusion, so that now and then words would leak from his pen that had naught to do with the argument he was upon, and he would find himself dispatching another piece of costly parchment, which for its price to his ledgers and thence to the crown did rile him considerably. At length he surrendered this procedure as bootless, and reclined back in his chair, and felt a heaviness and a dull agony on his cap that he could not have done with.

The shadows that played against the walls became object of his fixation. He stared at them sullenly, glowering into the dark and working his teeth against each other in a painful grinding. There was something upon that wall that did not please. These shadows were wrong, someway. They suddenly seemed to grow gravid and horrid to his eyes, as though demons there were dancing affrolick in the burnished light. He snarled silently at them and squinted his eyes away from them, for he would not be seized by such madness—he, who had lived at an edge of sobriety for all his many years—he would not cede to those dark powers now, would not offend his wonted habits at this elder age! Nay, his head would be his until the end, these phantasies notwithstanding... He clawed the air before him and muttered at those fowl depictions of darkness to hie away; but it seemed he could not have done with them—

"Thomas!" cried he, at the dark oaken door; and again, when no response was forthcoming, "Thomas!" with a shrill and broken voice. And at the second and more urgent call Thomas did indeed debouch from the door, looking himself haggard and pale, with the startled, disheveled glance of one who has been sleeping when he ought not, and has only just been awakened to those duties which he has been neglecting. "Thomas," muttered the Sheriff, from a voice that seemed suddenly as though it would fail him, "I do not feel i'the right. Gain me a draught of water." And Thomas, who saw that the Sheriff had become very pale indeed, awakened at once and obeyed, rushing to gather the draught requested. When he returned he found the Sheriff slumping in his chair, his hand rubbing numbly against a sodden brow; and so Thomas, much beset, called to the servants, who at once arranged a makeshift bed upon a wooden bench against the wall, whereupon the Sheriff was brought to repose his suddenly flaccid limbs.

There Thomas tarried about him nervously, unsure what to do; watched that great form, which he was unaccustomed to seeing in the prone, breathing oddly deep breaths, its great hands folded on its irregularly rising belly, and those sharp eyes closed, those seldom-smiling lips drawn down now into as fierce a frown in the mass of his cheeks and chin as ever they had worn in lucid hours. Now and again it seemed the jaw was working, and this alone quieted Thomas' concerns, and let him rest a little, thinking that his Sheriff was but fatigued—as who should not be at such an age, after such an adventure!—and would by and by rise up and be as if nothing had happened—

But time on he suddenly realized that the Sheriff had grown awfully pale, with a pallor that seemed horribly like to death; and he, much panicked, was about to call for help, when suddenly to his enormous startlement the Sheriff at a jerk rose up and sat, his eyes flying open and staring, dark and enormous, with terrible solemnity into void space.

"Shall I call a doctor, my Lord Sheriff?" managed Thomas weakly, gazing in blank fear at the specter before him, who seemed almost to have perished already.

"Nay, but thankee, Thomas," replied the Sheriff with a voice that was markably strong, not looking at Thomas, but ever at some invisible mark upon the wall. "There is no need of it. I shall get me some needed rest, and tomorrow shall be right as day. Methinks I am well enough."

So saying, the Right Honorable High Sheriff of Nottinghamshire, Derbyshire, and the Royal Forests laid him down to take his repose, never again to rise, but died that very night.

Merry Men

The Widow's Sons

ear that, dear brothers? They'd have the tale of the time Robin saved us from the Sheriff's noose!

WILL   Pity 'em, Brother John, for they'd not believe it e'en if it fell on 'em like an apple from the Tree of Life.

JOHN   What business is that of ours, brother Will? For our part, let us weave the yarn, and if they wish not to wear what's wove, what does it cost us? 'Tis no fault of ours if there are ears here too small for great events.

LESTER   Why waste th'breath?

JOHN   No talk of Robin is wasted breath, Brother Lester, and 'tis as much pleasure to me in the telling, as it will be pleasure to them in the hearing—whether they crede it or not. Hear, Brothers, how they call for't!

LESTER   'Tis only to mock us later, Brother. They want no part in truth.

JOHN   All men want part in truth. That is what it means to be man.

LESTER   E'en brother Will? Ne'ertheless, he is for once i'the right; they'd never believe it even if you fed it to them by the spoonful.

JOHN   And how could they not? Why, here we are, three solid witnesses. Men have been hanged on less!

WILL   Did you hear yon wag, Brothers? It seems that by the calculus of our honorable public, though three, we count to them as but one!

JOHN   Hah! Then my good Brothers, we must speak just so: one head with three voices in unison!

LESTER   Nay, but let us not speak at all, lest the authorities gain wind of it.

WILL   Authorities, pah! Brother, those days are long passed. A man can speak e'en of Robin Hood under pious King Henry and not worry for his neck. Let us wag our tongues while we may, for liberalism's a fickle thing.

LESTER   Still I say we should keep mum, lest other tongues than ours shall wag.

JOHN   Bless me! You are a right and true lester, Brother, and always have been. Given as named. But I say, I mean to proceed, though the Sheriff himself should try to give me the hoof for't. Enough of this bashfulness. Will, where begin?

WILL   Why, at the beginning, naturally.

JOHN   Right! The beginning. I was the firstborn—

WILL   Bosh! All know *I* was the firstborn. You came e'en after Lester.

JOHN   None came after Lester but Lester, and you came after me, and that's the order given by God and certified by the word of our mother herself—

WILL   Why, a greater liar...!

LESTER   Brothers, Brothers! What has any of this to do with Robin's saving us from hanging in Nottingham?

JOHN   Well, sure we could not have been hanged if we'd ne'er been born.

WILL   And sure we would not have lived such a life as risked us hanging, if the sight of a third twin born in a single hour had not sent our dear father to an early grave by bewildered terror, leaving our mother a widow to fend for herself, her swollen family and her sadly diminished belly.

JOHN   See, brother Lester, how 'tis one thing after another in this world?

WILL   Rather say, one brat after another.

LESTER   Rather say, one *fool* after another. If we are to proceed at this pace we will not manage ere Michaelmas. Let us hasten to more pertinent events, Brothers, lest our discourse turn obnoxious to its listeners.

WILL   Brother John, our brother is lesting us again.

JOHN   A more lestful man ne'er perceived the light of day, Brother Will. See you why I say he was born at the tail end?

LESTER   Yet for that I'll come straight to the head. We were to be hanged for poaching the King's deer. That's the long and short of it.

WILL   Precisely the charge levied on us! 'Twas all lies, of course.

JOHN   Slander.

WILL   Infamous calumny.

JOHN   Villainous defamation.

WILL   A woeful pack of mendacious, foul and incredible perjuries.

JOHN   Groundless of truth and seconded by no witness, neither living nor dead.

WILL   The work of backbiting and seditious cowards, antagonists of Faith and Crown.

JOHN   'Twas forsooth a very large rabbit we shot that day.

WILL   Aye. So large indeed, it touched the dimensions of a deer.

JOHN   And wore the antlers of one to boot.

WILL   A regular upland jack-a-lope. Nothing more and little less.

JOHN   Upon which beast, there was not then, and never has been since, any proscription against the killing, the cooking and the eating, and I defy any man to prove me the contrary by means of the letter of any law he pleases.

WILL   And for *this*, for *this*—alack!

JOHN   For this, we three, consigned to be slain, in cold blood!

WILL   O villainy!

JOHN   O cowardice!

WILL   O cruelty most cruel!

JOHN   O ruthless and callous heart of a naughty Sheriff!

WILL   A hard and cold and soulless man, if ever one were born in any lost corner of God's green earth!

JOHN   A monster unhinged, and a dire enemy of delectable coney stews!

WILL   A tasteless man, criminally numb to the charms of finer cuisine!

JOHN   An uneducated man, ignorant of botany, taxonomy, zoology and gastronomy alike!

WILL   Though, i'truth, one can hardly fault him the error...

JOHN   Aye. *'Twas* passing like a deer.

WILL   Why, had I known no better myself, I myself might have fallen into his same mistake—

LESTER   Brothers, Brothers! The hour, Brothers, the hour! (Jack-a-lope, indeed! *Jackanapes*, says I...)

JOHN   Onward, Will, lest our brother grow irascible...

WILL   Just so. Then here it was. We three, innocent as doves, apprehended with coarse hands by the Sheriff's toughies, who raided us most stealthily as we were about our honest venery, and caught us in the crook of a hill by the carcass of the aforementioned beast, which I believe was left there as food for the carrion feeders, to demonstrate once and for all the great value of the King's deer.

JOHN   Aye, left there to rot! As we ourselves were destined to be. For we were packed away most rudely into a barred and chained carriage, and trucked off to Nottingham, where (as the Lord Robert himself boasted most recklessly before us) we were to be employed as bait to lure Robin Hood to town, that he might succumb to the same fate that awaited us.

WILL   For the Lord Robert lost no time at spreading the word far and wide that the three most dashing, debonaire, handsome, fearsome and formidable members of the Merry Band of Sherwood (barring only Robin himself, naturally) had been seized by a group of his own lawless thugs.

JOHN   Seized, of course, after an honorable struggle.

WILL   As goes without saying! Five slain in a sortie fit for the storybooks.

JOHN   Why, I marvel at your memory, good brother Will! For more than just *five* fell before us that day.

WILL   I meant, five to Lester alone. He trailed us far in the count, needless to say.

JOHN   Troth! Ah, see how the poor fellow sighs and fidgets and grows russet, just thinking on't... Courage, dear Brother: 'tis no shame for the youngest sibling to fall well behind his elders in matters of war and love. Next time I do not doubt you shall prove much improved!

LESTER   What utter rot. We killed not a man of them, but they caught us as we were trying feckless to flee.

JOHN   Ah, come now, Brother, a touch of fancy!

LESTER   I am for the truth.

WILL   But what, Brother, is truth?

LESTER   Well, whatever it be, 'tis certainly nothing to do with your brazen forgeries.

JOHN   A brazen hypothesis, and one that would require a long and philosophic proof! I shall expect it from you at a more opportune moment. At any rate, this following portion of the tale, not even you, my dear punctilious Brother, could protest. There we were, billeted deep in Nottingham prison (where we found ourselves in the company of some of the most dangerous, malodorous and hirsute men in all the land), in bitter expectation of the abrupt end that awaited us when the rope grew sudden taut the following morn, and praying both that the news should find Robin Hood (for thus he should save our sorry hides), and that it should not (for thus he should spare his own).

WILL   But find him, it did!

JOHN   Aye, through our own dearest mother, no'theless, God rest her pure and noble soul! For she had word of our plight, and brought it straight to Robin Hood, weeping like a babe as she went. And he, good Christian as he was, found his heart melted at the sight of a suffering and outraged widow, and asked her what was the matter. "For pity, for pity, my children, my three boys, taken by the Sheriff!" she wailed at him, and he asked her what we had got up to, if we had outraged some prelate—

WILL   —or some girl, perchance —

JOHN   —or some worthy's worthy wife—

WILL   —or murdered, or pillaged, or set fire to villages—

JOHN   —or conspired against the King to o'erthrow the Monarchy—

WILL   —the which acts, of course, we had not committed —

JOHN   —nay, most certainly not! —

WILL   —on this particular day.

JOHN   And she, relating to Robin that we had been taken in
for the slaying of a monstrous hare —

WILL   —(whose shameless waste cried out now from the very
earth for avenging)—

JOHN   —did enflame his noblest heart with a desire to right
wrongs and set the scale of justice to its fit balance, and to stand
for orphans and widows and lapins alike! Up, up then, good
Robin Hood, and straight to our company of friends and brothers, the Merry Men of Sherwood, to rouse them to the task!

WILL   And planned they then a full out assault on Nottingham itself, with machines of war and fortified numbers, to arson that city to the ground and slay its inhabitants to a one, all
the which was to be carried out that very morn—

LESTER   Brother Will!

WILL   I say, Brother, you are singularly lacking in good humor.

LESTER   What shall all these exaggerations obtain for any man,
either now or late?

WILL   Naught but the delight of the heart and stimulation of
the mind in happy fantasy!

LESTER   That is a small grace to a great folly. As if men did not
utter enough mad things!

WILL   Our brother is a sourpuss and a curmudgeon, John.

JOHN   There's nothing for it, Will; always has been, and always will be. But we love him for't, do we not? In any case, he's
right, good listeners: for alack! there was to be no siege of the
city, in any classic sense of the word. Why, our band was hardly
fit for such polemical caprices, neither in its arms, nor its numbers, nor its preparation, nor its bent and mood. Nay, but

Robin and Little John worked up to a plan of lesser glow but greater glory, and, organizing everything in the arc of an hour or two, set them out to see it through.

WILL   Aye, got them thence toward Nottingham, and counting on luck to lead the way, for there was one key element to their scheme that had not yet fallen into place.

JOHN   But fall it did upon their very course when—by no luck, say I, but the grace of God alone—whom should they encounter on their way, but a jolly beggar, making his painted pathway up the road! And he all decked out in the most incredible motley a man ever saw, a rainbow robe of bags and pockets, such as caught Robin's attention at once.

WILL   And Robin went to him, to ask him, had he money hid in any of those prismatic caches—

LESTER   Robin ne'er once in all his days bothered a poor man for so much as a ha'penny, Will, and well you know it.

WILL   Indeed, Brother Lester, you are right, and have just jogged my memory: 'twas not so, but 'twas the *beggar* to beg *Robin* for alms. 'Twas just so. The beggar begged him for alms, but he replied, "Nay, for I am Robin Hood, known as friend of the poor and a poor man myself, and carry upon my poor person not a single farthing." But the beggar was skeptic, and would not credit his claims, saying that a thief such as Robin in the Hood would surely be deeply burthened with gold wherever he went, and begged him again, still more insistently, for alms. But poor Robin protested, saying, "I swear, good beggar, I am as much a pauper as the day my mother bore me, and if you should continue to cast aspersions on my frankness, why, then, my fist will be forced to defend the truth of my word!" At which the beggar grew right wroth, and set upon him with a fury like some manner of beast, and Robin had at him, too. They did long scuffle, beating at one another like two mad wildcats met there on the road. Why, never in all my life have I seen such fisticuffs! 'Twas a contest of blows and buffets! And they did carry on so, until Robin was at last sent packing with blood gushing from his ears—

LESTER   What a sorry mess. My foolish brothers should certainly fall into a world of trouble, were I not here to guide 'em straight out again! For I swear these two would roam over the whole sovereign face of the world, and yet never set foot within the farthest borders of their proclaimed destination. Tell me, Brother Will, if 'twas a mere beggar that Robin met, how was he to use this beggar's costume to our subsequent salvation?

WILL   Well, er... I suppose—

LESTER   In truth, 'twas no mere beggar that Robin met, but a palmer, and the proof of this is in what followed, if you would recall yourself an instant from the mere hot moment before you, and gain a goodly perspective on events and outcomes, as seems continually beyond you. And ne'er did they wrangle, Robin with this palmer, but Robin met the old man in great respect and honor, as he was always wont to give to the elderly and the holy. Or what, mean you to slander the name of the finest man of England still again?

JOHN   Aye, a palmer, a palmer! 'Twas so, 'twas just so, Will! Bravo, Lester! (You see, Brother Will, what we owe to our brother's sober memory?)

WILL   Nay, but now that I am recalling, there was a beggar first, *then* a palmer...

LESTER   What drivel! Will he never give in?

JOHN   Enough, Will! 'Twas a palmer, and a palmer alone, just come back from the Holy Land, and bearing on him the cross-bound palm he had fetched in that distant place. And he made his slow and faithful way upon the road, going then toward

Barnsdale (for he was a man of the northern country, and was homebound), when up to him strode bold Robin Hood, saying, "Salvete, good Father! And praytell, where have you been, that you bear the marks of a man at sojourn, and where are you going? For methinks I spy a crossed palm riding upon your breast, which speaks to me of adventure." At which the palmer recounted shortly his journey to the Holy Land and how he was now homeward bound. "Well returned, Father Palmer!" cried Robin at this. "And God bless you for your late pilgrimage. Pray well for me, Father, for I am in constant need of't. My name is Robin Hood, and I am this day set on a pilgrimage my own: a mission of mercy, to save three hotblooded young men from hanging for a crime of which they are guiltless."

WILL   But the palmer said, "And how, my son, do you intend to perform such a miracle? Have you evidences of their innocence?"

JOHN   "Nay," quoth Robin, "but I will get me thence and carry these boys before the very scythe of death, and truck 'em off by dint of wit or force as need be, safe to home and to the longing embrace of their widowed mother, who has no other good in all the world but these her sons."

WILL   "Well 'tis, then! But be wary of doing ill to any man there, good master Robin," cautioned that old man, "for verily the Lord hath said, 'Vengeance is mine.'"

JOHN   "Worketh the Lord not through his servants?" asked Robin. "Yet be at peace, Father Palmer, for I will harm no man as I can spare, and slay none, upon my word. Yet still I am in need of your aid e'en beyond your prayers and your sound rede, for decked out as I am I shall arrive no later than the town gate, and end up rather hanging side by side in doom with the same men I would succor. Would ye not exchange your robes for mine own, together with all my arms and possessions, including e'en these forty silver pieces?"

WILL   And the palmer replied: "For my consumed rags, your own fine apparel, weapons, and money withal? My son, 'tis a hard thing to make jest of an old man, just returned from a fatiguing pilgrimage of many long years. I beg you in the name of Christ, find some fairer pastime than teasing the elderly."

JOHN   "But no such scurvy intention would e'er I entertain, Father Palmer! And our Lord Christ as my witness. All that I have said is true. I am in keen need of disguise, and find it ready before me. May my own clothes keep you warm and sheltered, good Father, and my weapons keep you safe on your way; and as for the silver, I bid you use it to slake your hunger or your thirst after your long quest, and to see to any of your other immediate material needs, and to employ the remainder in such work or charity as suits you. And if you would rest this day in Sherwood forest, then upon my safe return, should God grant such to me, I would sit with you at board, and hear to an item of your enterprises in the Holy Land, and what you saw there, and what did. By your leave, I will send you e'en now with one of my men to our woody dugout, and there you may repose your weary feet and eat and drink to your fill, ere you, refreshed, set to the last leg of your journey." And the palmer, much surprised and e'en touched by this show of generosity and friendly dealing, did at last assent; though he swore he would restitute Robin his duds when they met again, for he could not abide any clothing but his own, and would ne'er go his way armed, arguing most sensibly that if arms had not served him these many thousands of miles in heathen lands, surely they should not do so now that he was on the very threshold of Christian home. He tried as well to talk him out of the pieces of silver, but of this, Robin would hear not a word. So the palmer said, "Then like I shall expend them on the poor." And Robin replied, "Words sweet to my ear, and true in my heart, Father Palmer! No finer return could these coins make, which once rode in a fat man's satchel, than to end in a thin man's palm. You have my blessing in't. Now to the exchange." And with this, they bartered skins, and Robin kept from out of all his goods only a dagger, his famed horn and a gray woolen mass contained in one of his pockets, a shag in the semblance of a beard. This last he strapped to his face, as he had a knack in doing, until he looked indeed superior in years to the very ancient before him. Then he ordered one of his men to lead the old man to their hideaway, without blindfold and with all honor and care. And guised thus as a veteran palmer, he and his contingent of men went their way to town.

WILL   Note well, good listeners! Of all these events, we heard alone. What follows now, we have seen with our own eyes.

JOHN   Or the most of it.

WILL   Or some of it.

JOHN   Or really, none of it ere the end, inasmuch as for the better part of it we wore sacks upon our heads, and stood blindly awaiting the final judgement.

WILL   But hear it, we did.

JOHN   Heard it with our own ears.

WILL   Ours and no others.

LESTER   What fools.

WILL   It began like this, that Robin found his way into Nottingham, and picked through the crowd until he'd come to the foot of our stage, whereupon we were about to play a great disappearing act—

JOHN   (— one way or another!—)

WILL   — and there below us he stood, chatting with the guard and inquiring after the weather, when who should suddenly stride up across the square to stand before the platform? None other on my honor than the King himself!

Lester   God in His heaven!

Will   Fine, Brother Lester, have your way of this one, too! There was no king at all, but only the wretched shire reeve. And this, Lester, you shall not gainsay me!

Lester   Nay, but 'tis so; Sheriff Robert did approach.

John   And Robin, just as smooth as you please, in a scratchy, weak old voice to match the very man's whose clothes he had donned—

Will   'Tis true! My own ears, keen as a hounds, did not recognize him in't!

John   Nor mine, Brother, nor mine. And Robbin, I say, in this exceptional mimic, queried, "M'Lord Sheriff, a word, by your leave: are these men to be hung for *murther*?" And the Sheriff said, nay, not for murther. "Then for *arson*? Have they perchance burned church or palace, house or hovel?" Nay, but did not pluck a single spark. "*Violence* against maid or nun?" Nay, so far as any authority could say. "What of *adultery*, then? Have they filled another man's shoe?" What, they, who could barely fill their own? "Or tried perchance to *assassinate* the King or some member of the nobility?" Blunderers like these? No, no, and no! "Then *what*, good Lord Sheriff, have they done, to merit this sad and most premature end?" Why, they have et of the King's deer! "Et of the King's *deer*?" Aye, et of his deer! "Why, then, surely they should hang not once, but thrice, and take their heinous crime down to Satan with 'em to shock the Prince of Shadows with such vile, deplorable, unexampled wickedness!"

Lester   Hah! He did say that, I had right forgotten, the merry maker...

John   Aye, Brother! Had that Sheriff on a run from the start. And then most sly he added, "But my Lord Sheriff, prithee, where is the hangman? For he seems right hung up!" And the

Sheriff allowed that in truth he did not know where his hang-man was dangling.

WILL   As how could he! For here, you see, the men of Sher-wood had been about their merry work. They had intercepted this same hangman only minutes past and strung him up be-hind the bulwark on a noose of his own until the life was gone of him—

LESTER   And killed a dozen men aside him, I suppose?

WILL   Nay, but *three* dozen, at the least—some twenty men in all!

LESTER   I have never been able to ascertain, Brother, whether your memory or your arithmetic is the more to be lamented.

WILL   Fiddlesticks! So be it. They did not hang this hangman at all (though he sure deserved it, the blackguard), yet tied and locked him in a wine cellar of a nearby tower, with an open noose about his neck (you cannot defy this, Brother Lester, 'twas Robin's own design!), and there he would remain the better part of three days, until a drunkard of a watchman de-scending thence to get him drink found the beggar himself, bound and gagged and on the verge of starvation.

JOHN   'Twould have been a sorry end for him, to be sure. But the man as brings death invites death, as my father used to say...

LESTER   *Your* father! And praytell, how did you hear of this say-ing of his, when not even I, the eldest of all, heard a single sov-ereign word from his lips ere his demise?

WILL   Well, the man fought a war, after all. Could not one imagine him saying something of the sort?

LESTER   Pah!

JOHN   At any rate, 'tis saying true, no matter who said it, whether my father or thine, or e'en Will's here. The hangman evaded his bonds and was saved in the end, and may be it e'en conduced to his salvation, for all we know. A man walks near enough the abyss, he is bound to change his sinful ways!

WILL   I fear he was bound to something more immobile than that, good Brother: a keg of ale such as not even Little John could have shifted. For which immobility he was sadly impaired of doing his duty that day.

JOHN   Aye! And so Robin asks the Sheriff where this man has got to, and the Sheriff admits he does not know, at which Robin exclaims, "Then my Lord will be in wont of a substitute! I am but a poor old palmer, but I am fit to shrive, and a man as is fit to shrive a man is fit to sheer one. If my Lord would offer just remuneration, I would willingly play the part of missing hangman, and see to it that justice is done by God's own grace with these three scurvy youngsters." And the Sheriff thought on't a moment, and said, "Old man, I am run clear of options. Thirteen pence will be your reward, and some clothing which reeks less and holds better, for I divine you have not changed your apparel since first you set foot out of England." And Robin replied, cheeky to the last, "I don my togs to suit my will, my Lord Sheriff."

WILL   And with that, they raced off to get him new clothes, and bid him enter them even (for the Sheriff remarked that it would not do to have offices of state carried out in such disarray), and made him ascend next to us. That was when he prodded John in the ribs and spoke to us in a whisper, the voice of which we withal did recognize, saying, "Fear not, my distraught friends, for the only thing to hang this day will be the murd'rous intentions of yon sheriff." And we rejoiced in our hearts to hear this welcome voice with such welcome words, and knew that we were saved. And then Robin stood before the entire crowd, and with voice stentorian, proclaimed, "Oyez, oyez, good people of Nottingham! Never have these hands yet slain a man"—

JOHN   Nay, Brother, that's not what he said! But rather, "I have worked me a dozen occupations since the day of my birth, have been butcher and beggar, captain and criminal, pirate and prelate, minstrel and monger, but never yet in all my life have I been hangman, nor is it a trade I shall take up this day; for the race of hangmen be cursed from the first of their damned number to the last!"

LESTER   'Twas the first speech he spoke; for verily, I never once heard him speak against hanging as such, but 'tis true that Robin Hood never once killed a man, by hanging or elsewise.

WILL   Hah! Is that so! And the seven woodsmen he slew which got him outlawed to start with?

LESTER   Four of these ne'er e'en existed, and two were ne'er slain. As for the last, 'twas another hand than Robin's that carried that crime. A white hand, by my troth.

WILL   Well, what of the twelve he killed when escaping from matins that day in May?

LESTER   The ones he slew before the door of the church?

WILL   The very same.

LESTER   Say you then that this man who risked life and limb to reverence the Virgin Mary, shed blood on Christ's own threshold to save his skin thereafter?

WILL   Well...

JOHN   But what of Guy of Gisborne, riding his pike?

LESTER   Another survivor. 'Tis a fable and a lie, that, and if I find the man as started it, I might set him on the same pike as he invented. I do not misdoubt that Sir Guy is presently happy as a hen back in Gisbourne, enjoying the high commissions that have come to him for a life of public villainy.

WILL   And the page that was riding to alert the Sheriff that time we caught the monk that dastardly betrayed Robin to the

Sheriff? The page I mean that Robin brought down with an arrow shaft at a hundred yards. What of him?

LESTER   What Robin, and what hundred yards! How could Robin have killed him, if Robin was at that moment in the Sheriff's keep? 'Twas forsooth Will Stutely as fired that shot, and the distance was no more than thirty yards. The page was not e'en killed, but only winged.

JOHN   Brother, you've heaped error on error. 'Twas Much the Miller's son as struck, and Robin struck *him* to in an inch of his life for't, threatening e'en to banish him from our band should he get up to such rash violence again.

LESTER   Quotha, you're right, John! Was Much indeed.

JOHN   Robin's very words as he beat him!

LESTER   Hah! 'Tis true. I had quite forgotten.

WILL   But Robin *did* kill the monk, at least, when he returned...

LESTER   I have heard variously 'twas Much as killed him, and Little John, and you yourself, Will—so which tale shall we credit?

WILL   Dead he is, at least.

LESTER   Aye—as dead as you yourself. The man was sent packing barefoot with his hands tied behind his back and a purse of weighted coins hung round his neck, to walk to Nottingham, or crawl there like an inchworm, as he could manage it. And if they say he is dead, it is only because he ne'er changed his ways, the crook.

JOHN   Ah. 'Tis so, 'tis so.

LESTER   But return us to the story at hand, lest we stray.

JOHN   Right! But after Robin had so declaimed before the crowd, then he said, "But rather than death, let us have us music! For though it is hard of the believing, I have robbed the clothes of Robin Hood himself this day, and in them find a trinket well known to him and his ilk"—and here withdrew the horn—"which I shall play this day in lieu of the ghastly hangman's harp. Hark!" And rose the piece to his lips, and blew a great blast on it, e'en as the Sheriff, sensing betrayal, let out a screech like an owl.

WILL   'Twas then that the men of Sherwood burst out of every third robe in that plaza, and Robin drew off our caps and cut us loose and Little John tossed us swords, and we set to, hacking down the guards and soldiers of the Sheriff like wheat, until full fifty of 'em—

LESTER   By God, Will, if you do not cease with these bloody innovations, I myself shall be tempted to fratricide! Why, if no body lies mangled and lifeless at the end of your tale, you seem to grow sick at heart. I wonder what went wrong with you in infancy, to make you so? Did we not issue of the same womb, shoulder to shoulder? Did we not come of age side by side?

WILL   The story was better as I would tell it.

LESTER   That most neatly depends, Brother Will. But here is how it really happened: Robin blew a mighty blast on his horn, and did indeed divest us of our hoods and cut us down, contemporaneously as a great wain commandeered by Little John came crashing through the crowd on the cue of Robin's call. And we four leapt upon it forthwith, and were carried off straight toward the town gates. And the mob that was there erupted in a fury such as I have never beheld, and began to swamp about the guards of the Sheriff, that they could not lay hands on any of us.

JOHN   Oh, how the Sheriff did cry and shout and rage for those gates to shut, to shut! But alack for him, they stood stuck as though rusted to their hinges. For the gatesmen were dreaming deep dreams, thanks to a few sweet blows from the Pedlar's cudgel!

WILL   And we rode like the wind through the opened gate,
with the soldiers of Nottingham hot on our heels—

JOHN   —right up until the gate clashed down before their
very eyes, barring their own exit! Ha ha!

WILL   Shall never forget their faces, Brothers, and how they
stared at us out from between the bars!

JOHN   Sadder eyes a beaten dog hath ne'er worn.

WILL   They seemed as children from whom a pie has been
robbed.

JOHN   Or a hound that's lost its prey.

WILL   Or a lover whose lover's betrayed him.

JOHN   The poor forlorn souls! I pray daily they were able to
o'ercome their distress, but did not die of broken hearts.

WILL   Ne'er fear, good Brother John, but man's spirit is
strong to misfortunes.

JOHN   So 'twas back to Sherwood with us, in haste, and we
abandoned the cart at the side of the road and took to the
woodsy paths with easy hearts and a joy upon us such as I shall
recall to my dying day. For to be saved out from the precipice
of death just so, as by an angel of grace, does bring a man to
tears, and to a weighing of all he has, and all he stands to lose,
and his life eternal.

WILL   Aye, wholesome and edifying thoughts, these, that last
as long as the first flagon of wine...

LESTER   You impious miscreant, Will.

JOHN   But back to Sherwood we went with these thoughts
on us, and joined our mirthy brothers there, and recounted to
them the whole of the emprise. And Robin and the palmer exchanged robes again straightaway, but this time the palmer
found himself wearing the new suit, courtesy of the Sheriff
himself; and when he was setting to protest, Robin laughed,

but said, "Good Father Palmer, if the new cloth rub coarse, take it up with the High Sheriff of Nottingham, for the gift was his. For my part, I fear it is wanting in luxury, for though he prefers silk and fine linen against his own frame, he is not so solicitous with the skins of other men, and I swear I have e'en seen him dressing their necks in hemp. So take such grace as God has given, Father Palmer, and let us give thanks to the Almighty for what He has rendered us this day. For all goods flow from Him, no matter the flotsam and jetsam that carry 'em to our hands." The palmer was much moved by this speech, and accepted the robes with gratitude. He recounted us then of his adventures in the Holy Land, and the many things he saw there—

WILL   —and the hundreds of heathens he slew along the way—

JOHN   —and Robin and he became fast friends. Atimes he would come to us in Sherwood on lesser pilgrimage than the great he had once completed, and would be greeted by Robin as a son greets a father. He would join us for a day or a week, praying alongside Robin, and exchanging many incredible stories, as for instance—

LESTER   Methinks a single good story suffices for this eve, Brother John.

WILL   Yet that one is not e'en done! For we spent the remainder of the evening of our salvation in great fest, drinking deep and carousing with the jolly palmer, who kept tempo with us to a flagon, and outdanced and outsang us to a man! And so drunk was he by the end, that he ended in fisticuffs—

LESTER   What bosh. The man ne'er touched a drop of wine nor a strip of flesh, but true to his monastic vows did eat with us in all Christian modesty, almost to put us revelers to shame for our excesses. And if you will recall, it was he who led that evening's prayers, and took almost even mastery of our little tribe for a night, so that none of us in truth was drunk by sun-up, quite against the usances of many of our folk. For he had over us a power of good that I had perceived in no other but Robin, though in Robin it was of a different stamp, and when he was with us, it was as if our men felt the call to saintliness. So speak not of drinking and carousing and fisticuffs, brother Will, for the truth as always belies you.

WILL   Ah, Lester, Lester...! You are ever the spoilsport.

Much the Miller's Son

ame's Much. 'Twas vengeance on the part of my dear departed mother, for when her first child was born a girl, me father, seeing her sex, said to me mother, "'Tis not much, Wife, but for now 'tis nough." And she, to teach him a lesson in manners and gratitude, called the girl Nuff, and when I came out called me Much. Me father would have none of it at first. I was to be an Andrew, and my sister an Agnes. But Mother would call us naught other than Nuff and Much, and would not e'en respond to me Father when he used the names he willed, but would pretend not to savvy. "Who *is* this Andrew?" she'd ask. "Who *is* this Agnes? *I* know no'ne of that name, Thomas Miller." Till at last the poor codger had to give in, as always, and began to call us by our right names. For me mother took the blows, but 'twas she as ruled about the house, make no mistake. So I was Much till I was Midge.

I take after me mother, God rest her soul, for I have always had an edge 'gainst authorities. A man tells me what I'm to do, I tell him with that much certainty what I'll not. 'Tis willfulness, said me father, but that was only because my will ran so counter his own as a tree to ground. Mother said I'd be a free wight, and I spect that's right, though God alone fathoms the heart. I know only this, that from the time I was a wee'ne I was in trouble with the local posse e'ery time I glanced o'er me shoulder. I wouldn't want to list out me misdemeanors from that callow age, for a fellow shouldn't criminate his-self, and besides, we've not time 'nough to list 'em to an item. But though I was a'ways in hot water with this or that co'stable, and spent me share of time in the gaol, I ne'er ran foul of the law to such a stent as to be driven out for't, nor had me enemies too powerful, until my fifteenth year upon this earth, when I shot and killed two of the wrong animals in Sherwood Forest, one upon th'other.

'Twas all the fault of that yaldson Pate. He was always getting me up to it, the rascal, Lord knows why I'd listen! He said to me one day, "Much, they say you are a true hand with a bow," and I said to him, "'A true hand at it, and an arm besides! Why, and a shoulder and an eye, Pate, by God!" And Pate says, "Why, then, could ye not prove it? For many a boaster is about these days." And I says, "What care I if ye believe me or not?" And Pate says, "Ah, 'tis as I 'magined, then, and as I told Ibb (that was a girl I was then most keen on), that ye are all lip and no finger." Well this is what got me riled, and I said, "Pate, ye are a right bastard, but I'll hit whate'er it is ye want at whate'er distance you term with a single arrow standing." "Anything?" says he. "Anything," says I, and stuck my cursèd chin out.

'Twas the chin that done me in. For he said, "Get me a four-pointed buck from Sherwood or I'll not believe your archery is worth the bark ye skinned off your shaft." And I said to him I'd do it.

I went that very morning into Sherwood and by luck (or misluck as time would tell), upon a hillside most at once spotted me a run of deer, and put down the biggest of them, a regular five-point, with a clean shot at forty yard. I was just going down to get him when I hear a blast of horn, and turn me 'bout, only to find two fat Norman for'sters riding down on me with three vicious hounds at their flanks. Well the hounds were coming fast and I had no choice but to climb me a tree and squat there in the branches like a crow. And the two idiots 'low me stalked bout in circles like fat dunces and tried to 'tice me down with treacle words. But I knew that the noose 'waited me in their hands, and that my best bet at this point was to sit fast and hope for a mir'cle. For I recked that they would not shoot me down, with me a boy, for it would mean too much 'splaining with the Sheriff. Rather they'd take me in live and kicking if they could and wash their hands of me with the ma'strates. With that fiend Lord Robert in the lor'ship I knew I was a gonner. I'd already seen a boy, and him no more'n twelve years of age, strung up in a Norman rope, the pigs, and I had no 'tention of suicide by any means.

So when they'd finished with their vain promises I 'splained to them in patient detail what sort of men they were. They grew red at this and started 'sulting me vilely, so my tongue gave them what they'd come for. We were long at the ol' back-and-forth 'fore the two fat fools finally wearied of losing face to a boy and sat down there right on the grass and set to playing some stupid game such as stupid fat men play. E'en the dogs had got bored and ceased their infernal whimp'ring and put their slobb'ry muzzles into the grass. I was 'ready starting to feel a might uncomf'table on me branch there, and was even considering shooting the scoundrels out of sheer desp'ration, though I thought it u'likely I could take 'em both down 'thout one of them stealing a shot off at me, and I didn't like the risk, with me in a tree and all. For their part, I s'pose they figured I'd come down when I got hungry or squirmy enough, for they did not know me. It would surely have come to ill, one way or another, if the mir'cle had not come.

He came out of the greenwood just as sure as you please, as if he weren't Nottingham's most wanted man (though I s'pose in those days he was fair unknown yet) and strode up to those men, and looked down at 'em, and up at me, and taking stock of the scene laughed a hearty laugh. "Gramercy!" he said, "I've seen hunters hunt wolf, bear, buck, doe, boar, fox, weasel, ferr't and stoat. I have seen 'em hunt women and wisdom and gold and kingdoms entire, and legend'ry treasures cross distant seas. I have seen 'em hot after duck and goose, pheasant and ptarmigan, partridge, grouse, raven and crow, and e'en on hungry 'casions the sparrows of the field. But by me lights I have ne'er in all me days seen men after so strange a bird as this as perches in yon tree. Say, men, but what manner of beast *have* ye treed there?" "A man!" says one. "Hah!" replies he, "looks more a midge than a man, by me bones! What could so slight a sprite have e'er done to seize so much fond 'tention?"

The guards stare at each other like dimwits and then look back at him.

"This boy here shot one of the king's deer and must pay the penalty," they say. "That is hard!" says he, and I swear I saw sparks from his eyes, "for the penalty for poaching is death, and this but a lad." "Old 'nough to shoot a deer, old 'nough to hang for it!" says the fatter of the two fatties with as stupid a sneer on his complacent mug as ever I saw. And Rob'n 'sponds, "Tell me, good friend, what is worth more in God's eyes—a boy or a stag?"

Well, they scratched their heads at this and looked at each other again, and then back to him. I swear there was ne'er a more moronic pair of dunces in all of England. "What is it you want, friend?" they ask him. "Will you help us to catch him?" And up they both struggle to their feet, the lardcatches.

And Rob'n just laughs. "Truly," says he, "I do 'tend to net this bird ere you are able, and take 'im with me to Sherwood, where he can roost in any tree he pleases. For the shot he fired at that deer would have been work of art for an adult man, not to speak of saplings like yon midge." "Then you saw 'im at it!" cried they. "That I did, by God's grace!" said he. "Then you knew 'ready he was guilty?" cried they. "Knew he was guilty of crime, aye, but of wrong, that's anon to be seen," says he. And peering up at me, suddenly asks, "Say, Midge, what 'pelled ye to shoot yon crowned buck, knowing full well that a greater crowned buck would have your skin for the skin ye dared to mar?"

"I's 'ungry, Lord," say I, lying through me teeth. For I considered that me 'forementioned skin was worth more to me than the truth in any case. "Hadn't eaten in nigh a week, nor me nor me Pah and me Mah, nor me little sister," I added. The "little sister" bit was I reckon a stroke of pure 'spiration, and might've been what saved me.

"Hear you this?" he asks, turning back to the duncecaps, and one of them says it don't matter what me motives were. To which he replies, "King's For'sters, I am at a loss for words. A boy kills a beast to feed his starving famb'ly, and for this you warrant he should hang?"

"Old 'nough to shoot a deer, old 'nough to hang for it!" said the fatter one again, and Rob'n said, "If you had as much wisdom as you have paunch, good man, you would let this boy run and think ne'er again on it." And the mutton-head says, "What business is this of yours, after all?" And he says, "'Tis 'tirely me business, for the boy is in me land and the deer that he killed was mine own." And the forester gets this wide-eyed stare on his idiotic face and says not a word for a moment, then starts laughing an idiotic laugh like a great laughing hog, taking this I guess for some manner of jest. But Rob'n says, "What will it take to 'vince you men to let this boy go untouched?" "A bag of coin!" jests one, still laughing his swinish laugh, and Rob'n, just as cool as you please, plucks a satchel off his belt and throws it down on the ground with as nice a rattle as you can imagine, and says, "Done as soon as said. Have over." And the two ogle that bag like it was aflame. Then they look at each other again, the nitwits, and at Rob'n, and the skinnier fatty says, "Nor he nor our honor ain't for sale."

And Rob'n considers a moment, then says, "Say what, let us have a contest of it, to see who will have their way." And plucks a long shoot off the tree I'm in and walks out upon yonder field and plants that stick at such a distance that you could just make it out, then returns to the foresters who had watched him mute the whole while like a couple of witless nunces. And he says to them, "The man that can halve yon reed shall take the boy with him wheresoever he pleases." Says the fatter: "Yon reed cannot e'en be made out." And he: "Then it shall have to be fancied. I'd wager half a pork that our Midge here could strike it cold from where he sits; mean ye to tell me that two for'sters of the Crown are the worse for it than that boy?" And that riled 'em up. Up they come a huffing, first the skinny fatty and then the fat fatty, and take their stands, and I watch in glee as they take aim like a pair of hefty nincompoops and let their arrows go sailing yards distant from the target that Rob'n had set. Then up he stands, and by God but I have never seen a man shoot so. He pulled the arrow to and seemed not e'en to aim but just let her fly, and true as a lark she went, and we could all see the twig in the field quiver and fall apart. Well Rob'n goes out and fetches the arrows and the branch and brings it back, and I swear it looked just as though a man had taken a knife down the length of it right through the center.

At the sight of it I like the fool pup I was take to hooping and carrying on, praising that shot with just about every good word I'd ever been taught, thinking that it meant me salvation. 'Twas my 'zub'rance as did it, most like, for the foresters grew stiff and glared at me and said that it had been a lucky shot, but even if it were pure skill as had done it, it changed little, for an arrow could halve a reed but not the law. "You will not do as agreed, then?" asked Rob'n, and they spoke enough to say that no, they would not. At which Rob'n suggested that a man, no matter his hefty girth, weighed only as much as his word, and this got them worked up fierce, and they drew their swords and threat'ed him to part or else they would take two souls, not one, into Nottingham gaol that day. Rob'n said he would not part 'thout me and one of the flapbellies moved toward him right menacing as though he would strike him.

Well this was just as much as me poor fool pup's heart could take, for I allow I had even then grown right fond of Rob'n, and before I e'en knew what I was doing I had notched my arrow and sent it off deft through that man's heart. Down he went like a right sack of lard, and the other took to jabb'ring like one of his curs, and all in a frenzy mounted his horse and rode away like the devil himself was after him, the hounds at his heels. Down from the tree I come then, salve and sound, and found Rob'n kneeling by the dead man and whisp'ring something, a prayer as it seemed. And I said, "Mean you to pray over that mound of grease?" Then he looked up at me and said, "Still your tongue, boy, and speak no ill of the dead. Halved the law this day, an arrow has," but his voice had no jest in it, and I knew better'n to laugh. He rose up and I don't know but I ever saw Rob'n so mad as at that moment. And he put his hand upon my shoulder and looked me square in the eye and said, "Boy, if I do not bring you in to Nottingham now, they will be after us both." And I defiant said, "Then you mean to bring me in, too?" And he said, "Nay, I do not. This man's blood be 'pon me now, and hence your blood as well. But from this day forth we are outlaws, you and I, for the deed you have done here, and you will pay your debt to me and begin your penance by dwelling with me in the greenwood and henceforth list'ning to me in all things, and ne'er gain firing upon a man so as to kill him. I will have all this by your word, sworn in solemn oath afore me now o'er my sword, and may God strike you dead if you should e'er dare to break it."

Well, I have said I am strong 'gainst 'thority, but Rob'n was different, by God, and I know not e'en how, but I sank to a knee and swore it, and have kept it e'er since. Or at least have done so much as I could, me nature considered in the bargain. Then I rose, and he asked me name, and I said it was Much; but he said it was rather little, and he would call me Midge, for I had a nice little sting, and he divined I would be buzzing about him for long years to come. And I asked him his name—

Zounds! What on God's green earth? Bah, look yonder... Seems a part of the roof has fallen in neath all this 'fernal rain. Will the sky never close! Well, let us go and try and mend it.

Guardsman

obin Hood? Fie.

Oh, *why* do I speak like that, ye ask me? What could anyone *possibly* have against Robin Hood? Well, friend, I'll tell you. He was a bloody fiend, Robin Hood was, a violent and disorderly man, that's what. What, *how* do I know? I saw him, friend—saw him drunk with blood on his hands, and I barely made it out of the carnage alive meself. I tell you, he was a demon. Or why do you think they call him the Butcher of Barnsdale?

This was years ago, man. He has been now some decade at least in the Sheriff's hold. Died, they say, of fear at what the Sheriff was to do to 'im, though no solider word have I had nor sought on it. I'm well quit of this cursed land, friend, and have only come back, God save me, to settle my dead father's estate. What, Sherwood? Nay, what has Sherwood to do with it? Robin was a Barnsdale man, everyone knows it. Barnsdale, I say, where all those vagrants go to congregate. What? Ye doubt it? Bah, did ye not hear me! I say, he did not habitate in Sherwood, like some manner of squirrel! I say, he was a Barnsdale man! God strike me dead if I'm wrong on't!

Well, sir, think ye what ye will on Sherwood and where our good Robin made his domicile. I could not give a fig the fewer. I will tell you this and this alone: it was in Barnsdale I saw him, and it was in Barnsdale I went to find him out with my captain, Sir Guy of Gisborne, the poor deluded wretch, may God rest his soul, and it was in Barnsdale that we found him, and it was in Barnsdale that he almost had my head, and did claim that of my captain. Now you tell me, gossip: what business should we have had in Barnsdale, if Robin Hood was keeping in Sherwood?

It was in spring we went, June, hard upon the very solstice, I recall it, and evening time. What's that? Where was Robin Hood, ye say? Why, he was in Barnsdale, man, are ye deaf, or what? He was there, in Barnsdale, drinking himself up the home brew as he liked to do and gargling to a host of his cronies in a tavern there. And here's the point of it, friend, and here is why I call your beloved Robin Hood a demon: this evening men lost their lives, and among them, the Sir Guy of Gisborne, that noble soul. What, now? Sir Guy, a rascal? Ah, he's been slandered, man! Slandered precisely as Robin Hood has been praised to the skies. They speak of Gisborne as a villain these days, and Robin Hood as a hero. Bah, the world is topsy-turvy, I swear it. These are upside-down times, friend, these are drunken days.

What's this, now? Why, we went to gather him to the bosom of the law, friend. The Sir Guy of Gisborne had patronized my services, nor for the first time, and those of another twenty men like me, all of us armed to the gills, to force Robin Hood to long-awaited justice. Aye, this was some decade into his mischief. What? Ah, in all I reckon he was at it almost two tenyear. He was anyway a long-known criminal in this time, and a wanted man by all hands of the law in all that piece of England, and it was a marvel he had not been caught yet. We went in to where the Sir Guy knew to find him, a seedy tavern there at the outskirts of Barnsdale, full of crooks and disreputable types of all kinds. And aye, we found him there, dancing upon a table and singing, man, like a madcap. Well, when we entered, you can be sure there was much quiet of a sudden. There were some thirty filthy knaves in there, but we had ourselves swords, and not one of us has never seen the right use of one. Nay, I reckon not a man among us had never seen gore on his blade. Sir Guy stood out then and demanded that the fellow come down from his perch—aye, friend, he recognized him, I know not how. And Robin Hood come down. What? Nah, he was a biggish fellow, if I remember aright. Fiery of hair and eye. A rough-looking sort, and no doubt. There was something wrong about him, friend, he seemed not right in the head. Or perhaps he was but drunk, who can rightly tell?

Well, Robin Hood come down, and Sir Guy said to him, "William of Loxley, you are under arrest, and will be asked to give news on the whereabouts of your tribe." William of Loxley—evidently that was his name, man. But he just laughed, I swear he did, and just stood there looking at Sir Guy and gaping and laughing in his face like some sort of madman, until Sir Guy ordered him to stop. Sir Guy was a nobleman and no doubt, and I have never seen him lose his self-control, but in this moment, I swear, friend, he was as enraged as a pricked bull. He drew his sword, and not even then did Robin Hood stop his laughing. There was something eerie about it, friend, something... unnatural. We did not know what to do—and I'll say it again, friend, we are not the sort to stand around with our hands sown to our sides in the midst of a cock fight. I drew me my sword, and tried to get me at the ready, but I kept looking over, I don't know why, at a wall of the room—like I feared something was going to jump out of it, right out the bricks themselves, to get us! Can't say, I don't know, friend, I lost my head completely. I was shaking like a leaf, first and last time in all my days, and I don't mind admitting it. And it seemed the others were in like state. I swear there was sorcering mischief on us.

I can't even say rightly what started us off. I remember only that in an instant we were all at it—us and all the men present, swords, clubs, chairs, everything a man could find to harm another, all trying to kill each other. Ah, blood was let, I know it, though I do not know for certain how many died. I myself killed no man, not that day, leastwise. Sir Guy was down immediately, and I haven't any idea how it happened, though I suspect treachery, friend. I believe someone came out of the shadows—there, over by the wall, where I kept looking, where I had the sense that—someone, don't know who or how—had a dagger, had a knife—sunk it in Sir Guy's back—bah. Why? 'Tis the only way I can square it all to myself, friend, for if not—

Well, however it happened, we all saw him down by and by, and it was a terrible thing. Someone shouted that we were to get out and away, and I did not question it, not even a moment, once our captain had fallen. Nay, I threw down my blade, and maybe I was the first to do so—aye, I'm none too proud to say it, friend, but that's how it happened, and it's useless squinting at the past—threw down my blade and made haste from that place. I fled out and concealed my poor self under a hay cart down the road. Methinks none saw me go there, for none came alooking for me, and I could peak out from there and could see the entrance to the tavern, glaring open like the mouth of a skull, friend, and dark of a sudden inside, like all lights had gone out.—Then torchlight, and singing, some awful song, and a terrible crowd came out with the dead piled on their shoulders, and blood streaming down their sides, celebrating, methought, and at their fore Robin Hood, all slick with gore, and the head of Sir Guy skewered upon his sword—

Fie. Here you have it—here is the reason they called him the Bloody Butcher of Barnsdale. I know not how long I stayed mired there in that muddy grotto. It was yet cold, and I began to shiver. What? Hey-ho! they had passed on, friend, at once and long ago, and they had made, methinks, for the wood, though I cannot be certain. And why did I stay there, under that cart in the dark, when they had gone by? Who knows? I was come over by an unearthly impression, friend. They were as fiends, they were possessed, and the monsters that had them were lingering. I swear there was a demon there in the shadows, waiting for me—over there in the door of the tavern—and as soon as I made myself seen from under that cart—*pahm*, he would have his claws on me. I didn't know then and never knew what became of the others, nor do I have any idea how many of them were torn to pieces by that band of crazed folk. I got me hence, friend, and have never looked back. They say the Sheriff took him the day following, there in that very Barnsedale, and no wonder! May be it was e'en the selfsame tavern, for he was a brazen sort, he was.

Aye. I left by and by, alright. Got me out and ran—ran as my life depended on it. Ran for London, and boarded me the first bark for the continent. I swear it. Nay, I have never set foot again in good England until this month, and once I am quit of it again, I will never stand on these shores again, and it is many years now I do not speak even a word of English, and perhaps would have even died that way had I not met you by chance here. I miss it not. 'Tis all rank, friend, and rotted through and through. It's the South for me, where the weather is fair and the demons are few. Up north 'tis dark.

Pedlar Gamblegold

 say, this universe was not created. *You* say 'twas, but I say—if this universe was created, then you must account for a thousandfold other facts that do not jive with your notion. As for instance, the corruption of man, the imperfection of material, the limitations of human reason, and most particularly, the existence of fortune, or that element in things which is not susceptible of man's prevision. For hear this, that our universe, if created, was created either by a perfect being or an imperfect. And in the latter case, you have explained nothing without surplus, for it would suffice to say, that this universe is imperfect and eternal, rather than adding to an imperfect and temporal universe, a god who is imperfect and eternal. And if your creator is perfect, then you must explain, *why* is his creation then not perfect? You say it is perfect in the whole, but not in the part? Well and good, but still you admit that imperfection exists—the which cannot be, if your god is perfect. For it is impossible to attribute what is imperfect, to what is perfect. *Quod erat demonstrandum.*

Whereas, I say, if this universe is but adventitious, why then, all's in it adventitious as well. And that an adventitious universe exists at all needs no explanation, for it suffices to bow to the iron rule of existence. It *is*, and always has been, and will be, and you cannot explain what is, by reference to what is not. So: I say, this universe was not created, nor is the product of chance, but of perfect law. And only so can you explain to me or to you or to any man, how it is that you or I or any man is, or that all things are, or in what way it is possible that anything should be.

Oh, but do not merit me with these notions, Sir Scholar! I myself gleaned them from the philosophers, who are men in hiding; and this I know, for I have all my life been myself a man in hiding, too. How, you ask me? Why, first to my own account, then from tyrannical men, then beneath a certain band of thieves. Yes, Sir Scholar, I, in a band of thieves, for some many years. 'Twas not reductive to my mental development, I find. As for our leader, he was as odd a sort as has ever walked 'neath Venus' light. You would know his name? Why, you have heard much talk of him already, and know his name well, though ne'er you read it on the shelf of a library. Why, his name's as common as water these days; common name for an uncommon man. *Robin Hood* was his given name, Sir, known to us as Loxley by virtue of a jest of his amongst us.

How did I come such an end? Why, Sir! Imagine it. A bent toward lawlessness was forced on me by the conditions of the times. I was already a man of nigh thirty when Robin Hood found me, and was making my way to Sherwood to dwell in hermitage; for I had just escaped from Lincoln, where I and my kin had been preserved by a hair's thread when the folk there turned against the Jewry, as they were much fond of doing in all of good England in that time. They came at us in mob, in the name of cross and King Richard, and we fled to the castle, where we were shielded by the King's men, for the King, though he loathed us, did not want us massacred in his own name. He had made himself a good Christian when he had flogged all the Jews of his court, and then expulsed them naked. Then his good Christian Englishmen resorted to Christian violence against us, and killed many of our number all across England, and the King like a good Christian still objected but would not defy such a mass of subjects. So in Lincoln we sought asylum in the King's castle, to escape the ramifications of the King's view; and I, upon leaving, resolved to get me to the wood.

Sir Scholar, your doubt is well phrased. But I bethought myself, what was I to do, in such times as those, when on the one side of me I found monarchical arbitrariness, and on the other, the law-defying ochlocracy? And I, with my tarnished blood! Nay, but I would get me to a bosky place and pass my years there in solitude and meditation. I feigned Christianity to boot—done only for good measure, for my race is not my faith, and a philosopher shall outward bend with the breath of the times—and got myself hence.

Nay, *I* did not find Robin Hood, but Robin Hood found *me*. For I had set me down beside a river there to eat my fare of lunch—a bite of stale bread, I warrant, and a wedge of sour goat cheese, and a meaty pie I had filched from a nearby peasant's hut where it was cooling on the window, for *necessitas non habet legem*. I was not much further accoutered. I had me a leather jerkin and a quarter staff with which I was not much alien, and a sword as well as some other goods which I had stolen along the way and had been a-peddling to earn my bread. Yes—stole and peddled, Sir Scholar, and without shame, for a man who finds himself in a state of anarchy must live anarchically or anarchically be destroyed, and that is certain right philosophical. So I got me hence, a Jew turned Christian with a pilfered blade, and, I say...—but where was I? Ah yes, I was having my lunch of meat pie by that river there in the wood, and was ruminating aloud with you on the three-fold principle of existence, of which you and I have discoursed many times; and so utterly lost in speech between myself (for as you know better than any, Sir Scholar, that is a vice I do much indulge, particularly now in my prisoning), I did not cognize the fellow sneaking up behind me until he had his arrow lined to my heart, and had spoken.

Well, Sir Scholar, although I had trained much in combat as a young man, I was unaccustomed to the truth of hostile encounters, and I leaped up and spun me round, and found none other than Robin Hood before me, grinning and with arrow cocked. He was as lithe and limber as a sapling, and devilish strong, with a beard of copper hue and teeth ne'er obscured by lips. He had himself a peculiarity, as well—his eyes were not both of the same color, but one was azure, and the other wont to alter its tone on account, methinks, of the mood of the man. He was nobly formed, and of that no question; for anyone who saw him would be forced to admit that he was attractive of feature and elegant of form, whatever such fleshy beauty be worth.

Now he stood before me with his bow chucked, as I say, and I helpless as

a puppy. I made indication of surrender, and he said to me, all out of the blue
and with no preamble, "Master Wayfare, know you what an ass is?"

But in gab I could not be so caught off my guard, and quick as darts
replied, "Such as you see before you, that could let himself finish in such case."

And Robin Hood laughed, and shook his head. "Nay, I do not mean in
that meaning but in the other. Say, Sir—what's an ass?"

I could not garner what he was driving at, and replied, "Why, 'tis a beast of
burden, made by God for the cargo of goods and humbler men."

"Excellent!" he cried, "a learnèd definition, I shall warrant. And I, Sir
Scholar, declare that I am just one such humbler man as you have sketched. Only
I have dreadful fear of cold, and yet must pass this river. Hence, in view of my
conundrum, and being as you are a man of sound reason, as I perceive, you will
allow that what I am most in need of, is precisely such an ass as you have limned."

"Yet I have none such sumpter," said I, indicating around me, "and so can
be of no aid to you."

"On the contrary! By your own admission, Sir, if I may agree with you
without offending you—you *are* such sumpter."

Now I did not at first cognize what he proposed, if it were not mere insult,
and expressed my perplexity, to which he replied, "See here! I take it from your
late speech that you are a good Christian and a Scholar to boot, and must suppose you know aught of the Golden Rule. Now taking that rule with care, be
pleased to weigh this delicate matter with me: were you in my stead, should
you hope for anything better than just such a wide and girthy fellow as yourself, that might bear you from one shore to the other? And hence—"

Now his dastardly intentions appeared before me in a flash. I folded my
arms, saying, "I see, Master Archer, say no more. Sure you are a jester, and
would have my coin purse."

"I protest!" he cried, and seemed verily appalled e'en at the suggestion.
"Gra'mercy! I am never in need of gold, for God has seen fit to sustain me all
my days, heavy with sins though I be. I am rather much in need, Master Wayfare, of crossing, and would be most obliged to you if you might minister to
this particular and presently urgent want."

I grew most indignant at this revelation of intention, and said, "Those are many words dressed in grateful good manners, Master Archer, but they are cast into an unlikely light by the nature of your request, and more sharply still by the arrow in your fingers.”

“What, this little sting? Prithee, do not fret over it; but as I have seen you armed so I sought to better arm myself, for these are, you will allow, troubled times, and there be dangerous and mad men abroad. If you would put your stave and your sword down some distance from your reach, then I will distense my string.” And so it was done on my part, for I had no other choice; and he did for his part lower his barb, and he sheathed his arrow and shouldered his bow, saying, “That’s better! Is it not? For now we may speak together as God intended reasonable men to speak—*sine ira et studio.* (I reconstruct with liberty, Sir Scholar; Robin had no Latin.) I was saying, Sir, about my need of bearing forth, and about the Golden Rule—”

But though I was much surprised at his use of tongue, yet here I interrupted him, for I have always had a weakness to jab at the weaknesses of other men’s logic. “Master Woodsman,” said I, “Supposing I did as you have entreated, I would be much obliging that rule, but abetting you in the breaking of it. For though I would be treating you as my brother, you would be treating me as your donkey. And as I cannot suppose you should wish another to treat *you* in such a way, ergo I conclude that you are equally wrong i’th’asking.”

“It is not comely to guess at the desiderata of other men,” tutted he, grinning still. “But listen, you do your part and I shall do mine, and we shall each discover our right duty on earth and just dessert in heaven.”

“I see,” said I, standing, to do what I now saw was inevitable. “If this is what must come, then this is what must come. And moreover, Master Woodsman, I do fathom your secret motive.”

“What motive would that be?” he asked in all innocent sincerity, and seemed e’en keen to hear my interpretation.

“Why, I warrant you have scented out what I am, you being one of these blood hounds and Jew baiters,” I said, “and you have determined to amerce me for my lineage.”

“I protest that you are most unjust!” he said, laughing outright in my face. “I am all for justice with my fellow man, and could not care a whit of what blood your mother was. Nay, but I declare: be you Norman or Saxon, Briton or Jew, I *will* ride you."

And so, seeing that naught could be done to thwart him, grudgingly I knelt down upon a knee and let him leap up on my back—and was surprised, for he seemed far lighter than I would have wagered—and set off trudging across the river, muttering all the while, me thinks, and sure contemplating how I would do, when we had come to the other side. And in the meanwhile, he, happy as a lark, did sing and whistle and loll on, and at one point e'en called out, "Hie now, Master Wayfare, and wary there of getting yon water up past the level of my toes. Ho, I would have my boots dry as kindling ere I reach our common shore, ye hear?" and set to singing once more, all of which was rankling beyond compare.

Now despite my exasperation I noted as we went a certain rhythm against my arm, something that was a-tap-tap-tapping, and inferred what it must be; so that when we came to the shore, I, fast as could be, dismounted my load flat onto his back, and in the same movement grasped at the tapping thing, which was nothing other than that man's dagger; for though girthy, I am quick when need has need. And flourished it at him, and held him off a ways at bay as he regained his feet, but near enough he would not dare to unsling his bow. And I said to him, "Well, now, Master Rider, that was, I avow, a brusque and re-freshing passage. Only that I fear I have most absentmindedly forgotten my sword and my quarterstaff, and worst of all, my meaty pie, on the far side of the river. Now, as 'tis so sultry a summer's day, I did wish to regain you the favor you have been so kind as to lend me, and give you the chance to cool your feet a little in this bracing water. For I am as you divined a good Christian, and obedient to the gilded principle aforementioned. And since I know you to be a weightless fellow, I will offer you, with my very form, even the weight to hold you down in't, so that you will not float off with the stream, featherlike."

Now I had expected of him some flare of anger, some show of rage, some childish frustration with which I might satisfy my craving for revenge. Noth-ing of the sort! But he laughed, in all evident good spirits, saying, "Master Wayfare, though you have called yourself a Jew, truly you are as Christian as any Christian hereabout in our England, and have proved the point with this kind rebuttal. I say, I was just beginning to suffer the oppression of this heat, and was thinking to make me a bath; but look, this water is chill, and I should have to work me up a sweat to bear the chill of it. What you propose, then, is fit to my need."

And so saying, he squatted quite voluntarily, and took me upon his back—I repeat, Sir Scholar, in those days, I was quite as girthy as I am this day, and it was no mean weight he took upon his shoulders—but with amazing fortitude did heft me and strode with me direct into the stream. And I, irritated by his nonchalance (for alas, *volenti non fit injuria*, and I was still something cross at the ill-use that had been made of me), took to beating him about the shoulders with the flat of his dagger and calling out at him as though he were an ass, and I must spur him on. He seemed to bear these blows with equanimity, and as we entered a deep part of the river that I for my part had avoided methought I even heard him singing again—which riled me considerably, so that I might have beaten him strongly or inclined the dagger somewhat upon its downward stroke, had he not suddenly disappeared from under me.

I do not know e'en how it came about, Sir Scholar, but of a sudden I found myself floating log-like in that stream with nothing beneath but water. I looked about me, to find where that prankster had got to, but saw him no where; and indeed he remained invisible for such a long term that I was beginning to wonder if he had not sunk and drown. When of a sudden I heard him laughing behind me, and twisted about to find him standing jaunty on the bank of the river, and something dangling from his fingers that I recognized as mine own coin purse. "Ho, filchthief!" I called, enraged now to such a pitch that I might have boiled that river, "That bag there is mine!"

"What, this meager sack, Master Wayfare?" he returned. "Why, and did you think there should be no coin to your crossing? This is the King's England, where everything is taxed."

"T'would be right scoundrelly of ye to strip me of it," said I, "I, who depend on those few metal disks as upon my very breath!" Sure I was starting to sweat for the strain of striding through water.

"Master Wayfare, ye are the queerest fish I ever espied, if ye must respire gold so as to live," laughed he. "But I say, for all your seeming, I perceived from

the first you were a man of some concealed substance, and your stash here
proves my intuition sound."

Bethinking myself, I paused in my hard journey, and lifted high his dagger,
and said, "Very well, let it be at that. Ye keep my gold, and I shall keep your
little blade. Let us call it a just barter, and it please you."

"Tell ye what again," said he. "Add in your sword and your stave here,
along with this most delectable meaty pie, and methinks with that we can call
it fare's fair." For it was true, I realized at once; he had gained the shore where
I had left my arms and my pie, and they lay abandoned not far from where he
was even then dripping. And by my troth, if he did not stride over to my pie
and lay his damp hand upon it and bring it to his mouth to enjoy the savor,
e'en while I, its right and natural owner, struggled 'gainst the current. (—Ah,
Sir Scholar, for a taste of that meaty pie now!—)

Now at this I swear I was bubbling over with rage, for I am an irascible
sort, and the pie had fired me over, but I gritted my teeth and roared, "'Tis
nothing to me, Master Rider! For the sword is stole and the stave easy substi-
tuted, and my meat pie sure no hasty pudding. Seize 'em all!" And was on the
cusp of adding, "And may you choke on that pie!" but had no time.

For he said, "I honor a man who knows how to season his misfortune with
a pinch of philosophy. Say, Sir Scholar, what might you be called?"

"Ralf Gambol," replied I, using that name I had invented to cover my
flight; and he returned, "And say, Master Gambol, this blade here, that you
admit to having rascally gambled from my person—can ye use it?"

"Can I use it!" cried I, still more wroth than before; for I am right proud
of my blade work. "Man, if ye took up that long blade there, I could trounce
you with naught but this stunted one."

And he, limber as a deer, strode on over to that sword and flung it to his
hand, and tested its balance a moment, before calling back, "Say what, Master
Gambol. Prove that claim to me, and you can have your coin purse, your
sword, your stave, your meaty pie, and your dignity as well. What's more, I'd
have proposition to make ye, and one that is perhaps not so inequitable as
those to precede it." And so saying he began to trudge back into the water toward me, grinning that madcap grin.

Well, now, I am not one to stand down from a challenge. I took his own blade at him, and though he was something practiced, and defended himself bravely. We were at a long dance of it, but by and by I disarmed him, gave him a slap on his shoulder with the flat of his own shortsword that must have left a pretty welt, and grasped my sword up from under the water whence it had fallen, and stood before him with two blades now, to his none. And indeed I pride myself to this day on having defeated Robin Hood in single combat. Though had it been a match of bows, or e'en of quarterstaves, methinks I should not have finished so proud.

Now he staggered back clutching his injured part, and laughed, delighted, it would seem, at having been trumped. And I came at him with both those blades, ready to flay him to the bone, for I was still much incensed. But he warded me off of my intent, waving and laughing and saying to me, "Good Master Gambol, I am mazed! Truly you are gold with iron. Now, before you cut me down, perchance would ye at least hear my offer?"

I stood back a moment, mastering my anger, for curiosity is the single passion of mine which is greater than wrath.

And he said, "Now, Master Gambol, I have had your name, but you have not so much as queried for mine own. And I swear, it is the nub of barbarism to kill a man before ye know what he is. So stand down a moment and learn from me at least as much as that, and then you may decide with due deliberation whether to hack me to giblets. I am the one called Robin Hood, and I dwell these forests with my band of men, to pluck trouble at rank authority and to prod at mirthless guts, gently or ungently, as case may require. Yet though I am well armed and provisioned by God and keep good company, I say, man, that my band, for all its arms, hands, legs, livers, and brawny breasts, is somewhat lacking in brains, which I do perceive you to possess. 'Tis vanishing rare to find one who has both spirit and flesh that do not flimsy at the strike. I do not ken your plight, friend, but I find you alone in Sherwood, which is sign enough already that you are mayhaps unsatisfied with that staid and too rigid structured civil life of town and court. Then I should offer you this: to come to the wilds with me, and leave aside the pampered odor of the city, for something that better approaches the pith and vigor of liberal life itself."

Now I, suspicious, looked him up and down, and said to him, "And my blade? Shall it be yours, then?"

"Only as you would wield it, Master Gambol."

"And my little bag of coin, shall it be divvied up meanly 'twixt all you fellows, so that not half a crown remains to me?"

"What, are we a city of pigs, that we must portion our slop equally between us? By my troth, good Master Gambol: that purse and all it contains is Gambol's gold; and their owner, as fine a Gambler of Gold as ever I happed across. Should ye seek to horde to yourself a veritable cache of golden coins collected through our various misadventures, after the better part has been duly dispersed to penury, why, they should stick yours to the end, and I myself will lay my solemn oath over them, that no man shall struck his fingers through them but as you have expressly permitted it. For my part, I am no purse-peek, and will not force free men's hands nor twist their consciences, as long as they leave mine own in sovereign peace."

Now I weighed, Sir Scholar, my options, and it seemed to me that the land lay thus: I could go my own way, divest this so-called Robin Hood of his bow and arrows, and take the twin blades with me to be sure I would not be ambushed by behind, and find me a grotto or the hollow bole of a tree wherein to live, as I had previously proposed, in holy reclusion, contemplating the nature of things to my spirit's content (for I was assured these would be my meditations in solitude) while living slim off the land; or I could join this Robin Hood and see where and how he dwelt, and divert myself at his company and his board, and perchance make me some riches through him, and so earn myself a vehicle of reentry into society when opinion had cooled against my blood (so little did I understand then the matter that has since and presently been made so appallingly plain).

And so the question was settled to my approval, and we gave each other our hand in signification of concord, and I was made one of those that Robin called his "Merry Men." Yet that was later, Sir Scholar, for in the moment, we but left that river to sit a while on dry land, where we built us a fire to dry our garb and divided my meaty pie in twain. And as we thus brake bread and made good of that shared meal, we entered deep into conversation. At first he asked me much and was a ready listener, and I, mistaking his silence, did tell him aught of me about which to any other I should have kept fast mum. As for instance that I played at being converted for sake of convenience and self-defense, about which he did scold me, smiling all the while, saying that it did not befit a man to falsify his spirit with mask and make-up.

"I scruple to say it, Master Robin, but this sounds as hypocrisy from your lips; for 'tis bruited about that you are the veritable master of disguises."

And he with that twinkle of his eye did retort, "Each mask Robin wears is but Robin's face again to those who know him, and never once has he lied by guise or fashion. Take that as my own dear confession, Father Gamblegold; for if ye would feint to be a Christian, why not live fuller to the role? I say, cease your gambols o'er these infertile fields of human fantasy, and make your act anew in Christ. 'Twill be God's will then to succor you, that, in this greater gamble, you might enjoy in full what you have so far bartered by half."

But I retorted that I would peddle whate'er counterfeit was needful to keep my skin on my back.

"That is taxing Soul to pay Body, Master Pedlar, and I wish you well of it, though I fancy you shall be the poorer withal. But come, let us now rise and go, for the greenwood is calling, and it shall teach us what we cannot elsewise learn. For I say, ne'er a finer master of virtue, professor of self-reflection, trainer in physical health, preceptor in spiritual growth, and educator in true economy has God made upon his green earth than this Sherwood forest, and I faithfully trust it shall do for you what my poor provocations cannot, instructing you, my good Pedlar Gamblegold, to the truer merchandise you should be trading."

And with this he did leave the matter off—and I got me my name and my title, the ones that he stuck on me and that I have in consternation worn amongst his Merry Men since.

I was long with him. Now, Sir Scholar, you know me for a wagging tongue, but from then on 'twas not I as did the most speechifying, but he. *Ab uno disce omnes:* once he said to me, as we were discoursing on a forest path, "See ye there, yon ant pile? Hours have I lain on this forest floor, belly down like a toad, to watch what those pismires got up to passing under my nose.

And I have seen wonders, as would any man who had patience enough to mark profundity 'neath the simple things. I will tell to you but one: All know how these bugs will build roads and pass in file for miles in length; but I have by and by spied an ant that does not pursue the way of his brethren, but, emerging from his grounded castle, does go his own true way, and breaks from those grinding marches. And he will gambol on for distances, and go about his chosen course as he please, until he stumble on food, and, beseeking himself no doubt a fine place to dine, shall port it back to the hill. And lo! but all his brothers, seeing the plenty his independence has discovered, follow the trail that he has forged. Now I ask you, Master Pedlar—do you think that our friend and vagabond, once these others have fashioned their tired old one-af-ter-another, shall put himself in straits with them and go the way that they are going, and that, once having been a free and liberal ant, shall now manacle himself to become but another mechanic and line-abider? Doubt it, friend, doubt it true. But woe to the hill if he should do so! for just as the many, if they disperse upon a thousand paths, will bring dissolution and ruin to the colony, so the loner if he coalesce shall pluck out from the whole its very eyes, mind and seeking fantasy. Each to his God-given place!"

Yes, Sir Scholar, I know 'tis a queer view, and speaks much to his sense of order, which I found hard of the grasping. And from this, he proceeded to speak of the threefold history of society. Threefold, Sir Scholar, for there are three forms of society—the monarchical, the aristocratic, and the democratic, in that order: for kingship cedes ever to the rule of few, and the rule of few cedes ever to the rule of many, and rule of the many dissolves always to rule of a single head once again in the form of kingship or tyranny, which is a corrupt kind of kingship. And the course from kingship to tyranny is a decline from the better to the worse, while the birth of kingship from tyranny is ascent to the better. But this last is rare, and the mystery is that man's societies tend ever to sink and not to rise. So far we fall within the classic orbit. But Robin told me that the driving force behind this decline of society is combined *Godlessness* and *envy*; for, said he, the human being, forgetting the divine law and craving what is not his own whether he merits it or nay, will bow to the death Adam brought into the world and succumb to the sin of Cain, and o'erthrow

the standing order within his sphere, be it great or small. And this is a punctuated decline, for at first it is the several already endowed with power that seek
to steer the ship of state along their self-chosen paths. But by and by the many
join together in a violent majority and, seeking resentfully to grasp the fine
things that have been restricted to the few, thus debase the whole, mobbing
together to fragment the crown from one into multitude, feeling it their right
to do so. Yet almost so soon as they have done so, but a single or a handful of
generations hence, some few rich or potent, seeing that the many are ruling
where they hold by rights they should, will o'erthrow the masses or elsewise
seize control of them. And it is an easy thing for a single bad ambitious clique
to grasp the reins of ochlocracy and to put some Antichrist in the seat as its
rider and master. Thus it is that men, forgetting God, seek their worldly good,
guided on by a worldly master, and are by envy impelled to precipitate the fall
of human societies—envy for what each does not have and yet craves to have.

Now, Robin was as right a monarchist as any man of the king, and held by
the King—the true King, mind you—to his dying day. But to my estimations,
in this he erred, for every king, being but a man, is unfit to rule a people; it
must be the philosophers that rule, lest ye shall see time and time again such
travesties as that which have hounded and injured me to this very moment.
And barring that—for it is hard to convince the philosophers to rule, and
harder still to convince ignorant men to obey them—barring that, I say, let
democracy govern; for 'tis workaday jealousy of common rights which one has
and would not like to lose, which impels the ascent from the lowest to the
highest; so if every man but guards his rights as a man, then the common order
will be preserved.

But my own conclusions aside, all this Robin drew out of an ant hill. Then
hear the myth he taught me of a spirit he called *Amnesia*, which, he said, was
granted to mankind as a sort of guardian angel by God himself. She was, he
told me in a parable, the only spirit to bear young, and was indeed eternal preg-
nant, she being the mistress and companion of all poets and musicians and
makers among men. He spoke to me of two kinds of man, and likened them to
a plate and a sieve; for he who recalls everything to himself is as the plate, which
retains all that falls upon it, the bone, the pit and the corrupted meat together

with the sumptuous and nourishing, 'til a man can make nothing of the heaped and rotting pile that results but throw it all out, or eats it to the detriment of his digestion; while he who forgets is as the sieve, that lets much fall through into his depths, that one might see the more clearly what is left. Or again, he said that these two kinds of person are like a pitchy trunk of tree on the one hand, and a spider on the other: the first catches everything that flies its way, whether carried by wind or breath or wings, while the other, being small and imperfect, must build itself beauteous nets in the very air if it is to capture anything at all, and lets the superfluous through to favor the substantial.

Now this was a doctrine much fascinating to me, Sir Scholar, for I have been blessed since my boyhood with a perfect memory, and can present to myself any moment of my past in completion. Hear what I said to you some time ago, precisely as I said it:

I say, this universe is uncreated. You say it was created, but I say—if this universe was created, then you must account for a thousand other facts that do not jive with your notion. For instance, the corruption of man, the imperfection of matter, the limitations of human reason, and most particularly, the rule of fortune, or that component in things which is not susceptible of man's prevision. For if our universe was created, it was created either by a perfect being or an imperfect. And in the latter case, you have explained nothing without surplus, for it would suffice to say, that this universe is imperfect and eternal, rather than adding to an imperfect and temporal universe, a god who is imperfect and eternal. And if your creator is perfect, then you must explain, why is his creation then not perfect? You say it is perfect in the whole, but not in the part? Well and good, but still you admit that imperfection exists—the which cannot be, if your god is perfect. For it is impossible to attribute to perfection, whatever is imperfect.

And so you see, Sir Scholar, that my memory is impeccable. Whereas Robin Hood always admitted the flaw of his own, and liked even to mock at himself, calling himself "Old Man Leaky Top," and referred to himself often a favorite of Amnesia's.

Yes, Sir Scholar, you speak the matter squarely and fairly; there are sound objections to his course of argument, and many times I did present them to him. To wit: that the human being losing his memory should, like the senile elderly, be incapable even of human speech, so that to call him a creative human being would be a kind of folly or an ugly jest; or that any right inspiration requires as well that one perceives the past with clarity, and the more perfect his recollection the more perfect his inspiration. But he would just laugh at these counterarguments, and call me logic chopper, thanking me for so succinctly proving his point.

But my cyclical view of things, Sir Scholar, is one of the principal points that I owe most to Robin Hood; for though he himself did hold in accordance with his faith that this world was a thing fashioned at a word by God and set upon a divine purpose, I inferred from his over-Christianized beliefs that all the world's a great cycle, or a spiral, that flies from order to disorder and back again, on a millennial and super-millennial pendulum, or a cosmic beast that reduces itself to rubble and dust and from its own ash is born once again like the Phoenix. But here is the mystery of it, Sir Scholar, which I have sought these many years since the death of Robin Hood to penetrate, without e'er being able: that this cycle cannot repeat itself perfectly, for, just as a year is never identical to any other, but each one comes with its own spirit and quality, so the cosmic year must be non-identical to each other; and this is shown also by the fact that in the world there exists never a perfect circle, but only ovular shapes resembling perfection, so that we may induce that any cycle cannot be a true ring save insofar as it be a ring that does not join with itself, or in other words (and adding to pure geometry the dimension of time) a spiral. Yet it would seem impossible, Sir Scholar, that the spiral could present any novelty, if the world has existed for an eternity; for eternity must mean as well that there has been time abundant for the expression of every realizable possibility. So the world must have begun at some inscrutable and definite moment. And if it began, then must it end. And if this is so, then the world's a race 'twixt time and matter, to see which shall exhaust itself the first; or put otherwise—there is possibility yet that the world will extinguish in the end. And that is a terrible thought, you will allow, though for that does not make itself less plausible, for the philosopher knows that there are terrible truths, and shrinks not from grasping them when they appear to him clearly and distinctly. So let us also resist the desire to find some compensation in this world, such as, that if the world may end, yet then it may also become divine in some way, and we wretched minuscule participants in it might pare our addition to its wondrous development, or perhaps may even ourselves some way become divine in the course of its many windings ere the end. But there is this problem withal: that the world cannot have had a beginning, for if it began then something brought it into being, which means that something existed before it, which means that what had beginning was only a part of the whole, which we call world, and not the whole itself; but if so, then the whole is eternal, and there can be no cosmic cycle save that which repeats itself perfectly for eternity, the which we have seen is in evident contrast to everything that we perceive, and so our pure reason must stand against our empirical reason. Then the only thought that might reconcile all these difficulties is that I heard proposed by Robin himself, which I will tell you here, in words my own: as time is in principle eternal, and all things upheld in their continued being by some Creator who, from love, will not destroy aught he has made, then possibility itself must be infinite, and the world itself reborn and renewed constantly of an unfathomable principle of divine creativity.

The Pinder

Ye'd heark once more what mischief Robin Hood got up to that day ere Michaelmas, would ye? That's a tale as ne'er wears thin. By my troth, I swear Robin Hood was a madcap. That day was one of the brashest I have seen of many in his company. Nay, friend, I say "company" to purpose: for ne'er I served Robin, but even bested him and his entire band of merry fools, one af'er another, on many occasions, as I have many times related. I know I look it not, old man that I am, but I was a strapping young buck once upon a yester. Aye, Robin owed me more'n I him, and that's solid fact, and all knew it. But he was a madcap, and no doubt, and now I will relate you again the solid proof of it.

Now he and I were set out in the wood to get us some meat from the hides of the King's deer and had been some vain hours o'the tracks of a herd of 'em, though I am a keen tracker of beast and men. And I could see that Robin was grown restless i'the hunt, for he dearly despised exertion, and was in general slothy and a bedabout, and atimes had little patience enow. I reminded him that the welfare of the men depended upon our venery, but 'twas of no use, and I knowed it. Nonetheless I am a stubborn crumpet and I followed the tracks of those deer unto the last, when I heard Robin say, "Methinks I shall go to prayer."

What prayer, I asked him, and what was he blathering about?

"Naturally," says he, "but to my devotions to Mary."

Now, I was some moments digesting this, and stared at him in the meanwhile, to find if he was jesting, but I saw him smiling as broad as the day itself. And I said to him, "Robin Hood, ye are wood mad. The Sheriff has men scouting ye out in all of Nottinghamshire, to speak nothing of the town itself and the building you propose, which, I should remind ye, is right at the heart of it. Ye should be walking straight into a prison cell, and your name craft o'er its door!"

"Nothing thus, master George," said he, "and I shall tell ye why: that a man who is looking large for another will fail to see what hides under his nose."

Now this seemed to me a barmy logic, but I held my tongue, for I kenned it useless arguing with Robin Hood in such a fey mood. And so I turned with him, and followed him toward the edge of Sherwood, where he was set by all determination to go, Cernunnos help us. Nor did we speak on that way, but he was preoccupied with his goal, and I much worried about the same, and much concerned with finding me a way to alter his course and turm him round. And I tried saying that we had not yet got us venison to provender the men; but he said, "Lacking meat, they shall better learn the nuts and fruits and toadstools of the wood, and that will be little harm to them and much boon to us." And by Cernunnos, he began to whistle.

Now I was right peeved, and all the more so, when he said, as I did loathe to hear him say, "Ah, Georgy, but my maiden is of a beauty such as to make a man turn in his boots."

"Ye are immedicable fond," said I, but Robin Hood only laughed, and would have strode on, had it not come to me in that moment, all in a flash, how I might turn him back round. "Tell ye what," I said to him, stopping, so that he must stop as well. "Methinks ye are a jolterhead to be going as ye are; but I know I cannot stop you, mule that ye be. So reck well: let us play a little at dice, and if they turn in your favor, then by Cernunnos, I shall go with you wherever you will, here, there, or the isles of the dead; yet if they are in my favor, then you abandon this insanity, and we shall go and gather us some mushrooms in lieu of our neglected carrion."

And Robin Hood, who was mad for dice and could ne'er naysay a game, was thus snared hard in my trap. He said to me, "By my faith, George-a-Greene, this notion likes me well!" And so we sat down there on a flat spot barren of undergrowth, and got us out my pair of lucky dice, and took to shooting.

Now, I had on me a purse half full of coin, and Robin Hood the same, and it was much back and forth between us for a time, to see whose bag would fill and whose would empty. But eftsoons I saw my stash exhausting, until it had dwindled down to naught but a lone coin. I set it boldly forth, and threw the dice over it, and found it vanquished.

"There," said he, "the matter's made. 'Tis Nottingham that calls."

But I said, "Nay, yet bear with me another toss."

"Ye've nothing to put to it," protested he.

"On the contrary," said I, "but I've this." And I laid out against his pile of coin my special talisman—that which I later lost, wellaway! 'Twas thanks to Robin and his antics that I lost it, and my life has been malisoned since. 'Twas a curled rabbit's foot with a mock of white fur on black, a periapt of exceptional virtues, which I had from a hex in the hills, and I have never since seen its like. "This foot and your gains, and then we shall see."

But he drew back, signing himself with the cross and saying, "Nay, George-a-Greene, I will not cast against such paynim amulets."

"No doubt!" mocked I, "For despite your Christian tomfoolery, ye ween them to be of a power. Come now, my foot against but a single of your coins. Or are ye superstitious of it?" And I saw that this had done the trick, for he was resolved now to misprove me. So he took up the bones and cast 'em o'er the pile, and my furry foot carried it. So I took my coin and my paw and put the first back to play and the second back to pocket. That coin made two, and two made four; and it was so until the pile afore him had dwindled to feed mine own, and he had before him only a single coin.

And I said to him, "Master Robin, keep your last coin, but I entreat you, come with me back into the wood. 'Tis time we were about our harvest."

And he responded, "Master George, the game's not over till there's nothing more to stake."

So I threw me the dice, and by Cernunnos, if I didn't win it! And I said to him, "I've won clear now, Robin, with no remainder, and do intend to make good on my claim."

But Robin Hood snatched up a satchel's worth of gold and leapt to his feet, even as I did the same. "Od, I've won!" said I again, hotly now; but he said, "Doxies do not wait on dice, Georgy," and turned to go. And I tried to seize him bodily, for I was irate with him, but he slipped away from me like a fish and ran on down the way. And I ran after him, calling out, "By Cernunnos, Robin Hood, I've won, and ye can't deny it!"

And he responded, "May be—but ye are not so swift as I am!"

And this was true, for he was yare as a squirrel. I could have thrashed him fifteen times on fifteen had he been within my reach, but just so it was as a badger pursuing a hare. So that I gave up the chase in little time, and, furious now, for I could hear him laughing up ahead, I bid him a hard *vale*, and I turned me back to Sherwood.

I was some time working my way back to our camp, and fuming at the trees for the slyness that had been perpetrated against me. And who knows why, but at a certain point I bethought me, and sat me down against a tree trunk, and took to flinging stones through the brush. I know not how long I was at that pastime, but suddenly I heard a yelp on the other side of the bushes, and a boy burst through, holding his eye where a stone I had cast had struck him. I got me up and asked him what in the world he was doing there, but he ran up to me and told me he was a page of lord Such and Such and that he had come to inform me that Robin had got himself into a pretty bind in Nottingham. Well you can be sure I cursed Robin's rotten name, but did get me on to the town to succor him, for I was foolish in those days and yet believed it profit a man to aid his fellows. The truth is that each man must do for himself, and be damned every other. But this I learned the hard way, I say, and at that time I made haste to Nottingham.

I came to town and cast through. I will not lie, I was skirty, for it is a surreal thing, walking where ye are a universally reproved enemy. And I imagined me that dunce, Robin Hood, who must have walked those streets as if they had been the very streets of his home town, and he a dignitary amongst them. And by my troth thinking that got me riled again, so that I might have beat who looked at me with crossed eyes.

Now I came to the house wherein dwelt his Magdalene, the wife of the Norman lord. I was in the nick of time, for as I rounded the corner I saw the Sheriff's men entering in through the doors. Cursing Robin Hood, I looked up to see if I could not guess the chamber of the Lady Marian; and divined it by the candle burning there in midday. I drew me an arrow and sent it clean in through a pane. I warrant that if the glass shattering did not wake the whole neighborhood then the shrieks of the trull within did to a certainty; and sure enough, but the cockalorum himself popped out there at the balcony, half dressed and all disheveled.

"Curse ye for a gull, Robin, they're in the very damned house to take ye! Get ye down, or it means a drubbing for you!"

"And how am I supposed to get down this-a-way?" he cried, all a panic.

"Did ye not get up that-a-way?" I retorted, much wroth; but he said he had not, but had crept in through a scullery, for he knew one of the hand-maids there surpassingly well.

"Damn you, Robin Hood, ye are ever the scapegrace! Jump, jump, and I shall have to catch ye!" And I put up my bow and widened my arms, to show him I would grab him as he fell.

The fool barely had mind enough to toss down his weapons ere he leapt down himself, and by my troth I almost missed him, and it would have been a pretty sight indeed with him broke on the thoroughfare and the guards about him like wasps, but somehow I managed it. I snatched him up out of air, and was not much emburdened by it, for he was a slight and scrawny man. Then we were away, and running down the street, and fled down a side alley to evade the sight of our foes. I spied me a nook between some buildings, and bethought me well, and we slipped in there and found a hidden place behind some scullery doors, where Robin could dress himself again; for a half-naked man may as well have been wearing crimson. And once he was again decently appareled we went out, and we all eyes; but they spotted us anyway, and were quick upon us. Wanion mine! for we had to make a dead break to the edge of the forest, and it was in this mad dash that I lost my foot, nor in the wrath that pursued us could ever get back to find me it.

Yet it must have shown me one last favor, for we somehow outpaced our foes and made it back to the refuge of the wood. Well you can be sure I gave him a sore thrashing for the trouble he'd put me to, and he bore the signs of it, but he told the men it had been a tussle with a guardsman that had so reduced him. And he recounted the whole tale with endless embellishments, how we killed a dozen men to get back to the wood. Every arrow we had ere spent on our venery that was lost now in the brambles he ascribed to battlement, and he counted these barbs each one as sunk into a Norman's heart. And he much diverted the idiots of Sherwood by describing me as his suitor, who came under his window strumming a string and cawing like a minstrel, so that he could do nothing other than descend to me, seeing as how I was too massy to get up to him. He knew he was safe then, for I would not dare smack him in the company of his rag-a-tags. That was always his way—loss and boast, loss and boast! Ne'er met a man as got through life making so much of so little, like a spindstress weaving gold from straw. But be ye not fooled by the old tales, and take it from one as knew him: that Robin Hood was a beast of a man in his heart, a harepig and not a man at all. Take it from one as knew him.

Gilbert with the White Hand

ah hah! By Jove, the very truth's in it, my friend. What is it they say? *In vino veritas—et gloria in excelsis Deo!* Spill out another mug of ale; I am in good spirits this day, and would give 'em good company.

Nay, I solemnly avow it: never have there been gestes to match those of Robin Hood! On this I could ante my honor itself. In boldness and mirth he hath never known a peer; take this, friend, from one who is wanting in neither quality! Oh, yea, I knew him well, as well as any man save Little John. Why, I was with him through all the long dark years toward the end, when Jack Lack-a-land was making good on his hereditary dearth and venting his malevolence left and right upon the barons. Ne'er did a king of England cultivate for himself so many enemies, but I do suspect His Majesty's scrawny heel carried no spine as deep as one named Rob. For a baron is easy work by the comparison: it suffices (let us say for the sake of argument) to imprison the baroness and baronet unto their demising, and send the baron himself to follow their example in exile. Egad, of course I speak conjecturally! Think you I would impugn the name of our much beloved King? But say: what's a mere baron? Why, against the thief of Sherwood, whom not even the wolves could track... I swear our cad Sheriff and his scoundrel of a deputy must have been tormented by the Crown for the years they failed to catch Rob in their hunt. At least the Sheriff was made to sweat a bit, the pig, before all the tributes that were heaped upon him at the tail of his life. I hear he passed but lately, and left a sum of money to pay for prayers on his soul. No one e'er told him that while even a pope might be bribed, never God.

How now? And all the Sheriff's men, you say? Ah, not so hasty with your tongue, friend! I myself was one of the Sheriff's busybodies. Did ye not know it? Aye indeed, I was years a ranger in his close employ, and 'twas by that very channel I met Robin Hood as he poached deer in the deeper woods. Nay, he was alone at the time, for much he loved to rove by himself through the green-wood, and many a scrape he got himself into by reason of this penchant for solitude. Scrapes, I say, but no more than that: never met a man who bled so much but scarred so little! Truly, it did lead us to suspect, until the day of his very capture, that there were no living man could murther Robin Hood. Yet I lost me count of the times we heard his horn ringing through the greenwood, calling us hence to his rescue. 'Twas a man who danced the razor's edge, Robin was. And a good thing that he almost always went out with John either in his company or trailing him, for elsewise, methinks this world would have been shorn of Robin Hood a mite too soon!

His equal among us? I shall surprise you, my fine and upstanding man, and tell you that I have never seen Robin Hood so tried as by a monk. Nay, I do not mean only physically—there were several among us who had him at arms, Little John and I myself (which success I owe perchance to my being gauche), though not Apollo himself could have bested him at bowfare—but I mean rather in that at which Robin excelled all the creatures of this merry earth: in wit, my friend, in wit.

Yet it was indeed the question of strength that first led us to it. (Revive my flagging cup, I say, and do not stop your pouring until like Vesuvius it runneth over!) I remember me the day as though 'twer yester, though in truth some twain decades have run the gauntlet since. Heed me now, friend: you can chase the curtails of Father Time all you would, but he will outpace you! Now, this day in question, they (by which I mean the inseparables, Robin and John) had just returned from an escapade with a certain shepherd. Seems that they had

come upon this venerable ancient a-lolling on the earth and slumbering in the
glow of the midday sun beside a great amphora crooked in his arms and a
haversack beneath his head, and a curious Robin, prodding him with his foot,
had awakened him to know what the jug and the sack contained. He, spry as a
goat and with a goatish face to boot, leapt up to his feet and began to caper
about in a rage at having been so misused, lifting high into the air a certain vine-
wound crook as in warning. I was not in my person present for this event, so I
shall not recount to you word for word what passed between them, but I know
this much: that when Robin again requested intelligence on the contents of
yon vessel, old Billy flared like a flame and refused to tell him, menacing him
even with a thrashing, and seeking to beat him about the head, at which Robin
drew his long-hilted sword and slashed the brandished crook in twain.

Our good pan fell into a veritable rage at the which, and called Robin himself a crook, and a coward to boot, and a wealth of other pesky names, to
which I do fancy our leader responded, as was his wont at such abuses, with
laughter and a clever return; and it would appear that Little John, whose humor was of another bent, demanded recompense of the man for his temper in
intelligence on the contents of jug and sack. And when he refused to speak
on't, nor to demonstrate to his contestors what these recipients contained,
Robin Hood was set to leave him, for 'twas his general policy to leave well
enough alone when there were no clear cause to intervene; but the fellow set
upon Little John with hoof and hand and a remarkable strength, and it was all
our giant companion could do to set him back down upon the same plot of
ground from whence he had arisen. Upon so achieving victory, Little John
knelt to rummage in the mystery goods of his vanquished opponent, only to
find the jug voided of its wine, and the sack a home to crumb-carrying ants; at
which discovery, the shepherd set to mocking them with vicious words. But
Robin announced with a laugh that he had new vintage and daily bread and
needed not the old, stale and outworn as it was; and our two victors set the
man packing and turned forth again into the wilds, and by and by to the camp,
where Robin set to recounting his adventures.

Upon so regaling us, and much vaunting Little John's victory o'er the
goat, many a murmuring voice disputed, indicating that the dotage of the

goatherd and his lack of company had surely made him but low-hanging fruit
for that shepherd to pluck. But Robin hotly contested them, saying that there
was no man alive as could stand against John Little in single combat, and that
he himself would stand as judge in any agon that might prove him contrary.
At the which there was much hot debate on this point—though toothless I
should warrant, for indeed no man of our company would have dared to challenge Little John, what with his seven feet and his deadly cudgel! But then
David of Doncaster, who had but freshly joined our ranks, and who was (as
the very day we found him) a sight too much in his beer (though for the nonce
at least miraculously awake) did rise up there to declaim that he knew a man
Little John could never fell. Much jeering did he receive for this outburst, but
he stood stalwartly beside his word, shouting that this man he intended could
not be swept to ground by hook or crook, not even by one so giant as our dear
companion and second-in-command, tiny Jack. Robin demanded to know
the name of this wond'rous human boulder, and David did reply that 'twas
one cowled friar of a chapel not far distant, stood in Sherwood itself; a monk
as wide as an ancestral oak and as stolid besides, with a strength superhuman
in its quality. This specification met with much reproach that no monk
should be subjected to violent hands, nor should know how to meet force
with force; but David did avow that this monk was no monk at all but a criminal rascal who had drawn the cowl about his compromised visage to avoid the
law's espying his features. Now, we were late to learn that all of this was but
invention and fourberie on Dave's part, for he had a grudge against this monk
for reasons that would soon be made plain; but at the time it riled us fiercely.

I recall not from whom the subsequent incitement came, but 'twas soon
urged upon us that we rise and go at once to seek us out this crooked eremite
in his mahogany guise. I warrant that David was not the only one that ex-
ceeded in his drink that day, but methinks we had all been a-toping a touch
toward excess, for we had in a most rare turn of events come across ale that
very afternoon (compliments of a wealthy merchant of Barnsdale), and were
much engaged in connoisseur-wise trying its quality. (The which reminds me:
tip more ale in this vessel as well, I say, for I would much like to better test its
quality!) 'Twas rare, I say, but now and again our merry men grew very merry

indeed—save Robin, whose was the sob'rest head I ever met (even when he did partake!), and John, which was abstemious as a rook. And soon in such a state we were all of us carried away in a veritable enthusiasm to find us this monk and sink John into a tussle with'm, and bets were a-flying amongst us, and before I knew what had come over us, we were storming away, wending through the truewood, led on by none other than David himself, who seemed determined as ne'er I had seen him before nor ever have seen him since, his arm lifted forth above him and his finger bravely pointing out the direction, as though he led no woody prank, but a veritable military expedition into enemy lands. Alas, I do reckon that, had he only scried it, the beating he was to gain for his troubles might have had a smothering effect on his willfulness.

The road was lengthier than David had intimated, and by and by the excitement had died down and the edge of the ale departed, and much was the muttering had begun to grow among us that we were being led on a wild monk chase. David was not well known to us yet, and needs must have felt the heat of his position, for by and by he began to sweat like a dog, glancing this way and that as if he had forgotten himself the road. Almost we abandoned the hunt altogether, but just as we had come upon the decision to send David and his lone cenobite arm in arm to Hades, lo! we came upon a greensward as handsome as any I have seen, with a runnel there edging it with water clear as heaven, and a thatched hut upon its corner—the very portrait of bucolic tranquillity! And there beside the hut, toiling diligent on all fours like a hog in mire, the man whose reputation had drawn us hence, in the midst of such a group of dogs as I have never beheld. There were ten of them if there was one, of every conceivable color, size and race, and some were running to and fro in search of food, and some were at each other viciously, and some were lazing about and panting in the sun. David informed us that this was the one we sought, and we advanced upon him, though slowly, for fear of his hounds.

The dogs noted us at once and set up a fearsome racket, enough to make a man freeze in his bones, and for a moment it was as though they would set on us and rip us to shreds; but their master whistled to them and they held fast, whimpering and whining for the remainder of our discourses. As for the man himself, he rose up as he saw us approaching, and methought his back and his knees seemed a trifle stiff for one who was to topple over John Little; yea, and his paunch a pinch rotund. Set he his one muddied hand upon his robèd hip, and leaned out over his hoe with his other, and, mouth agape to show tiny teeth amidst a somewhat trimmed beard, called out, in tones most incivil, "Stand ye fast, ye bandits, for I am but an eremite living in this glade alone and possess here with me nothing but my curs and what else ye see, and what I can gain by my singular weary labors. I have nothing ye would like."

At which Robin, advanced and laughing, called back at him, "'Tis mean hospitality to deny one's guests the pleasure of deciding for themselves what they should or should not desire. But peace, good Friar, for we are in no vein to rob you."

"'Tis false, ye bandit!" replied he loudly, "for ye have robbed me already—"

"—I protest, good Brother, not a man among us has not lain finger on your goods!" cried Robin, much surprised.

"—robbed me, I say, of my peace of mind, my silence, and a parcel already of my precious time, which I would fain dedicate to my potatoes here, the which want tucking in."

At this, one of our men cried out, "Do say, dear friar, are they fatigued by their daily labors, that they are now to be put to bed?"

"Aye, 'tis verily so," reposted the friar solemnly, his fat cheeks growing red in ire, "for if there's not earth enough over them then they will wake too soon and end all hollow stem and no fleshy bulbs—rotten of substance, like many a trespasser as has troubled my peace. But pray, if you desire an education in keeping tubers, do proceed hence, good bandit, and I shall tuck you in aside them to show you how 'tis done."

Robin again did laugh, and said, "Calm, Brother Tuck! for we have no will to irk you. We are but seeking us a certain friar of these parts, that was criminal, but turned monk to save his skin—a coward vested in the holy robes of a man of God. I do not suppose you could point us the way to your vagrant brethren, who is said to loiter in these parts, that we might set what is crooked to the straight and narrow?"

"The only monk as lives in these parts stands before you now."

"Alack, the straight and narrow would somewhat try your frame!" exclaimed Robin with a laugh, lifting his arms as though in hypothetic measurement, and the fat friar heaved up indignant at this, and retorted, "If ye mean to insinuate something against my character or my past, ye hasty gingerbeard, then I say, do not stand on ceremony so, but speak the charge open 'neath God's blue sky, and we shall see how much is in it!"

"'Twas only your impressive stature, good Friar, I mean to implicate. For the rest, I toss no accusations save as I've the merit of proof," retorted Robin. "We shall set this matter to trial, good brother, and see what verdict is to be drawn. I call to first testimony one David of Doncaster.—David? I say, David?—Bah, and where has he got to, the gadabout?"

But Robin twisted hither and thither in vain: for indeed our companion had quite dematerialized into the wood, evidently almost so soon as we had entered into the greensward, though not a man of us had seen him go. We all looked about us in amazement, and the friar alone seemed most pleased. He set up a hearty laugh and shook his tonsured head. "Ho ho! Many a fool has stumbled my way, Master Bandit," cried he, "but none ever towed in his trail an imaginary friend! This is a diverting novelty and no doubt!"

To which Robin quoth, somewhat irked, "The fellow in question is as solid as you or me, good brother, on my word. Why, he set us upon you like a tinchel round a deer, and tinked the bell to set us on our way, and indeed had tinkered the whole expedition together to begin with; and when I catch him, I swear I shall tink him straight through, the tinkerer, to discover just what's misfit in his head—"

And the monk: "Tell ye what, master bandit: get ye smartly hence to seek this ghost of yours, and may his vap'rous trail lead ye over a cliff fall. Leave me to my peace and my potatoes."

But Robin spun round, himself regained and smiling, and wagged a finger in the face of the fat friar. "Nay! for the trial is not over, good monk, though the witness be lacking. Still I have questions enow for you to answer, to see of what metal you are cast. And since you have ordered me to deliver my charges plainly, I shall sing them clear as a lark, and it please you. Question the first: you bear with you a fine heavy paunch, brother monk, such as it is vain for you to tuck in as you have done your potatoes; is that not a weight inopportune for a man who dedicates himself to God?"

And the monk: "'Tis God Himself has blessed me with such abundance, ye impious scoundrel. Get ye hence, and fast yourself straight through your last breath for all I care."

And Robin: "A solid answer from a solid source, I deny it not! And redolent moreover of Christian gratitude for divine gifts. I say, my men, his soul cannot be wrought of iron, for already with this reposte he shines a fairer luster than that. Then meet my question the second, good Brother Tuck: is that the telltale scent of ale I do perceive riding upon your breath, suggested as well by yon flaccid wineskin, and does this not betray somewhat a wont of Godly sobriety?"

So the monk: "He that drinks oft, sleeps much; and he that sleeps much, sins little. Now, by my selfsame beer, do bear yourself kindly from my presence and back into yon wood, where I invite ye to drink ale or wine or hemlock to your taste, until you sleep as sound as my potatoes under the very folds of the earth!"

Then Robin: "Had I found you snoring in the straw, this justification would have driven keener, good friar. But once again I shall brotherly take the point, for it be Christian indeed to evade the wages of sin by means most genial to each of us. I say, steel ne'er gleamed so fair as this. Thus far, friends, I find this man, if not guiltless, then of quite repentable material! Next, good Brother, answer me this third query: 'twould seem you are somewhat lacking in fraternal hospitality and charity; yet this does not accord with your sackcloth oaths. Or say, do I mistake me?"

The monk replied: "'Tis St. Paul who educates us to send rascals to the devil if they will not reform, so that they by the vile experience of the heavy yoke of the Evil One shall come piously to beg conduct again upon Christ's paths. Then I say again, in all Christian love: get ye hence to the old deuce and may ye singe your tails to a Christian nub and weld your forked tongue to an honest singularity, that when ye come before me a second time you have more grace to show for it!"

But Robin: "He knows the Good Book, does our good monk, both in word and in interpretation! That is little ill indeed, and I even wager 'tis right

Christian (alack, more in the theory than in the practice!). I say, copper were a metal too common for this. At the same time, even the hounds of Hell know their Scripture. Well, good scholar, in response to your pious wish, I shall change ye scripture for scripture: for while St. Paul hath spoken the Lord's own truth, the Lord Himself hath instructed us to be innocent as doves and sly as serpents. Thus my tailfeathers and my twain tongue alike I shall preserve, with the blessings of God."

The monk then cried: "This hypocrisy becomes ye, greencloth, for you are of the right hue for the latter beast, and flighty and airheaded as the former."

At which Robin declaimed: "And you, my good friar, are as irascible as a bear—a beast to whose mimic we Christians were never called. This forms indeed the pith of my fourth question to you: for I do say, good Friar Tuck, that I never met a man of God so lashing of tongue nor so quick to rage, nor one surrounded by such a host of feisty beasts. Wrath hath no place in Christian meekness, good monk, and I find me much amazed that it should so clearly mar a man of your character and uprightness."

But the monk retorted: "The Lord hath told us to pluck out our eyes should they offend, the which I could not do for reasons both personal and theologic: so I did instead bear my eyes to where they would not be tempted, by the workaday idiocies of our race, to crimes of dear cost to my body and soul. Yet you, kind sir, have in patent want of charity borne temptation before me once again, and by God I should not hesitate to pluck out *your* eyes, and so do both yourself and me a favor—"

And here Little John could not help but intervene, for nothing roused him so as insult and threat against Robin: "Turn from plucking and back to tucking, I do advise you, good Friar!"

The monk turned to him in amazement, saying, "What is that runt of a man?" And Robin answered him, laughing, "This is Little John, Brother, come all this way to try the aforementioned cowled criminal in game of strength, in order to punish a man for idly wearing cloth that is cut for men of purer spirit. For my part, however, I am disposed to consider you falsely charged of identity with that man, for by your answers various to my interrogations, you have proven yourself of finer metal than a hypocrite criminal is like to be. Nay, I do proclaim, you are innocent of the crimes aforetold! A sinner, to be sure, like all men—but one as knows his sinfulness and duly combats it, and thus a man of God withal."

But "Lies!" cried a husky voice in the bosky shades. "For yon monk is as enterprising a sorcerer as any devil e'er was!" All turned in amazement then to find that we had somehow been reunited with David of Doncaster, who, it seems, had elected to take a short snooze in the grass. But he stood now resurrected, a distance apart from us, grass upon his clothes and in his hair, wild as some meadow creature, and was pointing that eternal finger of his, only now in willful accusation. (By the by, follow you now where my own finger intimates, and reunite me, too, with my long-lost ale. For I am sore of heart to be so long without her...)

"David!" cried the monk then, and for once seemed at a loss for words. His manner all transformed, he strode forth into the greensward with arms parted. And John, beholding this scene in the same incredulity we all were feeling, demanded to know if they knew each other.

"*Do* we!" cried David. "This criminal Maelgwn is the very rogue that pawed my sister before cravenly robbing the brown of his current and most weasily garb!"

The monk grew abashed, his arms falling, and said, "Of the former I stand guilty as charged, David, and did indeed take these same vows to right the wrongs I had committed in my unrepentant and reprobate days. Never was I able to apologize to you for it, yet here God has set before me the chance I have long craved and thought should never come to me, to make aright what I have wronged—" but before he could speak another word, David, howling like a wild animal, had charged and tackled him, and the two commenced rolling about in the grassy floor like lovers. All the while they wrastled, the dogs about them began to grow visibly restless, and much did I fear they should come tumbling down upon poor David to rend him to shreds.

Now David was as fine a wrastler as ever I have seen, which was part and parcel of the reason that Robin had elected him to our ranks (as he had bested even Robin in a bout); yet I swear, in a trice the monk had him down, pinned him belly fast against the ground, and with his considerable mass, sat now upon his poor aching back. And from that post, the fat friar cried down to him from a reddened face, "Calm yourself, ye rowdy pup, for if ye will not meet me in Christian forgiveness I shall have no choice but to fore-give you unto the very earth, sitting upon your back until you sink deep into it, to keep us both out of harm—me in body, and you in eternal soul. I ask again your pardon, for I did seduce sweet Alice in my former wild and ignorant youth; grant me now your pardon, lest I mash it out of you as pulp from a spud!"

'Twas not much clear what David replied, for he was grunting into the dust, but all took it as sign of his willing forbearance, the good friar to boot; for he levered up his gross mass, leaving poor David rolling on the earth and complaining of broken ribs and crooked back. And Robin, laughing, said, "Methinks our brother Tinker here has paid the price of his constant tinkering. Meanwhile, Brother Tuck, tucking in his largest tuber yet, gained pardon for transgressions past. All's well in Sherwood. I do declare, good Friar, I am far impressed by the speed of your tongue and the might of your arm. I am the man known as Robin Hood, and by this name, I do solemnly invite you to join our humble forest band. I ween our ways shall please you and accord full with your intentions of sobriety, solitude, and repentance, for in truth, monkwise we do dwell in the dales of Sherwood, far from the world and its mundane travails. We retire ever to the loneliness of the forest, and anchored to its silence do like anchorites dwell. All that we possess we give as alms to the poor, and do oft fast long and hard in patient wait and faithful service to higher laws. By neither charms of politics nor lusts of flesh are we often tempted; human station we do foreswear, and seek us the free patronage of none but the virtuous and the brave. No earthly creature can impel us to bend the knee, but we dwell fast in God's Creation, and reserve all reverences to the Creator, or to whom He has appointed to right station. Humbly do we live, my fair friar, and humbly get us our necessaries. And if I may add a word cut to your own curtail, my courteous, if curt, cur master: little is the ale we see, but are sworn to general continence by dint of circumstance, save on days of feast, as commended by the Lord; and as for company, I reckon you shun it, but hear me well, that ours is merry company indeed, and of such high spirits that I do not doubt but even you, sour though you be, shall learn the art of mirth. Or you shall keep yourself in form, abusing us to our own merriment—for I swear, I never so enjoyed such lashes of the tongue as those you have delivered here!—and thus transform your principal vice into a boon to men.

"So much for the apophatic side of our style. To the affirmative, know this: that our band rights wrongs, gives means to want, succors widows and orphans, tends to the poor, uplifts the downtrodden, remembers the forgot, rights the bent, brings hope to the despairing, faith to the doubting and charity to the needful, embellishes the wilds with good works, gathers mellow fruits with manful care, embraces justice and shuns disorder, profits the virtuous and tames the haughty, fortifies courage and scorns cowardice, masters the passions, trains the body, sharpens the senses, refines the tongue, livens the spirit, elevates the heart, and in all and everything dedicates to God what God has given to man, that man's station in this world be perfected and his fate not forgot in the Kingdom to come.

"What say ye then, good Friar Tuck? Will you or will you not join us?"

The friar gave this some thought in somber reflection, a hand upon his bearded chin, and of a sudden cried, "And what of my hounds, Master Robin? For I cannot leave them behind me!"

"Care with curs is nigh our motto!" laughed Robin, and the friar, smiling broadly, exclaimed, "Then I declare it as good as a done deal, my cowled friend! For I and my curs shall gladly join you!" And, with a great whistle so sharp that it pierced the ears night to deafness, called for his hounds; and a mighty baying rose up in the woods surrounding, deafening us yet still further, and by my troth, but past the ten or so already present, dozens of dogs poured out of the forest like a river of fur and flowed onto the banks of the field there, surrounding us with a din such as I have seldom heard. But Robin rose up with a cry and somehow silenced the hounds to a one, and they sat around us in a circle and looked up at him, and he, laughing heartily, said, "Quotha, good Brother, with such a pack of curs, you are as true a Curtal Friar as ever walked God's green earth! I would wager that with such a canine army not even the Sheriff can dare to besiege us! Come, then, my men! Merry and alert! For today we break fast indeed, and celebrate the coming of a new man to our ranks! Forth, Friar Tuck—for from this moment on, Friar Tuck the Curtal Friar you are and shall ever be! Forth now with us to the green-wood, and alongside your dogs bring your spirits with you, for this day you shall tell a right prayer over our sustenance, and we shall with the blessings of God Almighty eat and drink in hearty thankfulness of all His gifts to us! Away, men, away!"

And so we returned more than twice the number that we had gone, albeit the better part of our new numbers were of the quadruped variety. (Say, double me as well my flagon, friend, for my thirst is not half abated. And cheers to you for't!) Each man of us had a whelp his own by day's end, named and numbered. And we came back to our encampment, where we had left the women and the children and some good men to keep the watch. Imagine their amazement as they saw us coming forth through the greenwood, a flock of hounds racing before us and we ourselves making our merry way, and in our midst as jolly a friar as ever has been seen, laughing and jesting like one of our very own! For though he was sharp of tongue and quick to anger, he was a right jovial sort with his friends, and knew how to turn his keen wit to pleasantries as well as insults. And though he now and then would tussle with one of us, and most times would win, he was from that day on as welcome a member of our little band as any we had claimed, and adorned our acts with commendations to God. For though we had never neglected such things, yet from that moment on, ne'er did we sit to meal nor set to venture, face danger nor feast on provender, without a meet prayer from the lips of the Curtal Friar, of such weight and quality that even the dogs would fall silent to hear it.

Simon Simoner

ah! What nonsense is this, that *you* could have had the better of Robin Hood!

What do you know of Robin Hood to deny it to me?

What do *I* know? Why, as I have told you, I lived with Robin Hood, you balmy fool, and was his man for many a year.

This balderdash again! Simon Simpleton, I do not believe you.

Yet it was so.

And what proof can you give me?

Here, I shall show you right proof. D'you see this little rock? Aye? I carry it with me wherever I go. And have ye any idea what it is? I took this stone, with my own hands, off a piece of the fortress in Sherwood—aye, the one that squats there overlooking St. Mary's Priory. Why, you know, the one that Sheriff de Vieuxpoint built, by will of King John, and which that fiend Sheriff Philip Marc saw finished and manned. Aye, that one, and none other. I sniped this piece of stone of it, after we with Robin Hood drove the soldiers out through constant harassment, and finally drove those soldiers back to Nottingham. We ransacked the place, though they had taken most everything out of it by then, and passed us a merry evening there, roasting the King's own meat in the King's own fire.

Ho, all your claims, riding on a stone the size of a horse turd! It seems one of these damned Robhod tales to me.

Does it, now? Eh, Tom, pass me another mug of beer! Get one for Arthur-a-Bland here, too. That's a dear fellow. He'll be needing his brews to settle him in for a nice long story that's comin'. A *tall tale*, does it seem, Bland my good man? Well, now, say what ye will, but I *was* one of the Green Men.

Well, master Simon, I shall tell ye, if you really were one of Robin Hood's men, then as of this moment, ye are looking at one who is your better.

My better! My better! And just how do you figure that?

Because I was proved your *leader's* better, that's how.

Robin Hood's better! Ho, that is ripe, and no doubt! Listen well, friend, for I shall not say it again. No man was better of Robin Hood.

Ah no?

None! Why, I have seen him heft a log that must have weighed ten stone at least. Why, I have seen him bend a horseshoe with his bare hand! He ran like a deer and he could climb a tree like a squirrel, and that's no lie.

And how was he for warfare, Simon Simpleton?

Why, with the bow he was first man, and everyone knows't. He is the first since Loys the Mighty to shoot an arrow through ten standing halberds, and I know it, for I saw him do it with mine own eyes.

I care not a shite for your bow, your arrow, your ten standing halberds or your eyes, man. I would know, how was he with a man's weapon—how was he with quarterstaff?

Quarterstaff? The best, Master Bland, and none better.

Hey, is that so? And what would *you* say, did ye know that I gave your Robin Hood a whopping welt about his crown, and another about his backside to set him well on his way?

I would say you are fibbing.

Yet 'tis so, Simon. By my balls 'tis so.

And just how did this come about, praytell, that you, Arthur-a-Bland, and Robin Hood joined in combat?

'Twas as I was marching through Sherwood, on my way to the far side. That bastard of a Robin Hood leapt out of the greenwood like a rat from a gutter and stopped me up short, and demanded to know where I was a-going. "Mind your affairs, Master Briarsnatch, and I shall mind me own," I tells him. But he persists—would know where I am going and why, and what I carry with me. "The only thing I have that need concern *you*, is this here pikestaff. For it would be a right pretty thing shoved up your arse," I tell him. And he says to me, "I am Robin Hood, and it is my right to know of all who pass through Sherwood." I say to him, "I give not a piss who ye are or what rights ye claim. I am going now to Nottingham, and I'll not have ye sticklefooting in my way, shite biter that ye are." To the which he replied, "Sir, I shall have ye speak cleanly in this wood, for it is a cleanly place." And I said to him, "God's bones, I'll speak as I see fit. Now get ye gone or I shall tan your hide as clean as yon wood." But bollocks, he would not go! So I took my pikestaff and I beat him about the brow with it, until he was right bloody. "Get ye gone!" I screamed at him again. But he brought up his stave then—a silly little sliver of a thing that must have been no longer than a prick, and said to me, "I shall have you fight me with something more akin to this!" But I was much outraged then, and swung at him once more. Now he was wary, the piker, and we began to battle it out. He was a hand with the stave, I warrant, but I gave him what he'd come for, and proved myself the truer man, and by and by sent him whimpering away into the forest. *There* is a Robin Hood for you, Simon, that comes to get his licking and then dodges off into Sherwood like a dog to lick his wounds!

Sherwo-o-o-od!

What's that? Who's that howling so? I say, what—who be you now, man? And what is the meaning of this?

I am Gilbert Greaves, if you would have my name, and I have heard out your tales. But I don't believe a sliver of either of them—neither yours, nor that of this man here.

And praytell, why not?

I have been in Sherwood, and know it for a haunted place filled with demons. And unless you and this fellow here be yourselves imps or woody sprites, I say, you are liars.

Ho! Listen here to this, Simon! This fellow here has called us both liars. And just what brings you such certainty, my good fellow, that you should question our candor in this or any other damned thing?

I say, I say! Were ye not listening? I have been *in* that devil's tangle!

We all have, gossip! What then?

I have both been, and seen. I went in there of an evening, years back now, when I was a boy, and Robin and his Green Men were still fey lords of that place. You see, my dear mother, may God rest her soul, did used to send me in there, telling me now to bring out this or now that plant or moss or lichen perhaps, as was her wont in those days... And I went, Lord save me! Went right into that forest, time and again, thinking that the worst I should have to fear me would be from wolf or boar! Agh, little does man know of Hell and its wiles. God save us from the darker! God save us from the darker!

Peace, man, and finish your tale...

I say! It was when I was a lad, and my mother had bid me gain her some herb. I was in there, in that demon-infested fen, and I was gathering me up a sprig of thyme and eyebright, and a garland of asphodel, for me mother was dear to that plant for weaving her baskets. I looked me up a moment, for something was not right, and glanced uneasy into the forest; but not a thing could I perceive, and so went again about my gathering. But something was grown in me, man, some sense that I was being hunted. Cannot reckon it to ye; it's what a doe must feel under sight of the arrow. I grew restless and bethought I would take my herbs and get me home.

And so? Hey, will you come to the point, or do you intend to stand around farting through your mouth the rest of the afternoon?

The point! The point! Here is the point: that I looked me up and saw me a *demon*...

What demon, now? More sense comes from my bull's backside...

A *man*, friend, or so it seemed at first. A man all green of skin, who was lurking there in the shade in a way that much disquieted me; and as it was grown evening I could not well make him out, though it seemed to me he was uneven somehow, or bent. "Hail, Sir! What is it ye are wanting?" asked I, much uneasy. Not a word from him. "O Sir, I say, are ye in need of aid?" I call.

And that's when he begins to speak it... a freakish gibberish, like he was some madman, only of such noises and sounds that I swear they could not be ripped of human lungs. I back me up a step, disturbed greatly, and say to him, "Ho, now, I say, are ye in need of aid?" But he rushes forward out of that gloom, and by the heavens, I do not know what to make of him. He seems a man, but he is growing horrible moment by moment. His face is terrible long and covered in a kind of—bark—

What now? *Bark*, you say?

Bark, I say—as though he had been a tree! But that was nothing, for as he come, he grows long, long, *long*—his limbs all wild and wavy. His hair is burning fire, and his eyes are round as saucers, and he is wailing—good God in heaven, methinks he's *laughing!* Oh, cackling with a hideous roar, like a bonfire—

Laughing, is he! And what then? Did he begin to belch, as well?

I got me hence in all haste! Dropped me satchels on the ground and raced off, and never came back into that place, nor went in to gather what I had left behind, though my poor mother implored me...

Hah! A tale indeed, what with this saucered barking fellow! And tell us another thing, master herbsman—

Aye?

—this demon here—did ye spot him *before*, or was it rather *after*, ye went on to the tavern?

Hah! That's a fine one, Arthur! Aye, truly, master herbsman, tell us once again—just what plants *were* ye eating out there in that wood?

And master herbsman—it mightn't be, that as ye were standing from your stooping and herb-gathering position, ye did not smack your head on a branch, so? The forest is dangerous for those low hangers, ye know...

Laugh! Laugh the lot of you! But the Devil has his voice in your laughter, and his hand on your hearts, and 'tis the loss of your souls, that vapor you expel of your mouths! This is a world of horrors, ye false fools, and there are devilish things amongst us even now. I can glimpse their hideous glimmering amongst us. What I saw—why, I know him, now, and he is waiting for us, all of us, he and a host of others like him, in the world that follows this one, if we do not set ourselves to right! I tell you, fools—

Pah! That's enough of this funmaker. Let's have him out of here. This is
no place for his damned preaching!

God save us from the darker!

Aye, God save us from the *barker*, indeed. And so away with ye! That's it,
boys, toss him out on his arse, and don't you mind his howling. He learned it
from a damned man-tree. God's britches, did ye ever hear such a balmy tale?
A shite-covered demon in the wood with eyes glowing like two fiery arseholes,
and what not. I say, this is one for the recounting! That fellow *was* assaulted
by a goblin, sure, but I do not believe it was in Sherwood. Unless this Robin
Hood of yours truly was nothing but a barky saucy fellow out there belching
in the undergrowth, hey, Simon?

You would know better'n I, Bland Arthur, for it is you that says I was
never a green man, and yet claims to have bested Robin in combat one to one.

Pardon, man, for I am a touch hard of hearing. Are you calling me a liar?

Well, one of us is!

Or the both of us together, for that. But Arthur-a-Bland ne'er lied about a
man that felt his pikestaff—nay, nor a woman, hah! Of that you can be certain,
Simon Simoner.

How dare you call me that...

Ah! Touched a nerve, did I? Why does it trouble you so, I'd like to know.
Tell, how *did* you get that byname?

'Tis no business of yours, Master Bland, but do not use it again, or else—

Or else what, Simon? Or else you'll set upon me as your Robin did, dangerous as a constipated duck, and learn me a lesson or two?

I won't tell you again, man, do not insult the name of Robin Hood!

I'll insult whomever and whatever I please, Simon Sot, at whatever time I
want and in any way I see fit—you or Robin Hood or that tree sarder as just
sadly passed out of our lives, or any of your respective mothers. Now say, you
who were a green man of Robin Hood and lived years in the greenwood, did
you ever see the barky terror that fellow was on about?

Nay.

Nor nothing of the like?

There are many things as dwell in the woods.

Are there, now? And enlighten me, Simon Sot. What dwells in the greenwood, apart from deer, grouse and swine like you?

There are gnomes and hobgoblins, to be sure.

Gnomes and hobgoblins! Hah! By my balls, wonders in this world shall never cease. First he claims he was a green man, and now he claims he's seen gnomes and hobgoblins!

I never claimed I saw any such, devil take you.

No? Cover your arse as you please. But tell me, if you have ne'er struck eyes on such, how d'you know they're about, Sooty Simon?

Well, members of our band did spot 'em.

Did they, now? Members of your band? Gnomes and hobgoblins? Zounds! You are a scoundrel, Master Bland, to so freely misuse your tongue.

You mind your own tongue and I shall mind mine, Sotty. And while you are minding your tongue, come and bid it tell me why it lies so about spirits of the wood.

I ne'er lied on it, gossip!

Nay, surely, not e'en once. But it lied on you, it would seem, and begat bastard notions a-plenty in that diseased head of yours. Or tell me what they told you, these gnome-spotters!

Well, there was Iain for instance—

Who in the blazes was Iain?

Iain the Scotsman, who was with us a time.

E'ery man makes mistakes, I warrant. At least *he* was sensible enough to get out.

Nay, he did not, but was killed, he believed, in defense of Robin.

That makes him less than half the man and more than twice the fool now, doesn't it? And so, what did this Iain see?

He was out in the woods and claimed he encountered a monster there, a man with the antlers of a deer. He called it Carnonos, or something the like, and said it desired something from Robin Hood.

Bollocks! Hob in Hood and a woodsy cuckhold. What a combination, by my mother's haggy soul! Then? What else?

Well, Will Stout's mother, for instance, who had a boggart and named it...

Ah, did she? Had one *and* named it? Well, God's britches!

Aye, she did—and named it. That was the trouble. For it wouldn't go away, but raised such havoc in that home that Will eventually ran off and went to sea on a fishing ship. And Robin Hood heard about it from this same mother, and went to get him back—

What, running errands for a ronyon, was he!

Well, Robin never would say no to a mother in need—

The sweet bastard.

—so he went out to sea as well, calling himself Simon—for he said he was fishing for men—

Bah! Simon! Not him, too! God's bodkins. Just what the world needed! A second Simoner...

That's it, I've had it—

—Come and get me you lardpacker—

—tear your hair out—

—You stay out of this, Tom, this is between me and Simon the arse master here!—

—You've insulted Robin Hood's good name one too many times—

—come and defend him, if you can!—

—Ouch!—

—Bastard!—

—kill you—

Hah! What's wrong, arse master? Too old to put up a man's fight? Or could ye never?

I'll show *you* who's too old for what!

Dire threat from a mumblecrust! I no longer have my trusty pikestaff, but I have this cane and these two balls and they will do the job just as well! Hah, take that you bilge drinker, and that, and that! Get gone, whoreson, and go simoning somewhere else, you pandermuncher. See? I've done for you just as I did for Robin Hood. So which man of us is proved the liar now, you flatulent dodderer? Now go find his ghost with all your antlered buggers and your green pricks out there in the wilderness and ne'er set foot in this hon'rable establishment again! I say: *be—gone—!*

Friar Tuck

calawag! I swear it by my soul, and may God strike me down for a liar if 'tis not precisely as I have relayed! 'Tis no fault of mine, you lardpate, if your eyes are two narrow to compass so large a tale. A man who will see only the mundane before him everywhere he goes can hardly be counted on to know the truth of things, that is a law, and by God 'tis why the Saints of our Church are few and far between. Why, most men cannot assess even what they have standing before them, else our Lord would ne'er have been hung upon a cross!

What, now? Ah, so that's how matters stand, you sly donkey! You disbelieve my story, but would know *how* it came to pass? 'Tis useless to put up a challenge as a mask for curiosity! You believe me halfway already, and though I do foresee you will strongly abuse and deride me as I run through the gauntlet of the past, e'en tomorrow you will be sitting on that selfsame stool like the sinful lump you are and recounting these events as though they were your own. No, no! Deny it not, my fat friend, for I know you shrewdly. What's more, I do not e'en hold it against you. Lord, forgive us our debts, as we forgive our debtors!

So here's my share of charity for the day, as a gift to a poor letabout like yourself who is in frank need of a brotherly hand. Follow where I lead, and do not be like the mule which perished of thirst because he would not be budged toward a pool of water. Let us work backward in time like crabs. There we stood, 'neath the great oak of the greenwood where oaths are bound, and the King Richard with his sword upon Robin's shoulder in forgiveness of all his wrongs (if wrongs they might be called!); and Robin on his knees before King Richard, in word and gesture of fealty he never once retracted.

Bah, listen to this fellow, trying to outpace me! As if I knew not how and where Robin wound up in the end! 'Tis true, you stickler, the amnesty did not stick. I wager Robin would have been at peace with the world thereafter, had good King Richard not been bolted fatally in the shoulder shortly thereafter, and our once and future King John Softsword not renewed his malicious ire against Sherwood. He disliked Robin fiercely, on account of court politics, I ween, and some matter concerning, if I do not mistake me, the Lord Robert of Duncaster, which I never clearly understood.

What now! Why, aspersions and slander most foul! How dare you, you runt of a man! I can hold my own in any fight, even now with my pate denuded by age and my limbs shaken by the burden of years! Why, you impertinent scoundrel, another such improper word from your flabby lips and I'll show you where my foot is yet capable of reaching! You had better hope you can outpace me, young upstart, for elsewise you shall rue the day your mother showed you the light of this world! Enough, now, get over here—

...Bah! Very well, very well. I shall let it slip this time, but only on account of yon maiden, who bids me hold my tongue and keep my peace. Benisons on you, my fair young lass, for the Lord has said that the peacemaker shall be blessed! As for you, stripling, I urge you, be wary of what you say, for I cannot always promise to be so forbearing in the face of wanton outrages, and the next time your tongue moves in such a wise, I shall fain tie it around your neck.

Now silence! I regain my tale. What concerns us is the sword on Robin's shoulder, and the hand that held it, and how the man to whom that member was welded had found himself in the greenwood to begin with. And the answer to that riddle is simply that I brought him there.

Aye, pork paunch, I, alone, unaided, and unaccompanied. Though hardly knew I the man I led hence. He was to me but a knight garbed in sable, some Crusader returned from hard years abroad in the King's Crusade, who wished to meet Robin Hood. Oh, I spied nobility in him, and a haughty attitude that brooked no rejoinder, that to be sure; 'twas right impossible to miss such traits. But beyond that, what knew I of the man or his quality, but the little that he told me?

Bah, listen to this fool, here! Boy, have you a stockpile of impatient queries up there in your head in need of disbursing, lest your neck collapse beneath their weight? What do you mean, *why* did I bring him? He told me he would know the Robin Hood of Sherwood fame, and I told him that the Robin Hood of Sherwood fame would know any good Christian that came in good will, and that was that. What was I to fear? That he, deceiving me, should single-handedly assail the entire Sherwood host and cut them down to a man? The fellow was neck deep in his own armor and could have been knocked over turtle-wise by a single blow from John Little, or a well-placed arrow from any one of twenty of our best archers. As for being able to find his way back through to us again—man, you know not how we lived. There was no danger of him finding the road again, and I knew I could count on Robin to measure his right quality and act accordingly.

Heaven grant me patience! Now the dullard wants to know how I myself could find the way back to Robin's encampments, when I knew the black knight could not do the same! These are secrets, man, that I will not even reveal now—nay not even now that the band is disbanded and our leader slain. And you start to keep up a more respectful silence, young derelict, if you'd have the rest of this story, or I'll wallop your head with a cudgel my own, and give you not a scrap the more!

So, as I say, we were making our way through the wood—agh! Mercy on high, did I not just tell you to bind your tongue to your teeth, you reprobate? I am just coming to that, and would get there sooner if your impatience did not fill your gullet with vain words at every single breath I am permitted to exhale! Now listen and learn: we were met on the way by Will Stutely and Gilbert, as I counted on, and I explained the situation to them. And I could already see that these two clever bears were already numbering the gold this knight likely carried in his satchels—particularly Gilbert, who was ever looking for a new penny, but I reckoned that if I could only get him to the Merry Men, the many would be saved for the sins of the few. So I told them to go and fetch Robin, and to meet us in a certain glade known to us all, with a great tree that Robin was most fond of for reasons his own. And so they went to gain him, and we to gain the meadow.

He told me on our way of his adventures in the Holy Land, and what he had seen there, and truth be told I felt he had been in it up to his chin. He told me marvels, and I would tell them to you in turn, if your mouth were not too full of your own regurgitated idiocies to masticate any solider food. And we did get to the meadow, and by and by were joined there by Robin Hood and our good men, and they with their hands already on their scabbards and smelling the gold they believed they would seize. But by my faith, though I often marveled at Robin Hood, never so much as this day! For he made an exclamation of sorts, and strode straight up to the black knight and sank to a knee before him, just like that, head bowed, to the shock and amazement of us all, and proclaimed his allegiance to good King Richard! And King Richard doffed his helmet then, and threw off his dark cloak, and lo! but the man shown forth in goodly silver and was splendid to the eye and indeed plainly and undeniably our liege and King! And we sank down beside Robin, all in awe, and trembling indeed as ne'er before we had trembled before any man beneath God's open skies. For we were accustomed to boldness with all men, as is the hard way of the criminal.

Ah, for once you put a fair question, good gabber, for I have asked myself the same a hundred times since: just how did Robin know him? How did he guess him out? I suspected what you have proposed, that perhaps he had seen him somewhere time before (for Robin's past was a mystery and any man's best guess), but here's the trick: the King had his helmet on and his visor down when Robin approached.

What, now? Why, what do you take us for? Of course we asked Robin about it! But Robin was such a man as, if he would not have you know a thing, would go to his grave ere he loosed it. His lips were not so flabby as some others I might name. Whenever we would ask him about it, he would only remark, "I'faith! 'twas the King who knew *me*." So make of that what you will.

It happened then like this, that the King drew his sword and laid it on Robin's shoulder, and said that by the law of the land he was entitled to Robin's head for poachery and divers high crimes, and Robin said aloud for all to hear that if the King so willed it, his head was duly forfeit. And I reckon that the lot of us must have issued a singular gasp at these words; but the King said, "If this head is mine to do with as I will, then by God, I deign to leave it where it stands, so long as its bearer shall promise never again to transgress the laws of this land while I wear the crown." And Robin said, "I do swear it, my liege." "Then so be it," said King Richard. "My blade, which too often has been forced to take life, now shall preserve it. Consider yourself pardoned, Robin of the Hood, along with all your men, and go now in Christian peace; and with this blade, which might have brought your life to the ground, I rather raise it up, for from now henceforth you shall be a knight of this Crown: Sir Robin the Green. What is more, I shall provision you each and all with special patents as woodsmen of the Crown and protectors of the peace of Sherwood, and entrust to you the care of this place, which you know better than any. You who have slain the King's deer shall now protect them, and you who have menaced the roads of Sherwood shall now stand warranty for them, and as the King's Foresters, you shall derive a just stipend for your good work. Rise then, good Foresters of Sherwood, and be glad!" And we, amazed, did stand and rose such a shout of rejoicing as has never been heard in those woods, and stood before the King, and all of us to a man came then before him and bent a knee and proclaimed our undying fealty. And there was a great feast that evening, there in that very field, in honor of His Highness, for worthier man has never worn the crown of England, and the King sat in state over it, and for the first and the last time we slew a fat buck with the Crown's own blessing, and roasted it on a mighty bonfire and ate of it with no cloud hanging over our heads. And by my troth, but the King and Robin exchanged stories all that night almost as equals, and we heard tales from our own leader that none of us, even Little John, knew; and the King would now and again look up at the stars over our heads, or at the woody bowers that circled us, and would let out an exclamation. And I shall recall it ever, for once he bent his face to Robin and said to him, "Sir Robin, verily I declare that you are a freer man than even your monarch, and rule over a fairer and doughtier kingdom. False were it for the King of England to envy any one of his subjects, but if there were a man beneath me who should wear my jealousy, he sits this evening at my right hand." And it was the first time, I swear it, that I ever perceived my leader at a loss for words.

We bedded down that evening on the ground beneath God's open sky, on pillows of summer grasses, as was our way, and our King, himself a man hardened by foreign wars and long privations, slept beside us that night as an equal. On the morrow he took his leave, and we bowed before him again, and I do suppose that if only he had lived the longer and been our king a few more seasons, there would have been a paramount time of peace and joy in England beneath such a man. But alas, it was not to be.

Ah, our young fool here is coming round to sense, and begins to speak like a reasoned man! For it is true, I have not told how he came to me to start. Then clamp your jaw again, and listen.

I was, you see, some weeks in retreat within my little hut, with no company to me but my hounds, and there I had gone to repent and pray, for I am a man as has always borne his share of the weight of our frail human ancestry, and above all that resentful wrath which led Cain to slay his kin. I had gone there, I say, for some weeks, and wished not a man to approach me there, for it was utmost important to my penitence that I should remain for that time an anchorite; but of a certain evening, past the browning of the day, there came a knock on my door. And I without rising from my modest repast called to he that had caused it, saying, "With no disrespect, but I am a man in fast reclusion, and would have no company but my own, so unless your errand be most urgent, I kindly bid you get you to another hovel and leave me in holy peace." But this was followed by another and still more insistent rapping, and I rose a-grumbling and opened the door, ready to give this man a round word; but I found standing before me a specter such as to make my blood freeze in my very veins, and by God, I feared that an emissary of death itself had been sent for me, to take me to my grave before I had had time enough to repent of my manifold sins. For before me stood a knight dressed in full armor and with his helmet pulled, and a black cloak about him, and it seemed the sky beyond was filled with bleak thunderheads. And I must have shrunk back in frank terror, for the knight drew up his visor, and said to me, "Man, I come in peace, but do declare that up to now I find this house dire wanting in Christian hospitality. I pray these impressions shall wane upon acquaintance." And without another word, strode straight past me and into my hut!

Well, I am not one to be pushed about by any man, no matter how menacing he may seem, and as I had now learned that it was flesh and blood that stood before me and not one of the Devil's own emissaries, I said to him, "Sir knight, I have invited you not into my home, and do not take kindly to harsh manners beneath my own roof," and would have granted him another ripe portion of my mind to boot, had he not stopped me with a gesture. There was something so imperious in his way and in the flash of his eyes that I found myself silenced—not a common occurrence, I can tell you!—and I watched in amazement as the man strode straight to my board and sat himself thereby, and, drawing off his gauntlets and taking his helmet from his brow, said to me, "If you have aught to eat, brother monk, I would be grateful." The head that had been revealed was a noble one, a strong bearded face with eyes that could turn from gentle to hard in a moment, and I perceived at once from the features of the man and from his way of speaking that this was a person of high rank, one much accustomed to being obeyed. In normal circumstances, this would not have stopped me from responding hard in the face of haughtiness, but I swear he had a way of putting a man to silence. And I, somehow abashed, said to him, "My Lord, you find me in time of fasting, and I have but modest food for offer, but whatever there is in this house, I will gladly divide it."

"That is more like," said he, "and I thank you for it. As for the modesty of your food, fear not, good Brother, for I am accustomed to far poorer fare than any which is given in Christian fraternity, and will gladly join you, whether in feast or in fast."

I was amazed at this, and sat at the table, and broke bread with him, but not before he requested I say a prayer over our mutual meal. Prayer I did say, and then we ate a simple portion of stale bread and stewed potatoes garnished with a sprig of rosemary alone, the which he consumed with relish and genteel words of gratitude, totally at odds with the arrogance I had previously perceived in him. And by and by he said to me, "Brother Tuck, I have sought you out a purpose, for I would find the man known as Robin Hood, and would have you lead me to him."

This of all things I was least expecting, but I said to him, using my actual amazement to my advantage, "Robin Hood! And why should I know where he might be found?"

"Play not the fool with me, Brother, but do as I have bid."

"Who told you that I could aid you in this?"

"Sir Richard of the Lea, and an honester man England has ne'er raised in the bosom of her nobility, so do not hope to persuade me that I err, nor strive to cheat me of my purpose; for you will find me hard to avert."

I thought on this in wonderment, and at last said, "It is much that Sir Richard has sent you. But prithee, what would you have of Robin Hood? For I will lead no man to him that intends him wrong, but sooner would die myself than so betray so excellent a man."

"That sentiment does honor to you and this house. But be at peace, Brother Tuck, for I do swear by this, my sword, which has preserved my life in dire moments and grave days, and which bears moreover in its form the sacred Cross of our Lord Jesus Christ, that I mean no harm to Robin Hood."

"What business do you have with him, then?"

"That business is mine and Robin's alone, and is not for general partaking. Take me on my word, Brother monk, or refuse me on't, as the spirit persuades you."

And I, hearing him in this, and sensing in his words naught but sincerity and good will, at last did concede, for I, though I had no proofs of anything he said, was somehow altogether convinced of his quality. And I confess, though a sin it might be, that I was equally curious to know what this man could possibly desire with Robin Hood, and wished with a burning desire to see this secret revealed. And I said to him, "Very well, my Lord, for something in your way convinces me of your honorable intent. By my troth, Robin Hood ne'er in all his life scorned the company of any Godfearing man, and why then should I? Tonight you shall sleep upon mine own cot, and on the morrow, come rosy dawn herself, we shall rise, and I bring you to the wood, and there we shall seek and find our Robin Hood."

"God bless you for it, Brother Monk," he said, "and repay you for your right trust as He alone knows how to do."

So I passed the remainder of the evening listening to marvelous tales from the Crusades, which this knight told with great skill and with evident piety, and the day following we set out, and everything else unfolded just as I have said, and may God truncate what remains to me of my wretched life to a day and a half if any word I have put to you was stated with will to falsehood. And I say again, England has never known such a King, and let us pray to God that he is not the last such sovereign that she shall know, and she would have been blessed by his crown if he had not been taken from us by some demon's plotting in time of war. But as another king may throw a shadow, so King Richard casts a light, and it outlast him, and shines even upon us now, even as the light shone by Robin Hood.

Bah, he is at it again, the garrulous mite! You may jest with me all you wish, vicious troublemaker, and scorn me as you would a dog, and doubt my words to your dying breath, but I am right in my conscience and know that all I have told you is good and true and conforms to the actual shape of the past. If you doubt me in it, and abuse me for it, and asperse me with foul tongue, the sin is on your head, not mine. May God forgive you, young rogue!

Little John

oy, what nonsense ye have heard of it. I never met a man more caught in the flock of stupid rumor than Robin Hood, but even now he is passed he draws these tales to him like stray hounds to a bone. Men are envious, boy, recall it to yourself always, and will lie about a man merely to wound him in memory when they cannot tear his flesh. Aye, even a man's followers—nay, especially they, for 'tis they who have most cause to envy him, as they are all directed toward one and the very same polestar, but are obliged to follow him as precedes them toward it, and lag always behind him, and fill themselves up with spleen at the constant sight of the man that outheads them.

I say, 'twas nothing like you heard that day. Maid Marion was well out of it, and that rascal pinder can have it up with me if he'd say otherwise. I am grown old but ne'er too old to crack him o'er the head with a rod of oak if it comes to that, and remind us both of better days. Marion had nothing to do with it, I say. 'Twas matins at church that Robin craved, for he had been long without communing and felt the pain for it. He had a devotion to the Holy Virgin, did Robin, and nothing rode hard on him about our exile but that he was cut off of church thereby. All were soothed when the good friar was with us, but Robin on more than one occasion got himself into large trouble in a narrow way for this devotion of his, and the time ye speak on was one of those.

What's that? Aye, 'twas a day of May, as the pinder said, but the pinder had none of it save the start. We went with Robin hence. Midge told him to take ten men, but he said no, and just the three of us set out. Robin and I quarreled on the way over some blessed thing or other—in all honesty I can't recall what, but I was a hot-headed man in those days, ere time and Robin's own hand tamed me—and I left him alone with that poltroon the pinder, to my shame. They went on. I headed back toward camp, but e'en as I went, by and by the pinder came a-racing up, cursing as he came that he'd lost some locket and carrying on about it, but I calmed him, and he finally told me that Robin had been chased into the church there by the Sheriff's men, and was presently holed up. 'Twas a hard moment's decision, whether to run and gather the men or to turn back myself to go to Robin's succor, but I kept my head on me and send the pinder for arms, and turned myself for Nottingham, ready for a fight to the death. I found the church, and the Sheriff's men loitering around it, but they would not enter. 'Twas Father Steven as held them off, I learned later. Well, I did not know what to do. Could not rightly leave Robin, could not rightly stay with him what with our men coming in and fast. I found a boy there and caught him by the sleeve and gave him a silver coin to go in and tell our men not to proceed into town, and I myself waited.

What! And the pinder says Robin was there in Marion's window for... The pinder is more worthless a man now than he was then, and that's the truth. He was indeed in Marion's window, but only because that's where he got himself to when he escaped the church, a few days on. I knew he would go there, and I was passing underneath it as frequently as I could without making myself suspect, for I reckoned rightly he would go there as a lodestone to a blade. Well, I knew that something was up, for I had seen guards suddenly flitting about like flies. Methinks the Sheriff got wind that Robin was no longer in the church, and had set met to find him in the streets of the town. So I came under that window, on my hunch, and looked around me to be sure the streets were clean, and I called up to see if Robin would answer. Sure as day, he stuck his head forth, and I said, "Heaven's gates, they're on to you, Robin!"

And he said, "Ye tell me nothing new, John Little, for they've been on to me all my life!" And, by my lights, he was laughing!

"Jump now, ye blessed fool, and I shall catch ye!" I cried, and he turned back into the room, not doubt to bid his Marion farewell, then lept down, and I caught him, and we were away. Aye, away we went, and I was running for it, but Robin stopped me, saying, "Little John, if ye were a guard, what would ye cast for the more than a man sprinting down the road, to all appearances willing to escape? Peace, but let us amble our way out of this place, leisurely as geese; and I assure you, they will not so much as glance our way." So we went, though I can assure you it was no easy prospect, and I tried hard not to keep gazing about me, for I expected at any moment our ruin, which, thanks be to God, ne'er came. We reached nigh the edge of Nottingham and had ere crossed the boundaries, but then it happened that someone as knew us spotted us—and by God, if I had only seen or e'en guessed his face, I would have come back later and erased it from the world—and yelled out for the guards, and away we bolted. Well, they horsed themselves, though this lost them precious time, so ere they had come after us, we had already taken refuge with a local cottier who was a loyal friend to us on many a hard occasion, and may Jesus Christ rest his soul and tenfold reward him for his boons. The guards could not find us, and we kept there all the day, and set back for Sherwood under cover of night, and cloaks to hide us.

That liar the pinder used to say that he was with Robin throughout this whole adventure, and was fighting even as Robin was bussing some girl, and that he himself slew some dozen men on the retreat, and that was how they got away. 'Tis a lot of stuff and nonsense, boy, first because the pinder was a great coward and in battle like that would have stood rather shaking in his boots and grabbing at his lucky charm, and second because Robin loathed the shedding of blood, though in his line of work not even the best of men could long avoid it. Men died in our time, but only those as asked keenly for the blade, and far fewer than some wags would have ye believe. I will tell you this bit of wisdom, lad, and listen well to me. Anything you take from a man he can get back, save life, limb, and honor, and if you rob these from him you had better be well justified in it, for these things shall hang heavier on the scales of the Judgement than any other weight of this our mortal lives. Shed no blood lightly, boy, for blood is weighty stuff indeed.

That's the true tale, and by my honor. So you see that Marion had no part in this. Though I allow other times Robin risked his hide just to catch a glimpse of her, for a man more enamored of his lady there ne'er was. What's that? You would know what kind of woman she was, as would turn Robin's head? Then I will tell you, boy: as rare a woman as comes. Here, I will tell you a story, to show you of what stuff she was made—and this a true story, not like that fable of the pinder's.

Robin had a habit of going out into the greenwood disguised as a mendicant, and I had a habit of following him, both to see as he wouldn't get into trouble, and, when he did, to enjoy the sport of it. One day he, arrayed in this fashion, and wending long the road to Nottingham, spotted what seemed the page of some worthy dignitary, a boy not much older than you yourself, for he had but a narrow line of a beard about his lips and chin. And as Robin ne'er let such a chance slip him up, he went straight out to this page, a-tapping with his cane like a veritable graybeard, and confronted the boy, asking who he was and what had sent him; and he said he was a page of the Lord Robert of Duncaster with a message for a certain man of Barnsdale. Foolish words! for at the name of Lord Robert Robin was ready to shed the lad of all he owned.

"The Lord Robert!" cried Robin. "Excellent good news, for Lord Robert is beloved of his people for his great charity to the poor, of which I am the first; so please it you, but give a poor old beggar man somewhat to aid him."

At which the page stopped up in his tracks and said, in a fair high voice, "With good will I give you this coin, the only one I carry with me, which you need more than I." And handed Robin the coin so mentioned, which he put into his pocket.

"Christ bless you, lad, and repay you hundredfold in life and in heaven," said Robin, taking a small step the nearer. "Do remember you now the solicitude of our common Lord Robert, and please it you, but give a poor old beggar man and his suffering stomach a bite of food."

The page eyed him a moment, but, reaching beneath his jerkin, pulled out a small satchel, and handed it over, saying, "Here are all the rations I have on my person, and now they are yours, for I am well enow fed that a fast of a day shall not injure me, and I ween you are in greater want of it than I."

"Christ bless you, lad, and repay you hundredfold in life and in heaven," said Robin, putting the satchel into his pocket and drawing another step the nearer. "Now be pleased to recall the constant generous donations of our common Lord to the dispossessed, and hand over all else ye possess."

And the page, swift as a lark, said, "And so I shall, and marry. Here, take you this single flower, which I have just plucked from yonder knoll; for, lacking the coin I have just handed o'er and the provender, it is the one thing on my person that is mine and not the Lord Robert's; and so with it I do indeed give you all I possess, and may it bring you better days than those I have known." And he handed him the flower, a stock flower as it seemed to me, which he had indeed been holding in his left hand.

Then Robin, taking the flower and putting it, too, in his pocket, and taking still another step nearer, said, "Christ bless you, lad, and repay you hundredfold in life and in heaven. Remember you now the Christian charity of our common Lord Robert, and, in his worthy name, but give a poor old beggar man aught too of what he owns: beginning with the very shirt from your back, which will keep me warm on this chill spring day, and which moreover is of a sweet and womanish scent."

Well I saw the page blush at this, in anger as first I thought, and he stuttered, "That I cannot do, Master Beggar, for the Lord Robert has entrusted me to vouchsafe only a single possession of his own, and that is the message I carry in my skull."

And Robin, taking a final step closer, said, "Then let us have the message, good lad, and we shall rest content with it in place of the many other things the Lord Robert owes us."

"Nay, but the message is not meant for your ears, and I will not so betray the trust that has been placed in me. Now kindly step back, Master Beggar, for there is no need to stand so near to me!" For indeed, over the course of this conversation, Robin had, little step by little step, come up so near to the poor boy that they were nose on nose, and it was all I could do to hold my tongue from laughing, and nigh broke my control entire when Robin cried out in wild response, "Pardon, pardon! but ye are a sweet-smelling boy, and I lost me head o'er your dear perfume."

But still he did not step back, and the page at last was forced to do so, though I could see it nettled him something fierce, for he said, with a harder tone than before, "I must be on my way now, Master Beggar. I bid you good day and Godspeed." And moved to round him, but Robin side-stepped quick as you please, standing in the way of the page, who tried again to round him on the other side, to the same result. "I most strongly urge you let me pass," said he, growing red again.

But Robin said, "First a boon, and answer me this query. Is our Lord Robert not a generous man?"

"Generous as the beasts of this wood," said he.

"And not a Christian?"

"As Christian as the next man."

"And not a most eleemosynary and benevolent Lord to those as depend on him?"

"Surely we as depend on him most closely must say he is. Now let me pass."

"And so I shall, good lad, so I shall—the very moment our good and common Lord Robert has made good on his generosity, Christianity and benevolence, and given what is worthy of so great and generous a soul as his own—shirt, and message, and also the sword you wear."

"Charity forced is ne'er charity!" cried the boy, his chin up.

"What, forced! Would he not bless the gifts with his own good name? But tell him that you encountered the King of Beggars on Sherwood road, and could not do other than what lordly compassion compelled. Then, if I know our Lord, his heart shall swell indeed and the blood rise e'en to his cheeks, so quick shall it flow at the news of good done!"

"I shall not do it!"

"What, and so blacken the bright fame of your Lord?"

"'Who are you to speak of blackening, who meets passersby with such cunning and deceit?"

"Tut, tut! For this is not so charitable as before, dear lad. But I willingly give you the space of amendment. First the sword, I think, and then we can come to the rest.”

“If you so keenly desire it, then sword you shall have!” cried he, and leaping back did indeed draw his sword, but in such a way as to make known that if he would give it to Robin, it was to be point first. “Now let me pass, lest I will force a passage!”

“Where there is will, there is a way,” said Robin, laughing, and, from beneath his heap of rags, produced his own sword, to the page’s evident astonishment.

“You are no beggar!” cried he.

“How? Have I not been a-begging?” said Robin.

“But falsely, by my troth, for that sword in your hand is worth more than mine own!”

“’Twas but a noble gift to a poor fellow from a certain wealthy gentleman. Or do you begrudge me this yard of steel, with which to defend my beggarly kingdom?”

“I know you! You are a highway man, as I perceive it now, and would rob me of all I own!”

“And how? For all you own was freely given, my lad, by your own assessment! What cost it you, then, to give me in the bargain what is already another’s?”

“It cost me my honor!” said he, a shrill note come into his voice.

“Now that is one thing I’d take from no man,” said Robin, laughing again.

“Then I pray let me pass!”

“Why, ’twould be firm against the principle just affirmed! For ’twere right dishonorable for a Christian lad like you to be about menial services to gray names.”

“Then say I am here of my own accord, and grant me leave to pass on that account!”

“What, and give you leave to lie? God forbid it! For that, too, is prejudicial to the honor we both would so dearly preserve in you. Nay, my lad, but call me a friend; shed yourself of all that is the Lord Robert’s, and be back now upon this Sherwood way, disburdened of these dishonorable accouterments as the day you were born, and ready to begin anew in life.”

"Count this my final warning! I must pass! Must, must, must!"

"By my troth, you smell nothing of must, lad," laughed Robin a final time. For then the page lunged.

There followed such sport as I have seldom had the delight of watching, for Robin was a sure hand at the sword, and the page proved his equal. They were at each other in a flash of blades, and it was thrust, parry, counter-thrust across the road and back, and the forest rang out in the clash of steel. For a time it seemed they were a perfect match, for neither could get the better of the other, and each throw of the blade was met by a swift return. But by and by I could see the page was gaining on Robin step by step, and I saw a growing alarm on his face that was so misplaced there that it cast me into a fit of hilarity, and for a time I saw nothing more, but was rolling in the green grass and sobbing with silent laughter. When I regained myself and glanced up again, however, I saw the page, blooming red now on his pretty cheeks, had disarmed Robin and thrust him down upon his back, and had the sword point at his neck; and it was marvelous to see the best of men so clean defeated! Then I heard the page say, "Now, Master Highwayman, let us have back the coin, the food and the flower that anon I gave you."

"What, and betray the very charity with which they were given?" said Robin, who in defeat had as usual full regained his composure.

"Nay, but fulfill it: for it has been proved that I am more in want of these trifles than you, and so the charity is owed in the other direction. Thus is equity made in the world, and thus may you count me the friend both of God's law, and your honor."

By God, boy, but this was the first and the last time I ever saw Robin tongueless! By and by he laughed, and said at last, "Good lad! I am fair beaten. You have earned this day what I will give you, and I even have an offer to make you besides."

"I want none of your offers, but will have what is mine and then be on my way. A word the more from you and I will slash your neck to stop your words at their root, is't understood?"

There was no mistaking the seriousness of his tone. I could perceive at this point that Robin was in need of my aid, for to ask him to hold his tongue was tantamount to asking a waterfall to change its course, so rising I came out of my hiding place, stave in hand, and moved toward them; but when the page saw me he gave a cry of fury and flung himself at me, sword at the ready; and what could I do but teach this sapling a lesson for pertness? So with a single blow of my sturdy oak, I sent his sword flying from his hand, and he sprawling back a dozen steps upon the ground, a wound upon his brow. And as he went, his cap flew from his head, and before our amazed eyes it was as if a cascade of gold had bloomed there, and I swear for a moment I believed I had given the lad such a blow that his own auric soul had spilled from his skull!

We ran to the lad, who was cold witless upon the earth, and, as I found at once, was no lad at all, but as beautiful a lass as e'er I had laid eyes upon. The beard I had perceived on her face was smudged upon it: it had been painted there. As for the gold, it was none other than her hair. And Robin cried out madly and, tearing his faux beard from his face, sank beside her in a horror. He found her lightless but living. "'Tis the Maid Marion!" he cried to me, confirming what I had already wist, and then knelt fast beside her and kissed her bloodied brow. "You have struck the very watch from her. Come, Little John, a kerchief, or e'en a rag, imbued with a little water, for her sweet brow!" And I raced thence to a spring of cool clear waters near at hand and sank beside it, and tore a piece of cloth from my own garments and soaked it fast with water, then raced back.

But when I came there I found her already awake, and she was gazing at Robin in wonderment. "Are you well, my Lady?" he asked her, and to my relief I saw her nod.

"Robin! I might have killed you!" I heard her say wanly, but Robin only laughed.

"Nay, m'Lady," said he, "but only had you yourself been killed!" And he took the cloth from my hand and cleaned her brow and e'en wiped away the beard and mustaches, so that her radiance shone forth full, and then helped her to her feet.

"I beg your pardon, my Lady," said I, stuttering badly and making a hash of it, for I have always been right nervous around womenfolk, and I felt the blood in my cheeks. But she smiled at me and said to me that a friend of

Robin's who sought only to defend him required no pardon by her or any other man but Christ Himself, upon whose forgiveness we all depend; and by God, as she excused me, I felt as though a weight had been lifted from my soul, and I could have wept before her like a babe. She had eyes that could cut right through a man. When she was ired she was a hellcat and not to be trifled with, and you could see it from the fire in her gaze; and I have seen her do worse to a man than what she did to Robin that day. But when she looked with fondness upon a man it was like she was melting him.

Robin said to her, "This bold swain who has been so generous with his strength is my first mate and the finest warrior in all of England. I trust him as I trust my very soul. His name be Little John—little for his girth, and John for his heart. I need not defend to you the power of his arm, for I fear you have tried the half of it."

She laughed then, and her laugh was so like to Robin's that I wondered, as if it were but the fairer sister to his manly mirth. "If that is but the half, then God save the enemies of Robin Hood, who must feel it in the full!" And she offered me her hand, the which I took, and, bowing, kissed it, marveling in my heart that these delicate and fairest fingers had but lately disarmed e'en Robin Hood, and might have slain him. I knew not what to say to her for her great magnanimity, and I allow I must have blushed so that my entire face was red, for she saw that I was landed in grave difficulty, and herself said, "Well met, Master Little John, and God bless you for so well defending this man, who is dear not only to me, but to the whole of our England."

We asked her then if she would hence to the greenwood with us, but she told us that she could not, for she would soon be missed at home, and must return to the house of Robert. It was for this she had come, for she had indeed a message from Robert to Robin, though truth be told she was not the one entrusted to bring it, but he had been counting on rumor to do the work for him. Robert had with that scurvy Sheriff of Rottingham determined on a trap to lure Robin to sure imprisonment, for he had planned a contest of archery, and had already sent invitations to the finest archers of the land, knowing that Robin could ne'er resist such bait; and so they planned to catch him out and bring him to chains.

"I will go, forsooth, and beat 'em to a one!" cried Robin at once, as I could have bet my soul upon. But she urged him hotly against it, saying that it was certain death, to which he responded with a laugh that he feared neither Sheriff nor Lord, nay, nor duke nor baron nor king, and would go where he pleased as the free man he was.

"They will kill you for it, Robin!" she cried, but he replied, "Hark, Lady! For you are much afeared of my demise, as though I were as fragile as the flower you have but lately gifted me. Fear not, for a man's time comes when it comes, whether he will or not, no matter what he does to preserve himself, and all our lives are in the hands of God. Or say, was I born to die?"

She attempted again to dissuade him, and as she spoke, not once did she complain of the wound upon her brow. But when Robin asked her about it for the third time she waved him away, saying she would tell the Lord Robert she had fallen from her horse. And she spoke of Robert's plans with boldness and surety, and left out no detail, but in all things gave a man such a sense of self-possession and courage that I was amazed that such a woman should have been brought up in a lordly house. For by my troth, boy, she seemed in luster and quality like to the gold of noble halls, but in strength and resistance like the steel of the women of the country, who must face hardship and perils and necessity with grit and resolution.

These were but my first impressions, brief indeed, for soon she left us. Ere she went Robin gave her back her coin and food and flower, but the flower she would not take, saying that she had brought it for him; and he kept it nigh his breast to his dying day, folded in a piece of vellum. We made our farewells, and I feared that I would ne'er again lay eyes on her. But I was to spend many a day with her, later, when she fled for good that life of vainglory and came to dwell with us a season in Sherwood, and so remained until the tragedy struck, of which you well know. And I say, in all my days of knowing her, and gaining her confidence, and even in her presence finding my own (for she was, in all those days, as sweet and dear with me as a sister, and I credit her with my marriage to Meg, for I should not have dared stand in my wife's presence had she not goaded me to it)—I say, not once were my first impressions bent back, but e'en confirmed and made strong and living as an oak. And there were times she saved us all, as in the siege of our castle. All of that was, of course, much later, and only after Robin saved her from marrying one of those rich scoundrels—

What's that? The Sheriff's archery contest, you say? Why, of course he went! Have ye not heard the tale, boy? Ah! Well, you must hear it, there is no question of that. But 'tis for another day, for at present I fear I am grown tired of all this recounting, and must to bed. Old age does not agree with me, lad, and things have been hard since my Meg passed on. Tomorrow we shall see.

But for now, remember you this one lesson from my tale, and forget it not. Do not believe half the tales you hear of Robin, nor any of the evil. There are many as would call him a rogue, boy, and belike he was, but a brilliant rogue. Know it, methinks a man like that is exception to much, and being of greatness, need not follow the rules set down for general mediocrity, not by God, whose rule is golden and universal, but by man, whose rule is silver and often enough copper or tin. Nay, *need* not—but *ought* not! Aye, he got up to mischief, boy, but it would have been scoundreliness sure in another man, whilst in him it was but his great spirit that would not settle. For if ye were to say to a kestrel that it must fly low and gentle like a dove, and feed on grains, and coo softly in the morning light, why, ye should be setting all things topsy-turvy, boy, and denying the natural vein of things. And that is so with men, too, my boy, that some are doves and others are buzzards and a few eagles, and it is a thing to marvel at and conducive to God's greatness and his perfect preparation of the world, that all parts fit together and nothing is superfluous nor nothing misplaced, but each man like some member of a great human body has his fit and proper role and place—I say, it is a thing to thank the Almighty for, that there be regions yet untamed by the hand of little men, where larger ones might live widely by their brighter lights. And I tell ye, boy, that this to me is as sure as God's own day: that if ever men do seek to order the world diversely, so that all things upon it, all the land, the goods, and the men themselves, are owned and divvied and governed by a single yoke meant for a single neck, or governed by buzzards that feed of carrion, and every acre of it cut by a grid, and every head bowed beneath a single man, why, that will be the conquest of Devilry on earth, and the reign of Satan himself.

Will Scarlock

ark, friends! I've a song for weary ears. Up with you, up! Upon your feet, wake, and rouse your drowsy heads! And you, sad Sam, do not mill so in your beer; and you, melancholy Mike, pick up your ear from the floor where it has fallen abed, and heed my words. For I've a lay on a theme that I know likes you well, and I will spill this song into any waiting chalice. Then hark, up now, and listen! For I am in a vein of song. My tale concerns Robin Hood when he was still among us, and a gambol he took once in the long ago, and the outcome thereof. And I know you know I speak true of it, for I have been longer Robin's companion than any man, and ken whereof I speak. Then up, Listeners! Ope your ears, your eyes, your hearts, and your hands, and grab with 'em all that I aim to give you! For the lay runs something like this:

> When that April with new green shoot
> does break the frozen crust of earth
> recalling life to bold rebirth
> and blessing bud and branch and root,
>
> then Robin'd rise, leaving home and hearth
> to walk the easter-going way,
> midst cherry bloom and scent of bay,
> in glad piety and manly mirth.

In wreath of olive and basil 'rayed
flush as the beast for whom he's named
he'd sorcel and conduct the games
that all the foresters anon shall play.

I say! Were e'er a king so richly famed
as Robin on his ivy'd throne?
Mere dynasties are come and gone
ceding to mind but hollowed names,

and ciphers 'cized upon the bone.
Hammurabi's but basalt code,
the Pharoahs mummied without blood.
What face bear Henry, Edward, John

or any of the Roman's brood
of emperors, or tyrant Greeks,
or Gallic hosts of King Louis,
fat or green, feline or good?

Mere syllables! But one yet speaks
with fluency that's not erased,
and visage that shan't be effaced,
by finger, tongue, jowl or cheek:

yet ne'er was a scepter braced
in his dextrous hand, if not a bow
or oaken reed; ne'er did his brow
wear crown or diadem emplaced,

if not the flame and rosy glow
of summer health and vernal fantasies.
King Robin in his doughty wood decrees
law to our day too, 'neath which are darkly stowed

the bones of monarchs in the mucky lees
of mold'ring pits, mute and pow'rless.
But behold! for the fields this day are dressed
in meadow sprigs, and anemones 'neath the trees

raise their silv'ry gold-hearted heads
to praise the God-granted grace of sun.
'Neath emerald-budded boughs there run
and scamper rousen beasts, o'er mossy beds

all hemmed in kingcup and columbine.
Noon and eventide birds sing alight,
as if even the very shades of night
should by the mirroring of timely moon

be made votaries of the bright
and supple springtide rule of day.
Thus Robin too doth wend the way,
oft in guise to gainsay sight;

and in alloy of gravity and play
doth try alike the bad and good,
the poor and rich, the meek and proud,
to see of what metal they be made.

Lo! a stranger strolling midst the wood
a mourner or a mendicant,
a monk, a minstrel, an elding man,
may 'neath robe and rag hide Robin Hood.

So once passed angels o'er the land
obscured to eye by dissemblement,
to ear by voice made inclement,
to prove who would with gen'rous hand

match hospitality to patent want;
and so again did Richard Lionheart
once fashion him the beggar's part
and try the Sherwood way, to the haunt

of Robin and his men, there to regard
their woodland arts and himself to gauge
what sort of men therein had pledged,
and, if goodly, his homage t'impart.

But Robin cann'ly guessed his siege,
uncloaked this occulted royalty,
that one single time ere he'd die
he'd bend the knee before his liege,

to swear great oaths of fealty
to the God-appointed crown. Down,
upon the mossy enflowered lawn,
did Robin kneel in signal loyalty,

ere this monarch's leaf was blown
by autumn winds illegitimate
and the sorry imposture of miscreant.
Thus war and peace by one bond are bound.

Then ask not why Robin went
asly beneath the em'rald roof,
or why 'twas his warp and woof
to try in fire the hearts of men.

'Twas duty mixed with pleasure then. Aloof
of common etiquette
and with merry intention set,
so oft did Robin prise the proof

of the mettle of the men he'd met.
Thus once did Robin rise and go
sojourning 'neath oak, ash and mistletoe
hunting such game as prized him. No fret

in heart, nor inner lies to slow
the quickness of his eyes and limb,
with jollity and ready vim
he trespassed the wood. So 'twas neither doe

nor stag he found, but such megrims
as did well like him. For at a spell,
as he passed a certain wishing well
where fey spirits dwell in eldritch dreams,

a somber procession was sudden seen, bells
a-ringing as though to ward away
ev'ry beast or man of the living day:
lo, the Bishop's long rank and file!

A score of guards in grand display
did company the wayward train,
in mem'ry no doubt of the peine
that the Merry Men so oft defrayed

'pon such worldly splendors. Robin gained
their sight, but was not himself espied,
and quick as squirrel deftly dived
behind the well's stone wall, nor had lain

the length of a robin's call when arrived
the long ungainly and paltered troop.
He heard them pass in solid group.
But of relief he was fast deprived:

his hope did stutter, his solace droop;
for a voice as shrill as a copper whistle
did make him freeze and coldly bristle:
"Halt, ye men, turn back, recoup!

For a word I'd spend at yonder well. Thistles
and brimstone: halt, return!" And indeed
the mass did backward slowly speed;
then a bejeweled hand launched a golden missile—

a ringing coin, o'er guardsman's head,
toward the yawning earthen maw:
but as if thwarted by some higher law
this mark the gold did some exceed

and landed instead at Robin's craw.
He, who ne'er'd waste a chance
at once leapt up with doubloon in hands,
and laughing did race away. So the Bishop saw,

and shrieked in wildest rage, "Sprite! Imp! Brigand!
Outlaw! Catch me fast that devil thief!
Take me coin and head, be brief!
Flesh or ghost—bring me the fiend!"

But Robin ran at haste, and was lief
to leave his pursuers tangled
far behind him; and thus angled
o'er stream and boulder, through brush and sheaf

and thorny bramble. The Bishop's men were mangled
there and could not keep the pace,
but each moment lost still more the race
against their jaunty quarry. And he headstrong fangled

himself a path where none ere had graced
the greenwood waste, dodging the darts
that deadly sped toward his heart
from the strings the inept guardsmen laced

into the waiting nock. Farther and farther apart
grew hunter and hunted, until at last
Robin outpaced 'em, and, chuckling, cast
coin into fist, and steps for woody fort,

there to relate to his merry band o'er fair repast
his run-in with superstitious prelate
and soldiers maladroit. But, God-given fate,
Robin's misadventures were ne'er past!

For behind him the guards, fearing irate
reprimands, did conspire to pursue his tracks
for all that day at least; as turning back
would sure mean demotion, lash or hate

from one whose animus was rending. Alack!
Robin, creding he was well evaded,
was leisurely a-strolling, whistling in the shaded
bowers and relishing his lackadaisic trek

through the spring bounties of the gloried gladed
wood. Was all lost in birdsong, he;
was all in mood of sunspired dreams,
wending as the crystal streams that braided

'neath the oak and ash. Scented and a-beam
with light was the air that buoyed round him.
Squirrels chattered in the dusky limns
of flower-woven glebes and meadows, and raceme

blooms like clustered pearls from honey locust limbs.
Warm the breeze that sloughed the trees,
causing them to sigh and whisper. Ah, May revelries!
All creation to its Creator rose gladsome hymns,

Robin no less than any, but in grateful ecstasies
his joy he did extol, and so a-singing went,
rambling reckless of malice, and innocent
of the eyes that hungrily spied his ways.

The Bishop's guards, like hunter's hounds hellbent
on trace of hare or feathered pheasant, did scout
his song-strewn path with pointing snout
until they'd found him. But Robin was not meant

to die. Ill should true have fingered him out,
and he fallen to th'greater force,
if one of his stalkers, blundering on spiny gorse,
did not fall clattering down. A cry, a shout,

and Robin's warned! Nor deer, nor ass, nor horse
should faster bolt from wolf or lion's onslaught.
And hence the guards, much distraught,
fretful and a-flailing, sought to mend his course.

But he like fox seeking some safe spot
of hiding did scamper on, until lo! ahead he glanced
a hut upon the cusp of humble hamlet, and danced
nigh for joy at such deliv'rance, and thanked God

for having spared him through risk and chance
to so fair a port and happy harbor.
Breaking free from his wonted arbor
he dashed to th'hovel and thrust himself in. Lance

and sword did follow him: but slow now, ardor
damped in caution then, lest he, entrapped,
rain on them in arrows keen, and cap
their brows in deadly diadem. Fervor

was upon them; but like the huntsman's cur, rapt
and tense upon its mark, shakes
in fierce excitement, but brakes
its forth impulsion, till its master's tapped

his tongue and called the sign, so stakes
were on the guardsmen's limbs, dread
their master, both behind and ahead.
Like ships buffeted by winds midst shoals that break

the ribs of vessels and the limbs of men, sped
on midst ruin by the tempest's bout,
so they meandered 'twixt desire and doubt.
But the strangest silence was o'er their heads

and not a single whistling thistle did flout
their coming, nor bear them from life's shore.
Until at last they reached the hovel's door
and, sweating and grunting like pigs at rout,

did fling it open. There they found better'n spoor:
the prey himself, his back on them,
strangely stooped, standing at window open.
And they raced inside and spun him 'bout: poor

the eyes that first beheld that sight! Oh man!
Death is e'er hidden, concealed within
the blushing face of swain and maiden,
in might of thew, the slender grace of woman.

How the heart did freeze within those guardsmen
who first clapped eyes upon that sight!
For there before them no outlaw, but wight
decrepit and aging, wrinkles marring skin,

its hair all blasted by some winter blight,
its eyes clouded o'er in a dead'ning mist.
Shaking it rose up a skeletal fist
and, fey and jeering, the toothless fright

began all brazen to mock them. "Ye missed!
Ye missed! Missed again yon Robin brave
who's again outkenned ye." So the banshee raved;
and the heart in these men was frozen. Whist,

the guardsmen withdrew in fright: the grave
they seemed to glimpse in flesh,
rising rank before them. The mesh
'twixt man and ghost was rived. But: "The knave!"

cried one skeptic then, a boy still fresh,
who yet disbelieved his own demise; "The scalawag!
He's taken the guise of yon old hag
and through yon window's escaped us!" In a dash

all awakened to this pauper's truth, this sprag
to hold the ceiling o'er 'em; and one,
their leader, stood forth grim and dun
(for umwhile was much dismayed). "Lallygag

us not, old nag, or there'll be hell to run.
Tell us now, and don't ye lag, where the snipe
has gone!" And she but chortled. "Tripe
and trash!" she cawed in glee. "Naught and none

could ye take from me, but me very life.
And that a service would render me,
for I am old and suff'rin'. Or get ye
gone, ye nincompoops, and take yer strife

back to him as loves it well! Flee,
oh flee, milksops and minikins! Rattlecaps
and loiter-sacks! For 'tis time for me nap
and I am sore unwell. Begone!" And they

indeed did leave her fast, and flapped
like ducks in dire distress from her lair.
But no sign was seen there in the square
of any misdressed bandit or masked madcap.

And though the remnant day they fared
here and there about her door,
and e'en laid hands on many a beldam poor,
no sign nor spoor did they again regard

of the man who'd stripped their purpled lord.
Nigh dusk did they, like hounds dismayed,
tail drawn and muzzles drooped, return the way
they'd come. But as for Robin, one meeting more

was reserved to him this fated day.
For as he walked the thoroughfare
that winds the Sherwood way, bare
of arms, and garbed as an ancient maid,

slow and stooped as with age and care
as not to summon the sense of foe,
he was passed, upon the broad old road,
by a pair of priests returning there

toward the Barnsdale way. With a yowl to slow
'em, he shuffled up beside 'em, and cried,
"Pray a moment hold! Fathers kind, Fathers right,
won't ye spare a bit for a poor old widow,

lost her man to th'scruffles and her child to blight?
Pray, holy Fathers, won't ye lend us a hand?"
The two priests, one fat and red, one pale and thin,
cast each upon the next a knowing sight.

"Daughter," quoth longshanks, "by your deprivation
though we sorrowed be, we cannot succor thee,
for 'twixt our needs and divers acts of charity,
I dread that not a free coin on me stands.

But I shall pray for thee this day, rest easy,
and remember thee to God." And with blessing
and sign of holy cross, did make toward pressing
on. But quickly she: "Fathers kind, Fathers worthy,

could ye dream it not to spare a jot? Stressing
is me need, for I'm poor and can't afford
me bread. Have ye but a crust to ward
away me hunger?" "Daughter," quoth hamflanks, "distressing

though your need, yet we, alas, are fasting hard;
I've not a speck nor crumb upon me!
But I shall pray to God for thee."
And with blessing and cross, twisted his lard

upon the Barnsdale way. But quickly she:
"Fathers kind, oh Fathers good,
if ye have neither coin nor food,
could ye at least a moment with me tarry

to speak a prayer upon me soul? For demons brood,
I fear, upon me way, and dire's me state."
And they spoke as in a single wit:
"Daughter, we dearly wish we could,

for we are called to aid the indigent.
But Church business drives us hard this day
and we've not second to spare. But pray,
pray for thee we will, and that without stint,

in vespers and matins, and upon our way;
so go in peace, good child!" And did spin
again on the Barnsdale way. But Robin
heard, as they turned, a telling clink, and made

out strange lumps on the fat one's person;
and so called again, "But Father's kind,
one moment the more, for I've a mind
to propose to ye a right exchange: half what's in

your pockets, for all that's in mine..."
And the priests turned all mazed
upon this apparition for to gaze,
who no bauble, trinket nor lockets fine

was liable to own in all the world. Crazed
she seemed to them, and with a laugh,
smothered by proprieties, the daft
priests stuttered objection, in words all phased

by the suddenness of this auction. "Soft,
Daughter, for we've naught to fix!
'Twould be half of nothing for all of nix.
Prayers, penitence, and patience, then. God aloft

shall succor thee!" But she: "Good Father Sticks,
what's this me hears when quick ye turn?
What's this in your pockets chinks and churns?
Half in yours for all in mine. No tricks!

But ye shall be the richer for't." He spurned
Robin then with harsher phrase:
"Perjure me not, woman, nor dare accuse,
for I'm true in word, lest in hell I burn!

Away!" But she: "Of much I be guilty, but ne'er abused
the truth nor an honest man. But hold:
Good Father Sack-a-Lumps, may I be so bold?
Are yon bulges 'neath yon robe a ruse?

They do belie the severity lately told
of your pious fasting. No doubt the insides
of your drooping cassock can well abide
to halve their leanness, which in fulness of gold

some meat to spare bones I'd provide?
Half for whole, Father, and naught to lose:
thus strictly ye follow fasting's rules!"
But he rose up in embonpoint pride

and quoth, most vexed, "Why, ne'er shall a fool
make light thus of men of the cloth!
Begone, harridan: swift now, be off!"
But to their mazement, Robin most cool

the cowl about his visage did doff
showing to daylight a smiling beard,
and, speaking in manliness whilom unheard
cried, "Thank God this day, Fathers, and Christ aloft!

Thanks be! For this uneven weight ye both do bear
hath not gone unnoticed to honest eyes.
He hath appointed one to cut off vice
and free you at last of your worldly cares."

And shedding full his erstwhile guise
 he straited his back and stood him tall.
"Warlock!" cried th'one in terror; but th'other withal:
"Prevaricator and fibber foul! Know ye not that lies

the Lord will chastise and liars exile
to Hades' sulfured lanes?" "Yet for your pains,"
reposted he, "good Fathers, your gains
shall be equal great in heaven. But a while

ere accusations: some order first. Each in train
must be weighed on the scales of honesty.
First ye, Father Bones, for all to see:
turn your pockets on their heads, for I'd fain

know this day if you've lied to me."
And that worthy priest, fearing no doubt
grave misuse by some vicious gadabout
did as bid, and his pockets fast emptied;

and lo! for upon the ground there flowed a spout
of cash; and he, cringing back as from a cane,
cowered before this bearded dame,
his hands before his face. But turning to the stout

companion, Robin said, "Father Stones, shame's
in the pockets of your worthy peer;
let us see now how you will fare.
Your pockets bare, and if it proves the same,

we shall know then what type of virtue you wear."
And that priest, contemplating fisty defense,
yet demured and withdrew the contents
of his inner garb: bread and hams and cheeses fair

did line the road before him! And Robin bent
to gather in single heap the load
at his feet, seeming not least annoyed;
but rose smiling, and quoth in happy accent,

"'Tis true, good Fathers, your pockets are void!
And you proved honest men at last:
One is poor, and the other shall fast.
Now, to test the metal of my own word!" One coin

of gold he then withdrew in hand unclasped.
"All I have is here, 'tis yours i'th'round,
to prove my word is certes sound:
for half of nothing by God's still half!"

How they marveled, for't o'ervalued their gathered mound!
"I'd scribe on this coin but one request,"
continued he: "So listen close to my bequest.
This holy gold is ransom for such as are bound

in nets of vice, deceit, self-love and list,
that they might purchase freedom therefrom
through a dear and condign martyrdom.
Then give half the worth of this gold disc

to widows and orphans, the pressed, the dumb,
the downtrod and wretched and all that pine.
Half of what's yours, for all that's mine."
And so saying, handed o'er the gilded crumb

and sent them grumbling on down the lane.
But he turned round, and to the same
hamlet from which late he came,
did bear his gains: and ere the eventide had waned

had disbursed the lot to the pained, the lame
the misfortuned and dispossessed,
and to that antient widow whose very dress
had saved him that day in life and limb. His fame,

already wide, at this deed did far surpass,
for nor copper nor crust of bread did he retain
but to the cent and speck did make it plain
and offered it to fingers trembling in hard duress.

The grateful host did demand he full explain
this great windfall that he bore,
but he: "'Tis but a scrap of forest lore."
But they would not rest at that, and asked again.

And so: "'Twas the largess and careful store
of two Barnsdale curates, the which I know
you know. I met them as they did go
down the Barnsdale way, and did impress

inequalities on their consciences. They bestowed
willingly on me, to bestow on thee,
the fullness of their fortunes." But these
twin priests the folk too well did know,

and exchanged many a disbelieving eye. "Fie!"
cried sudden the same saving dame: "Notions
rare! For these crows but filthed their stations,
nor gave drop of water to thirsting need.

Praytell how then, by what evocations,
did ye bewitch them to Christian charity?”
But Robin smiled. “M’lady, ’twas no wizardry.
I but reminded them of God-given vocations.

’Twere simpler than to teach ’em economies,
additions and divisions and their kith.
But calculation’s speculation at its pith.”
“Should’ve hanged ’em in th’Barnsdale way!”

cried a voice, but he: “Nay, Ken Taft! for King’s grith,
God’s will and Sherwood’s way all shield
a man from violent ends, save he as wields
a blade first to kill. I’d play the locksmith

with a man’s own heart, but ne’er yield
to passions, passion’s fire to put out.
I swear ’tis a drake that each time shall rout
the best of men on its uneven fields.”

Then another: “Yet old Robin sure as day did flout
those dirty selfish nobs! For he robbed
’em blind and left ’em nude. By Bob,
he did ’em well!” But Robin: “Nay, Cob Stout!

For I swear I ne’er robbed a man, in hob
nor in will for good. They are richer now
than ere we met, by my lights I trow,
and richer yet shall be, if they do not snob

my exhortations to ’em. I allow
we shall know when they return:
for a man transforms as he has learned
the Way of Christ and brotherhood. Stow

your resentment 'til then, good men, and spurn
not these priests when they again show face
at your doors, your squares, and your holy place.
By their fruits then ye shall know them." "May they burn

in hell's dark pit!" cried a third. But he: "God's grace,
Aldebrand, that 'tis God and not man
who determines our final destination:
for else all would cook, each saint and scapegrace,

in Satan's fiery nook! May He stay his righteous hand
when He comes again to bring us justice!
And may ere then I have trained one soul vice
to shun and virtue embrace. 'Tis not by what ye've gained

or lost, robbed or been robbed of, that Christ
shall winnow ye to wheat or to chaff:
but what ye've done on His behalf
to bear your brethren to good." "And the heists

of Robin Hood then?" cried again Ken Taft.
"What are they, oh solemn preacher?"
"I am a hard and hardy teacher,"
reposted Robin with a hearty laugh,

"and spare my pupils not. But 'tis just feature
of my own vocation, for 'tis man's craft
to forge him burdensome crown and gilded haft.
Man's soul's a stiffened pleacher,

a bitter scion to be sweetened in graft.
I cut off no heads, but do willing amputate
that which rides 'em: frondy excess, unwieldy weight,
crown of prides and greeds afore and aft.

I go richer, that they may go light,
and with my pelf I do aright
such physic wrongs as are the blight
that avarice is wont to cause, or spite,

envy, or the many-headed hydra of vice
which excess in gold is sure to pay.
And they then go upon their way,
to sink again or to rise in flight,

as their will should have it. But I say,
if will will will to leave unfulfilled
the chance that the day has spilled
like riches in their laps, or turn away

the gifts of Godgiven luck; then will's
willing's not will's, but imposter's foul
in his place. Enow, good friends; for a bowl
of moonlit wine shall make my fill

and slake my thirst this night; and a ready cowl
shall keep me hid from owl or foe
as dare I now the Sherwood way to go;
and whip-poor-will shall with sorrowed call

guide me true to to and fro. Lo!
The woody path does summon me,
and I've never yet its summons fleed,
though dread had I that mortal bone

should break or flesh should finely bleed.
But God shall succor me, and see me on't."
And thus he did turn his face for his haunt
against the villagers' desire, who did much plead

him to stay there the night; but "Gaunt's
the eve," said he, "and full the morrow;
I should no longer daylight borrow
'gainst hypothetic gains, nor barter the font

against the sup. By my very pith and marrow,
God protect you all, and Godspeed on me!"
And went he then the Sherwood way
all bathed in frosted moonshine; and fallow

fields did ring him 'bout beseechingly,
begging the plow and harrow. He spoke
to the land in loving tones, and woke
their denizens with his singing; the trees

did seem to bend and bough, the folk
of the forest arising. Slumber past,
they shook their eyes of dust
and rising did they follow: the yoke

of sleep they shook off at last
and found it light and hollow. In cortege gay
'neath murmuring leaves they wended their way,
procession as has not been massed

since the Fall rendered man strange and fey
to the mistrustful race of beast.
Went they then to a midnight feast
and feasted them until the day,

when Robin, merry, did leave to go,
did rise again and go, the fields to plow
and the deepened wood to till.
And so he would and would again until

the end would come to him, and the Death,
as must to all mortal men, his breath
would steal, his flesh expend,
past all hope save God's own mend.

But perchance then his spirit's abroad still
'neath the oak and ash, wand'ring still with willing will
to test meeting souls in Robin's way,
to measure each man to the living day.

The Rogue

I

ark! all things in this vale are passing, and grace that it is so. For
eternity of anything in a fallen world should be falling eternal,
and it is in holy contrast that glory lies.

’Twas Christmastide of that year, and he was leaning back in
a chair of rough cut oak that had to it more years than any man there could
recall—a weathered and beaten old furniture that had no form to it but the
minimum necessary to keep it on its feet, as though it had been hacked of raw
timber and nailed together as the warp and woof of the pieces would stick.
Was leaning back, I say, and gazing into fast nothing, his chin upon his fist, and
he evidently much abstracted—though there was much to distract him, and
quite enough to keep any robust man in his senses, or far from dismal
thoughts. Bawlers and slick players were seated round at games of chance and
tales and bickerings, and rough red faces and grizzled beards, and glowing
bawdies at many a manly side. ’Twas all a noise and gambol, a wild and vulgar
display. Much shouting was there, and much harshness of tongue, and much
hacking hilarity. Of hilarity contrariwise there was none on *his* visage, but
rather a strange and winsome sadness, perchance, as on the face of one brood-
ing on nostalgia, or in the eyes of a refined soul that must despite itself con-
template the coarseness of things.

Had been about that inner gazing some time, and would like have remained at it some time the more, had it not been for a slight fellow beside him

who, filled to the rim with ale, carried his gesticulations too far, and, losing his balance, collapsed awkward and all akimbo into his lap—the which brought about general laughter and fingers pointed at the scene of the two of them trying to disentangle each from the other. And he, too, was laughing, though a laugh, it would seem, that was cored by some darker emotion.

"Hi, Loxley man," cried out a trim, handsomish fellow, "say now, what devil's got your tail! Ye seem hardly in your right spirits!"

"Why, he's at his *dreaming* again!" exclaimed a tart, sneering. She was a buxom, wrinkled thing, aged years beyond what was for her profession the prime, and was dressed in handsome raiment that was all for a younger woman, and rode upon her aging body like a second skin to furbish the tarnishment of time. "He's *always* at his dreaming!"

But he lifted an elegant hand, and was rewarded sudden silence, as faces turned upon him as upon a lodestone. He smiled sadly into their countenances. "Friends," quoth he, "I am sour."

"Sour!" slurred a gruff old fellow. "Hey, that's a pretty tune! 'Tis winter and the ale is in us, and there is a fire roaring also in yon hearth. That's fire within and fire without. What's there of sourness here? Get ye a wench, man, to warm your blood!" So saying, he shoved a woman before him, a slight lass of tender years who was bewildered still in this life she had fallen to, and who glanced about herself nervously with dark, timid eyes.

"Aye now, don't lose your way!" cried another drunkard, who grabbed this same girl hard by the arm and flung her roughly into his lap, where she cowered from the blows behind her and from those she might expect from the man to whose attention she had collapsed.

But he lifted that same elegant hand and caressed her blushing cheek with it, even as she drew back from his touch, as one who has known too many times the bad strength in the arm of men. And he smiled into her eyes, and helped her to her feet, she taking his hand with growing but still timid faith.

"Love is the madness that even reason craves," said he to her, "and this before me is a flower among women, whose beauty almost reminds me—But I say, friends, there is no right season for love. Lo! I would have a plum, I go to the tree in June, and there find myself the drupe ripe hanging. For grapes it is the summer vineyard, and apples the autumn bough. But 'tis another matter with the fairest fruit of the earth; for it grows in any time and in all and in none. Friends, I swear, the spirit is not in me for it, and my fingers are locked tight these frozen days." The poor trembling creature backed away from him, her eyes blinking, and she was snatched up at once by a pair of callous hands; and he smiled somehow tenderly at her passing.

"Then sing us a ballade, Loxley!" called out an old bearded man with a voice weak with its burden of years, rolling his wrist upon his cane. "They say ye are a fair voice!"

"My good man, you are a naughty flatterer, and a tempter rank!" admonished he, clucking his tongue and wagging a finger. "For music there *is* season, and winter, by my troth, is not the one for't, save lays and chants in due reverence of the incarnation of our Lord and Savior. The rest is not for me. I have consigned my lute to trustworthy hands, and shall not bend my fingers on its strings in these white days—nay, not 'til the blossoms are crowning the apple trees and petals are clinging to the buds, and the ground is white with pearls and not with hoarfrost. Come to me then in Sherwood, my good man, in lusty May, when emeralds and peridots glow i'th'eye, and I shall ply for you whatever tune you may desire."

"What might lift your spirits, then, Loxley?" came another voice, from somewhere in the crowd.

"Three months of the corkscrew sun around this mortal vale, friend," sighed he, "and the thawing of yon river."

"Ye are eating your life up in spleen!" cried the tart of before, whose face was reddened with some angering emotion. "Say, hard times are ever on our wretched race—but is this the way to face 'em, pouting there in your corner and pouring out bile? What kind of a man, what kind of a man!"

He took these words in a moment, and suddenly smiled, seemed to rise in his seat. "By troth, my lady, 'tis truth you speak!"

"Of course 'tis truth, man of Loxley!" cried she, her eyes wide and indignant. "Where would ye seek for knowledge but in a bawdy's mouth?" And suddenly she cackled vulgarly. But he smiled with such a smile as could smelt gold from filth, and sprang sudden to his feet.

"I say, friends!" cried he, "When the present cannot delight, 'tis the way of men to look to past or future. Now I say, the future is sought in vain by prognosticators, sibyls, palm-readers and haruspices, whose eyes are bent to transfix this veil of time, but in spite of their vain devilry, the morrow is God's alone. Yet all of us are future-bound, and it is our pleasure to build our castles on the hour to come. But speaking idly of our prospects is among the greater vices there are; for 'tis in the doing and not the pronouncing that future and heart alike are provisioned and proved. As for the past, it is a garden, friends, even when it is a midnight glen. Thus the winter, which freezes the garden about us, is the season for the garden within. I say—the winter is time for tales, epoch for epics. Who would give us a proper tale to keep our spirits high and warm through these dim, chill days?"

"But Loxley, who better than *you*?" sneered the harlot. "I say, who has lived better than *Loxley* has lived, and seen more of this world than *he*? Who could *possibly* have more to tell us?"

"I?" cried he with a mock of humble surprise. "I am but a sojourner upon my sliver of earth, Madam, and have lived only as well as God has given me to live." But many voices arose in dispute, and he, laughing, said, "Very well! *Vox populi*. But prithee, good folk of Barnsdale—you who have assigned the worker must apportion as well the task. What story would you hear?"

"Tell us the tale of the Bloody Butcher of Barnsdale!" cried with enthusiasm a young man, callow and with but the first down upon his lip; and at once he blushed, not from timidity, but from youthful awareness of too much awareness on him. He glanced about, and added with an air of defense, "For I have heard it telled in many a way, and ever and each time the new tale argues with the last. Well, then—I say—that is, I'd have the truth of it, I would! And from the horse's mouth—that is, not to say, of course—"

"Hey ho!" laughed he, throwing his head back. "I'll take your point by the flight of it, my young friend. Lo, here I am, a jument that shall carry ye all hence, if he may, and neighing merrily as he goes, though his poor back must sway beneath the weight of ye!"

And so saying, the rogue leapt forth.

"Now say, friends, I will recall you to a time long past now—so fast does the arc of time throw its dart!—when the county fair came to Nottingham. And it had been a fine year for apples and cider, that, and many were the able and red-cheeked cheeries who came, and barrels of the autumn's good stock, and the air had on it the scent of spices. 'Twas hard on May, in the days following Holy Week, and I swear in the wake of the Resurrection of our Lord the whole world wore on its aspect that same rubicund freshness and apricity, as of blood and living and the freshest blossoms of the new year. I say but not a day passed that the better part of the folk of Nottingham were not drunk on one or the other of these living saps, and truly it was a time of Godly mirth.

"Now it happened that, through the greening meadows and the leafing trees, one day did come through my very domain—for domain I call mine own that forest of Sherwood there, and if any man would challenge me for the rule of it, he has but to find me there in the warmer season, and dislodge me of my mossy throne—I say, one day did come through my domain a carriage all weighed down and heavy, and a figure driving the horses of it, he all wrapped up in hides and hunkered over his reins. And I upon seeing him did say to myself and thence to my good and ready men who were with me, 'Lo! that carriage meseems is weighted with riches of a sort. Let us go and have ourselves gander of it.'

"Forth we went, and in a glimmer had surrounded the carriage and stalled the horses; and one of us lay wait in the brush and sent an arrow forth to lodge in the side of its timbers, to alert our good driver that he was not only beset in ambuscade, but nigh surrounded by dozens of wild men. He, simple soul that he was, almost fell from his perch at the sight of us, and only with some alacrity of mind retained his post and his composure. He drew into his hood and glared down at us in fear and in hatred. 'Friend,' said I, 'for friend you must be, if you come this way bearing not even so much as a dagger to threaten the wayfarer—friend, I prithee, have no fear of me or of my men, notwithstanding this arrow that even now trembles in your carriage wall; for that is but my common mark and sign, I being the king of these woods, friend to all who are friend to all, and enemy sworn of whomever is friend to none. Say then, voyager—for I have interest in this thing that goes beyond my thieving name—what do you carry in this landed bark of yours?'

"'Meats!' shrieked he; and I do not know if it was the terror on him or some native reticence of character that kept him at so brief an inventory.

"'Meats!' I laughed. 'And say, of whom or what are these meats, and whence would ye be hauling them?'

"'Of me cow, sheep, and goat, Master Hod,' he said, 'or of what *were* me cow, sheep, and goat, ere I took 'em from 'em. And thus of me meself, Master Hod, are these meats. I carry 'em to sell 'em at the fair for fair price. And I beg of you to let me pass in peace, Master Hod, for I am a simple man, and depend upon these meats as upon me very breath.'

"'Verily, without his meats a man is naught but skin and bone,' quoth I, and said, 'Tell me, Master Butcher, whence do you hail?'

"'I am a Barnsdale man,' said he—with meet pride about him, I might communicate to all now present, since you are to a man his kinsmen. And jutted out his chin for the first time in that exchange, to show me that I was facing, for his heritage at least, a person of substance.

"'Well for it, Master Butcher of Barnsdale. I have a bit of business I should like to pass ye by, as ye are passing us. Now hear, and mark me well. How much could I pay you for everything ye have before you, save that beard of yours and whatever meat is attached to it?'

"'How now?' asked he, most suspicious. 'For this poor cart, and the mule that pulls it, you would know the price?'

"'Aye, Master Butcher,' said I, 'and not only, but the reins, wheels, spokes, bolts and screws that hold it from falling to shambles. And the whip in your hand, the cloak upon your back, man, and these leathern trousers here—even the boots that stand ye up. Also, and most especially, the meats that this carriage bears upon its worthy spine—save whichever of them cling to your soul.'

"'What?' cried he, 'And I, without me meats?'

"'Why, man, ye shall have the price of them to justify their loss.'

"'What?' he cried once more, all alarm now. 'And I to be left naked then by this road, with no transport to bring me neither fore nor back?'

"'That is the way of it, my most worthy friend, Master Butcher of Barnsdale. 'Tis promised by worldly sorts that gold can warm a man and carry him e'en to heaven and back. Dream the matter well.'

"'Master Hod,' said to me then this poor wretch, drawing back upon his seat and peering at me from under his hood, not yet sure whether to play it shy or sly, whether I was going to rob him in the end, or he me. 'These meats is me very livelihood, and that to a working man's his life.'

"'Then, Master Butcher,' I replied, smiling, 'you must sure pick ye a meet price.'

"I saw him deliberate the matter. I knew he was about such, for the knots his tongue was tying in his throat as he glanced from the ground to me and back again. He was measuring me, my friends—measuring me as we measure a man who might be demon and might be angel. And by and by, he set his jaw, and tossed back his head, and said, "I could not abandon me here by this road, naked and with no transport and no cent to my name, for aught less than three pound.'

"'What!' cried I, feigning amazement. 'Is *that* all ye would have? As said, so done!' and clapped my hands as I watched the poor fellow's gaze go out like a light, at the prospect of all the riches that might have been his, but for his excess in caution. His poor jaw set to working like the blade he used to saw his meats. Yet certainly he could not up the ante now that the deal was ready sealed, and so he clamped his tongue like a vice and swallowed his bitters like a man, though he was frowning a-fierce. And I marveled, and not for the first time, that a man may lament that his fine fortune were no greater, and weep bitter tears over the very treasures that God's good will has heaped at his feet.

"Yet I shall say this in favor of our good butcher, that this poor wretch, once the deal had been struck and the agreement stuck, did descend from his high carriage with face up and back straight and all the humility of a Christian, and got him firmly onto the ground, where he began at once and without complaint to divest himself of every sad rag upon his back, save for that barest minimum which could account for dignity and decency. A box of coin was apportioned out by my men from one of our local caches, and brought straightaway, as our good butcher stoically did show his milky breast to sky, birds, and sun, which babyish skin I am certain had not seen the blaze of day for a living lifetime. He took the box offered him, and set at once with great sobriety to counting out every last coin within it; and when he had satisfied himself that we had not robbed him of a cent, then with a dignified word of gratitude he did stand, and set forth along the road to Barnsdale, barefoot and head high, hefting thence, together with his own and not inconsiderable personal meats, a box of gold, and hiding with each weighty tread the suffering he felt, that his burthen was not greater.

"Now, friends, I set me about it. I donned me our friend the butcher's scattered garb, bethinking sure of those cities of lice and fleas that called it home, but willing in the name of the public good to bear the weight of these minor kingdoms. My own clothes I padded in about me, to mimic the meatiness of any self-respecting butcher. I explained to my men what I was about, and, though they were somber and trist—no doubt because they are much loth to part with me—yet I loaded myself onto my newly got wagon, and, towing behind me my freight of newly got meats, left, alone, for the fair town of Nottingham.

"Arrived I thus with the weight of many a murdered beast on my back, and came hard into a square, me all filled with life and livers. And I got me off of my carriage, and looked about me a moment, before setting up the call. 'Hey—oh!' called I then to the fair folk of Nottingham. 'Hey—oh! Meats a-sale, meats a-sale, a tithe the price! Hey—oh, meats a-sale oh!'

"And by and by, hearing these tidings of tithings, a few skeptic heads did approach my wagon. 'Hey, Master Butcher,' said they, 'whence do ye hail?'

"'I am the Butcher of Barnsdale,' proclaimed I loudly, in all due pride at the cachet of this title, 'and my meats are a-sale.'

"'And this price, Master Butcher,' ventured they, 'sure it means that these meats are green and almost at reeking?'

"'Have a gander with your own eyes—or noses, as ye would fain,' countered I, 'but these meats are fresh as daisies. New meats and salted meats have I, meats of cow and sheep and goat, and all the various parts of all the various beasts; and 'tis all as you see it and as I say it, a tithe of the price you will find in any butchery in any corner of England.'

"So saying, I opened my meats to the light of day; and lo! for our good butcher of Barnsdale did not lie, and his meats were many and glorious to the light, iced about to preserve them, pink and tender and of every good sign of quality and health. The skeptics stooped and stared and sniffed and tittered, and at length did willingly open coin purses and pockets, and began to buy my meats by the pound, perceiving in me no doubt a fool or a madman, and only too eager to take advantage of my congenital weakness. Thence they went, carrying the good tidings with them, and I for my part kept up my declarations from aside my wagon. 'Hey—oh!' cried I, 'Hey! Meats a-sale, meats a-sale, ne'er a lesser price for greater meats! Hey—*oh*!'

"By and by a swelling crowd assembled about me, and there was I with meats in my hands distributing to all callers left and right, and there were they flying at me with gold. 'Good butcher, good butcher!' they cried, and gave their orders; and I, fossicking amongst my meat wagon, did like a proper merchant return with meats a-shucking from my fingers. A hunger was on the poor folk, and I doled out my meats to fill their need with such alacrity as I could muster, until the wagon was nigh voided.

"Now it happened that, catching wind of the good news, a man of the most riotous Sheriff of Nottingham did carry the word of my meetings to his employer, which worthy got himself at once hence, bethinking himself that some mischief must be about, if anyone were divesting himself so liberally of so much hard-earned flesh. Woe to us all, that the least little sign of Christian largesse doth prick doubts in the heart! And so he came himself in person, our fair Sheriff, attended by two men, to see what I might be about, and to sniff out the deceit that was sure in't.

"I was by then at the last of my meats, a poor trifling sample of what marvelous abundance I had lately boasted. I spied the Sheriff a-riding with most interested visage up to my wagon, where I had lately finished haggling a humble dame down from the offensively regular price she was trying to swindle me into taking from her. I perceived the great man's coming as I dislodged myself from the bowels of my craft, where I had been cutting off a bit of rib for a blind old codger, stooped by the wayside. I handed this fellow the rib with my blessings, bethinking myself that as God had once borrowed a rib from all us male folk, I might with the Lord's permission reestablish it to this man as had been born e'en without eyes. And had just in time given him a portion of his lost inner parts—*gratis*, of course, for one does not pay what one has lent—as the Sheriff said to me, 'Master Butcher, might I ask for a pricing of your goods?'

"'My Lord Sheriff, my honor to serve! My meats, whatever they be, are a tenth the price of whatever it be—the going price, that is, in whatever butchery, be.'

"'And how is this tithe arrived at, good Master Butcher, when the price does vary from butcher to butcher?'

"'Why, my Lord Sheriff, I am a humble and trusting man, and leave it to my customer to 'stablish the price—whatever it be. The world has ne'er yet maltreated me!'

"'And for example that steak there, my good man—if I were to offer you twopence for it?'

"'Then I would say that 'tis a meet price! And my Lord Sheriff would be most welcome to it!' cried I, and at once went scrambling to get him his steak.

"But he held up his hand and said to me, 'Nay, my good man, nay; I am in wont of no steak. I asked for curiosity's sake. For I marvel that any meatmonger can hawk his goods at so low a price.'

"'Does it not seem to my Lord Sheriff a fair price?'

"'Fair or not fair I would not know, my good man. 'Tis not the price that goes.'

"'It seems to me the price goes handsome well,' replied I, even then passing off some meats to a happy huswife.

"But ignoring this, he said, 'And tell me, how is it that ye are able thus to pay even the feed on your beasts?'

"''Tis simple enough, my Lord Sheriff! My beasts roam free.'

"'Roam free!' exclaimed he, much taken aback.

"'Yes, my good Lord Sheriff! For my Lord Sheriff must understand—I am a fortune-struck man, that not long ago was starving. One day a-wandering at the border of Sherwood forest in search at least of berries or edible toadstools, I did come upon a herd of wild cattle, ranging there in a meadow, owned by no man and so now owned by me. Since then I have lived of 'em. I take a tithe of their meats each month, and ask in return a tithe the price of other meats, which seems to me a fair price, as 'tis that I ask of my kine. They live by tenths of me and I live by tenths of them, and all pay me tenths for the tenths that I take; and so is equity made in the world.'

"'A herd of wild cattle...!' exclaimed the Sheriff, who had not heard be-yond this news, and the beautiful prospects it opened to his marveling eyes.

"'Aye, a herd of God's own bovine!' exclaimed I. 'In fact,' I added at once, giving to my voice all semblance of eagerness, 'in *fact* I could show my Lord Sheriff just what and where they are, my beautiful cows! What pleasure to show him what a fortune I have found! Nay, I know—my Lord Sheriff is a busy man—but if he would take just an hour of his time, to share in the joy of a poor chance cattle farmer, like the good soul I know him to be...'

"'Just what and where...?' he echoed, somewhat numbly, methought; and I saw at last what I had been searching in my Lord Sheriff—that same hunger for meats that had late been glimmering in so many a patron's eye about me. For my friends, I was born to minister to the needy. Barely did he hold himself back, by force of what was seemly, from licking his thick lips. 'Why,' said he, giving his voice that deceptive measured tone that a man will put to it, who hopes to pull a fast one on his neighbor, 'why, that would be most generous of the good master butcher indeed, and I would gladly see what luck has be-stowed upon him. For atimes and truly, it does one's heart good, to see a man as has started rough but ended well...'

"And thus 'twas easily arranged. The Sheriff, in his great impatience to seize these cattle, chose to part with me alongside the two men that had ac-companied him. I offered the rest of my meats at the usual price to a well-to-do sort, who recoiled in disgust from them, and so I gave them off to a pair of urchin boys along with the same money the gentleman ought to have paid me, out of an interest in balancing the books; and, gesturing most animatedly to our friend the Sheriff, did urge him to follow me hence, toward the wood—I alone and unarmed, and they in three.

"By and by we came to that key point in the Great Highway, in which I, knowing what I was about, stopped my carriage and drove it off the road, and behind a mossy mound; and unhooked my donkey therefrom and seated my-self upon him, saying to the Sheriff, 'My Lord Sheriff will understand, of course, that these wild cattle do not keep by the road, they being shy sorts—yet they are not far now, I swear it!'

"And I saw the eyes of the Sheriff and his men drift uneasily over the

densing foliage of that wood; but the greed had the better of them, and their
hearts were made bold by a certain hunger. They assented to follow, bethinking themselves, no doubt, that before them was but a poor idiot butcher of
fortune, and that the dirty deed they must soon perform would really be all
the more comfortably played out in some hollow of the forest, and not upon
the thoroughfare itself—particularly as it was a fair day, and they could count
on many travelers beating the dust of that road into their heels.

"So they followed me. I would glance back at 'em from time to time, to
relish me of the nervousness etched onto their faces, and also to gesture most
eagerly at them, whispering words of bovine encouragement. Glanced I as
well to the trees and the brush, and saw there sign of silent company, which
could not help but make me smile, as to how wild we had become to move so
swift, invisible and sure. And the Sheriff on the other hand, nervous and
placid as a cow himself, did follow obedient and muzzled, manacled by the
thought and dream of the same pasture I had claimed for my herd. I say, my
friends, it was leading cows to cows that day.

"Now there is a spot, not far from the highway, as I had indeed promised
them—a little glade that nestles into the elbow of a brook, with shade-giving
trees grouped about and fair pasture to be had in the warm sunlight, and at its
center a great oak, the king of all its kind in Sherwood. And I knew this spot
as a favorite of the deer of the wood; for I would often go there, not indeed to
hunt—for such would be to ruin once what might forever yield me
plenty—but to stalk my game from there, or atimes simply to loll in the forest
as a stag myself, and train my limbs to otium to better ponder the world. I
brought the Sheriff and his fair men to a spot not long distant from that
meadow, where the meadow itself could easy be surveyed from a point of
some repair; and, as I had measured me the wind, I knew that we were safe,
there, from disturbing the beasts that would be a-roaming in that place. And
lo! God favored me that day, for there were more of them than even I might
have dreamed, a veritable herd indeed, of deer and doe and buck and fawn, all
grazing and capering and lying silent in the shade of the oak—I say, more than
I had ever seen before, as though they were in on our little joke, and meant to
delight in the Sheriff's bafflement as well as I!

"So we stopped there on that rise of ground, we four—a fool and the three greater fools that had dedicated themselves to the robbing of fools; and I saw the Sheriff gazing about with that narrow gaze of his, striving with all his poor intellect to comprehend me. I, eager, pointing toward the glade, filled to its brim with beasts of the wood; and he, following my pointing finger and striving to capture its intent—but finding there, the poor fellow, not even a single of those cows that had grown so precious to him in late hours. 'My Lord Sheriff, see you not my cows?' I cried at last, puffing big with pride; and saw him blanch as he found me indicating, no cattle at all, but a herd of the finest of the King's deer.

I shall not reproduce the blasphemies he uttered, but sure it was that an entire herd of cows in that instant were slain to the world, and a thousand flanksteaks and beefsteaks and bowls of ground liver went up in great bitter puffs of smoke, metamorphosing against all natural principles into but sacrosanct and awfully unsaleable deer. His hand flailed by for his sword. But there is a moment, my dear friends, in the mind of poor man—that beast who is chained cowlike to expectation and perception—there is a moment, I say, in the dawning of novelty, when the shadows stretch too long and cover the eyes with too great a darkness; a moment, I say, when our witness, failing to understand how he himself could ever have been so mistaken, is shocked and muted to respond. By the time the Sheriff had drawn his steel, my own men had already surrounded us, arrows set upon the Sheriff and his two worthies. And he found me there smiling before him, not at all the butcher he had dreamed.

"'My Lord Sheriff,' announced I, throwing back my cloak and divesting myself of my falsened belly, 'welcome to Sherwood, in whose abode and kingdom I call myself the warden and steward. My Lord and his men have come far this day to gaze upon my battening kine; the least I can do in recompense for time spent, is offer them a meal of the meat of these self-same cattle. For truly, you shall be well meeted here!'

"'These are the King's deer, you madman!' cried the Sheriff, thinking still, no doubt, as his mind labored to regain the sprinting moment, that he was talking yet to a fool.

"'Aye, Lord Sheriff, 'tis true; these be the King's own cows we find before us. And I myself am the King himself, my good Sheriff, within the airy walls of this bosk. Then I am most at my rights in expending these bovine as I please.'

"'Treason, man!' he sputtered. 'No man is King but the King!'

"'He is King of a thing who has right use of it,' smiled I, 'and I see that our poor King of England is much too tasked to consume even the enormous and rich fare that his cooks heap before him. Poor King! A kind of Sisyphus he is. Each time he clears his board it is at once filled for him anew, and his devouring never finds any repose, but there is always something novel to swallow. 'Tis a shame for any man to become a gullet. Pray, let us all now take a little weight from off our monarch's tortured and tumescent belly, and aid him in consumption of his obligations, for our poor King, misapprizing his abilities, has claimed of this land more than he can digest. I say—let him be the King of his table this day, and we of ours.'

"'You, man, who are you, that should dare...!' cried the Sheriff; and I marveled at him, that ingenuity should be so hard dying in his bestartled mind.

"'Why, my good Sheriff!' chided I, 'almost am I offended to be so unrecognizable to a face that I know so well! At least my Lord Sheriff's sense of context should do for him, what his memory cannot. But be that as will.'

"'What treachery is this!' cried the poor Sheriff, yet visibly at loss.

"'Who speaks to me of treachery, Lord Sheriff?' parried I. 'And tell me—what was it when three men followed one into a forest, he with intent of sharing a morsel of his good luck, and they with intent of robbing it of him whole?'

"'But you were the one that lied on't!'

"'After my Lord the Sheriff had well stuffed the bedding,' laughed I. 'In any case, fear not, Lord Sheriff—for we are generous and Christian folk, we folk of Sherwood, and would not have any guest of ours go forth barehanded or barebacked. My Lord Sheriff has come to this wood in search of meats, and it would be in offense of good generosity, to send him back wanting.'

"So saying we took the arms of the Sheriff and his men, and the gold they had about them, and a number of nice trinkets to boot, and their horses as well, which truly were magnificent beasts, telling them that it was a shame to keep such excellent specimens stalled up and penned in, but rather that it was the better part of wisdom to let them to their natural roaming, alongside the King's cows. And we took three fresh steaks cut of the venison of Sherwood, and tied these to the breast of the Sheriff and his men, and with the same ropes did lash up their wrists behind their backs, to be sure that they should arrive safely in Nottingham with the gifts we had gifted—those ripe steaks, from which the juices were still streaming, so that our good Sheriff and his two worthies would be truly red with them by the time they made it home once more. We dressed them in skins of bucks but lately killed, head and antlers and all, and accompanied them to the forest road—for such was the minimum obligation of our hospitality—and gave them a warm and hearty farewell, to send them on their way. Though I was not there to see it, I hear that the women of several houses at the gate to the town, and even a few manfolk as well, did faint straight out upon seeing their poor Sheriff stumbling back home, his arms having evidently been cut from his torso, and he garbed as some demon of the wood, and his heart gushing out blood. Well can I believe they reacted so; for it was sure the first time they had ever caught sight of that particular member of the Sheriff's body, or even suspected its existence. We, for our part, had ourselves a fine feast that day of our own meats, and celebrated thus the honor we had received at the visitation of so great and worthy a functionary.

"And that, my friends, is why they call me the Bloody Butcher of Barnsdale."

Much did his audience revel at his tale, and in particular at the final image of the Sheriff and his men, bedraggled and footing it, dressed as deer and bleeding to boot, as they stumbled back in after miles of road to Nottingham, only to produce such an effect on all the eyes that witnessed them. And cheers were raised to the daring and courage and wit of the tale; and one fellow in particular called out that he was a most inventive spirit indeed.

"Inventive!" cried he, smiling at the word. "And say, friend—do you mean, inventive in acting or inventive in telling?"

"Both, I should say!" cried he; then, bethinking himself, "But of course, in this present case, more inventive in the telling, to be sure..."

"Ah! And why would you put stress upon *that* point?"

"Well," hesitated he, considering his position with a sudden care, as a man who is called out to give account. "I mean to say—this is but a high tale, and not a story derived of fact itself—"

"Was ever the difference drawn by teller or tale?" smiled the rogue.

"Well, I cannot say, but... That is to say—beggin' your pardon, but, these things did not really *happen*."

And he, rather than responding, but smiled and put his hand in the air, and, splaying the fingers, turned his palm toward his own face, and, so displaying his digits, showed the entire room the two rings he wore—one on his index finger, a band of silver with a seal in it, of an eagle with wings braced to air; and one on his ring finger, a band, it looked, of polished wood. "This ring," said he, pointing to that with the seal, "is none other than the seal of the Sheriff of Nottingham, which he would once wear on his right hand. 'Twas confiscated from him the day in question, for an animal of such nobility should not adorn a beast of such swinishness. I wear it upon my left out of contrariety and will to mark as mine what is said to be by rights another's."

Much did all marvel at this ring, which seemed against all sense or credibility to prove all that the teller had told; and they gazed at one another and muttered to each other in perplexity.

And by and by, another of them, a wiseacre and a prankster, spoke up, saying, "O Loxley, well enough that ye've espoused the ring of another; but my question is rather for that ring that seems to have spoused you. Say, why do you, who is eternal bachelor and sworn to singlehood, wear the signal of matrimony on that finger there—that finger 'twixt the useless and the vulgar?"

"What!" cried he merrily, retracting his hand at once, and touching the finger that had inspired the question. "And how do you know that this head is not wed?"

"All know it, Loxley!" cried the witster, right willing to play. "For a man that lives as you are wont to live, almost as a wolf or a fox—say, what could such a man do with a wife?"

"What, but adore and revere her as the sun?" parried he.

"But ever from due distance," parried the other, "and far from any proper hearth she might dust for 'im."

"There is a hearth in the heart itself, my young master," said he, "and it is there a man will go to warm his deeper bones. If he can find his love there, then I say—that is a blaze that none other can mime. Say, what would you tell me, if ye knew that I was wed?"

"I would say bullocks—with respect to the famosest name in all of England," said the other, with a mocking bow.

"Then I will say to you, young master, that ye are too fresh a skeptic," smiled he.

"And what is the name of Master Loxley's bride, then?" asked the rake, none shaken in his certainty.

"Marion, she is called, and by all is known."

"Marion of Loxley, is it then?" mocked the other once more.

"Nay, but Marian de Gils."

This remark was met with a silent amazement in that hall; and verily, even the young rake was taken aback at it. Muttering went from mouth to ear, and one old drunkard was heard to laugh, as though this had been the cleverest jest of the day.

"Marian de Gils," repeated the rake, his smile seeking the edges of a frown; and said no more, as if the tone of this affirmation itself would suffice to reveal the absurdity of the claim.

"None other than," replied he, calm as can, "*if* you would have the name that convention has given her. If you would have her true and rightful name—then I will tell you she is the Rubicond Rebel."

"I know not what I think of that," countered the skeptic, shy, as men will be, of oddity, "but a Marian de Gils I know by hearsay, as all do, for her beauty and her wit are renowned. One Marian de Gils, I say, I know: and know her, as again all do, for the wife of Sir Humphrey de Gils."

"Then see, young friend—you are not as uninformed as you have so far made out!" laughed he; yet something sad was about his smile once more. "Yet perchance you are the more confused. Mind the brand that the thief has stamped upon the goods he has robbed."

"Robbed!" scoffed the rake. "How *robbed*? She has been wife of Sir de Gils now since they were wed—and that was nigh fifteen years back! How *robbed*? They have seeded se'en children together, Master Loxley, have mingled flesh and blood in a septet knot. How then *robbed?* She wears the band on her finger that marks the prime link of an invisible chain, which leads back to her master's hand—how then, Master Loxley, has she been robbed from any man at all?"

"By the laws of all that's seemly, you are delivered, my lad. But breathe with care your first breath of honest air. I would ask you, my good man—if that chain is invisible, how do you mark where it ends? And as for these other signs and evidences that you propose—why, what's palpable in 'em? I say, time's as invisible a chain as ever were, and skin is all seeming, and its roots all inward. Ye are one well fit for appearances, lad, if you play so freely the joker of the gamesman."

"Strange words," proclaimed the rake, embittered, and shrugged, and spat upon the floor.

"I would not waste so much spittle over so small a critique," said he, smiling wide once more, and not taking this lad up on his challenge. "But lo, I am gifted the power of gab this day, and I will gladly tell you a tale to make you the master of these events, that you can judge of 'em with grace and right, rather than speaking, as you are presently doing, as a man in the dark, of matters darkened. Hear first, friend, and then I will have your word on't. Are ye accorded with me, as the string to its lute? Yea or nay..? Speak out, man..! Oh, I have said I would not play this day, nor song nor ballad, but I am set to make myself a lyre. Say only—*will* ye listen? Or is it I that's mum, or mere a mummer? Then God bless ye, lad! For a man without ears is like a fish of no gills.

"Hey ho! I was young once as ye; and as is sure the case with ye, I was a game and cocky fellow. This blood was hot and fiery in me, and did bring me to course and range over all the hills and dales of all the land, seeking out violence and adventure, and over and above all things, my fairest lady—that shining one whom I might call the love forthright of my life, and light her like a lamp in my skies to provoke Venus herself in the glowing. For I have known since my years were green that I was bound to one, and one alone, and no matter the forms that should fall betwixt my arms, curve of bow or tree or mare, yet those arms could bend to fit around a single waist alone, and my spirit mesh and mold with a lone other. And I say, man, I knew her as I saw her; for the eyes that are in my head were crafted for the vision, and it fell on them like a body to its shadow. She was Marian, son of Gilbert Gracy, and in those days still a maid; and I, fool and outlaw that I was, took to win her favor as any knave could—by treachery and surreptitious movements of the body and the soul. Letters I would write to her, to entrust to her maid, who favored me, and notes to tell her by what sign she could mark me among the crowd, to see in the distant shining of my eyes the love that I bore her. Machinations myriad did I weave around her, and left her sign of me in all the places she would go, to point ever and once again to this still and constant soul in me, that was and will be forever hers alone. Poetry I composed for her, and sang it to her on occasions various, whilst showing to eyes not in the know that I was but a poor wandering minstrel or a drunkard bawling in the street. But *she* knew, I warrant; she heard me, though she did ignore me many long months; and her eyes sought me out though her spirit resisted. I say, what is a woman whose heart needs no conquering? 'Tis a drake bereft of gall and gold, a fortress abandoned. Anything would I have done, and many absurdities did I accrue to an already much absurded name, to demonstrate the loyal flickering of this heart's flame. I would have done as much merely to glimpse her. Perhaps some here have seen her? Then they know what light is.

"Long was my courtship. That first word from her lips was hard earned, I swear it. I would have measured deserts out with my body like an inchworm for such a sup of joy. Many were the months even after that before I gained the first glimmer of her trust—that trust which is as hard of the earning as of the losing; for, once given, 'tis never retracted.

"God bless me, but her heart by and by was mine, and I was drunk on the world itself. Alas! it was a thing from the first doomed. How was I, this rapscallion, to hope to wed her? Yet she protested she would come with me. How was I, who loved her, to rob her from that plenty in which she found herself, and subject her to a life of modest means and uncertainty constant, consigning her children to a life of equal or worse doubt still? Yet my heart protested that our love would be a palace, and the flesh of our flesh could grow from no richer mulch than that which paves the informal roads of Sherwood. I do not know, friends, to this day, how I hoped to marry her, or what we hoped to gain of it. Perhaps only this: a knowledge that what lay between us had been welt in the fires of heaven, though those of Earth should quaver before soldering two metals of such diverse origin. In such things, I swear it, two minds are sufficient for the knowing and the memory. Love is a second world.

"Imagine it, then, how my heart was rent, when I learned that her father would have her the wife of another—a nobleman, to be sure, of at least a worded honor. And it seems to me now as then that he did this, not only with scope in mind of fastening his family to one of higher stature, nor of securing for himself and his progeny a good name and good means; but also because he had somehow divined the power between us, and knew that his ward was in hazard of being filched by a bard. For she was taken from me, her very hand-maid exchanged for another, and all the fleeting and narrow avenues by which I had since pierced her cloistered bower were of a sudden shut closed to me. My queen became a kind of ghost, and was no longer seen in the living light of day; but her father sowed her up tight in a cocoon of his own making, and in this chrysalis did propose to make her a different kind of creature than what she had been. To me 'twas reversal itself; she had been the butterfly, and he would make her a kind of crawling and begging thing for the remainder of her days.

"I was in torment and woe. These past bitter days appear to me, compared to those, as blessed and halcyon indeed. I went my way dispirited and heavy of soul, and much did I dwell on death, as a man will hope for the coming of a dear friend who can win him from his troubles. I do not know what should have become of me, if my fellow John Smallman did not come to me one day bearing tidings that seemed to him sorrowful, but to me the pith of mirth.

"For he had found, had John—and to this day I know not where nor how—had found the date, the hour, the place, and the company of those wedding ceremonies. 'Twas a modest and little-known chapel, and but a few souls standing at the ceremonies—enough as should suffice for formality. For Marian's father, as jealous men will, had clutched so tightly that even what he was holding was squeezed out his fingers. He thought to avoid all danger in secrecy; but little did he know that I am the prince of silence.

"Oh, I embraced John and kissed his blessed hairy cheeks and chortled like a bird! I might have married him, so delighted was I, had I not been betrothed to another. I gamboled about the forest all that day as a child of the wood. I say, I was reborn. For I knew then that what was mine should be marked as mine, and I who was Marian's should finally be Marian's; and if the show of the thing could not be ours, then at least we should have the truth of it.

"The day of the wedding, there upon the church's stoop, there arrived at the very cusp of the ceremonies three men. One, a dwarf; one a beggar; and one a minstrel dight fast in scarlet. This last was I, and I beat upon that door until it was answered by the Father of Marian himself. And I said to him, 'Greetings, milord; I am but a humble minstrel, benamed Alan-a-Dale, who has divined that this day two souls are to be bound in holy matrimony, and have come in present company to make gay the fest with music sweet and dulcet to the ears of the beloved and her lover.'

"'What is this?' cried he. 'How did you hear that a wedding is here to be performed?'

"'I am friend of birds, for they are creatures of song; and one of them did communicate me this dear news. I have come to celebrate, milord, the joy of milord's ward and the man she has chosen for her own.'

"'Impertinence!' cried he, much heated and reddening of his whiskered cheeks. 'I say, we want none of you here!'

"'Does milord's daughter desire no dulcet dancing to delight this diamorous day?'

"'The choice is not hers, but mine own, ye blackguard, and if ye do not get hence, I will have your tongue out for't!'

"'Tut, tut! This tongue bears too many words yet in it to lop it from its root,' smiled I, 'and the choice is yet the bride's. See ye the point?' And so saying, did press a dagger through my cloak and into his side, so that he stepped back, amazed, and regarded me with horror, saying, 'By the dickens, who are ye?"

"'Why, I am called Will Scarlett,'" said I, "'so named, let us say by way of hypothesis, for the blood I have spilled.'

"'And what would you have, man?' whimpered he, much terrorized.

"'Be gay yet, milord,' I smiled in response, 'for I, too, would have here a wedding this day.'

"We entered into the chapel and closed the door tight behind us; at which,

John drew back his cloak and my jolly friend the Friar—for such was to be our officiate—drew off his cowl; and John, made larger by virtue of his favored crossbow, saw to the guardian of the bride and the father of the groom, as well as naturally the groom himself, divesting them of the little arms they carried and herding them into a corner, where they would pay right witness. The priest was corralled there with them, and there they waited, John menacing them as necessary with his deadly bolt, as I drew my dear bride to me, and gazed a moment into her eyes. Few words were we able to exchange—sufficient to promise each to the other for all that might come—and then we bid the Friar to gain the altar. He did, and there he did preside over that ceremony and saw us bond and wed with every necessary formulation, and added to boot a touch all his own; for he pulled from his pocket a favored tome of his which he carried on his very person, and read aloud from it a verse condign:

> *Haec cum superba uerterit uices dextra*
> *Et aestuantis more fertur Euripi,*
> *Dudum tremendos saeua proterit reges*
> *Humilemque uicti subleuat fallax uultum.*

The rings that had been promised brought to seal the false marriage I did confiscate, as tax upon the ceremony—for truly, by then, I had furnished all that was necessary for that event, save the testimony of those who watched from their corner—and I presented my bride the rings that I myself had cut and carved from the bole of the oak tree aforementioned. We hung these rings about our fingers, and were given to each other by the word of the good Friar, who, when his offices were concluded, cried, in his usual good cheer, 'And may you be wed long and prosperously, and God bless you both!' And at that happy word I kissed my bride for the first time; and so was espoused to her for all days of all my life, by law of man and God, in this world or beyond it.

"Thus happily we were wed, and that bond ne'er dissolved in heaven or on earth, but was supplanted by the great thief Father Time. But for that tale there is no season at all, my friends, and I have not the heart to speak anent, nor ever shall."

"This stands well against the common sense, singer," observed the skeptic.

"All that's common is bland," smiled he.

"I do take you for a clever man—but mendacious no'theless."

"Grant me at least *splendide mendax*! But I shall console myself that you are starting to take me seriously."

"Not yet. Would you have us believe you, sirrah? Then explain in detail what happened after you were wed."

"I told you I would not."

"So you will not tell us why you were ne'er punished, or how she came to wed de Gils, or why your own marriage to her was not brought before the banns?"

"And say, *did* she marry him?"

"All the world knows it! It's in her name, by God!"

"Much that all the world knows is folly. Always doubt the name. A name's a fickle thing."

"Aye, 'tis!" cried someone, "for who ever heard of Will Scarlett?"

"I've heard of him!" cried the old man. "A minstrel and a dandy he was, a fair bawdy fellow; of such a sort as'll die young, even should he die old. Aye, I know him, that's a fact…"

"Then he's real, this Will Scarlett!" marveled another.

"And say, Master Loxley," put in the skeptic, "if all's as ye say it was, then—why that name above all others?"

He smiled. "My young friend is ne'er sated. Alas, the past is passed; all that's left of it is rumor in the ashes, and smoke on the breeze of voices, and ears sniffing like noses at the scent of what was burning. Only the word of God, I say, lasts against e'en a secular fortnight. You doubt well, my young man, you doubt well. Nonetheless, this thing is as I have said, and the name was mine by rights to use."

"How? Do you know Will Scarlett?"

"Know him! Hah! Friends, how does a man know his son, how does he know his father or his brother? Measure me thus. Now I say, I have weighed this thing out, and determined upon it: I shall tell you a secret. 'Tis one I have for these many years of my life hid up in me like a jewel. But I feel myself nigh at the end of things—no, do not scoff, good friends, looking upon my not-so-antique limbs! For a man feels it in his heart when he is fit for parting. And that is true of places and of times and of folk, and of life itself. I say, I keep a few things locked in this heart that shall go to the grave with me, and there with me lie in the cold cuckold earth, to keep me in good company; and I swear, they are hard enough that not even the worms will get them, nor these bones of mine outlast them to the moldering and slow-consuming flames of rot. Such are the locks about them. Yet this, perhaps, is not one of them; I can spare you this jewel, friends, for I am come rich enough for that. Aye, verily, let me unlock a little. I will tell you then the secret of a name—"

But at that moment there was trouble heard beyond the door of the ale-house, the shrieking of a woman who seemed to be battling with someone; and the rogue stood straight upon his heels and looked direct at those doors, as though he should leap for them. Others lent their heads to this side and that as if to ask each other and the facts themselves what was afoot; and the skeptic seemed bemused. Then the doors burst open, and gave leave to a gust of the frigid air, and a man came tramping through the door behind it with a woman almost riding upon him—a girl, even, of no more than sixteen years, and snow clinging to the hems of her skirt; a lass that no one therein knew, of red hair that was straying wild beneath her bonnet, and frail and slender form, but eyes that burned with a fury so that no one could tell even the color of them, and the rogue watched her with strange consternation. She was knocking at the helmeted head of the soldier with tiny fists reddened by the ice; and fallen snow was flying from her clothes. She was a lovely thing indeed, riled there with a wrath that that small form could not even for the best of it express; and she was screaming, "Ye shall not have him, ye shall not have him, get ye back!" But the guard put guantletted hands to his head and shielded him from her little fists, which cut open and began to bleed upon that metal; and he flung her off and away from him and shook himself like a dog come in from the rain. She fell to the floorboards with a thud, sobbing, and rose at once to her knees beseechingly, though she had been hurt; and in that posture tended toward the rogue with her arms outstretched imploringly, as he stared down at her. But another guard was fast upon her, and grabbed her by the waist and drew her up; and in that pose carried her, though she was shrieking and flailing and kicking like a mad wild foal, out through the door and into the dark. Then the tavern was full of them, guards armored and armed, and at their center a well-kept and clean-looking sort, with an expression upon his face so dead of emotion, it was as if he were but a shell. He glanced about the place with heavy lidded eyes; and when his glance alighted upon the rogue, those eyes did pause, and he drew up a quick finger, saying, "You there, man of Loxley—your day is ended. You are come with me."

And the rogue regarded this apparition a moment, as though in contemplation of some distant and unrelated thing, before at last coming back to himself, and smiling easily, and bowing, and saying, not without a certain cheer, "It shall be as the right honorable sheriff commands." And easy did he step forth, and offered his wrists to the bindings that were bit hard on them, nor even protested as they set a death's hood over his skull and drew him out and away into the snowy deep.

"Zounds," murmured the skeptic, from whose face all the blood had sapped out; and he looked in lost amazement at the folk gathered round.

II

Black and cold had become his element—those two principles of the world which he most abhorred and dreaded. He trembled in chill silence there, pressing wretchedly against the walls of the tiny room into which they had hurled him—so little a space that not even kneeling was possible, but he was forced to stand and stand, until the muscles in him gave out and the weariness drove his weight painfully into the rough walls about him. Thrice a day they handed him a fistful of stale bread; twice again, a cup of brackish water; and thus five times did that petty imitation sun burning at the end of the guards' flambeaux pass his sight, and cast upon his world the ruddy simulacrum of day. And he mouselike consumed that bread, and as a frog did sup of that water, and batlike did blink his yet hungrier eyes at the glare of the torch—all this to keep the living spirit wakeful in him. For it was the one rebellion left to him, to grip tight, not indeed to his life, but to his living; for in precise proportion that the one thing grew cheap, the other grew dear. He alone with his thought and his idle genius did pass those long tormented hours; and, as many another prisoner once condemned to death, did console himself with the blessings and midday visitations of a spirit invisible to all eyes but the inner.

The dungeons below the castle of Nottingham were a network of tunnels and hovels as though some horrid worm had once set itself to scouring out the sandstone that upheld the gargantuan mossclung structure above it. The dark was oft full of the moaning of some old man he had glimpsed down the way, as they brought him, cuffed but free now of vision, to his final berth. That old head complained of searing pains within the skull, and sometimes for hours would not have off of its animal lamentations. And he listened to the man's lugubrious moaning in silence, and prayed constantly, but would not join his voice to it in a doleful or infernal duo.

'Twas long enough in that forgotten place that he did lose track of all time and all days, and could no longer say, maugre the feeble instinct in him, where the bright sun did sear through the canopy of the sky, or if sun there yet were in the world. Madness crept through him and he through it; an interpenetration it was, and a deep mutual delving of the one with the other; and all things he forgot, save for his own name and his own love, and it was only by his prayers to the living God that he clung to a scrap of sanity through it all.

When the iron grate in his door one day opened, he was much startled when no hand bearing bread was forthcoming, but only a shadow burning there beyond the window, so intent and silent at first that he did fear some fiendish and wicked specter, or the death himself. But it was a human voice that spoke to him then, in accent of Nottingham, and confirmed its carnal reality with the gruff common speech of it.

"Speak, prisoner! Do you live?" And the blaze of the torch was lifted blindingly to the gate's aperture.

The voice so long unused in him would not come in response. He lifted a shaking hand before his eyes, and saw the silhouette of spindly fingers before him. The door was unbarred, was opened; rough hands drew him out by the enfeebled arms, and dragged him along the hallway with the spectral flickering of the flame chasing corrupt shadows on the walls. And that guard did not hold back for the agony that rode in that prisoner's long unused limbs, and the miserable arrows of pain that shot along all the lines of his body and shore through his atrophied tissue. Yet silence did he keep despite that torment; nor a mutter of pain wet his lips.

He was brought to a room, and cast within, where he fell crippled to the floor, and where he lay for some time, a form ruined and as if shorn of its vital principle. But by and by he gave the lie to those appearances, and in agony he pressed himself up, grimacing against the furious pain, to slump upon the wall; and there at last finding a dolorous repose, he gazed dully about him.

It was a room with a torch of its own hanging on the wall, and its flame cast a steadier light upon things. Even this small fire was at first near intolerable to his darkness-blinded eyes, but soon they grew accustomed to it, and he could make out his surroundings. He found himself in a hovel carved into the stone, an ocher-walled burrow in the earth with rounded corners, and nothing to suggest floor nor wall nor ceiling but the brute principle of gravity itself. A stone bed there was, and a reek from a depression in one of the corners as of the fresh ordure of some late prisoner, carried off perchance to hang. He thought to rise, to go to the bed, to lay himself upon it; but a slackness was upon his wracked bones, and he held his slumped position against that wall, and drowsed in and out of terrible dreams.

By and by the door opened and he was stunned to a dizzy alertness as a guard wordlessly lugged into that cell a wooden chair, which he carried to the corner most distant from the cesspit, and set it facing the prisoner; and as wordlessly as he had come, so he left, glancing at the man slumped upon the floor with utter contempt. He did not even close the door behind him, but left it agape, as though in mockery. For while such a sight would have been tempting to any lusty body, the prisoner could not so much as lift an arm, and glowered at that portal from out of burning eyes, which burned the more, the longer it did stand there empty and inviting.

Thus at length he saw the flame's light casting on the wall beyond the door, and the long stretch of approaching shadows; and heard the clipped tap of the all-too-regular steps. Round the corner came fast pacing the Sheriff of Nottingham, and stood above the prisoner, hands behind his back, gazing down at him in great scorn; then turned upon his heel and strode to the chair, and sat straight-backed upon it, his right hand upon his knees, something anonymous held in his left, in the posture of some potentate or idol. His great empty eyes gazed on the man before him, and his fleshy lips frowned in disdain. In silence he gazed at him, and in silence did the prisoner's eyes, made baleful and dark from his captivity, gaze back, unstinting. Then the Sheriff spoke.

"I need not tell you why you have been brought here, for you know it well. For your crimes, and for my own pleasure, who do hate you not indifferently, you are sentenced to death."

The prisoner seemed to make an attempted to sit up, but little did it avail. Yet he smiled, and, with great force upon his lungs, croaked, "Only?" The Sheriff drew up in a rage and snapped his fingers; and at once a guard appeared from beside the open door and, going to the prisoner, knelt beside him and struck him smartly across the face once with the back of his hand, so that the stricken man's weakened head lolled upon his neck, and his mouth fell agape. Then the Sheriff gestured to the guard, and the guard disappeared into the hallway again.

"Smile no more, man of Loxley," said the Sheriff, "for the time of weeping is come."

The prisoner swallowed, and strained his head upright once more; and said to the Sheriff, haltingly, his voice hoarse and debile, "Much folly... have I nurtured...but none...so foolish...as to weep at death, when there is such good news brought to this wretched race of men, as bids me rejoice."

"Keep your tongue for better use," spat the Sheriff in disgust, which was the one emotion to well animate those features. "Your days of jesting are o'er, and ne'er again shall you have the pleasure of putting me to public shame. I have questions, and this time you will answer them, if I must tear the answers from your breast. But I begin with an act of simple grace. I will spare your worthless life, though I should much like to pin it on a pike, if you will answer me: where are the others?" He held up the object he was holding: a vellum manuscript.

"Gone," said the prisoner, smiling, but his eyes lingering almost feverishly on the manuscript.

"What mean ye, *gone*?"

"Ours is a moveable feast," said he, and began at once to hack and wheeze, which the Sheriff took for a cough.

"Play no games with me, Loxley," seethed the Sheriff, rousing. "It has been my pleasure to stow you in that shaft on account of your silence, and I can as easy as not return you to't and leave ye there till the rotting of your bones. Speak straight with me, man. I say—where are they?"

The prisoner worked his jaw, and stared off and away for a moment. But he said nothing again, and finally turned burning eyes upon his oppressor.

"Where did last you see them, then?" said the Sheriff, waxing impatient.

"'Twixt a shepherd's grotto and a hoary oak," said Loxley at last, "nigh the eyries of eagles. I would seek them where I have dwelt—far beyond the tyranny of longshanked Edwards or mad brat Richards or their slavish henchmen."

"Would you add treason to the foot of your list of crimes?"

"Did it not already crown them?"

"I warn you again: rile me not, Loxley."

"What then, shall I draw a map?"

"Hear me: paper and quill and ink shall be borne to you, and you will scribe me the names and the quality of all the men of this band, to a one."

"Would you have the truth about them, or the rumor?" asked the prisoner, smiling again against his feebleness.

"I would have the straight facts about 'em, and devil take the rest."

"Truly, if that be the condition, the devil shall take all, and without fail."

The Sheriff grew dark, and glared upon the man before him. He spoke again, then, with slow and cold words. "You misheed me, gossip. You are faced with two choices, and I will have your answer now, or ne'er again: either you will hang by the neck until dead before the jeering of the crowd come the first break of tomorrow's sun, or you will personally lead me and my men to your vile collaborators, a week tomorrow, or whenever you have regained sufficient of your strength to ride a horse. I say, man, you will give me the head of these outlaws, or you will lose your own. What is it to be?"

The prisoner had watched him with a long gaze from his uneven eyes, which seemed to flicker at times in the firelight and to grow larger as he took these words in. But after a moment's silence, he sat up, in all his frailty, and announced, with a voice, though yet husky, suddenly grown strong, "I, bring you to them? Man, I would not lead you so far as the refuse in yon corner!"

The Sheriff's eyes narrowed; but he nodded curtly, and rose, and went out, as the prisoner's eyes followed his going, until the door swung shut behind him with a clash.

That eve the rogue came down with the ague, and was borne to his bed. It was the order of the Sheriff that he should be carefully cured, for the Sheriff would have the pleasure of his head.

A nun, knowledgeable in healing, was brought thence, and made to descend into the deep under Nottingham Castle; and timid and fearful, did follow behind the guards and clove to them like a child to its parents. But when they came to the room and she saw him shaking and trembling upon the stone bed, the fear left her, and she flew to the side of the ailing man, and knelt by him. His teeth were chattering and his body rigid, but his deep dark eyes were still as he gazed into her own; and she but glanced with a certain pity at that fixed stare as she went about her work. She ordered a blanket brought to him, and one of wholecloth was tossed over his wrecked form; and she brought a wooden bowl and lay it beneath his wrist, and with a knife crafted a neat incision into the skin, to bleed from him the bad humors that were fretting him.

He said to her in a whisper, "Your touch is gentle, sister," and she glanced at him shyly and blushed, and nodded once to show that she had heard and understood; but elsewise did not respond.

It was the nun that kept watch that first night, as the fever rode him, and would not leave him. For a time he was seized by fancies and freaks and moaned and called out strange names, and seemed to be engaged in some manner of battle or duel. But by the morning it seemed the bleeding had had its way, for the fever had already broke, and a calm settled down upon him and upon that grotto in which he had been borne. And we speak of night and day with the liberty that is permitted to surface dwellers, though it was known only vaguely to the nun what hour it was, and to the moribund, no longer even remotely.

He did not know that even then above him in the wide sky the sun was casting its first rays upon the castle's spires, or that the jays were stirring in the eaves. He did not perceive the light that soaked into the wintry hillsides, nor saw the eagle gyring in solemn circles above the very place he lay, as he himself bent glazed eyes here and there about the room, restless and without stop, until they settled at last on the clear face of the nun who was removing the dampened rag from his forehead. And suddenly smiling a weak smile, he said to her with a hoarse and wrecked voice, "Why do you cure me today, sister, if the very morrow they shall have my head?"

She glanced at him and away, and continued to see about his blankets and to fuss over the bandages at his wrist. And she said, "It is none of my affair what *they* do. God has given me to tend to what I do."

"Aye," formed he with his mouth, and nodded, but did not make a sound.

After a moment she added, a certain decision in her voice, "God has given us the moment to care. The day and not the morrow."

And he looked at her strangely but he did not speak.

Time on—and who could say how long in that place, forgotten as it was by all cycles and all rhythms but those locked within and vouchsafed to the body—he turned to her as she sat quiet in her corner, and he said, "All my life I have ne'er passed by a man in need but as I sought to succor him; and now in my own direst extremity the Lord in His mercy has sent me the hand of kindness itself to minister to my fading life. Sister, were I not bound to die, I swear by your loveliness alone I should heal."

And it was true. For though the costume of the convent is meant to obscure all earthly beauty and to insist upon a sobriety and simplicity that belongs to the Kingdom, yet she was lovely, and her large pale eyes looked startled at the rogue as he made this proclamation, and her fair cheeks drew to a comely russet. But she replied, "Beauty is fleeting."

"Beauty, fleeting!" he cried. "My God! Good sister, all beauty is in God, and God is eternal."

But she shook her head. "'Tis nothing how I seem or do not seem. We are all of us bound to death, save as Christ will grant us life. If good has been done this day, then give the glory to God."

He nodded softly, his eyes inward. And then, looking up at her once more: "Yet God has given us the moment to care." And she glanced at him and then back to her work, but it seemed she smiled.

III

He requested and was granted final unction.

He complained again of fever, and she was moved to pity, and drew the lance once more into his veins. But as she cut the blade down against him he jerked as if in a shiver of ague and the lance bit deep into flesh. She drew it back in horror, but too late: the jagged cut had been made and could not be unmade. She bandaged the wound and worked swift with hands slick with his spilling blood, but he grew pale and faint before her very eyes, and soon whispered to her, "Enough, good sister, the thing is done. Now cease your ministrations, and heed me closely. Two boons I would ask of you. The first is this, that you find a man known as John Smallman. Inquire with Father James, who will know where to send you. Find you John, and ask him to lead you to a certain oak tree he will know, the one which bears a crimson-feathered arrow. For once long since did I shoot a dart as high in an arc o'er the wood as my arm would send, and vowed that my resting place would fall where'er the arrow did land, and it was this very tree that my arrow found. I am not in power to see my vow to completion, but go you there in my stead, and into the bole of the tree, in lieu of my body, cast this ring, that neither flame nor worm should take it. There too you will find a manuscript well preserved in a lockbox, and this you must give over to John, who will know what to do with it." With some difficulty he took the ring from his wasted hand, a tawny trinket, the one thing that had been left to him of all he owned in those dark days, and gave it over to her milk-white fingers, which received it trembling. With a force of will he smiled at her and looked into her eyes, wherein was captive the last of the sky he would ever see, and continued: "The second boon I would ask of you, who have already been angelic kind to me, is to deliver a message I shall entrust to you. I ask that you report the following speech to the Sheriff of Nottingham, word for word, or failing that then in nearest spirit: that, since my infancy upon the shores of Lake Lee and ere I was e'er carried to the king's domain, I have been my whole life about a kind of honorable theft, and that I leave this life in the same spirit, lest in my parting I betray my calling. Here, at my end, may it be known—I will rob e'en my own head."

"Commend yourself to God!" she whispered, frightened, staring into his dimming eyes.

"Much mendment is wanted indeed," muttered he, with a pallid smile. "May Christ our common Lord forgive me and have mercy in my soul. Pray for me, Sister, in the name of the Father and the Son and the Holy Ghost." With that he made the sign of the cross over his breast, and fell silent and spoke no more. He sank deep into a slumber by and by, and was left there upon the bed, though she would not have done with him, but sat in that corner next to him and stared uneasily upon him, now fussing over him in great futility, now chewing upon her lip and bearing his clammy hand clasped in her own. During that night, the last of his breath left him, and he expired, and she who had not left him a moment in his silence nor eaten since she had entered his cell wept over him a bitter hour.

The Sheriff fell to a mad fury when the message of these final words was brought to him, and would have had the nun whipped had she fallen to his power. But by the holy arm of the Church she was defended, and was swept away into the safety of her nunnery. The body was discharged in fashion most cursory, and no man knew the whereabouts of the grave into which it had been consigned—nay, nor if indeed it lay at all in the dark earth. For it was whispered that the rogue had feigned his own demise, and had in wanton mock of law eschewed that yawning gape of soil, to wander once more in Sherwood and to resume his accustomed liberty, singing his lays and reciting his verse and playing the bandit to the delight of those who witnessed him. And indeed, by and by many a lusty sort did rise and, inspired by his tales, took up the name, or not the mantle, of Robin Hood, and many another did seek these out to know the truth of the matter, and if Robin Hood lived yet. But in each case it seemed that the seekers met with disappointment at imposters who pretended a name that they had not won, and it became commonplace to speak of the Rabunhods of the wood—the false Hoods that made trouble in the forest, but a trouble commonplace and all too easy of resolution. Mere rabble and bandits and rebels were these, though some of goodly will and minded to aid the poor and needy; and not a one of them had in him spirit such as might outrest his form.

Spirit to outrest form! That indeed is troublesome; that indeed troubled many a head, and even the sober, calculating head of the Sheriff himself unto his own grave time. It came to be bruited about that while the rogue had died in truth, still his immaterial vestige haunted Sherwood, doomed to linger in this potter's vale, loitering there in vague attachment to the ways it had once cherished. It was whispered that of a twilight eve his voice could be heard singing yet, calling men to a truer destiny than that which had befallen them, or leading them astray thereby to their very deaths. This was said even then, even of Robin Hood.

But the final resting place of these twin souls is in God's hands alone, and this much alone remains to us mere mortals in our mere human limitations: *Robin Hood* remains, though many centuries now have lapsed since he perished to this world and was made the stuff of song and was brought before a particular judgement infinitely higher than any sheriff's. Spirit to outrest form, and a legend in a name—a name that has come down to us and rests also on our tongues and on our pens and on our minds, and calls to us as well to strive with it and to emulate it and to revive it ever anon. And this is immortality of a sort, will assure us that master of Sherwood, with his dozen faces and his dozen monikers—he who, though not still living, is yet not still dead.

Note to the Reader

If, good reader, these humble words of a wandering singer have pleased, humored, diverted, amused, or in any small way gladdened you of an idle hour, then kindly "give a poor old beggar man somewhat to aid him" (to rob words from Robin Hood) by leaving your reviews in any of the going places, as for instance Amazon.com or Goodreads.com. A bit of what's yours for all that's mine—and I will be grateful to you, and much the richer for it.

If, to the contrary, you found naught to gratify you in this work, or aught to displease you, or much to censure, then be pleased all the same to leave your critiques in the aforementioned spots, both to forewarn others from similarly abusing their time, and to aid this writer in improving his craft—and I will be grateful to you, and much the richer for it.

John Bruce Leonard

About the Author

John Bruce Leonard was born in the Stanley basin in Idaho, began writing at the age of seven, and, despite all his noblest intentions, never managed to stop. To add insult to injury, he studied letters and philosophy in college, emerging therefrom with great expectations and poor prospects.

After a young life spent ping-ponging between the north and the south of the Great American West, he finally pulled the string back taut indeed, straight overshot the Atlantic, and landed his arrow in Sardinia. There he dwells with his wife and son in the straw-bale house they built, amidst olive trees and an alarming number of animals, in whose merry company he continues to patronize his literary vices.

johnbruceleonard.substack.com

johnbruceleonard@gmail.com

@JohnBLeonard